THE GREEN
AND THE GOLD

Also by Christopher Peachment

CARAVAGGIO

Christopher Peachment

THE GREEN AND THE GOLD

AN HISTORICAL NOVEL

PICADOR

First published 2003 by Picador
an imprint of Pan Macmillan Ltd
Pan Macmillan, 20 New Wharf Road, London N1 9RR
Basingstoke and Oxford
Associated companies throughout the world
www.panmacmillan.com

ISBN 0 330 48733 7

Typeset by Intype London Ltd
Printed and bound in Great Britain by
Mackays of Chatham plc, Chatham, Kent

For Vivien.

A double minded man is unstable in all his ways.

James 1: 8

one

THE GREEN

1. Biding My Time

'Tis all enforced, the fountain and the grot,
   While the sweet fields do lie forgot:
Where willing nature does to all dispense
   A wild and fragrant innocence:
And fauns and fairies do the meadows till
   More by their presence than their skill.
Their statues, polished by some ancient hand,
   May to adorn the gardens stand:
But howsoe'er the figures do excel,
   The gods themselves with us do dwell.

Marvell. 'The Mower against Gardens'

My sisters were too old for me. The youngest of the trio was only three years my senior, yet it made no difference. They were all grown long before me, and formed a cabal against me, which I could not enter.

When I was little, just six years old or so, I became intrigued by women. I had always liked their smell. I know now that my mother was not the most demonstrative of women, but on the rare occasions when she held me, to comfort me when I was sick or had hurt myself in a fall, then

I liked the smell of her. I tried to describe the smell once to a friend and the best word that I could come up with was 'plowder'. Even though I was young I was already well tutored from my father and his young curates in Latin and Greek, and also I had my letters down well from a chapbook. True it was before I went to school, but I already had read my Aesop and some Homer and a little of Virgil, and had even begun my Hebrew. But I could not find a word that I wanted, and so made one up even before I thought about it. It just came to me, and still, now I am in my forties, when I repeat that word again to myself, her smell almost returns to me.

Just one word, a nonce word that I had made up, and my nose pricks and my eyes fill as if I were about to sneeze, and a faint crawling sensation at the back of my throat brings her back to me. Above all else it was a smell that promised warmth. A smell that arose from soft folds of flesh and the pores of a woman, which must be so different from those of a man. God built us different.

She used no perfume that I knew of. My father had been to the most puritan of colleges, but he was easy, and so not a puritan himself. He was a pious man and well learned, and he was a Conformist to the established Rites of the Church, though I confess none of the most over-running or eager in them. He was a middling sort of Reverend then. Neither was he poor. Even so, we were not extravagant, but rather plain in our living, and so my mother used no scent. But when I nuzzled my face into her neck and her hair became unpinned slightly and brushed against my face, I felt warm and safe. That smell that she had I will always associate with that state of mind, that feeling of safety. When I wish to feel more secure, I search out one of her old handkerchiefs that I keep in my chest for that very purpose. I had tried keeping them in oilcloth to start with, but the smell of the oil overwhelmed the smell of the lace. So I had a small glass box made, for glass has no smell, nor can it absorb odours. The lid was sealed with hard wax, which again has no smell once cooled. Each time that I need comforting, I have to break the wax and later reseal it, and so it is not an easy matter, but one which requires patience and a little inconvenience. It means that I can only use it for special occasions, and I like it so. The smell is growing dim with the years, but it is still there however faint, and it can calm me even when I am at my most disturbed.

The smell of geraniums will do the same, for different reasons I will go into later.

As I said, I became interested in women. It was their smell that did it. I wanted to know where it came from and whether they were all alike. And why they took so much time in their dressing. And how it was that their appearance was so carefully rendered. They did not wear paint or powder such as *ladies* do, but none the less they would pin their hair with much care and work upon their brows and eyes and cheeks and lips and do other things before the glass, which they would not let me see. My father would often rail against vanity and preach some sermon about how women were weak in that vein, but I knew, even as a child, that it went deeper than that. Yes, it was vanity that made them alter their appearance (how? I wanted to know *how*), but it was something else, some other quality I could not put a name to for I was young, that made it all worthwhile. They knew something, they had a secret, which made them realize deep down that the world was a better place if they spent a little while in front of the glass each day and prettied themselves.

You will know all this, you are a grown man, and acquainted with the ways of women; and so I am too, to a limited extent for I have not married; and you will be saying in a few short words what I am struggling for with many. Brevity was never my strong point in speech, though it is true I write short, but then I use the words of others, and Latin is a good master for keeping to the point. Stay with me if you will, I am sinking back to when the world was newgreen, and petticoats were all that I would think of.

You will be thinking that it was sex that was working upon me. Well, you may be right. I was young, but I was advanced for my years, in learning at any rate, and I do not believe in childish innocence, there is no such thing. Watch a child at play, and it will exhibit all the motions of the soul that you will see when it grows to manhood. Do you know a greedy man? He will have been a guzzler when in his cradle. Is this or that man a libertine? He will have had kinder sisters than mine, who would have caressed him when young, perhaps too much and too privily. Do you know a bully? He will have made his younger brothers and sisters live in hell, even when he was five. In the childhood of Judas was Christ betrayed. Truly is it said that the child is father to the man, and all we do, and all we be, is prefigured by our youth, right from the smallest age. There is no escape.

I wish my sisters had been kinder to me, for I would have turned out so very different from what I now am, a condition that I hate so much. They were only a little older than me it is true, but they were all three close in age to each other and so good friends, as far as any woman is a friend to another. They often quarrelled over nothing, the way women do, but why they had to treat me so unkind I can never understand. I was but a little thing, not ugly, nor horrid, and they could have used me as their own child or baby, to practise upon for when they had children of their own. I did not know that then of course, but I know it now, for I have seen older sisters pet their little brothers and cradle them and dress them up and play with them as if they were little poppets. Such girls have no need of dolls to teach them to be good mothers, they have the living breathing thing before them, which God gave them for good instruction.

They could, as I say, have done all that with me, and I would not have complained. Complained? By God, I would have loved it, for I do so love it now when a woman is busying herself about me, fixing my hose or straightening my stock, or flirting a little. It is a weakness of mine. But they did not. They ignored me in the main, and when they did not ignore me, it was only to order me about and make me fetch and carry and run errands for them. They would give me orders even when they did not need anything fetched. I was but a servant to them, and not a valued one. An annoyance at best, at worst a slave.

I did not like their smell much. It was not like my mother's. But they had something that I wanted to know about. I had rested my head in my mother's lap, and I knew well enough how it might have been figured. I knew well enough that there was a lack there, a lack which men do not have, but I had not seen the thing itself, and I will always want to see things for myself even now. Curiosity has always marked me, I know not why. And so I spied upon my sister, the eldest of the three. Her body had filled out, and she was almost become a woman. I followed her around from a distance, always keeping myself hid, and for the first time in my life, I knew a secret joy. There was something delicious, almost voluptuous, in watching her while she did not know it. It made me very excited, even at that age, before I could produce seed.

Truly man is fallen from the moment of birth, there is no age of innocence. To talk of the innocence of children is to lie to oneself. It is to draw a veil over the truth that one can remember if only one is honest enough about it. But men are not honest about themselves. They may be honest in their dealings with others, but they will not admit to themselves what they dare not. They deceive themselves in order to flatter the soul, and so they live in bad faith.

I will always be honest with myself, and to others I will dissemble. I will be the reverse of the common.

We lived at that time without the city wall, in a house provided by the charitable foundation for which my father was a Master. It was a middling sort of house, not large, nor fancy, nor yet mean, but it had several acres of garden, some of it wooded, and I grew up surrounded by flowers and trees, which I did love very much. For the flowers gave me beauty and the trees gave me hiding. My sisters would often go into the woods, for they had a little bower where they met to talk and laugh. It was well hidden from the outside, deep in a spinney of trees, and while it was not exactly a secret place, yet it could be used as such, for if anyone were approaching it, they could be heard quite easily by the rustling in the undergrowth and breaking of twigs underfoot. The girls would stop their giggling, and pick up their books and look grave, as if they were declining their verbs or reading scripture or some such, and my father would see them and would go away much pleased with his devout daughters. The hypocrites.

They thought I did not know of the place, for I was always under the eye of one or other of them. But I did. And I knew of much else besides that they did not know I knew, but I kept it all to myself, for that was my one weapon against them.

I too had a secret part of the wood. There was a box hedge which ran nearly up to the house, and bordered the parterre. It had been there for generations and was cut regularly by the gardener to keep its shape. It stood as high as two tall men, was as broad at its base as a carriage, and I discovered that it had a nearly hollow centre. If you parted the glaze green foliage at a point I discovered, you could crawl inside the hedge, and the greenery, the colour of a copper church steeple, would spring back in place behind you and cover your entry. Inside was a tangle of roots and branches, but it was possible to crawl the length of the hedge unseen. It was dusty inside, not a household kind of dust, but a dark brown heavy dust which flaked off the branches of box, and it had a strong resinous smell which always makes me think of alcohol and strong drink, even though I had never tasted that when I discovered my tunnel. I loved this place for a long time just for itself alone and because it was all mine. Then I found out what it could do, and I liked it even more.

By crawling to the end I could penetrate the woods. Not quite all the way inside, but that did not matter. The important thing was that I could get into the trees without being seen or heard. The paths were mostly gravel, which is noisy; and if you approached by the grass, then you could easily be seen crossing the open spaces by someone hidden not even very deep in the trees, but my secret hedge was like a tunnel that the engineers build beneath the walls of a besieged city. From it, I could invade my enemy.

And invade them I did. I used to creep up upon my sisters and stay within a deep thicket close by to their little bower with the pool of standing nile-green water in it. I would listen to their talk for hours, and looking back now I realize that they said absolutely nothing of the slightest interest to God or man. But that was not the point. It was not the intelligence I wanted. It was the act of watching them and hearing them while they did not know it, that so delighted me. I was not born a spy, it was my sisters made me one.

One hot afternoon in August, the house was empty. My father had gone into Hull on business with the Committee of the Charity and also something to do with shipping, and my mother had taken my sisters off visiting, and left me in the charge of the maid and the gardener. She was busying herself in the kitchen, he was working with his scythe upon the greenth, and I was left to my own devices. As the only male child, I was often alone, and have always enjoyed my own company. I went to my box hedge, taking care not to let the gardener see me, and drew back the branches and slipped inside. The sun shone only a little through the dense leaves, making the outside edge branches dappled with yellow and brown, but deep inside it was a cool ultramarine green. I crept forward slowly, with my mouth firmly closed, inhaling deeply through my nose. The resinous smell left me light-

11

headed and I drifted through the heat haze as if swimming through a sluggish oil.

Presently I came to my spot in the woods. No one was around, but still I went for my nook in the undergrowth, and nestled down in it silently, packing the leaves and ferns down beneath me into a sort of bedding. I plucked a long stalk of yellow-green grass, and chewed the end and sucked the juice from it, which was both sweet and brackish. There was a quiet hum of insects and the occasional quick slap of water from the pool, as some bird dipped its beak in, or a gold fish surfaced and smacked its lips. And then I saw my oldest sister, and nearly gave myself away by starting. I had thought she was off with my mother, but obviously she had managed to slip away on some excuse. She was standing quietly by the water gazing intently upon her reflection in it. She smoothed her hair slowly, and dabbed a little water on her eyebrows and wiped them into a downward curve, and gently rubbed her cheeks with water to cool them, it was so hot.

Then I could hardly breathe for I knew what was coming next. She stepped out of her dress and lifted up her shift over her head, so that her small white arms were clear above her head for an instant as she stood there naked. And I saw her breasts, and the faintest bulge to her white belly and her long thin thighs. Her hips were not broad like my mother's, yet they were wider than a man's. Between her legs I could see nothing, for it was part covered in hair like a dog or a mouse. I did not expect that at all, thinking that they were all

12

smooth, like a doll. I thought perhaps that that was all they had there, just a patch of hair such as men have under their arm. Did they? What is there, and how may I know?

She stepped lightly toward the nile-green water on tiptoe for she was barefoot, and she placed her left arm across her breasts as if to support them, though they were not so heavy. Gently she lowered herself into the pool with scarce a ripple, and sank with a sigh into the cool water. Her arm stayed across her breasts, holding them quite tight, and her right arm she sank into the water and it bobbed gently in a rhythmic motion as if she were very slowly strumming a guitar. Her head she rested on the grass of the bank and her eyes were softly closed and she breathed gently through her mouth, just faint but audible above the thrum of insects. After a while she hummed a song to herself, a sweet air, which I did not know, and have sought out over many years, and never have I found it. It stays with me though.

I had seen her and I loved what I saw.

What excited me even more, was that I was not supposed to have seen her. I was beginning to tremble, my arms and especially my thighs, which were rubbing together with an excitement I could hardly bear. My eyes became heavy as they do before sleep and I fainted dead away. But I must have come around quite quick, for I came to with a start, and a terrible fear gripping my innards and my heart hammering in my chest, for there stood my sister, towering over my nest and looking straight at me. She was clothed now, and her eyes were straining from their sockets with the whites showing all around the centre and her brows were lowered and minced together so they met above her nose, and her jaw was tight shut so that the muscles on her cheeks were bunched. She always was something of an actress, the silly bitch. It was as if she were playing some fireside game, and someone had said to her 'Mime anger.' She even had her arms akimbo, resting on her hips. There was so little natural about her, she was always putting on airs like my mother.

She did not say any word of accusation, which was strange, although she must have known I had been watching her. And I knew what was coming. And I knew I was in for it. I started to give an excuse, but stammered badly as I always used to when caught out, and I coloured till I thought my head would catch fire. She gripped me by the shoulders and shook me and said, 'This time I really will tell on you.' She was always threatening to tell my parents of any bad behaviour that she had caught me in, though she hardly ever did, and it had become an idle threat. This time I could see she meant it.

Then, she turned upon her heel and strode off. Yes, she really did that. I mean, anyone else would just have turned around and walked away. Not her though. She truly did grind one heel into the ground and swivel upon it, then strode off at a military pace, swinging her arms furiously as if she were in the local militia. God knows where they get it from, girls I mean. I suspect that the theatre and all drama written for it would die out if it weren't for girls. They just love an act.

Off she stalked, and I was trembling uncontrollably and grizzling, for I knew my mother would be very cross and like as not to tell my father when he returned. I am not sure why I was so frightened, for my father was not a violent man. My mother would often slap out at me, but it was brief and unconsidered. My teachers had sometimes threatened me with the rod when I was backward in my learning, but my father always forbade it. He would talk to me quite sternly about my behaviour and chide me most bitterly till I felt very sad that I had upset him so. Yet never once did he raise his hand to me, or to the girls. He treated us all quite equally in his affections, he was very scrupulous in that respect, but here I was in my bower and I was afraid. What had been my secret, my own to enjoy entirely by myself, was now about to be known to the rest of the family. I was both fearful and angry in a strange combination, so that I felt like both stamping my feet and throwing myself about, and weeping at the same time.

I crawled away, and went to the far edge of the woods, furthest away from the house and found the little hut made of stone there, with no roof. It had sometime been used as a privy, but was now ruined, with broken-down machicolated walls, though a wooden stool was still there, and I sat upon it and put my elbows on my knees and rested my chin on my hands. Slowly my eyes dried, but I did not move and stared out at the distance to where the huge sky met the far land in one long, flat, estranging line, and fused with it in shades of grey. I sat there without moving, staring and staring, my thoughts jumping around for hours in some terror.

And I sat, knowing that they would be looking for me, and might not find me, for no one came here any more, especially my sisters who were always joking about the old privy and its broken down state, as if it were another thing that were beneath them, like almost everything else. Often I had the urge to run home and brave whatever awaited me, but I did not. By a large effort of will, I stayed anchored to my spot, and wondered if I might stay all night, and what would happen if I ran away completely. I had never travelled further than the short walk into Hull, and there I was well known as my father's son. Where I might go I did not know, but I considered it. My young mind took no thought of where I might find food or shelter. I simply pictured myself wandering as far as London, wherever that might be, and perhaps further afield, to places where they spoke the Latin and the Greek. No one spoke Hebrew, I knew that much. But to go far abroad, that would be a great game.

After an hour or two, the fear abated, as it will when you apply your reason to it. The worst that could happen would be a beating, and that would smart but soon be better. Or else a stern talking to, which I hated more than a beating, but still could be borne. Or what else could they? My fear, as I said, died down, but what did not was my frustration. They knew my secret, they would know what I wanted to keep for myself entire, and it was that which I could hardly bear. So I sat and I sat even longer, and I learned patience, which is really very easy when you have a landscape to watch and a few thoughts to think on. What I called patience was of course stubbornness, and what I later heard men call procrastination, but I did not know that then. It was not until I was at University that I first read of Fabius Cunctator, the Roman general who defeated his opponents simply by delaying tactics, and it was then I knew I had found my man.

It was the gardener found me. I heard him walking quietly through the grass toward the little hut with a steady and undeviating tread, as if he knew exactly where I was. Which in truth I think he did. He was a quiet man, and near invisible, but not much went on in his grounds that he did not see. I expect he knew of my tunnel in the hedge, though never would he let on with a wink or a smile. He stood in the doorway, blotting out the evening sun, and he had a scythe over his shoulder, whose shadow fell on my left in a long, thin curve. He hefted the scythe into his right hand and laid it carefully on the grass, blade-down, and pointing toward the wall, for it was frightening sharp, and he leaned the long cranked handle against the outside wall, so that the whole thing was safe and could not be knocked or trod upon by accident. I have seen novices cut themselves to the bone with that fearful thing, but he was a master of its use.

He notched his massive hands under my arms, and lifted

me up most gently and placed me upon his shoulder, and thus he walked me through the long grass, away from my small ruin and back toward home. 'Just like the return of the conquering hero,' he said quietly, and though I did not feel at all like a hero, yet it cheered me.

He placed me at the open kitchen door, and with only a brief salute to my mother, who was bustling about inside with the maid, he turned and was gone, as quiet as he had arrived. With no flourish my mother gathered me up and pulled my chair from the wall and placed me on it, and fetched me a bowl of some soup from the range and a spoon and then carried on with her business with the maid. Not one word was said. Nor was there that studied sort of silence which often occurs after I have been caught out in something I should not have done, and after a brief outburst of temper my mother says, 'Well, we shall speak no more about it,' and purses her lips for about an hour in case any injudicious word should escape her mouth. I dread those silences more than a scolding. I wish much more were said about it all, rather than those accusing silences. No, there was nothing like that here. Just she and the maid pottering about at the stove, doing whatever it is that women do to keep busy in a kitchen, quietly muttering nothing important to each other.

I had it in mind to begin some explanation as to why I was near the pool and so excuse my behaviour, but wisely I kept silent. Silence is so much more effective than a lie.

After a while, my father came by, returned from his business in town, and asked what was for dinner, and why I was not in bed. And so I kissed him, and climbed the stairs to my room. From over the balustrade I saw two of my sisters, the eldest that I had looked on, and the middle one, coming through the hall. And they did nothing out of the ordinary. They did not studiously ignore me, nor did they scowl at me, nor did they tug their sleeves and point and look superior as they so often did when they were plotting something. Just a brief glance from those twin pair of malachite eyes with no special acknowledgement and they went on their way for something to eat.

I could not work it out at all; the whole household seemed oblivious to my crime. It was not even as though they had discussed it and decided to ignore it, I would have known that from the lowering atmosphere immediately. It was as if by the time my sister had returned home she had forgot about it entirely. And that is what I truly did believe for a long time afterward: that my crime was hardly more than a misdemeanour in her eyes, and she was too busy with some other scheme to even mention it. Her scolding by the pool had been purely routine, just a way of telling me that I must not spy on a girl bathing. Or more simply yet another way of keeping me in my place.

It was many years before I realized that perhaps she had enjoyed it all. For I knew nothing of women when young.

But then, I had seen her naked and I had loved the sight of it; and I had loved her for it too. And all I wanted was for her to love me a little, for I was only her younger brother, and not much of a threat to anyone, least of all her. It would have cost her nothing, and it would have gained her all the world. But she did not. And so my love died and burned out almost as quick as the fuse had been lit. Never again would I show my heart so openly, not to any woman who might break it, for I was more badly hurt than I knew.

But I learned a useful lesson. Sit long on a problem without stirring and it will pass.

That is all you need to know of my childhood. It was otherwise passed with the same mix of joy and sadness as marks any other child. Our memory of our childhood deceives us. Most people, when they look back, imagine that they passed an idyllic time through their early years. This is not true. For we choose to remember only the pleasant memories, and suppress the ill ones, and the way that a child sees and feels the world is neither happy nor sad for most of the time. It is *vivid*.

When I look back on childhood, what I see in the main is boredom, bright flashes of joy, and long concealment, but then that is an enduring condition with me.

The gardener is dead now. His name was van Dieman, and he taught me the names of flowers and how to mow a field, though never did I need to in later life. I honoured him none the less in my poems, I will tell you how at a later date.

The Green and the Gold

Of my life, I have set out the following events, not in the order in which they occurred, but in the order in which they seem to me now to have became important to me. Contingency has a chronology all of its own.

2. At Cambridge

. . . one Mervill, a notable English Italo-Machavillian.

James Scudamore, a Royalist living at Saumur, France, in a letter to
Sir Richard Browne at Paris, describing Marvell and his pupil Dutton,
a ward of Cromwell's, both of whom visited Saumur.

My father sent me to the university at Cambridge when I was
twelve. It was the first time I had been away from home on
my own. I was glad to be rid of my sisters, but I missed my
mother more than I could ever admit to anyone. My father
took me to Cambridge and made sure I was well lodged with
my trunk of clothes and as he was gathering himself to say
goodbye and take his leave, I began to tremble, and was close
to tears. He clapped me on the shoulder and looked quite
stern, and told me to play the man, but then he softened and
held me to him in an embrace and I gave way to weeping. He
was really a most tender man, for he could not harden his
heart for long. I often think now that that is the reason my
sisters get away with murder. He could not bring himself to
be strict enough with them. I sometimes daydream of seeing
them get a good thrashing. It is one of my happier reveries.

It was not the unhappiest day of my life, but it was close.

After he had left, looking a little uncomfortable but smiling for my sake, I unpacked and sat on my bed staring out the window, without thinking of anything much, but chewing my lips in worry and frustration. And I took the little piece of cloth handkerchief which had been my mother's, and I had taken from her room, and secreted in my trunk, and I lay back on the bed and draped the cloth over my nose and mouth and inhaled deeply. Her smell came straight back to me, and slowly I felt comforted and presently fell asleep; and my dreams were so sweet that when I woke, I tried to sleep again, and continue with the same dream. But I have never managed to do that, I do not know why. Surely a man should be able to will a dream into being.

Now that I think of it, that is surely what man must never be allowed to do. It is assuredly what Cromwell tried to do in my later life, and look at the disaster he made of this country. If man were able to control his dreams and make them real, well . . . Our nature is too fallen ever to encompass such a thing. But I get ahead of myself.

My college years were dull. I was a diligent enough student but Cambridge is a dank place, full of mists and fogs and rising damps from the surrounding fens and marshes. It is hard to keep warm, even in spring and summer, and in the winters you will often pull on a clean shirt in the morning only to find that it is damp simply from the moisture in the air. No wonder Puritanism thrives here. I believe that they do things quite different over at Oxford.

The rules were many and strict. One had to be up at five in the morning and there was a one-hour service in chapel before breakfast. I did not mind my studies at all, which were taken in four-hour lessons, for I proved very capable at my Greek and Hebrew, and I was surpassing good at Latin, for it was my true love. I liked all of it. I even liked Julius Caesar, whom most of my fellow-students detested, for his plain prose. His *Gallic Wars* is a model of clarity and I like the very exact way he describes his military campaigns. So vivid are his descriptions, that I can see the battle in my mind's eye. He fired an interest in military tactics in me, and I went on to study the writings of King Gustavus Adolphus of Sweden, who is a great strategist, and the more recent Dutch generals, who are perfecting the art of war. I do not have it in me to be a soldier, but with luck I might witness a few battles and write commentaries on them.

My greatest love, however, was for the poets, most especially Horace, for I found I could reproduce him well in translation. The exercise was quite a stretch, but I would sit for hours in my spare time, trying out different rhymes and metres, and matching his sentiments in English.

Which was just as well, for most other ways of passing one's spare time were banned to us. Taverns were forbidden, and so were harmless games such as skittles and boxing matches. Needless to say we would go off secretly and play them, indeed we played games which we otherwise would not, even had they been legal. Dogs and fierce birds were not allowed in our rooms, so we used to borrow them and sneak them in anyway. We did it just for the hell of it, and to get back at our tutors, who were pinched and narrow to a man.

I would like to teach, if only to pass on this great store of knowledge I am acquiring, but I will not do it in any of the great colleges. If I do it, it will be as a private tutor to some young man. And I have a great yearning to travel. Perhaps the reason for that was my growing up in Hull, and watching the ships roll in to the harbour, and wondering where they were bound when they set sail again. I never did see a ship leaving without wanting to be on it. Though when I tried it, I became horribly seasick. One of my wretched sisters married a man in Hull who has a marine trading business, and he took me to sea a few times in one of his many boats. And every time, I spent most of the voyage at the taff-rail, heaving my breakfast up and feeling that I wanted to die. There is nothing worse than seasickness, for you cannot step off the boat. I would like to die a dry death.

Still, the desire to travel never went away. I look at a ship, and I want to be on it. Then I look at the boat again and realize that I don't want to be on it at all; what I really want is to be wherever it is going. It would be nice if one could arrive at a foreign place, without having travelled at all. At least not by boat. Horse I can manage. To fly would be wonderful.

The Green and the Gold

Most young men wish to set sail, and I was no different.
I just didn't want to set sails.

When I was eighteen my tutor told me that a certain professor wanted to see me. I knew of this man, although I had
never met him, nor even seen him about the town or college,
which was somewhat strange, for one usually bumped into
most of the teachers there at one time or another. But I knew
exactly what was coming, for I had heard rumours of this
man's reputation.

I am sure you can guess what happened, for everyone
claims to know of at least one friend of theirs, or a friend of a
friend, to whom this happened. The story is always the same:

Called into the tutor's study . . . asked to sit down
immediately . . . offered a glass of sherry . . . the talk less
formal than usual . . . enquiries after your general health and,
um . . . what you might do when you go down . . . observed
throughout your stay here . . . like the cut of your jib . . . a
reliable young man . . . just the sort we need . . . when I say
'we' of course, I mean, well . . . say no more . . . would you
care to do something to help your country . . . patriotism is
such an embarrassing word . . . no money in it of course, but
expenses . . . you wouldn't be out of pocket . . . and we, I
mean the powers that be, can show great *gratitude* . . .

I had heard of this story countless times from fellow
students when we had been outside the city on an illicit
drinking spree, and over the years I had assumed it was just

another myth, along with the ghost of Trinity and how you had to be a pederast to get into King's. But no, here it was happening to me.

The litany went on:

Nothing underhand of course . . . nothing a gentleman need be ashamed of . . . just a bit of travel to start with . . . your Latin is good and everyone speaks that, sort of *lingua franca* . . . learn some languages, say French, Spanish, maybe a bit of Dutch . . . make a few contacts . . . get to know our ambassadors abroad . . . deliver a few packets and letters for us . . . diplomatic pouches, nothing illegal . . . study troop movements, your interest in military matters will stand you in good stead there . . . help open trade and commerce routes . . . good for economy . . . a few simple codes so your letters won't be read . . . and take a travelling companion . . . know just the fellow, nice young man, show him the ropes, tutor him in his Latin . . . together you'll have a lovely . . . good, good, so pleased to have had this little chat . . . do think it over . . . couple of days . . . my door is always open.

Well, I would have said 'yes' there and then, so keen was I to get out into the wide world, but I wasn't completely wet behind the ears, so I hung on for a couple of days just to keep them waiting, before returning. And I read a book I found in the library about the reign of Queen Elizabeth, and about Sir Francis Walsingham, who I assume came from the Norfolk place of the same name. He was the chief spymaster to the Queen and he was excellent at his job, although he nearly beggared himself in the process, for the Queen was notoriously stingy with money. He realized that the key to it all was information and was prepared to pay good money to get it.

He studied counter-intelligence from the Venetians, a crafty people and past masters at deceit. He also employed a master-coder, a white magician called John Dee, who recovered the lost secrets of Trithemius, Abbot of Sponheim, in a book called *Stenographia*, which Dee found in a flea market in Paris. He thus could both decipher those letters that his enemy had encoded, and encipher any letters he did not wish his enemy to read.

I read and studied all the usual codes and became adept at cracking them, for they are mostly based on the frequency of letters which occur in English, or on simple grid systems. There are suppression-of-frequency systems, but again I can crack them in no time.

The thing is that once you know that you are looking at a code, then the challenge is there, and there is no system devised by man that cannot be broken by man. Francis Bacon believed that the best code is one that does not look like a code, but if you have a letter before you from one ambassador hostile to your country to another known trouble maker, and it is all about what his wife did on their last trip to the dressmaker, then you are looking at a code, one in which 'tight laced corsets' means 'barrels of gunpowder'.

Bacon's idea was to change the typefaces around to some agreed system, but that looks very much like a code to me, when I see it. And one I can crack too.

The book code is the best there is, for all it requires is a common agreement on the book to be used by both parties, and anyone else intercepting the letter might never know the book in question, and is therefore forever in the dark.

Unless of course one had either sender or receiver in custody, and then judicious use of the rack would surely yield up the title of the book. But then judicious use of the rack would yield up whatever treason was being plotted anyway, and so you wouldn't need to crack the code.

Unless of course, it was imperative that neither party knew that you were privy to their secrets.

Oh, it goes on and on and round and round; the ramifications to this spying game have no end, and I will enjoy them all, I am sure.

It strikes me that the surest code of all would be a very rare sort of language, which it is certain that none of your enemies can speak. We have sent ships to the vexed Bermudas for example, including my friend the Reverend John Oxenbridge, who went there to escape the rage of Archbishop Laud. (There were hopes of setting up a new colony there, a veritable Utopia, but, alas for human frailty, some ambergris was found washed up on the shore line, and the men fell to fighting and killing each other for it. I wrote of the enterprise in my poem 'Bermudas', later in life; but it was a lyric, and so I omitted the unpleasantness. I will recount it later.) And some sea captains have returned from there with natives who speak a strange tongue, which no one outside these isles will have heard. Get the Bermudans to send letters to each other in their own language, and then get them to translate it into English, and you have an uncrackable code.

Except that you will need one of them at either end of your route of correspondence, which might be tricky if you want to know what is happening in the court of the Tsar of Muscovy, for example. And no one here has yet managed to understand one word of what they say.

The other slight problem is that Bermudans are illiterate. Paper and pen has yet to figure in their culture. In fact anything at all has yet to figure in their culture, aside from sitting around getting drunk all day. Civility and all its benefits have not taken hold in the West Indies. Also I think the Spanish might have gone there by now. Still, it's a good idea, and one which I will think on some more, for there must be a way around it.

I said 'yes' to that mysterious professor I told you about, and he introduced me to a lawyer from Essex. His name was Thurloe. I didn't pay much attention at the time, but mark that name well. As I am sure you know, he will re-appear from time to time, and was already more powerful than he pretended. When a man becomes private secretary and top intelligencer to Mr Cromwell, then he has no need to trumpet his power.

He had the good sense to be Postmaster General too, thus having control of all letters, and could crack them open to discover their secrets whenever he wanted.

Thurloe employed a master-coder called Dr John Wallis, of Oxford, a man who claimed to be able to decipher any code known to man. He invented the 'Pig Pen System', which is with us to this day, and is comprised of dots and squares. I broke it in less than an hour.

The professor also introduced me to John Milton. You will know of him, I am sure. He had been at my college before me, a very handsome man, but boils had scarred his face, so he had the look of a poxy cherub. Mr Milton speaks many languages and would have me do the same. I will travel for him, and he will provide me with a covering story.

Just before I left Cambridge, we put on a play, on the pistachio green lawn that runs down to the river. It was midsummer, and we decided on *Twelfth Night*, for we wanted a comedy. I was asked to take the part of the Steward of the Lady's house, and at first refused, for I have no experience of this kind of thing, and moreover I was worried about my stammer. It had been quite severe when I was young, but it had slowly faded over the years until it had now all but gone. Just occasionally, however, when I am caught unawares, it returns. It happens under those circumstances that make some men blush. I never blush; with me, my tongue congeals and the word is stopped at my teeth.

So I said no at first, but soon relented, because I am an easy mark whenever anyone asks me to do something. I am not sure why, but I always find it very flattering just to be asked, and am so pleased that I will comply. Now that I think of it, I was ordered about but never asked to do anything when I was small. My sisters largely ignored me, as I told you, and my parents, if they wanted something done, would ask my sisters. I was left quite unregarded. Looking back now, I did not know how lucky I was at the time to be left in peace, but it marked me in strange ways, and one of them is that I find it hard to say 'no'.

Moreover my father was very much against play-acting, for in his book it was pretence, and tantamount to lying. Also, the playhouses of his youth were notorious as places of assignation and peopled by women of loose character. Certainly, my father's old college would never have allowed such a thing. Neither did mine officially, but it was a less Puritan sort of place than most at Cambridge and so a blind eye was turned to student merriment on the green.

I learned my lines quite quickly, and it was not difficult for me, perhaps because I have read so much now in the library that I am getting a good memory. What I remember is not so much the words themselves, as their place upon the page and the patterns that they make. Once I summon the picture to mind, I can remember whole chunks of text quite easily.

We rehearsed for about two weeks before the performance, and a strange thing happened to me. I changed. I grew
a little and became taller and more proud, with my nose held
higher in the air, and I walked about with airs and graces, and
astounded my friends with my new-found confidence. It did
not happen overnight, but slowly, as I immersed myself more
and more in the speech of this finest of men. I had never
thought such a thing possible, but my old self fell away, and I
felt much happier, for with the loss of my former identity
went all my worries and fears. It was like travelling to a
foreign place where no one knows you. Your old self, and all
the baggage that was hanging from it, drifts away.

I did not notice any of this until after the play, when I
reverted back. I know it was only an act, but what a strange
sensation! I can see the attractions of the theatre now and
why people are drawn to acting. You become something else,
quite outside your self, and you slough off your old skin like a
snake. But it is a danger too, and a delusion. For when you
are acting you are bathed in the brightness of adoration,
and are never challenged by the dismal light of life.

The Steward does not strike me as one of nature's easiest
of men, but he has a correct nature, and he is cruelly abused
by the lower orders in the play. The trick played upon him
seems to me the worst kind of practical joke, and not at all
funny.

So for my parting line, which, as far as I remember it now,
went, 'I will be revenged upon you, every man-jack of you,' I

let my voice rise slowly along the sentence until it was a high pitched shriek of rage on the last word, and then I swept out. It was a great touch and much remembered. To this day I believe they still talk of Malvolio's great marvel. Oh, to be young again, and applauded on a hot afternoon.

I left before taking my degree. I was too full of books and wanted to be busy. I am sorry, I meant Marvell's great Malvolio, a Freudian slip.

3. Mr Richard Harrington the Puritan

The Puritan hated bear-baiting, not because it gave pain to the bear, but because it gave pleasure to the spectators.

Thomas Babington Macaulay.
History of England, vol. 1 (1849)

Mr Harrington stood at my door. He had been one of the congregation of my father, the Reverend Andrew Marvell the elder, and he never liked the man, for my father veered too close to Romish fancies for his liking.

He brought me the news of my father's death, for he was first to hear it from one who was at the scene. The walk from the Charterhouse is some little distance, perhaps two or two and a half miles, so he had about half of an hour to think carefully about how to break the news. I ushered him in, and looked at him most gravely and steadily, for I could sense that he brought bad news.

It happened yesterday, the twenty-third day into January, and an uncommonly windy one. My father saw a young woman whom he knew arguing with the ferryman that she must be taken across the Humber in his Barrow-boat, for she had promised to be home for her mother who was sick and most worried at her daughter's absence. The ferryman was obstinate in his refusals, and rightly so, for the wind was getting up all the while, and the river was swollen and choppy. Worse, his boat was sand-warped. The Reverend Marvell was passing, and seeing her distress, prevailed upon the man, and promised that he would accompany them both. I dare say the ferryman looked on that as a good sign, for the Lord would surely look kindly upon one of his own Ministers, however much he was given to the arrant ways of Rome. And ferrymen are also famously stricken with superstitions. No doubt it comes from their forebear Charon, who lived before Christ and is therefore in purgatory I understand.

About halfway across the river, the boat began to fill. The boatswain was seen furiously baling with an old bucket, with the Reverend Marvell joining him, and the young woman sitting in the stern looking fearful. And it became clear to my father, before the ferryman, what his fate would be. He was seen to stand up in the centre of the boat, with much difficulty due to wind and wave, and with his right hand he flung his silver-topped cane to the shore, where it landed in the mud, quite clear of the water. Then he gave a great cry, which could be heard by all who were standing in horror upon the bank: 'Ho for Heaven!' and then they sank, never to be seen again.

'I have here the cane, sir,' said Mr Harrington, 'and am

pleased to give it you, though very sorry for my news. He was a good man and a fine preacher, and he will be missed.'

At this Harrington bowed his head. I ushered him out, him looking suitably holy and long faced, and me looking neither happy nor sad. He went through all the right motions, holding his hat humbly in both hands in front of him, and lowering his head slightly and cocking it to one side in sympathy, and speaking in a low and respectful voice. And he backed out the door in deferential manner before turning his back to me, but not before I saw the gleam of satisfaction in his eye. That look was more than just the pleasure that any man enjoys as the bearer of bad news. I know this man's name, but am not sure where from. Harrington, Harrington, hmmm – it will come to me.

As to the story of my father's last cry, I do not believe it for one moment. 'Ho for Heaven,' indeed! He was a pious man all right, but no kind of Puritan, unlike the grey-clad, greasy Mr Harrington, who was squirming so much with suppressed pleasure, he might have been wearing hair drawers under his trousers. Puritanism is the haunting fear that someone else might be happy.

The cane bit rings true though. His last thoughts would have been of me, or at least, of his offspring, though he would have known that the cane would come to me, and not my sisters. It is a fine thing, of good stout thorn, well-japanned to a gleaming black, and with a neat S-shaped cross piece for a handle, chased with a little piece of silver at its top. Nothing fancy, but then nothing plain either, just well wrought and discreetly ornamented, pleasing but not barbarian.

I could see Mr Harrington disapproved of such frippery. His stick was oak, unvarnished, and splayed at the tip, with no handle. Which is just fine as far as I go, if that is what he wants for a stick, let him have it. But what I can't abide with these men is that they think whatever little they want should be enough for all men. They rant on about freedom for all, but when a man expresses another opinion at variance with their own, just watch their love of freedom fly out of the window, and suddenly it's all talk of heresy and burning. I am not joking. It is not just the Papists who burn people. Later in my life, there was an outbreak of witchcraft in Norfolk, halfway to London from here, the first for two generations, and the person who most enjoyed finding the witches out and burning them was a special general, appointed by Cromwell for his piety and zeal in all things. More of that later.

I went to look in my father's papers, and after a short time of leafing found a correspondence he had had with our friend Harrington. It was from some seven or eight years previously, when Harrington had complained to the Bishop about the way my Father preached and his love of a little humour now and then, and had also written to my father as follows:

'Your later letters are full stuffed with swelling, snarling, biting, belching terms of disparagings, false accusings, rash censuring, challenging, and threatening, all of which smell rankly of a proud (to say no worse) and haughty spirit.'

I found a copy that my father had kept of his reply. It was on a single sheet and simply said:

'Mr Harrington, You teach me to write shorter.'

I doubt it shut Mr Harrington down. I doubt if he even saw the joke. His kind never can, and can never achieve the humility they wish upon others, for they have no joking in them. Watch them in a group of men standing around enjoying a joke. His kind will always laugh at the wrong moment, or too loudly, or not at all, for they know they have no understanding of humour, and that is the saddest state of all. It were better they lived in ignorance of it. A good fuck would sort them out. Oh, the hypocrites.

They say that you should not kill the messenger if he brings bad news, but I think that that is often a good policy. Harrington was long faced as he gave me my tragic tidings, yet he could scarce contain his gloating. I am glad I will not see him for a little while, else I might strike him down with this very cane. In fact, had I known then what I would get up to in my later life, I would have killed him stone dead there and then.

I like this cane. I think I will get it turned into a sword-stick, or at least a stick with a dagger concealed inside. I cannot fence yet, but I will learn. I am not a fighting man, quite the reverse, but it may prove useful.

As to my own feelings about the death of my father: very little in truth. I was sad, but cannot say I was grief-stricken, and I was happy at last to succeed to the full state of manhood, which does not fully come upon a man until his father dies. Yet I was also a little fearful of the new responsibility. I swelled in my mind, yet I shrank a little in my chest. Indeed I became quite bowed for a while and got a crick in my neck for a month, but it was soon better, after which I think I grew an inch or two in height. It is strange how the tremors of the mind do often limn themselves in our bodies.

I was now the head of my family, thought I doubt my sisters would acknowledge it, the cows. Not that I care either way what they think. I will inherit whatever my father left. They can make shift perfectly well, for they have married men in the shipping business in Hull, and will be well set up. At least that gets them out of my hair.

I have not yet discovered the pleasure of the opposite sex. I am not yet sure what to do about it, for I am prudent. I do not want to be in its thrall, and I do not want a wife.

4. The Edge-hill Fight on 23 October 1642

For Death thou art a Mower too.

Marvell. 'Damon the Mower'

The harvest was in, the fields mown flat, and the sheaves stacked. It was a cold clear autumnal day, with just the first taste of winter on the wind when I arrived in Banbury, to the north of Oxford. I had left the University at Cambridge in 1641 at the age of twenty, but I still returned occasionally to see my old tutor John de Hunt. I had gone to Banbury straight from Cambridge, under the instructions of de Hunt, who had heard something was under way from his own intelligencers. He is a cunning spymaster. I would report later to Mr Milton and perhaps to that lawyer Thurloe.

There had been skirmishes some days before, at Powick so I had heard, when Prince Rupert had lined some hedges with his Dragoons, and there might be a fight, or even a campaign very soon. A spark may sputter and die, but every inferno began as a spark.

People think there will be no campaign for this fight will

prove decisive, or so they believe. Myself I am not so sure. The English have not fought each other for many, many years, not since the Wars of Lancaster and York perhaps. I think their heart may not be in it when they confront their fellow men. We shall see.

I wrote the above ten years ago now, and how right I was to be dubious. The intervening years taught me much about men's ways. The war dragged on interminably, with little by way of decisive result, and it brought out the worst in men, and very little of the best. Still, I now return to my contemporary account.

Men always go to war when the leaves have turned from green to sere-yellow and are falling.

The Dragoons were on good form. They may have cheap horses, but their chosen weapon is still the long musket, rather than the short carbine which most mounted men prefer, and so their firepower is killing big. Their *enfilade* volley took Parliamentary troopers and their Colonel completely by surprise, and since they packed the lane for nearly a mile, all that they could do was gallop ahead as fast as they could to escape the withering fire from the hedgerows. When they finally broke free of the lane and bridge they were crossing, they emerged to a field where Prince Rupert's men had rapidly mustered, having quit their hedges and mounted fast. There was a charge and the Parliamentary men were scattered back down the road they had come up, as fast as they could manage, fleeing as far as Upton and even Pershore.

It was only a playground bout, no more than a dogfight really, a minor spat between two boys who were left with bloody noses, but it presaged worse, for already the forces were massing for a battle, and from what I had heard of Rupert's cavalry tactics, things did not look good for the Royalists. He is a charismatic man, and a leader with courage and flair, and he may have bested Parliament's men in a mean hedgerow fight with a bunch of heavy Dragoons, but when it comes to the crunch, I do not think his tactics are sound. When he does not have the element of surprise, he will have to rely on sound drill and order, and I do not think he has done his studies well enough. He has read my essays on what I observed of the Dutch in their intelligent campaigns in their recent wars, and how they drew upon and improved the Roman military order, and also on the Swedish King Gustavus Adolphus, who completely reshaped the line of battle to suit a modern army. He models his own tactics on Gustavus, but they are a little old now, and do not conform to modern military practice. I know he has read well, but he is headstrong and impetuous in the way only a twenty-two-year-old can be. He thinks he knows best, and may well have insisted on his own theories being put into practice. This is all very well, but he has never been in a battle before. He may have dash, but it is men's lives he plays with, and a King's honour at stake, and it is honour that drives him, not the careful plotting of a sound battle. He is callous too, which may be a good thing in battle, but cannot recommend him to me much.

Behind him, leading his second line of cavalry, is Lord Digby, a perfectly gallant man, but he has seen no action either, and is unsure of his duties. This is the problem with the King's men. All of them sound, no doubt, but amateurs to a man.

Parliament's men are under Rob Devereux, the third Earl of Essex, and their Captain-General. He is very wealthy, and a haughty man, but his haughtiness is a front, for he was badly scarred as a child by the execution of his father. Worse, he has had two bad marriages, the first dissolved for his impotence, the second for her adultery. He puffs upon his pipe as an aid for thinking, and his men like him, and call him 'Robin'. His men may be equally untried, but they are trained well, can expect reinforcement, and have a cause. He says that they are 'the most resolute foot in Christendom', and there is no reason to doubt it. Prince Rupert says much the same of his cavalry, and no doubt he is right too. Rupert as I said is unblooded, but Essex fought with the Dutch army as a Colonel. That is worth a lot.

We shall see.

That is why I am here. To observe the battle.

The cannonade began at the second hour of the afternoon of the twenty-third. Shot was exchanged for about an hour, to no very great effect that I could see, since I think that both sides were short of grape and canister shot, and instead were using heavy ball fire, which is a waste of ammunition against scattered troops. The Parliament men were better supplied however and gave perhaps two shots for every one of the King's. There was much powder and thunderous noise though, and it played upon men's nerves. I often think I would like to go around the ranks after a cannonade, and gauge the men's morale and inquire what they are thinking. It is a fearsome thing, and there is nothing they can do but endure it. Most men hand around the bottle, to stiffen their resolve and blunt their nerve. Which I can only take to be a good thing, but a good soldier must learn his limit exactly. A falling-down drunk on the field would be no more use than a coward.

It occurs to me that either commander could easily order his men to lie down on the green. I notice the grass is taking on that brassy, darkening hue, such as happens before a thunderstorm. One or two might be unlucky enough to have a ball fall upon them, but the majority could lie there and watch the balls fly overhead, and harmlessly smash the copper-leaved trees at the far distance. The cannoneers might just try lowering their muzzles to aim more directly at the ground, but it would be a very tricky thing to execute. A colonel could thus save himself the lives of a good few hundred men, but I don't think they ever will. It looks too much like a licence for cowardice.

I noted that the Parliamentary cannons were focusing their fire on one part of the King's forces, and I ran to a trooper in the rear, and he told me that it was much suspected that that was the place where the King himself was on his horse. His standard could be seen, and also much of his colours.

Now that is interesting. The King himself would never issue such an order, viz. that his cannon should concentrate upon the area where he thought his opposite number, the Earl of Essex, was standing. He would consider it most ungentlemanly to have something so impersonal as cannon fire take out an aristocrat. Indeed he would hold it cowardly. Cannon fire may well thin out the ranks, but the ranks are cannon-fodder. A Lord should be granted the courtesy of face-to-face combat.

Clearly, the Parliament men have no time for such nicety. The enemy is the enemy as far as they are concerned, and if they despatch the King early on then the whole thing is over and done with, no more waste of time or life. I must say that their vulgar course of action is the more logical, and makes more sense to me, deplorable manners though it may be, but then the Parliamentary cause always did slice straight through to the kernel of the matter. They cut the Gordian knot, you might say. They lack subtlety though. We shall see.

During the exchange of fire and stone, Rupert's Dragoons were up to their old tricks of lining the hedgerows again.

Really, they are very thick, those Dragoons, wobbling around on their knock-kneed nags, and tripping over their long barrelled muskets. Just because it worked once, they think they can pull the same stunt again, within only a few days.

Which as a matter of fact is exactly what they did. The King's Dragooners beat off most of the Rebel musketeers from the hedges that flanked the main field, which was the intended fighting zone, and the way was now clear for a Royal attack.

Which was the very first attack of what became the Civil Wars, though no one knew at the time it would be so long drawn out. It was believed this fight might decide it all, and they would all be enjoying peace once more come Christmas. Poor fools.

I am coming to admire those Dragooners. Give a man freedom of space to skirmish around, away from the ordered line of battle, and he can achieve much if he has the will and the courage, and a good understanding of the ground on which he finds himself. A small map might help each and every one of them. I must think upon them and their possible uses in future, after this thing is over. You never know which way is the best way forward in martial matters. Some new device is always welcome if it can be used. Who knows, future battles may well be fought by easily manoeuvrable skirmishers, with no orders to follow but their own good sense and experience. They could wreak havoc on a trained army, biting at its edges like fleas on a helpless man in a tight suit, forever scratching but never finding them.

Prince Rupert charged, and what a stirring sight he made. From standing quietly in ranks three deep, in the Swedish formation he had learnt from his reading of Gustavus Adolphus, they spurred their horses to full gallop without benefit of a first cantering and were soon charging across the clear ground with a roar like rolling thunder. His best troopers were in the front rank and he was ahead of them, his distinguishing red plume near horizontal in the wind, and his long, curled locks waving out behind him from under his iron helm. He wore no face guard, and his hawk-nosed features could easily be made out.

He rode a coal black horse, somewhat shorter than the others, but most pretty, for its head was more upright and it charged most proudly. Alongside him ran his pet pudell dog, a handsome big beast with black curly hair called 'Boy', charging into the fray with great enthusiasm, spurred on by his master's cry of 'To them, Boy.'

Rupert had already taught his men to use only their toes in the stirrups. Most cavalrymen push their boot into the stirrup up to the heel, but that is only necessary if they are lancers and need the extra purchase, and so they galloped on across the field on their toes.

His two long pistols were sheathed in red leather saddle-holsters, which were chased in gold filigree. Other than a simple cuirass over his buff coat, he wore no armour, and his sword looked light. His front rank favoured heavier swords of the older cavalry type, and one man to his left carried an axe. They all wore scarlet silk sashes from shoulder to waist and their breastplates gleamed gash-gold vermilion in the sun. Their thunder rang across the field like the wrath of God.

Parliament's men were keeping steady. They stood in Dutch formation, that is eight lines deep for infantry and six for cavalry. It is more modern than Prince Rupert's Swedish style, and I think less of a gamble. They stood, and they stood, as the enemy approached, like a great wave rolling up to the shore. Their tactic was to meet the enemy charge at the halt with solid fire from all available carbines and pistols. There were also, I could see, some 300 extra foot musketeers, who had been placed at random among the ranks of the horsemen, to increase their firepower. Other musketeers were placed in the hedges at the edge, in emulation of the Royal Dragoons of which I told you above. There were even three cannon wheeled in to play, to back up the assembled fire.

They stood patiently, while the Royalists came down like the wolf on the fold.

First, the men in the pale green hedges were pushed back by those cunning Royal Dragoons, and so one line of defence was lost. Then the three cannons let off an early volley, I think before anyone gave them the signal, and so the shot soared clear over the heads of the charging troopers to no effect at all. There went the second line of defence.

It all now depended upon the mounted men, standing so patiently, their flintlocks at the shoulder, and the foot musketeers, with older matchlocks, their slow-burning matches fizzing in the crisp afternoon air. And on the charge came.

They roared up to the fifty-yard mark, which a London man had secretly staked out in the turf with a short stick so that Essex might have an idea of scale. It was then he gave the command, having reckoned that it would be but three or four seconds before the charge would be upon him. I felt a huge crash, as if a giant's hand had hit me hard upon the chest. It was loud enough to the ear, but the sensation was more physical than auditory. The shock wave from the assembled gunnery rolled past me and almost knocked me over, and left my ears ringing from the pressure. There was a large amount of black powder smoke too, surrounding the mounted men and cloaking their heads.

I looked at the charging Royalists, expecting to see carnage.

It had hardly made a blind bit of difference. They continued forward completely undismayed. A few men had been shot and fallen from their mounts, but the main charge was neither halted nor even broken slightly. Even the riderless horses stayed with the main body, galloping still at full stretch. I could hardly believe what I saw, and neither could the Parliamentary men. They sat there, still at the halt, their mouths agape, and then the first wave was upon them and a huge cry arose from both sides as they engaged with a clash almost as loud as the volley of shot.

No man at a standstill can withstand a horse at full gallop. The sheer inertia of a speeding line of cavalrymen is too great. Parliament's lines were utterly smashed by Rupert and the King's cavalry. They reared and turned and wheeled helplessly under the onslaught, their horses screeching in fear, and many of the men too, I have to record, and each man did as he could best in order to escape. They were crushed in an instant and whosoever was not killed scattered very quickly and retreated at full tilt.

Then it all went to hell.

The centre and one flank of all the mounted Parliament men fled for their lives, and the Royal men, whooping with victory, pursued them until they were all out of sight. Worse, the second line of Royal horse, under Digby, lost their heads and joined in the charge, and soon disappeared over the horizon with the first line. They were supposed to be held in reserve, but were too overcome with enthusiasm for what looked like an easy victory. And so, in the space of minutes, the entire Royal cavalry was removed from the field, leaving their foot to fend for themselves and at the mercy of one small wing of Parliament horse who had survived the charge.

I have never seen anything in battle so utterly stupid.

If the King loses this battle, and he surely will now, he will have only his own nephew, Prince Rupert, to blame. Honour and glory in a young man are all very well, but without discipline and order of line, you might as well surrender before the first volley.

The King's cavalry had won a victory with their first charge and they threw it away just as soon as they had it.

Then I saw a sight. It was Sir Jacob Astley, who commanded the King's infantry, who now stepped up to his place at their head, knowing that it was his turn to take the field. I could see his proud bearing even though I was some way off behind my wall. He was well into his forties, but a fit man. His blond hair was long and curled, and his goatee beard, very like the King's, was streaked with grey, which looked most becoming. Like Rupert he wore a red plume, the better to be seen by his men. He had his top-boots unrolled all the way up his thighs, and he stepped forward and raised his sword high above his head. The ranks fell silent, and he spoke some words which were lost to me on the wind, but which I later learned from a survivor.

'O Lord. Thou knowest how busy I must be this day. If I forget thee, do not thou forget me.' And with that he rose up and cried out at the top of his voice, 'March on boys!' and they followed him at a brisk pace to their drummer's beat most gallantly. It strikes me now as a most excellent prayer. Pious, short and soldierly.

They marched forward steadily, their colours, a proud flag

of a red cross on a field of white, whipping in the breeze. There were five brigades of them in line of battle and they closed with the Parliament men at a ploughed patch at near dead centre of the main battlefield. Of the fight on foot, I can say little, for it was the usual terrifying muddle, though here and there I could make out patterns and incidents, of which I will tell you. Early on for example, I saw Wentworth's brigade failing to close *to push of pike*, and therefore were held in check simply by Meldrum's smaller regiment.

The pike is a most noble instrument for a gentleman of rank and if used properly is most effective. I saw, way across from where I was standing, Sir Philip Stapleton's cuirassiers charge down upon Lord Byron's Brigade, but to no good effect because Byron's men were able to form a defensive ring of pikes, all of them eighteen-footers and all firmly held at the heel, at a low angle. Not one cavalryman could penetrate that ring of steel, and indeed the horses were most fearful of clashing with it. It was like the worst thicket thorns in a forest, no beast could hope to get clear if once it fell in, and so the horses tended to shy away, no matter that their riders spurred them on. The pike is truly excellent at both defence and offence.

There was a rogue troop of Parliament's cavalry under Sir William Balfour, which had not taken part in the first charge and so had not been forced from the field by Prince Rupert. They had the field to themselves, since all the other horsemen had charged off, and they were therefore engaged with difficult work behind their enemy's lines.

At one point they broke clean through a regiment of King's foot, who had rallied under a virid green banner, and fought all the way back to the King's artillery. Here they found many cannon, including two of the biggest, known as Demy-Cannon, and Balfour called for nails, for he wished to spike the guns. A great cry went up of 'Nails. Nails', but the few men who had been deputed to carry some in their wallets had been killed or lost, no one knew where. So Balfour had to be content with cutting the heavy ropes attached to the cannon. It would stop them being used almost as effectively as spiking, for they could not be man-oeuvred without their ropes.

Note for the future: every tenth (?) man in a cavalry line to carry at least one nail in his equipage. It would be invaluable. A cannon with a nail driven deep into its powder hole is effectively dead to the battle. To remove such a nail requires a skilled carpenter with an iron screw as well as heavy lifting rigs, and cannot be done in the press of fighting.

Balfour killed all the cannoneers and pursued the ones who fled half a mile upon execution.

If he had but known it at the time, he came close to capturing the young Prince Charles, the King's son, who later became King Charles the Second, and also his brother James,

Duke of York. They were under the close protection of Sir Will Howard, and he had seen Balfour's body of horse approach but had thought it to be their own side's cavalry. Balfour's men were easily within musket shot, when Howard realized his mistake and quickly took his charges to a nearby barn, where lay the wounded of the King's men. Balfour's men, upon seeing that it was a royalist dressing station, withdrew. Never did they know that if they had pressed their charge they could have taken a future king of England and so easily changed the course of history, to such a degree as to be unimaginable.

To think: Cromwell might well have reigned with Charles beheaded, and the two sons, Charles and James, forever held in the Tower. England would be a Republic till the crack of doom and might never have had another King. Ah, take a simple step to the left or the right and the whole perspective changes, and then we say, ah, what might have been?

But Balfour missed them. After capturing a few more cannon, he retreated to join his own forces again, and shot a man in the hand who was approaching, because he thought the man was of the enemy. The man was simply waving his hand in greeting.

Note for the future: one must have not only standards to rally up to, but also some identifying colour on each man which would be different from the other side. Green would be appropriate to Parliament's men. It is a revolutionary colour. Either that or insist on eye-glasses for each officer in charge.

Two other things I saw which are worth recounting, for though very different actions, they bear a similar moral lesson.

The King's standard was captured at one point. In fact it made little true difference to the outcome, but it is amazing how it can affect the men who are fighting beneath it. It is symbolic, and I have seen men throw down their arms, even though they were winning, simply because they had lost their standard.

It was carried by Sir Edmund Verney. Now I know Verney a little, and he is the finest of men. Like many, including myself, he was in two minds about the Parliamentary cause, and could not decide which side he should join, for he had been at the King's court for most of his life, yet he began to deplore the way the King behaved, and did truly believe that the King must have a Parliament to modify his tyrannical behaviour. Then he was called on to choose a side, and he could not. What it came down to was: he was torn between duty and conscience. His conscience knew of the justness of the Cause of Parliament. His duty lay to his King. He sat and pondered long and hard on this, and then wrote a letter to his family, which I can quote from memory. The salient part went:

'I have eaten his bread and served him for near thirty

years, and so I cannot do so base a thing as to forsake him.' Instead he did 'choose rather to lose my life – which I am sure I will do – to preserve and defend those Things which are against my conscience to preserve.'

So, without benefit of arms or armour, nor even of a buff coat, he stepped quite naked of defence on to the field to carry the King's standard. I saw it waving most proudly in the very thickest of the fighting. Then there came a moment when it dipped. I could hardly make out what was happening, but later learned that the King's men were crumbling under sustained pressure from the opposing combination of horse and foot, and Verney adventured among his enemy's soldiers, armed solely with his pennant, so that his own men might be encouraged to follow him.

There followed a desperate fight around the standard, such is its power and appeal to both sides, for it must be captured and taken to demoralize an enemy.

He was cut down, even as he was waving the flag, and trying to use it as a pike in his own defence.

Alas, his body was never found from the heap surrounding the flag, and I fear the locals later buried it too quickly before he could be identified, but the standard was found, and still gripped about its pole was a severed hand. When they removed the glove they found Sir Edmund Verney's ring on his mid finger, which had in it a miniature portrait of his King. His hand was returned, with the ring, to his family, who have preserved it to this day.

When I think upon such bravery words first fail me, for I feel it was glorious, but then I become indignant at the loss of so good a man, and then quite cynical, for the man did not so have to throw his life away as if it were worthless. He had a family who needed him as much as did his King.

Oh, the glory of it, and the waste.

The other curious thing I saw concerned Fortescue's men. The ill-named Sir Faithful Fortescue had raised a troop of horse to join Parliament's army, and they were to be sent to Ireland to put down yet another rebellion from the Catholic swine. However, before it could even set out for Ireland, it was pressed into service with Essex's men for the Edge-hill fight. Now, Faithful Fortescue was perfectly happy to go and butcher a few hairy Papists who were still living in mud huts, but he was damned if he was going to attack his own King.

So, before the fight began, he sent his Lieutenant, a man called Van Girish, to carry a message to Prince Rupert on the other side. The gist of it was that, once Rupert charged, Fortescue's men, on the left of the line of Parliament's cavalry, would fire their weapons into the ground and yield immediately, and change sides.

Unfortunately, Rupert did not have time to convey this news to all his commanders, and so some of Fortescue's men were hurt by the Royalist charge. Mostly, however, it had a saddening effect upon the Parliamentary cavalry, to find so great a number of their own men shooting off their pistols into the ground and yielding to the enemy's cause and even turning and fighting for them.

I do not think it was a decisive gesture. I think that Prince Rupert's horse would have broken through and routed the Parliament men, whether there were turncoats or not, but it was of interest to me, for none complained very much about the affair afterwards. No one accused Sir Faithful of any cowardice. No one, from either side, reproached any of his troopers for their little plot. And the reason for that I think is that almost all men here feel the same. Their minds are divided, and when they find themselves fighting for one side or the other, it is mainly a matter of timing or exigency or sheer blind fate. They know perfectly well they could have been on the other side if they had turned left and not right at some crossroads they had passed.

As I said: a step left or right, and the whole perspective changes.

There was cowardice and there was bravery, in equal measure and on both sides, as there always is in any fight, and I do not wish to dwell on it. Who among us can say that when the hour is at hand we would behave as we would wish to be remembered? So much malign fate can intervene, as to turn a man's best intentions to dust and ashes.

By way of an example, I give you the fate of just one man, who was called John Smith. No, that truly was his name, I am not making it up as a general example. He was a Captain of

Lord Grandison's Troop of Horse: not a humble person, nor yet a very elevated one either, a middling sort of man, which I often think that this island is very good at producing. The middling stations in life here are very sound. He was on the Left Wing of the King's horsemen, and was rallied with about 200 others of like mind, under Sir Charles Lucas.

After the first charge, when the Royal cavalry broke the ranks of Parliament's troopers and pursued them from the field in the disastrous way I have described, for some reason that I cannot find out, he did not follow them, but suddenly he found himself almost alone on the field, but for one other horseman.

I remember seeing him at the time, though I did not know who he was. He stood up high in his stirrups, and twisted his neck around and looked in every direction, and I swear that I could see his brows furrowed and a frown on his face, even though I was too far away. His whole body spoke of a perplexed man. And so he relaxed his reins slightly, wheeled about, and ambled back towards his own lines, the other lone horseman following suit, for all the world as if they were out for a morning's leisurely canter.

As he tracked back across the field, he saw a party of Parliament's men carrying a rolled-up flag. He looked at it, and thought he could discern the Colours of His Majesty's Life Guards, and so was not too troubled, since it was not actually the King's Standard. Besides, there were six of them around the flag, three Cuirassiers and three Harquebusiers on horseback, all guarding a seventh man on foot who was carrying the banner. So, outnumbered, he turned his horse and rode wide around them. An entirely sensible course of action. He was not a Life Guard himself, and so the Standard meant little to him. Let each man look to his own flag.

But then this boy comes running up, I know not where from, probably one of the luggage-train sent on an errand, and tells Mr John Smith that the flag that the Rebels are carrying off is in fact the Royal Standard.

I wish I could say what he thought in the next five seconds. I certainly know what he did almost immediately, but what thought prompted his actions, and how long he took to make a decision about his course of action, I do not know, and I dearly wish I did.

He charged the knot of men, and wounded one of them immediately in the chest with his sword. It was in fact one of the Earl of Essex's servants. He followed through with his thrust to try again, but one of the other Cuirassiers swung a poleaxe at him and wounded him through the collar of his doublet on the neck, though not severely. There was much blood, but there always is from a neck wound.

Then the rest all pulled out their pistols and started blazing away, and after five clear shots, he was still unhit. True they were all mounted and whirling about their man, but still, he was more than lucky. Or was it luck? I have so often seen men steel themselves to take on the impossible, when hopelessly outnumbered, and then fate smiles upon them. Or perhaps it is the enemy who are unnerved by a single madman taking them on. Whatever it is, I do often find that fortune favours the aggressive man.

I digress. He was left with nothing more than a face blackened by powder and some singed eyebrows. His enemies looked at him and gaped in surprise. So he squares his shoulders again, and makes another thrust at one of the Cuirassiers, and runs him through the belly. The man fell, and at that the rest of them ran away, leaving their captured banner behind. They probably thought he was a demon, or at least a man possessed. There was a long silence as he looked at the flag, and calmed his breathing. He wiped the blood from his neck and chest, I could see that too, and after a minute or so, he called a foot soldier over and asked, most politely, if the man could hand him up the flagpole. I do not think the soldier even knew what it was, but he handed it up to our horseman. And he rode back most content to his King with his flag.

The next day his King dubbed him a knight banneret, an ancient and rare honour, and now he is Sir John Smith, and I have spoken to him about the incident, which I witnessed from my high vantage-point, and he says that he scarcely knows how it all came about, or even whether he truly deserves his honour. He is a modest, taciturn man, and I do believe him. Another, bolder man might have recognized that his hour of glory had come around and seized the moment. John Smith, I think, was swept along by fate, and rose to meet whatever the blind bitch had thrown in his path, by dint of good nature and sound sense.

He is not an imaginative man. I have noticed that men with fanciful imaginations are often not courageous. They too easily imagine the worst that can happen, and that can make a coward of any of us.

Not content with all of that farrago, Smith also rescued Richard Fielding, who had been captured by a party of ten of Parliament's men, after his Brigade of foot had been defeated and fled. I did not see that.

By God, he was going it some that day. Men fight best in groups, I have perceived. What we call courage is often the desire not to let down one's fellow soldier. Nor to be seen as a coward in the eyes of one's peers. Or sometimes the strong desire to protect a loved brother-in-arms. But Smith was all alone, on both occasions.

May his sons, and their sons, and their sons inherit his modest courage down the years for as long as it please the Lord for his family to prevail. It is a fine quality to see in a man. He was killed eighteen months later in a fight at Cheriton.

I saw men run from the fight too, men that I knew of, screaming at the tops of their voices and begging mercy of the Lord. It was a shaming sight, but I cannot hold it against them, and I will not name them here. It would be hard enough for any man to live with himself after a thing like that. Their God and their conscience will know of it, and that is good enough for me, let it be good enough for you too.

The firing continued till night put an end to the dispute. Late in the day, the King's Secretary urged Lord Wilmot to make one more charge, for by then, many of the Royalist cavalry had remustered, after having charged off in all directions so disastrously. But Lord Wilmot replied, 'My Lord, we have the day. Let us live to enjoy it.' And so they did not, and they did. Typical cavalier behaviour, I may say. They did not have the day at all, though they could not perhaps have known it for sure. Still they were arrogant enough to believe it, and lazy enough not to be bothered with one last push, that might have secured them a sound victory.

The Royalists retired to the high ground, which they had held at the start, and Parliament's men returned to their village, where they had been quartered the night before, and I must say I think they had the better of it, what with a good fire and hot food and a roof to go home to after a day's fighting.

The dead were left where they were for the night, and later were buried by each side with the help of local men. The official count, ordered by the King, reckoned on one thousand slaughtered, and three times that number wounded. Barber-chirurgeons and their assistants had laboured as long as they could searching for the wounded, but soon darkness hampered them, and they were forced to wait for morning. Many of the wounded and dying were left all night on the cold field. It was not a fate I would wish on any man.

Both sides faced each other the next day, and both had a forlorn look. Neither would advance to the fight, they had no stomach for more. Both sides bragged of a victory, though both were equally dismayed at their losses. Nothing was decisive.

The most that could be said of the outcome was that the King's objective of marching on London had been slightly advanced. Essex's objective had been to prevent him, but by the end of the fight, and the final skirmishes, the King and his men were left marginally closer to London than their enemy. That was the best interpretation that could be put upon it all. And little good it did either of them.

Prince Rupert was for dashing to London and taking it. He could certainly get there quicker than Essex's men, but once there he would have been lost. He does not know London at all, and thinks he can canter through it until he reach Whitehall. He knows nothing of its narrow lanes, in which a simple thick chain laid across two buildings could thwart a whole army. Wiser counsel prevailed and the King's men marched slowly on the capital, until they took Brentford and then reached Turnham Green. There they were confronted by an army of 25,000 trained men. The Royalists all swallowed heavily, turned on their heels, retreated to Oxford, and didn't stray from their snug quarters for the rest of the winter.

And so it proved for the whole of the rest of the wars. The Royalists would come within an inch of victory and then retire into their comfort for lack of resolve. Had one side or the other prevailed and smashed the enemy utterly, killed them by the hundred, spared no prisoners, then enslaved all their families, and sowed their land with salt, if they had done all of that, it would have been more humane, I swear it.

Because of lack of a strong result, however, the war continued for years, and dribbled on and on like an incontinent old dotard, and took off too many of our young men, and made brother to fight brother, and caused so much misery throughout this land as to be worse than a plague. The thing about a plague is that it is God that sends it and so it must be endured. Men do much worse, and all of it with good intentions.

God rot this stupid fight. I will watch it without flinching, for I can watch anything. My heart is cool, and my mind is strong, I am not governed by emotion, and so nothing can make me avert my gaze. Yet I know no good will come of it. It may be a cause worth fighting for, but it is not a cause worth dying for. No political cause ever is. I would prefer to be ruled by a king and a parliament, rather than just a king – and if there be a choice in the matter, perhaps I would rather just be ruled by a parliament of like-minded gentlemen – but if there be no choice, I will take whatever comes along and make shift.

But I speak of the overall picture, when I should be attending to the particulars. For it is in details that I deal.

> Edge-hill:
> I looked out over the field and saw the quick and
> the dead. And however we toil, we all will sleep at
> last on a field. And all shall rust amid green. As last
> year's scythes are flung down and left in the half
> cut swathes.

And now you know how I feel, I will take myself off before my mind changes again as it usually does. By tomorrow I will feel different, and will tell you a different tale.

5. After the Fight at Edge-hill

He will be looked on by posterity as a brave bad man.

Edward Hyde, Earl of Clarendon. *The History of the Rebellion* (1703)

> *Then burning through the air he went,*
> *And palaces and temples rent.*

Marvell. 'An Horatian Ode upon Cromwell's Return from Ireland'

'Mister Murvill, I thank you for coming.' He was striding fast as usual, his gloves were tucked in his belt, and the tops of riding boots were not rolled down, but flapped heavily against his thighs. He would have been able to walk much easier if he had folded them down, but there was always something impatient about him, I have often marked it. If it were not his boots, it would be his stock awry, or his laces undone, or his buttons fallen off, and never would he correct it.

As in his dress, so in his politics. It was as if he could not be bothered to attend to the details of making the world a better place, but he would bend it to his desires by sheer force of will. As always with men like that, they expend twice as much energy to gain their result, than if they had done it patiently and carefully. But then, I have to say, patience and care do not win the day at a fight. Brute strength and bloody-mindedness are what you want on your side there, and Oliver had them in spades.

And here we were, come together at his most express request, the day after the fight. He had arrived late with a troop of horse and had taken no part in it. He was only a Captain in those days. We fell in step quite unconsciously even as we talked, and strode across the grass together, towards the killing ground.

We crested a low rise in the ground, and oh, dear God what a sight was there! It pulled him up to a dead halt, and me too, even though I have been studying the wars for a long time now. There was a long pause between us, as he studied the scene in general at first, and then in more detail, his head turning from side to side, and his eyes like a hawk. I noticed his nostrils were flared and he breathed quick and rather shallow, as if he were short of air.

'Not your first time for such a sight, I imagine Mr Murvill,' he said. 'Please bear with me for a moment, for it is certainly my first time.'

'You are right, sir, I *have* seen much of this before, and it is surprising how quickly you might become inured to it. Like a barber-chirurgeon,' I said, and I knew he understood me well. For a headstrong man, he is very understanding of others. He might not allow them to live, because of their opinions, but he understands them all right. 'But I saw all of what I know about battles abroad. Never did I see Englishmen like this before.'

I was lying. This is my first battle. I had only read of them before in my studies.

'No, I imagine not,' he said and shook his head, and snorted through his nose, 'And worse than that, sir. Not just Englishmen, but Englishmen killed by Englishmen.'

'It is a sorry sight,' I said.

'Sorry for anyone who looks upon it, like you, sir,' he said, 'but I will have to take a part in it, and I beg you pray for me, when I do.' Then he turned quickly and shook off his thoughts, and was all business again.

'Tell me your observations on cavalry, sir. I have been raising them, and I have not yet got enough, but I will do, I surely will. It seems to me that they are mighty important, but we do not use them wisely.'

'You are right on both counts, sir,' I said. 'First: they *are* mighty important. The cavalry is there to provide the victory . . .' and before I could finish, he interrupted, 'But what of the poor bloody infantry, will they get no credit?'

'The infantry, sir, are there to provide the casualties,' I said.

He looked at me with a sombre knowingness. He knew what I had just said to be a terrible truth, but never would he admit it, to his troops or himself. What must be done by a leader in battle must be done.

'I am sorry, your second point, sir?'

'On the second score you are also right, sir,' I said. 'Prince Rupert there, of the King's band, is a dashing man and no doubt his bunch of whooping Lords on horse would follow him any way, but they do not have the right idea.'

'And you do, sir? You do?'

'I have studied it, sir.'

'Then let us walk the field, and you may talk me through it.'

'I would rather not, sir, there are too many men down there busy dying.' And it was true. They had lain there all night in the cold, and though the pallet-bearers were moving through them and picking them up as fast as they could manage, yet still the ground was littered with men. Some were still moving, lifting their arms to heaven. And over the whole field, a hideous quiet.

So we turned together, and skirted the edge of the killing ground, and talked long and hard upon the use of cavalry, and I told him what I had learned from both Gustavus Adolphus of Sweden, who was the first to rethink the use of cavalry for our times, and from the more modern Dutch approach. Gustavus it was who insisted that the sword be their primary weapon and not the pistol, for the pistol may be a good frightener, what with its noise, but it is very inaccurate when fired from horseback, and then cannot be reloaded at all easily. Also I told him what I had learned and seen from the Lowlands, and from witnessing manoeuvres in

Spain, which were greater refinements on the Swede's ideas. I had not seen them, only read of them in books.

'And so to sum up,' I said finally, 'the chiefest thing to remember is to round them all up after the first charge. That first charge is vital, as we have all seen – it will scatter the enemy's infantry to hell and gone, and frighten them out of their wits, as much because of the horses' hooves as from the cavalry's weapons – but once the cavalry have broken through the lines, then the horsemen tend to scatter and gallop off in twos and threes, pursuing whoever they feel like. It is as much to do with the psychology of each man as anything. The rider feels such a gleeful satisfaction at having charged down and broken through the enemy lines without being harmed, that suddenly he is king of the world and wants to celebrate by cantering off into the twilight, haring after a few stragglers.

'What you must, must, *must* impress on each and every man-jack of your cavalry, is that once they have broken through, then they must wheel and remuster. Form a single line abreast behind the enemy's broken ranks, it need not be a perfect line, and then charge once more. Do not waste time reloading your pistols, use your swords instead. You will not face pike-men this time, and most of the enemy will be disordered and scattered. Charge them once more, and then keep re-forming and charging again and again. After two or three smashes, you will find them crushed utterly. That may sound cruel to you, sir, but in point of fact it is more humane.

The battle will be over the quicker, decided more swiftly, and so there will finally be fewer killed and wounded by the end of the day.'

'You may find this odd, sir, but that is what I devoutly pray for, even against my enemies.'

'I find that unusual, but not odd, Captain. You are an unusual man in many ways.'

'What of pike-men, sir, what is your opinion on that matter.'

'Pike-men are invaluable. A solid front rank of eighteen-footers, held low at the heel, is almost impregnable to a cavalry charge, and they need only two things taught to them. The first is the standard pike drill, as I have laid out in my manual to you, and can easily be printed up in picture form on pamphlets. I know that most of your trained bands are learned men, and can read from their scriptures and so on, but there are some who are unlettered. Besides, a picture is a great aid to learning. So, they can each have a pamphlet to carry and look at over their food, and discuss. The drilling once learned is a great aid to discipline and morale, two most important factors and hard to quantify, but most important as any leader will tell you.'

'And the second thing, sir?'

'It sounds the simpler of the two, yet it is the harder. Indeed it is the hardest thing of all for a foot soldier to do, and I do not know how you teach it. It is, simply, to stand.'

'Ah, indeed, to stand.'

We gladly let a long pause pass between us, for we both of us had yet to experience the terrors of battle, yet we understood only too well.

'To stand firm, in order of line, while your comrades fall on either side from shot and ball, and not run ... well that takes a special kind of man.' There was a silence while he thought upon it.

'I talk to my men, you know,' he said finally.

'I have seen you, sir, you are a great one for talking.' Indeed he was. He may have been short and stumpy, he may have had a very plain face with warts upon it, he may have had colourless, straggly hair of no great beauty, and he certainly had breath so bad that it could slay a mule at ten paces. But he could talk. When he opened his mouth, his words were to the point and freighted with conviction. When he spoke, you listened.

'You are inspired,' I continued, 'and your men are grateful for it. No one on the King's side talks to their men. As far as the Lords are concerned, their men are a bunch of rabble who will fight simply because that is what they are paid to do. And no doubt they are right, in their way. Your troopers are often old and decayed men, and men such as innkeepers and the like. They face an army composed of gentlemen and men of quality. The spirit of a base or mean man will always consider itself to be the inferior of that of a gentleman. You must find men of spirit, sir, men who will go as far as a gentleman will go in this fight, or you will be beaten.

'But talk to your men, sir, persuade them of the rightness and just cause of your fight, and I do believe they will fight the better for it. A man will fight for a cause he believes in much better than for money.'

'Aye, and die for it, too,' he said.

'Oh, men will die for any damn fool thing,' I said.

'But the cause is just, sir, and the Lord is with us.'

'Don't you think that the other side says that too?'

'They may very well, but they are wrong,' he near-shouted.

'Our Lord Fairfax,' I said, changing the subject rapidly, 'who is rising fast and may be a leader soon, does not think anything like that, but he will be a very great General none the less.'

'He will be a great General,' said Oliver through gritted teeth, 'but he lacks the final resolve.'

The final resolve, eh? What you really mean, I thought, is a taste for never stopping the slaughter until every last opposing man on the field is dead, and then killing and raping the women and children too. You are a butcher, sir, and my Lord Fairfax is not. He is a good soldier, and he is the better man.

'The final resolve, sir?' I said. 'You may very well be right, I think. And do you plan perhaps to supplant my Lord Fairfax in time as General of our forces?'

Then he looked at me angrily, but said nothing more, and walked away, pulling out his sword, a heavy, old-fashioned cavalry weapon, slightly straighter than more modern ones which have a curve, and began swinging it and hacking at tufts of grass.

We had not even finished talking. There was more, much more that I could have said to him about tactics, and more, I suspect, that he wished to ask, but he is short-tempered, and head-strong, and mighty full of himself too. He will walk off simply to make sure he has the last word, let alone if he is annoyed at something. I think perhaps I revealed my hand too much when I asked about his plans to take over from Fairfax as leader of the Parliament troop, but by his temper he made it clear that that is exactly what he has in mind.

'You are granite, sir,' I called after him, though he made no sign of having heard. And the Royalists, I thought, they are the rain. They will wear *you* down, drip by drip.

There are times when I dislike you Mr Cromwell, though never would I show it, to you or to any other. But you should beware of my dislike. Best keep on the good side of Mr Murvill, *sir*. And learn my name properly. That would only be a common courtesy, yet it might save you my enmity, and perhaps spare you some pains later.

Although, now I think about it, Fairfax is a splendid soldier, but I suspect he would rather retire from a fight against his own race, no matter what their political allegiance may be. He has his own politics, which are loosely against the King, but he is sane enough to know that there may be an opposing view. He has no stomach for killing his own kind, and has a delicate conscience. Besides, he has his coin and medal collection to look after, at his home in Yorkshire, and a fine wife and a little daughter.

The Parliament claimed the victory here, and so did the King's men, but they were both wrong. The outcome was indeterminate. As I have told you, had one side smashed the other for all time, it would have been a blessing, no matter which side won. As it was the butchery continued. And so I took off. I can watch anything without turning a hair, but do not ask me to take part. Had I stayed in England I knew I would have been called to choose and then fight at some point, and I could not do that.

I went abroad and stayed there for as long as I could, passing myself off as a tutor to whichever son whose family would pay me enough to din some knowledge into his thick skull. Cromwell even gave me his ward, young Dutton, for a while. He was a nice boy, and it was intended by Cromwell that Dutton marry his daughter.

In fact I was also acting as a spy for Mr Milton, which I will tell you about later. I went through Amsterdam, France, Switzerland and Rome, where I met Mr Flecknoe, which was so boring I do not think I will tell you about it, and Ronda and Madrid in Spain, where I learned about swords and also the bullring and much more besides, but mainly about the teasing nature of women, and what a nuisance that is to a man. *Nuisance?* It was an abject nightmare and I will live celibate rather than deal with it again. And if a woman gets me to the brink of her bed once more and then refuses, no matter that she be the last woman alive on earth, I will strangle her with the guts of her sister and plead mitigation. Celibacy, thy name is balm.

6. Sketches of Spain

Anecdote. Short account (or painting) of an entertaining or interesting incident. First used by Marvell. From Greek, *anekdota*, things unpublished.

In Ronda I took fencing lessons, for I had neglected my martial exercises thus far, being content to study the wars only from books, but I live in troubled times and, besides, every man should know how to bear arms. I had the sword-stick made from the cane left to me by my father, but I preferred to keep that my secret, and so sought out one of the better armourers in the town, who are gathered mainly around the bullring. I could find none that I took a liking to though and so went for a short walk along the main street as far as the gorge.

Ronda is a strange place, built high up on a cragged mountain and spanning a steep gorge, which divides the town in two. The chasm can be crossed by an ancient bridge, resting on long tall thin supports, which sometimes sway when the ground quakes, so they tell me, but seem sound enough.

I leaned on the parapet and looked down to the jagged

rocks down the side of the gorge, and littering the bottom of what looked like a dried up river bed, fringed by stunted moss-green plants. Nature here was mainly brown and mean. I was doing fine, admiring the view downwards, when I felt a passer-by behind me, and I began to twist my head without due thought, and was hit by a terrible attack of the vertigo. I stood up and clutched at my head, but also had to reach for the rail, for I was swaying violently and could not stay upright on my feet. I stumbled against the safety wall, and fell, first to my knees, which I barked, and then further till I was sprawled on the ground in a sitting position.

A man came up, I think the one who had first unsettled me, and squatted down beside me. Taking the back of my head most gently, he pressed it forward until it was crouched between my knees. 'There now,' he said, 'that is better, the blood will flow more freely, and now you must breathe more deeply and more slowly, for you were panting just now like a dog.' He unplugged a canteen and poured some water on his hands and wiped the back of my neck and my temples, and continued crooning things that I could not catch, perhaps they were in Spanish, but they were most soothing.

'You were looking for an armourer,' he said after a while, when I had calmed, but was still sitting. It was not a question.

'How did you know?' I asked, and he just smiled by way of reply. Oh spare me the enigmatic foreigner stuff, I thought, please, I am sick of it: 'We Spanish, we may not say much, but nothing escapes our . . .' You know the sort of thing.

He helped me to my feet, and I must say that I was less dizzy now, though I did not turn to look over the parapet again. I have not had one of those attacks for many years now. I must learn what brings them on.

'Are you troubled?' he said.

'Yes,' I said, 'I have not had the vertigo for a long time.'

'No, I meant from before that. Are you troubled in general? In the mind or in your circumstance?'

'I do not think so,' I said, though I was.

'Well, that is strange,' he said, 'for vertigo can often be brought on by a man's troubles. He may go near the edge for years with no problem, but if he is too troubled it can bring on the giddy spell. I often think that the root of the problem is not the fear of the height.'

'Oh, and what then can it be?' I said.

'It is the desire to jump that frightens you,' he said.

I garrumphed and made rubbishy sorts of noises, but later, upon reflection, I had to admit that he had something of the truth. The abyss has a pull to it.

He was tall, and walked with a swagger, which may have been a limp, I was not sure. He was about my age, and handsome, and he was very black, with swarthy skin, long dark mustachios and the darkest eyes, which in bright sunlight turned basalt green.

As he was helping me to my feet, he held his hand out to

me, and as I took it, I had the most profound sense of feeling completely safe. His hands did not seem especially large, but it was just that he seemed very capable in what he did, and handled himself with a sharp economy. He did not pull me to my feet so much as lever me upward by leaning his body at exactly the right angle, and without expense of energy. When he moved he almost seemed to dance, so light and effortless were his motions, and all done without any evidence of thought or effort. He did not mince like the courtiers do.

'Come with me,' he said, though I knew already that I would go wherever he wished, 'and we will find you what you want.' We walked away from the bridge back into the centre of town, and he led me off the main street and down a few dark alleyways. After a few minutes we stopped outside a house, which had two wide doors like a stable's, both thrown open. From inside came the sound of hammering, though of metal ringing on metal, not wood.

He ushered me inside, through the small hallway into a courtyard, open to the bright sun, but shaded here and there by canvas awnings slung from the edges of the roof. The flagstones were of chessboard pattern, most pretty in altern-ating naphtha green and white, and hazily dappled by the shadows from the canvases. The air was thick and heavy, but two or three young men went about their work, hammering and inspecting sword blades. There had been no sign on the street as to their employment, and so I can only suppose that people hereabouts just know about them. Perhaps they must have a reputation.

My new guide went to one of them, and chatted to him in low tones, without interrupting his work. The sword smith had a blade flat in a vice, and was working on some chasings with a bottle of nitric acid and a feather. It is strange how the acid will eat into steel, but will not harm the feather. I could see the work was very fine, like filigree. The blade was old though, for I could see that its handle had been removed, and the hasp was darkened from ancient dirt and sweat. It may have been old, but it caught the sun and threw it off in a spark like golden lightning.

My guide turned to me, and the smith stopped his workings, wiped the blade, and looked at me, a little shyly, but quite friendly, yet without smiling. I note that they do not smile much, the Spanish. They are lofty, and every man, even the meanest, thinks he is a *hidalgo*. Unlike the Italians, who do the same, there is nothing comical about it. I do not mind it, indeed I would find it charming, if ever I had permitted myself to be charmed by anything.

'We are rather short of good steel, at the moment,' my companion said, 'but I sense you are a beginner. This will serve for you, until you have found your style.' He motioned me over, with a steadying hand in the small of my back, and once again, I had the curious feeling of being shepherded, not against my will, but yet abandoning all resistance. There was something about him that was most persuasive.

The smith stood respectfully aside. 'It is old,' said my man, 'but it is fair. It is from Toledo originally, where as you know all the best blades come from. This is not one of the best. The foible here,' and he paused to balance the blade across his forefinger to find its pivot point, then pointed at a spot about one third towards the point, 'the foible is just a touch too close to the point, and so throws it very slightly off balance. But that would only affect the style of a master.'

He paused and thought a moment. 'No, on second thoughts, I am wrong, nothing would affect a master swordsman. He could do down his worst enemy armed with a rusty lump of steel no better balanced than a broomstick. No, I was altogether wrong. For you to start properly, you must have a blade that is perhaps not quite so pretty, but at least well balanced. That way you will not pick up bad habits.'

He handed the blade back to the smith, and I found myself intervening. 'No, please,' I said, 'I find that blade most appealing. May I just try it? I am not entirely a beginner. I have a sword-stick . . .' Once again I found myself talking too much. They were regarding me with their dark eyes, as if I were an interesting new breed of cattle, and just in time I halted my babbling.

'Very well,' said my man, hefting the blade once more and handing it back to the smith. 'Leave the chasings for now, and just fit the handle back on. We will go across the way for a little something to eat and drink and be back shortly. May we have it on approval?'

The smith spoke for the first time, but only softly and briefly and deferentially to say that of course we could, that was perfectly all right with him, we were clearly both men of honour and would return shortly either with the blade or with whatever money we took to be appropriate for the weapon.

I think he spoke perhaps three words, but he managed to intimate all of the above, complete with gestures which were both dismissive and friendly, like a priest waving you off after church.

We went across a little cobbled square with a well in the middle. I wondered how deep that went. The town must be a good five hundred feet above sea level. The well must go deep. 'There is a cistern underneath it,' said my man, noticing where I was looking. 'We keep it filled at all times, by pumps from the valley, or when that fails, by handcarts.'

'In case of siege I suppose,' I said. He nodded his assent. 'But no one would besiege you. You are too high and impregnable.'

'True,' he said, 'It has been easier in the past for armies simply to go around and ignore us altogether. The Moors often did, and later enemies. It is how we have remained so independent, and so different from our neighbours. But still, you never know . . .'

We settled at a table in what I thought to be an inn at first, though when my eyes had adjusted from the sunlight to the interior gloom, I found to be more like a large kitchen. A woman came over from behind the big stove and planked a small earthen dish of mushrooms on the table. I tried one and it was delicious. It had been cooked in olive oil and had some shavings of brown-white root in with it. 'Garlic,' said my guide, when I asked him.

'We do not have it in my country,' I said.

'Yes you do,' he said, 'it grows wild, you just do not use it for cooking.'

'How do you know? Have you been to England?' I said.

'I am English,' he said, and smiled. 'I was born in Liverpool.'

I was amazed, but covered my wonder pretty well. 'But your English,' I said. 'It is good but it is not perfect, and besides you have a strong local accent.'

'I have been here many years,' he said. 'My name is Higgins. John Higgins.'

'Are you a seaman?' I asked, thinking perhaps of one of our oldest links with Spain. Except that is Portugal; I was getting confused.

'I was once,' he said. 'That was why I came here when very young. And I am a Catholic too, for which reason I found the locals more, ah, congenial, than my fellow country-men. Now I am a fighter,' he said.

'Ah,' I said, as if I understood everything. 'You must be a mercenary, what the Italians call a *condottiere*.'

He looked at me a moment, as if he were waking up to

the fact that he was answering an awful lot of questions, and not all of them to his liking, but he seemed affable still.

'Not at all,' he said. 'I am not a soldier, although I do still deal in arms and armour. It used to be my main earner. Now though I fight bulls. There is much money in it. Big crowds, a lot of money.'

'Ah, the *corrida*,' I said. 'I have heard all about that and I would like to see it very much.'

This time he did smile. 'Of course,' he said. 'I will show you. We will pick up the sword and you and I will try a few passes. Then tomorrow you may watch me fight a bull in the ring here. But first, let us eat. Here comes the next dish.'

It was pieces of pork, stewed in a piquant green sauce, made I think of peppers and also something metallic-tasting, perhaps coriander. I scooped it up on some flat bread and wolfed it down, for my vertigo had abated and I was very hungry, as one always seems to be after a stomach malady has passed.

It was very nice but the dish was only small and I wondered whether to ask for some more but, without prompting, the woman kept them coming. There was some salted cod, with a strange porridge of corn, and some small sausages, most spicy, cut into discs and cooked in red wine, and some little pieces of a chicken, I think perhaps the gizzard, boiled in parsley and cream, which were most pleasant. Each was like a little taster for a main dish that was coming up, but never actually appeared. After six or seven of these dishes, I felt most full.

Higgins ate sparingly but appreciatively, without much talk. He called for more wine after we finished the first small jug. It was dark ruby red, and tasted of fruits such as the black berry as well as the grape. Perhaps it is the local version of the *port* of which I am fond in London. Oh no, that is Portugal again, I am getting confused.

Higgins noticed that he was drinking much more than me. About three glasses to every one of mine, although in truth I was dissembling as I usually do when I cannot refuse to drink for fear of causing offence. I was raising the glass often to my lips, but not swallowing any. He clapped me on the shoulder and urged more wine on me. I demurred, saying that my stomach was recovered, but still delicate, and I did not wish to strain it.

As you might guess, it is my old rule. Never drink in company. I drink quite enough by myself in my lodgings to make up for it. Never will drink make me let slip a secret.

We went back to the armoury and got my blade from the young man, who had been chasing it. He had not quite finished he explained, but would be happy to do so at some other time, after I had begun my first few lessons. I looked at his work closely, and it was very refined. I could see no evidence of anything half-finished.

'Oh, it is there if you know where to look,' he said, 'and I wouldn't want you to be disgraced in front of an expert who sees it. Incidentally, never show your sword to another man who asks to see it. Heegeenz will tell you why.' And he tapped his temple with two fingers. It is a local gesture rather like the Italian tapping of a finger to the side of the nose. It means 'I am in the know, and so will you be.'

I picked up my sword. It was now nicely fitted with a wooden handle, not new, but burnished by a former owner's palm.

I gripped it in my fist and swished it through the air a few times. It made a noise like the scythe that belonged to my father's gardener van Dieman, a noise such as I have not heard since I was a boy. The faint tearing noise through the air, like tissue paper being ripped, brought back to me the smell of new mown grass, and it filled the back of my throat and the upper part of my nose so strongly that I sneezed.

Higgins clapped me on the back again, not hard, and his hand lingered a little, pressing me on the spine as if in encouragement. 'Do you like it?' he said.

'I do,' I said. 'It seems . . .' There was a pause for I did not know the right word to use, and I feared making a fool of myself by not knowing any technical terms, but Higgins waited most politely, an expression of interest and encouragement on his face.

'Comfortable,' I said finally. I half expected him to laugh

and say that only a feather bed is comfortable, but he only nodded gravely.

'Good, it may not be a word that a swordsman might use, but I know exactly what you mean. It feels right in your hand doesn't it? And the right weight, and the right sort of well balanced. So, it's a good start.'

We left and made our way back towards the bridge again. After a few glasses of the wine, it held fewer terrors for me. But before we reached there, we came to a small space of clear sand, well shaded by trees surrounding it, and set apart from the cramped houses of this part of the town.

'So,' he said. 'First. The on guard position.'

'I know of the on guard,' I said, and duly adopted the position, one foot forward, one foot back, weight evenly distributed, right hand forward, elbow slightly bent, left hand on hip. I flexed my knees a little and sprang back and forth, quite jauntily, I thought.

'You have done this before?' he said.

'No,' I said, 'I have simply observed.'

'Mmm,' he said, and walked around me, looking closely. He then began to correct my stance with his hands running along my limbs, and patting the side of my knee and lowering my shoulders. This took several minutes, and by the end I felt I was bent out of all shape into something grotesque.

'Are you uncomfortable now?' he said.

'No, no,' I said, 'I am doing fine.'

'You are not,' he said, 'you are uncomfortable.'

It is true I was.

'And you look like a ruptured duck,' he added and began to laugh gently.

This is not a good start, I thought, and twisted my neck slightly to get it out of my collar a little. I was feeling hot under my stock. Well, it was a hot day.

Higgins ran into a nearby house, I presume his own, and returned with a glass and held it up a little way from me. What I saw was an ape on a string, frozen in an insane posture, waving a metal stick about in front of his nose like a blind man searching for obstacles.

I stood upright again, and sighed very sadly. 'It does not suit me does it?'

He looked at me equally sadly. 'No, it does not.'

Then he smiled, and said, 'You must use your pen, Mr Marvell, and stick with that I think.'

'What? Mightier than the sword and all that?' I said.

'No it isn't mightier than the sword, but at least it keeps you indoors and out of harm's way,' he said.

'But suppose harm comes my way. I am *expecting* harm, I *want* harm,' I said, almost wailing.

'I will show you a trick,' he said. 'There is one infallible winning stroke in sword fighting, and it never, ever fails.' He smiled again, this time wickedly.

'Well?' I said eagerly. 'What? I am all ears.'

'Always strike the first blow,' he said, and turned most deliberately, for he wanted the lesson to sink in without discussion, walked back to his house, and then just briefly flung over his shoulder, 'Be back here tomorrow in the morning. I'll show you how to fight a bull.'

I am not sure I want to fight a bull, but I wouldn't mind seeing it, and so I went back to my lodgings and, alone at last, indulged myself at last with two more bottles of that good local wine, and composed a short letter to the Latin secretary in the Madrid office. It related my observations of Ronda and its possible military significance, such as fortifications, and how vulnerable it might be to siege, and how many men it would need to defend.

I looked at it from the point of view both of a possible aggressor and of the inhabitants. In other words it got my usual double-minded attention.

I also alluded briefly to my encounter with the Englishman bull-fighter and possible mercenary, though without too much detail. He may or may not be of any use to us in the future, bearing in mind that he may have been English a long time ago, but he is also Catholic and now more or less Spanish by country of adoption. We could play upon his English birth, and stress how he should be patriotic to the land of his fathers. We could certainly play up to his long time residence in Spain, for that would gain him an entrée to places any other agent or diplomat such as myself or our man in Barcelona could not.

And we could use his Catholicism in one way or another. Either we stress that he should fight for his faith, and if he do right by us, the Catholic cause in England will be advanced a little. Or we suggest that there are many Catholics in high-up places who have formed a secret cabal and it is only a matter of a few years before they seize power, which may not be so far from the truth, now I think of it. Charles hankers for Rome occasionally, and his wife is a Papist. Or if that fails, I find out something he is ashamed of (all Catholics have that) and we put the blackmail screws on him.

One way or another he could be useful. Nothing is happening between us and Spain right now, but you never know what the future might bring. They are a vicious and cruel race, and may well declare for war against us once again just for the pleasure of it. A man on the ground in Malaga might be useful.

But I did not say this, since I need to learn more of him before committing myself. He seems a pleasant enough fellow, but with something of the night about him. There is a sadness, a lack, a hidden mournfulness which shows through when he is thinking his private thoughts, I cannot quite put my finger on it. He is certainly far from idle. Perhaps he is like me, prone to melancholia, and so keeps busy in order that it not gain too strong a grip upon his soul.

I must confess I am uneasy with the way he moves. It is so graceful I would almost describe it as like a woman dancing, except it has none of the artifice or the self-consciousness that women have when they are skilful dancers. Besides I loathe dancing. I cannot do it to save my life, and I am not fond of looking on it, for it reminds me of my inability. Needless to say the Puritans hate it because the people dancing are having a good time. I hate it for the same reason a crippled man will hate ball games. I always keep to the wall at a dance, but I look on it, I do look on it, as I do with all human life.

I look on human life with a cool eye, and everywhere I look I find that nature is divine, and man's hand in it disgusting.

I would not be upset if the world ended tomorrow, provided it were done by a man's accident. If a man's greed or a man's rage or a man's cruelty brought on the fire and brimstone of the latter day, I would think it just. You might wonder then why I continue in my employment as diplomat and spy. Well, a man has to do something to get him out of the house.

My lodgings are at one end of the town, in a large and pleasant inn. You approach it from one end of the main street, like any other gateway with a short path up to the front door, but it is around the back that it is most rare and strange.

It has a lovely garden, with well-arranged green shrubs and gravel patches, sometimes even coloured with sands and paints in the way that we do them in England, and there are shady trees well-planted in short avenues and bowers with vines and rose growing up them. You walk through, conscious of a large expanse of sky above you, but putting that down to the fact that the town is so high above the plain. One is closer to heaven here.

Then you reach the edge of the garden, furthest away from the house, and here is the marvel of it. There is a sheer drop down a cliff face of, I would guess, five hundred feet or so. There is a sturdy metal fence at the edge, but none the less, the effect is extraordinary, and leaves you stock motion-less with surprise.

I have sat here on a garden bench many an hour and simply immersed myself in the view, and after a while I get the distinct feeling that my thoughts are enlarging, and flying clear across the landscape from my cliff, over the darkling plains below, clear on over to the distant sea-shore line that can be seen far but distinct on the horizon. The sky there is divine-blue. Then they return, the thoughts I mean, as if they had rebounded on the edge of the world, and made an answering echo. They return to me in seconds, no more than an echo might take, but they have grown larger, and finely tuned themselves, so that what was once a question in my mind, or even not quite a question, but an unformed idea, comes back to me as an answer, or as a more perfectly-formed notion. It is wonderful. Like drinking the purest, coldest spring water and feeling instantly refreshed, in a way that one is not from murky water, or that feeling that comes some two-thirds towards the bottom of a bottle of wine, that you have found not just peace with the world, but the answer to it all as well. Alas, I know that that second one is only the wine talking, but it is worth having all the same.

This view is a clear and present comfort to me, and a great aid to thought. I find I shudder with pleasure when I get my thoughts clear, and I even gain a delicious sexual frisson from . . . no, I will not go on. I have not told you of my strange private thoughts, nor do I think I will.

After I had finished the letter in English, I translated it to good ecclesiastical Latin; and then I transposed it by using our book code and burnt the two originals, leaving only one sheet of strong parchment covered in illiterate scribblings that would baffle anyone. I sealed it with wax, but did not use my signet for fear of it appearing too important. The Secretary will know my hand anyway on the outside of the page.

It will go by a Thurn and Taxis messenger tomorrow morning and it should be with the Secretary in two days, the route being clear of bandits at this time, which gives me a four-day breather before a reply. I will observe my new-found, Catholic, part-time-armourer, bull-fighter, almost-Spaniard friend from Liverpool. (What are the odds on finding all of that in one man, I wonder?) Also I will enjoy myself I think. I deserve a little treat. What are Spanish women like, I wonder?

7. Help me Ronda

Had we but world enough, and time,
This coyness lady were no crime.

Marvell. 'To his Coy Mistress'

The world when first created sure
Was such a table rase and pure.
Or rather such is the toril
Ere the bulls enter at Madril.

Marvell. 'Upon Appleton House'

Dark, hairy and smelly is the answer – not that their smell is objectionable, just very strong. I will explain it later – and regular spitfires too. Ye Gods, they have a temper on them that would make the shade of Torquemada stir in happy contemplation. They have faint moustaches on the upper lip. It is most attracting. And they can tease a man to death.

She was a married woman, otherwise she would not have been allowed out without a chaperone. This country is much more strict about such matters than we are. I have often noticed this behaviour among Catholics. While praying for the best behaviour from men, they expect the worst. It is the same with Puritans too I notice now. A strange paradox, since they loathe each other.

Even so, it was hard to find time when she was not attended, either by her husband or her maids, or her mother, a fearsome gorgon, but find time, she did. I had had a letter of introduction to her husband the Don Coyote, an important man around here, although one that I found I had no time for. He was yet another example from the corrupt and idle courtier system that the Spanish affect. They have more aristocrats than they know what to do with, and much time is wasted on pomp and show. They had a fine young man, in the age of my father, for example, who led the Armada. He was a sea-general and his name was Medina Sidonia. The armada was of course a failure as far as Spain was concerned, but still he was a good warrior, done down I do believe by sad circumstance, and they gave him his due reward. The family name lives on though, in a fat eunuch of a son (and a worse grandson) who is content to rest upon his father's glory, lord it over the populace, and give nothing to his country. What is worse is that no one complains of this behaviour. The Spanish seem to think it perfectly natural. It will do them no good in the long run.

I first noticed her in a church, where I had gone to investigate the service. You will recall that I had allowed myself to be seduced by the Catholics when very young, in London, and so the format of the service was not a mystery to me; I knew when to bend and when to stand. However, there is something about the Catholic ceremony, with its stress on bright theatre and ritual, which is disgusting to the Puritans. For myself, I am against it by instinct and by intellect, for I was raised to be plain, but I have the most extraordinary confession to make: I find it all sexually arousing. It seems to work upon my nerves, for when I am attending a mass, all I can concentrate on are the women in the congregation. Is there anything more alluring than a devout woman, possessed by the love of the Holy Spirit, in a posture of ecstatic devotion, whether on her knees or even just sitting? I long to tear the coverings from their hair and the veils from their faces and teach them the true meaning of the 'bride of Christ' there and then. It is blasphemy I know, but I cannot help it. I find blasphemy arousing too. Am I strange?

I saw a production of Kit Marlowe's *Tamurlaine* once in the theatre, his play about the worst tyrant after Gengis the Khan, called Timur the Lame. He was a man who makes mountains out his enemies' skulls, and beats the brains out of rival Kings, and has his chariot drawn by a team of conquered Princes, and puts whole populations to the sword, but the moment that had the most effect, the moment of truth in that play, was when he dared defy Mahommet. He raised his clenched fist to heaven and called down the wrath of God upon his head, just to get Him to prove that He existed. Otherwise, he, Tamurlaine, would cease to believe.

I saw women faint dead away at that blasphemy, and not from horror either. They were in the throes of tremulous debility, their limbs shaking without control, as if they had the Dancing disease, and their husbands ushered them off to a carriage very quick to take advantage, before they could calm down and lose the moment.

Where was I? In the back row of chairs in the small dark church which serves as the main cathedral here in Ronda. The walls were decorated with paintings of saints, in interesting postures of suffering. The candles, guttering in the faint breeze and painting the walls with flickering shadows of the faithful, gave off a heavy, soporific scent. She turned her head slightly as if to ease a stiff neck, but truly I think because she felt my gaze upon her back.

Her eyes were large, and dark as raisins, and bulging slightly in their lids, as if she were short sighted or had a thyroid condition. She wore a dark peppercorn green bodice with full skirt, and her hands and wrists were tightly clad in pale buckskin gloves of thinnest skin. Gripped lightly in her right-hand fingers was a lovely fan of off-white turtle shell, picked out in *piqué*-gold. Her arms were covered, as is the custom, but the extraordinary thing was that her breast was half-bare so that her full pale cleavage was visible. The rest of her face was invisible behind its black lace, but her gaze lit on mine for the briefest half second before she turned back, and her wide brown eyes latched on to mine, and in that instant I thought I would suffocate.

The Green and the Gold

I steadied my breathing, and began to calm myself by thinking. I am not a love-sick young man, I never have been, and so I find it easy to govern myself. But I *must* have her. No remedy.

I left the service early and waited in the square. The faithful duly filed out after their devotions, blinking in the bright sun, and breathing deeply, as people do after church, as much from relief I think as from the exercise of rising from their knees.

She was alone, completely unescorted, which I found very unusual, but I suppose her husband and family must have reckoned her safe at her devotions. She saw me, and turned quickly and started to bustle away, her black skirts kicking up behind her in the dust. I wondered where her maids were.

I followed, but at a distance, as she wended her way through the warren of streets, once more in the direction of the bridge where I first had my turn of vertigo. It wasn't going to get me this time, though, not if she stepped across it in her silver sandals. I was ten-men resolute.

Then I lost her. This was most unlike me, but she had turned a corner, and I had carefully not hurried to it for fear of alerting her, but when I too reached the corner and turned, she was nowhere in sight. The street was full with people, and so I launched myself among them, but nowhere could I catch sight of her. I marched at double pace to the end of the street and then retraced my steps. Still no sighting. I estimated that she had been out of my sight for perhaps ten seconds before I rounded the corner, enough for her to have entered any of the first five houses on either side of the street, which certainly narrowed it down a bit. I could easily cover the houses without them noticing my surveillance. The problem was that there were also a couple of narrow alleys on either side of the street, right at its beginning, where I was now standing. She might have slipped down them. One was a dead end, and filled with rubbish, but the other three were open, and led to other streets. The possible permutations were large. Ah well, nothing ventured, nothing... Faint heart ne'er won ... Please forgive me the clichés. Love turns a man's brain to mush. It will come dribbling out of my ears, unless I find her and have my way. The blood is throbbing in the drums of my ears.

I wondered whether to find a *putana* and slake my desire, but I could not see one immediately, and anyway do not yet know where they hang out. I really cannot let this thing get the better of me, it will govern my every action unless I get it out of the way.

I went down each of the three alleys to their end, but they each gave on to more and larger streets, with no sign of the woman. I went back to the street where I had lost her, and sat a while in the doorway of a cantina, enjoying a glass of rioja and a small cigar, watching the world go by and wondering what to do next. Fortunately, before I took a drink, for it would have blunted my senses, however slightly, I knew that someone was watching me. I always know.

The eye sends out an invisible ray which, when it strikes a distant object, rebounds and returns to the eye of the beholder. I often think that this ray must be composed of countless tiny particles which are almost weightless, yet which strike the distant object with the faintest of blows in order to be reflected back. If one is alert enough, one can feel the blow of someone turning their gaze upon you, especially if it is a concentrated and inquiring gaze. Most men cannot feel another's gaze upon them, but then most men are insensible beasts. I, on the other hand, am a man of feeling.

I sipped my drink, and carefully emptied my mind of thinking about who the watcher might be, and where, and instead concentrated on something else entirely. Horace, since you ask. I am often troubled about how one could render his odes in English. The metre is easy to mimic; even though it doesn't quite conform to English patterns of speech, it can be bent to fit. What is trickier is the sentiment. What one might call the tone of voice. It is one that came easily to the Roman, but we Christians are, at one and the same time, more ironic and less robust than the stoic Roman. I digress, and so will leave you there, for it is a problem I will soon solve, and then may show you my efforts.

There! You see what will happen if you let your mind wander where it will and concentrate on whatever you find? You forget entirely where you were. So it was with me, and so it is with me each time I do not want anyone to know that I am watching them. I concentrate on something else, and

I become invisible. After some moments of looking at the table and thinking about iambics, I went inside for a news sheet, and also borrowed a small glass mirror from behind the bar, which the waitress uses to primp her hair, and returned to my seat, with the paper unfolded in front of me. My hat was pulled low, and the paper I held up quite high, as if I were a bit short sighted, and trying to catch the sunlight upon it. I could feel my eyes were in shadow, and so without moving my head, I let my eyes roam over the nearest houses.

They all had the shutters over the windows, for although it was late in the afternoon, most would still be enjoying the siesta, a habit I could never get used to, however hot the weather, but almost instantly, I knew it was the second house from me, on the other side of the road. The upstairs window to the left of the door was shuttered, but they were not closed fully and latched, and I once or twice detected a movement, the faintest flicker of a black shawl or dress behind them. Normally it is the whiteness of skin which one can pick up straight away, but, if it is who I think it is watching me, then she still has the veil and mantilla from her church visit covering her face. The clever minx.

Nothing more to be done, I thought. I know where she lives, and I know she is watching me, and I don't think she knows that I know, or perhaps she is playing a double game, the way women do, but either way . . . I can't be bothered to think about it any more. My passion has died down. The day is getting cooler, the wine has blunted my feelings rather than inflaming them, and just thinking about women's ways is always enough to deflate me. It is God's curse that I carry this sex desire for a woman, for when I have one, she is no sooner had than hated.

I thought I wanted a little treat. Now I find that I don't really want it, if it means the trouble of chasing a woman. But the itch is still there, no doubt about it. I wonder how other men manage? Actually I do not. I couldn't care less. Just let me indulge in a woman, once in a while, and then have them clear out from under my roof.

I returned the news sheet, and the glass even though I had no need of it, paid for my drink and left the bar.

The next morning, up betimes, I called first at the armourer's workshop to return the sword which he had so charmingly given me, but which did not suit me after all. I explained about what had happened, and he was very understanding and also most polite and tactful, not giving me any reason to lose face over my inability to strike even the on-guard position with any credibility. I said that I did not need it after all, and he asked if perhaps I had some other weapon about me, for the streets here may in fact be pretty safe, but outside the town, well, there were the usual hazards of brigands and highwaymen. I said I had my sword-stick, and while I could not strike a pose for a fencing class, yet I knew one end of a sword from another and could make shift in a brawl pretty well. As indeed I did many times, which I will tell you of later

He smiled and said 'quite so quite so,' and slipped me a little pistol, which fitted most snugly into my coat pocket. It was a neat thing, with a smallish butt, which suited my womanly hands very well, and a short barrel, which will only be accurate over the length of a room or so, but will serve. The lock with the flint in it has been filed down. It is now harder to cock it, but the point is that it will not snag in my coat pocket, should I have to draw it in a hurry. I practised it many times back in my lodgings, and quite got the knack of it. I even fired it a few times outside the town, and demolished a cactus, which shouldn't have been standing where it was.

It fires high and to the right, a foible which is easily compensated for. I will just aim a little low and to the left. I like shooting. Destroying things is often more satisfying than creating. (There speaks a poet. Every writer will tell you that the waste basket is his best friend.)

When I offered to pay, he smiled and said that Señor Heegeenz would see to it, and I was not to worry, and if I had any problems at all, and he said again, *any* problems, to return and see him and all would be worked out. He was most obliging. I think he must be the chief villain hereabouts. I asked him where Higgins was, and he inclined his head towards the bullring across the way.

'Just near where you first tried the duelling positions,' he said. 'He is preparing.'

'What for?' I said. 'Oh, of course, he told me. I will go and help him.'

'Best not, I think,' said my man. 'It is a complicated process and, well, he is facing an ordeal. He is nerving himself. You could distract him, and distraction from what he is about to do is the very last thing he wants on earth. In fact,' he gave a short dry laugh, 'distract him, and it would indeed be the last thing on earth for him.'

So I loafed over the bridge, in vague search of something to eat for lunch, feeling slightly hung-over and ill tempered, for I wanted to see more of my new friend. And there I saw my dark lady again. And felt a little better and friskier. And also a little worse and frustrated.

She had two other women with her this time, a maid and I think perhaps a sister, for she was more intimate with the second woman, clasping her arm and whispering behind her fan, the way they do. They were passing me on the bridge and I bowed rather lower than I would to a complete stranger or slight acquaintance, as if to acknowledge that we had met. The sister looked straight at me, and smiled. My dark lady stared straight through me as if I did not exist. She shouldn't have done that, for she has given herself away. It means she is interested in me, which her sister who smiled is not.

Oh fuck, well I knew that already didn't I? What with her playing hide and seek all over town yesterday, then observing me from the shutters of her boudoir. She has thick brows and is as dark as an Indian, and I must have her, God's boots

I must. I will make her squeak. Time is running out for me though. I must be gone in a week for Rome and then back to London. More packets, more deliveries, more of the usual dull business that spying is. Oh I need more time to pursue her, she is so shy of me, and I do not have it. Damn the woman, why can she not be more forward? She might have guessed I am in a hurry.

I went for a lunch. Spanish omelette, which is vile in comparison to the French: green peppers yet again, which is a bully of a vegetable, a very nasty poison-green, and infects everything it touches with its cacky metallic taste, and a long insipid-green-streaked root, like a pale cucumber, but watery and tasteless. The innkeeper said it was a courjet. Fine, just so long as they never export it.

I called for meat, and ate a piece of horse.

Feeling better after that I wandered back to the bullring and took a seat inside under the shade of the awning, among the richer townsfolk, for the heat was rising. I hoped that a death would brighten an otherwise dull afternoon.

I saw four acts of brute butchery, done with all the finesse of an abattoir. I had been told of the grace and mastery of it all, but all I saw was men in a palpable state of fear worrying a beast to a slow death with a thousand cuts. My gorge began to rise after a while, what with the strong smell of blood pooling in the sand, and the matadors' legs slippery with it, and I got up to leave in some hurry. But then my friend Higgins appeared and walked toward the *toril* gate, where the bulls are kept, and which they call the Gate of Fear. They are a dramatic race.

And so I sat down again.

He walked forward with that faint swagger which I recognized and which I now thought might be a limp. I had seen a previous matador get nicked on the thigh by a horn. It was not a deep wound, but he had bled like a pig, and I think it hurt a muscle. Higgins looked most cool, with a face of quiet concentration.

The bull came in, pounding a hollow din from the sand. It was black as pitch and glossy. It swerved away from my man, earning a few boos from the crowd for its cowardice. I do not understand this practice. The bull lacks human understanding. It may be brave or it may be cowardly by human standards, but the bull itself knows nothing of that. All that this one was showing was an entirely sensible desire to save its own skin. Believe me, I would have done exactly the same if I had been peering over the fence and seen what had happened to the other bulls, but no, this mob went on booing the bull, which just confirms their stupidity and the good sense of the bull.

Higgins was altogether more composed. He began to work the bull with his cape, shaking and rattling it so the beast could not overcome its own curiosity. Slowly Higgins began to tease him. Just the faintest of movements and then he would turn and walk away, his back to the bull. Then turn again, and flick his cape just slightly, until he had the bull's interest again. I could see what he was doing, and it would not be very long before he was playing the poor animal like a musical instrument. It was curiosity killed this bull.

I am sure you are ahead of me. I am sure you can see which way my mind is working. It is all so very symbolic is it not? Also bleeding obvious. Sometimes the gods do not so much whisper in your ear, as bludgeon you to death with a message. This was the whole nine yards; comets, shooting stars, tidal waves, earthquakes and any other kind of portent they chuck in our path by way of warning. If I do not break off my interest with the dark lady, she will do to me what Higgins is about to do to the bull.

Now there's a funny thing, don't you think? You would think that the matador would be the epitome of manliness, but in fact it is he doing the teasing and luring to doom. He is acting the woman's part. I must tell him afterwards, when I see him, about this interesting paradox. No doubt it will tickle him, having just escaped a hideous death.

Then the bull made a charge, all two tons of it, and by Christ, I thought that there might not be an afterwards, for Higgins didn't budge. He was backed up against the wooden wall, and it looked like he was going to be pinned there for all eternity with a horn through his guts, but at the last minute he gave a leap in the air, the bull sank its horns all the way into the wood with a noise like the crack of doom, and Higgo sprang clear over the top of the beast's head and down its back and clear on past its rump before dropping down the other side. I couldn't help but think of the cult of the Minotaur and the bull jumpers I had learned about in my Greek when a child. Roars of approval from the crowd, standing ovations, calls for his immediate sanctification, deification, possible kingship. I do not know what the manoeuvre is called, but no doubt he will lecture me on it at great length this evening.

The bull pulled its horns out of the woodwork and went berserk. It bucked up and down like a firecracker, and went charging hither and yon, even though it was still reeling from the blow to the head, and half blinded to boot by the blood. It was out of control now, but instead of taking advantage of that and finishing it off, Higgins began to play it again, calming it down. I could see he wanted an elegant kill.

Well, he got it. After some few minutes of flirting, again the bull calmed and they faced each other across the sand, which was now quite black in patches. The bull lowered its head and I knew that here was the moment of truth, and Higgins called 'Toro, Toro,' just twice, quite softly, and charged too. The bull and the man were one. Just for one brief moment, they were one, and then it was all over.

At least that is how I heard one man describe it to his friend afterwards. He was a bearded man, with a barrel chest, and sunburnt, grizzled face, and he sounded like some sort of expert. What he said quite deceived me for about an hour. Until I thought about it.

No they weren't. They were nothing like one. The bull

was dirty, and half-deranged from the spears that the horse-men had stuck in its neck, and thoroughly annoyed at being teased with a cape and being put on display as a spectacle for a bunch of reeking thrill-seekers. It was also already half-dead, from exhaustion and loss of blood, what with three great long pics still stuck into the spine near the shoulders. It could hardly raise its head anymore, and blood was pouring from its mouth. It was three-quarters on its way to being a side of meat even before Higgins got on its case.

Higgins by contrast was young, fit and handsome. True, he didn't have horns and was fighting about one and nine-tenths of a ton out of his class. But he had a sword and he had a human will and that will always win hands down.

The bull stank. I could smell it clear across from where I was sitting at least twenty yards from it. I could smell it above the crowd of Spaniards, who God knows are not the cleanest of men. The bull stank of blood and fear.

I couldn't smell Higgins at all. He and the bull were not one. Oh, I know all right what that man I overheard was on about. The sacred rites of blood sacrifice. The dark bond that exists between hunter and the hunted. The hard-won route back from the artifice of civilization to the truth of our primeval state, when man was more nearly an animal, and he danced the sacred dances to attract the attention of the gods and to imitate his quarry. The respect of a man for his foe. 'We will kill him in battle but honour his memory as a worthy . . .' you know the sort of thing. There was a lot of bull shit around the ring that day.

I was impressed enough at the time, but not when I thought about it all. And it is reflection upon a thing that separates us from the animals, and prompts us to behave better. What appealed to the crowd was the cruelty. Just as it does with bear baiting in my homeland. Let there be no hypocrisy about it. The crowd were sadists, and they wanted their green lust slaked.

They were not one, they were man and beast, and he killed it, and there's an end on it.

It seems to me that if you want cruelty then you should go to a whorehouse and watch a man whipped. At least a human has a choice in the matter, and no one holds a sword to his head. Taunting dumb beasts is for children.

I think that my rant above would sound better if I had just stepped from the ring, having killed a bull myself. I know that a moral precept holds its truth, whatever the sinful state of the speaker. (Don't forget my father was a vicar. He taught me well.) But I can't help feeling that my strictures would count for a little more if I had just faced a charge from an enraged side of beef with sharpened horns, and me without so much as a box over my balls. It's all very well for me to mouth off from the safety of the crowd.

So I did go and see Higgins afterwards, in a state of a little contrition, and surprisingly he was alone in his tiring room, taking off the complicated costume and draping it over a chair. The room was otherwise bare, except for a single burning candle.

'How do you feel?' I said.

'Alive,' he said, in a very plain voice, not at all the elated soul I expected.

'Yes, indeed, you did well to survive. Some do not, I believe.'

'No, I meant, *alive*. More alive than I do at any other time. At any other time at all, even when I am with a woman.'

'Ah, you are invigorated, by the exercise and by the nearness of death,' I said. I was acting the devil's advocate I know, but I wanted to get to some truth that I had just witnessed but might have missed.

'No,' he said, 'nothing like that. It is just that there is nothing more exciting than being threatened with death to no effect.'

'What is that like then?' I said, but I had missed my chance. The rhythm of the argument had gone and I had missed the beat. Perhaps he was tired; well he would be wouldn't he? Or then again perhaps fired up to life again, just as I saw after the fight at Edge-hill among those who survived. But he seemed neither one thing nor the other, neither tired nor invigorated. He just seemed quite calm and locked inside himself.

'The moment is over, quite gone,' he said, 'and now there is nothing. I must simply continue in my round of daily affairs until the next time.' I wish I understood him better. As far as

I can make out, he only feels fully alive when in the ring. This might explain his air of slight melancholy at other times. Life for him is when he faces the bull. The rest is waiting.

I have encountered the same attitude among the mountain men of Switzerland. They are not happy unless hanging by their nails from an overhang in an almighty gale. It is not the danger so much as . . . what? Well that is just the way they are. It is in their nature.

But what is this man's nature? I must get a handle on him, if I am to report back to my office in Madrid with a view to using him as one of ours.

'Would other thrills excite you?' I asked. 'Might other risks make you feel better, or distract you from the crush of the daily round.'

'They might,' he said. 'I seek them out all the time, but nothing can really compare.'

'You have been kind to me, Señor Higgins, you took me up quite without prompting when I was in trouble, and you have shown concern and kindness for me since. I am a stranger in a strange land, and was much at the mercy of foreign men and circumstance. True, you are almost a countryman of mine, but you did not know that when you extended the hand of friendship, and besides I do not think that which land you hail from weighs too much with you, in the general scale of things. I like you sir, and I care not who knows it. Forgive me, I do not wish to embarrass you, and I am windy. However, there is a point to what I am saying, and I will get to it. But not just yet.

'I must be on my way from here in three or four days, and there then may be some ways in which you may help me, to your advantage, both in monies, and also by way of the excitement you seek, and the diversion from a life you find dull. Bear with me if you will. I cannot say more at present, but I will do so, before I am gone.'

He had finished unwinding the bandages from beneath his stockings now, and was reaching for his linen breeches. I paused while he pulled them on, and fastened them with his belt, and then with his sword belt too.

He turned to me, and bowed low without a word, nor any expression bar the usual grave dignity one finds on all the locals. Then he said, 'I too must be gone for a couple of days, for I have another fight, and some business matters in Madril.'

'Where?' I said.

'Madril,' he said.

'?'

'The capital,' he said.

'*Ah.*'

8. Don Coyote

My vegetable love should grow
Vaster than empires and more slow.

Marvell. 'To his Coy Mistress'

As I stepped into the bright late afternoon, I felt terrifyingly
aroused again, and went in search of my dark lady. I wondered what brought it on. The death of the beast no doubt.
Death does have that effect on people, I have often noticed.
Let death into the room, and life will start reasserting itself
like a madness. Many a funeral of a good man I have
attended of an afternoon, and been in the widow's bed that
same evening.

When women weep beside a grave, you may be certain
they will cry out later that night. And not from grief either,
but from the moment of truth.

It is something I have often noticed, and indeed I put the
conceit somewhere in one of my poems, which was about
Mourning. I cannot remember quite how it went, something
along the lines of:

But sure as oft as women weep,
It is to be supposed they grieve.

I like that 'supposed', I am quite proud of that. It's the sort of word your average speaker would pass over quite quickly without giving it too much thought. The line seems only to be proposing the most commonplace observation, until you think about that word a little, and it pulls you up short. 'Supposed'. Hmm, so they may be dissembling then. Or not; whoever knows about women's wiles?

I can say that I am proud of it because I am not always proud of what I have written. Indeed, I can hardly bring myself to go back and read it again. I can write prose, official reports and such, quite quickly and without revision, but poetry will always take longer. When you are a poet, you do not approximate. It must be the *mot juste* or nothing. So I will quite often leave blanks in the line where a word should be, and wander off for months until the right word comes to mind. I often think a man might make a fortune composing a book of nothing but words and their definitions and their synonyms.

Then, once I have got the work to its perfection, and finally dropped it, then I feel as though I have purged something from my system. It is gone from me, and there is something stale and nasty about it, almost the stench of decay, if I return to it. 'Like a dog returning to its own vomit' is a phrase bandied about in this context sometimes, although the speaker usually forgets that returning to their own vomit is something that dogs *like* to do. The smell pleases them, and so they will do it again and again.

No, with my poems it is more like those parents who have spent much care and expense in raising their children to maturity and then watch them set sail into the wide world to find a life for themselves. Many parents still worry about their offspring, but most are delighted to get shot of them. Nature ensures that there are enough black marks against children as there are joys, in order that the parting of parent from child be less painful to the parents. So too with poems. They are scarcely less painful to give birth to, and, just like childbirth, the pride and the joy in the new-born outweigh the birth pains. But one soon tires of the newness of it, and so I push my poems out on to the wide sea, where they cannot wake me in the middle of the night demanding attention.

Unless I am drunk, late at night, and then I can look upon them and think that they are the best poems that have ever been written, surpassing Virgil's delicacy of thought, surpassing Ovid's cerebral eroticisms, surpassing Shakespeare's better sonnets, oh so far ahead of any of the vain scribblings of Donne, that lewd Dean, as to be of a different angelic order. Well, you know how it is when you are drunk. Plain women look pretty when you are drunk, pretty women look beautiful, and you might even see your way to marrying one of them. Even my landlady has a certain *je ne sais quoi* about her, and believe me, in the light of day, her face could cause a miscarriage. Thank God for the morning after. God gave us hangovers to punish us and to make us see things in their true light.

That really is quite enough philosophy for one afternoon. I must have her.

I stepped into the bright late afternoon, feeling terrifyingly aroused again, and went in search of my dark lady.

I found her quite quickly, just by ploughing my way back towards the fearsome bridge through the early evening crowd, all come out to parade as usual about the town before dining. They like to dine late here, and they enjoy strolling around, seeing and being seen. Unlike my own kind, who stay at home with a decent modesty.

This time she was alone again, and it struck me she might be married. I do not know why that had not occurred to me before, it is usually the first thing I inquire about. No matter, I am short of time, and it makes no difference. This time she acknowledged my presence, though coolly.

I made some comment or other about the weather, and she agreed, or did not, I cannot now remember, and we made a few other pleasantries. Then I knew what must be done. Either I could tip my hat, bow and say how pleasant it was to see her again, and that would signal the end of all that. Or . . .

'I like your mantilla, very much,' I said. 'Forgive me, but of course we do not have them in my country, and so I am

124

intrigued. Yours seems to be made of the finest lace, and it hangs so well . . .' and more and more in that line. She smiled and gladly told me where it was made and by whom and what it signified and so on, and she made no move to leave. I knew I had her.

'It is so very hot,' I said, fanning my face with my hat, and before she said that she was used to it, I said, 'My lodgings are not so very far, if you would like a little shade and something to drink.'

'Kind of you,' she said, 'but my house is closer. See it, we are almost there.'

She quite brazenly took my arm, and together we sauntered back to where I had sat at the café on that first day and she had watched me from the shadows. Her house was on the dark side of the street and very cool. Her maid Nadine greeted me in the hallway and took my hat, and top coat, and ushered us into the parlour and set wine down without her mistress having said a word. Some silent understanding passed between them, and I could not help noticing a naughty twinkle on the maid's face. Female intuition? Oh, bugger all that, they just planned it all together is my guess.

'My husband is Don Coyote,' she said with a bold look upon her face, as indeed she would since he is about the biggest man in these parts: big in business, big in terms of hard cash, and big in terms of hulking. He also has a big temper on him, and an unbecoming attachment to his wife, probably because he is fifty and therefore just short of being an impotent dotard, and she is only half that age.

'He is away on business,' she added, looking even more bold. Really she was so brass-necked, I wonder that she did not lift her skirts with a cry of 'Take me now, English stallion.'

'Hmm,' I said, and took a judicious slug of wine, 'And how do you amuse yourself while he is absent?'

'Oh, my maid and I are very inventive,' she said. And a vision came swimming to the forefront of my mind, such as I never dared entertain. Oh, the pair of them, together, now that would be something I had never hoped for before.

I felt that, should it arise, it would be impolite to refuse such an offer.

'And now Mr Marvell, you must be hungry,' she said. I was about to say, 'Not at all, no, no, please let's eat afterwards,' when the maid came from the kitchen with dishes of something. Dear God, she is up to her old tricks again. She is a raging tease, and I hardly know how to contain myself. It is appalling the games that women play. I sometimes think that the flirting is all they enjoy, and that love's true end is finally a bore to them. She wants to play the long game, but I only have a couple of days left in Ronda. A couple of days? Christ, that might as well be half a life-time, for my balls will explode if I do not have her within the hour.

So we ate, and I managed to force something down, in spite of the heat and my raging hard-on, and I also took the opportunity to drink a little more wine, just enough to remove my inhibitions, but not enough to dampen the urge.

The maid cleared the dishes and withdrew. Actually she didn't just withdraw in any way you or I would, just leave the room in other words. She 'withdrew' in the way that conspiring women do, making a big show of leaving us alone together, and all but tapping the side of her nose and winking at us both.

So, another green light I thought, and indeed so it proved. My Donna Julia (for such was her name I discovered as we prattled on) allowed herself greater and greater licence and, well I am so sick of relating all the byways of her deceits and evasions, I will get to the point, we found ourselves in her room, on her bed and naked. All of which was to the point and was very much the sort of thing I happened to think ought to happen. And I was just about to commit myself fully, when the door bursts open and in rushes the wretched maid, crying at the top of her voice, 'Madame, Madame, flee, your husband Don Coyote approaches, with all his servants. He is outside in the road and has a certain look about him.' Which pulled me up in very short order.

Although why Madame should have to flee I am uncertain. I think the silly maid got it muddled. Madame can remain where she is with perfect equanimity, since it is her very own bed in which she lies. It is me that will have to take a flyer out of the window and take to my heels in nothing but my under-clothing with my old sceptre charging in front of me like a hat peg. But not yet because there were clearly men still outside, posted no doubt by the lady's husband with wicked intent.

I heard the front door open, and the sound of men mounting the stairs with a very fixed sort of purpose in their tread. Why they should care what happens to Don Coyote's wife I do not know. Perhaps they are all very much married and do not like the idea of adultery becoming available to all and sundry and so intend to make an example of me. You know what the Catholics are, almost as bad as the Puritans in that respect. Damn.

I wondered where my pistol was. In the pocket of my coat, was the answer, which was in the corner of the cupboard over by the wall. I wondered whether to dive in but realized that it would be the first place old Coyote would look. He might miss the coat, but he wouldn't miss me. Things were not looking good, but the maid came up with a very good idea. She started ruffling up the bedclothes into a great heap, and jumped in beside Donna Julia.

In burst the men, all bristling brows and thunderous looks. Julia started, as if she were just awoken from her slumbers, and cried out a sharp little squeak as if she had been frightened by all the horrid men, and then put on an air and got her retaliation in first. 'Why husband, what can this mean? How dare you come in here with your rabble, as if I were a common whore.'

And at that word, she made a sharp intake of breath, and

widened her eyes and clapped her hand to her mouth. 'Oh,' she said, 'now I see. Is that what you think? That I have someone here with me. Well, aren't *you* the old fool? Search the room why don't you?'

Don Coyote pulled himself up to his full two yards, stared down his nose and with the haughtiest tone he could manage, which was pretty haughty given that all his rough-neck hirelings were milling about him, pretending not to notice anything, but laughing up their sleeves at his predicament, said, 'I will.'

The maid clutched the bedclothes tight up around her neck and wailed. Don Coyote could not see anything wrong with her being there, so presumably Julia and the maid often slept double. Hmm, what a nice thought! Though little good it did me, huddled where I was.

The Don rattled around with a grim and suspicious look on his face, peering under the bed and in the cupboard. I was right, he missed my coat, too dark I suppose, or else he took it for one of his own. His men did nasty things like run their swords through the curtains. They gained nothing but a blade-tip blunted on the wall, but it made me wince a bit.

Meanwhile old Julia kept up a fair barrage of high dudgeon. 'Call for my lawyers,' she shrieked, 'I'll not endure this behaviour from the silly old fool any longer. Do you all realize (this to the servants who by now had taken to rummaging through the linen chest) what I have had to put up with through the years from this dotard? It is amazing I have not gone mad. I have been so virtuous a wife that I especially chose a confessor too old to arouse suspicion, and never had he reason to give me penance. Was it for this that I refused the advances of the Irish peer Lord Malpractice?

'I have had two full Cardinals make advances to me. And the Russian Count Lobachevsky was under such pain after my refusal, he drank himself to death. The Italian tenor Count Fazzi-paparazzi sang under my balcony for six months in vain. Dons from Madrid and Barcelona too numerous to mention have plied me with their favours. Not once did I so much as lower my lids at them. And now this! Is this how you treat a good and honourable wife?' Her voice was beginning to get hoarse, but the Don was visibly beginning to wilt as the volume and the sarcasm increased and his search proved more and more futile.

'Is the moon full by any chance? Are you growing hair upon your hands? Perhaps you would care to beat me,' she cried, pushing her luck a little I thought. 'You, with your men with cudgels, and your drawn sword!' I winced again. 'Don't you cut a pretty figure?'

He was growing ever more unsure of himself, and she redoubled. 'There,' she cried, pointing, 'you have ignored the chimney. Perhaps it is a sweep you seek. And over there, the window. Perhaps I have been wringing out the man servant's chamois leather. You have not checked the flower-beds and borders for footprints. And there,' she pointed again, this time under the bed, 'have you checked the chamber pot? Perhaps my swain is a midget and crawled in there.'

The Don began to waver, and so she resorted to the time-honoured female tactic of hysterics (optional use as a clincher to round three, or in an emergency give it a full blast for the finale). She began to sob and simper and pretty soon it turned to an angry wail as she sank her face in the pillow and begged a handkerchief from her maid, and then stopped abruptly and hurled more abuse and imprecations against her now rattled husband, and then was off crying again. Finally his nerve broke.

He ushered out the men, and with a bad tempered 'Damn,' he left the room and closed the door. And not a moment too soon. I staggered out from under the maid and the bedclothes, and gasped in great lungfuls of air. I was half-smothered, half-ecstatic at such a happy form of death, and half-terrified still of the Don and his possible return. Thank God I am still slim, else I could never have lain close-packed among the bed sheets undiscovered. That maid has lovely thick thighs I tell you. Oh, welcome death, among such flesh.

But, oh God, Coyote will only have to dismiss all his myrmidons and then he will surely return to his spouse and have it out with her. Or attempt reconciliation. He is married to this appalling woman, and I will bet good money that she just loves to kiss and make up.

She kissed me hard and I licked her tears (at least they were genuine) and ran my hand through her tangled locks, and she said, 'There is no time for fooling now. Into the closet, double quick. He'll be back.' So I joined my coat, and pulled out the pistol from its pocket just in case, though I did not cock it. To be up on a charge of adultery is one thing, murder quite another.

Sure enough Don Coyote returned and ordered out the maid with a brief seigniorial gesture. She curtsied and withdrew, taking a candle with her. So there was even less light in the room now.

He simply begged her pardon, which I must say I thought exactly the right thing to do, and perfectly done from where I stood. They certainly can lay on the dignity, these Spanish. She in her turn half-withheld and half-granted, the way they do. Then she began to lay down her conditions for a reunion, which no doubt would have included copious gifts in the gold and precious stone department, as well as the denial of any conjugal visits for the next few months just to rub in the lesson. She was just about to warm to her subject, for Spaniards also do like their revenge. When, lo! He paced across the room and stumbled on a pair of shoes, and they were not his. Oh bugger, my teeth began to chatter, my veins to freeze.

Coyote took on an air of fury and left the room to find his sword, which he had hung up outside. Julia flung the closet door open, with a muted hiss of 'Flee, flee for thy life. The door downstairs is open. You might slip through. It is still dark, and no one is around. Run.' Alas, it was all too late.

Coyote re-appeared in his dressing robe, waving his rapier about like a berserker and uttering curses and death threats, with extensive detail as to what tortures he would put me to beforehand. So I reversed the pistol in my hand, and fetched him a beauty on the nose, which knocked him down, stepped over him and made for the door. Alas, he grabbed my foot and twisted, and we started to wrestle in unseemly fashion, banging around on the floorboards like a pair of drunken peasants.

'Eek,' shouted Julia. 'Rape!'

'Oh *no*,' shrieked the maid. 'Fire.'

Not a soul in the house stirred. Either they were insensible or they'd heard it all before, and were leaning on their elbows enjoying listening to the fight.

After thrashing about a bit on the floor, I realized that the Don hadn't got a clue on how to fight with his hands, so I cuffed him again on the nose, which left an impressive amount of blood about the place, boxed both his ears with the palms of my hands so that he was temporarily deafened, and left in a hurry. He managed to grab a handful of my shirt-tail and it all tore away.

So it was I found myself in the street, naked, my blood up, and a painful erection still in progress after at least an hour and nothing to show for it. I legged it back to my lodgings, trying to hold down the unruly member, while at my back I could almost hear ten pairs of vengeful feet hurrying near.

Fortunately no one was around, and the night porter was

fast asleep over his bottle. Exactly thirty minutes later I was dressed, packed, relieved of my hard-on quite guiltlessly, and out of the door, on my horse, heading down hill for Madrid, and all of it before dawn had broken. No sense in hanging around for Coyote's hired furies to begin their search in what would be the most obvious place to look.

On the road I turned in my saddle and looked back at Ronda, just as the rosy-fingered dawn was illuminating it with a red-gold halo, and I thought that living there would be like being married to a beautiful but demanding woman.

No doubt you read about the divorce in those semi-literate accounts by Wilson.

> *But at my back I always hear*
> *Time's winged chariot hurrying near.*

My very best couplet in years I think, and now you see where I got it. I do not want to give too much away about my craft, for then it might stop coming to me, but I couldn't help but recall that feeling of having twenty footsteps thundering after me. I originally wrote, while still very much dry-mouthed and heart-pounding from the experience:

> *And at my back I clearly hear*
> *Ten Spanish cut-throats hurrying near.*

Which was funny enough and might just be good enough for

a mock-heroic narrative poem, if and when I want to do one of those, perhaps later. However, I must say that I was pleased with the final version of 'To his Coy Mistress', which I did once I had calmed down and was recollecting the whole saga when reclining in some tranquillity. No one will know who my 'Coy Mistress' was. She will be like Shakespeare's 'Dark Lady', the object of much future curiosity. Let men wonder.

9. The Madrid Office

Console-toi, tu ne me chercherais pas si tu ne
m'avais trouvé.
(Console yourself, you would not seek me if you
had not found me.)

Blaise Pascal. *Pensées*

And to Madrid, to the office there, where I told Our Man
all about Mister John Higgins, formerly of Liverpool, now
adopted by Spain, part-time armourer, mercenary (I suspect)
and bull-fighter extraordinary.

I related all the virtues peculiar to the man, and why he
would make so good a spy for us, since his situation seemed
almost heaven-inspired for such a task. Speaking Spanish
like a native, behaving like-wise, quiet, not to say broody,
courageous, well versed in the martial arts, well placed in
Ronda, and a hero to the bull-fight aficionados of the
western hemisphere, why, the Fates themselves could hardly
have placed a more suitable candidate in our path.

'Indeed,' said Our Man in Madrid, 'my thinking exactly.
Which is why we have already recruited him.' My heart sank
and I felt first foolish, then annoyed. Somebody might have

told me before I was sent to Ronda. 'In fact,' continued Our Man, 'I have received this very morning, his report on the surprise visit of a certain Englishman to Ronda. Would you care to read it?' he said with a smirk on his face. I disguised my eagerness, and took the folded pages from him with sullen lack of interest, sat back in my chair and began to peruse them lightly.

' . . . conducting some sort of clandestine affair . . . do not know with whom . . . very difficult to follow . . . skilled at evasion both physically and verbally . . . cannot make out the fellow at all . . . impossible to get close to, in person or in understanding . . . moderately amusing, though not always intentionally . . . a mite chilly . . . completely unskilled in the use of sword, and likely to remain so . . . carries a pistol, somewhat awkwardly . . . something of a philosopher, though unwilling to share thoughts . . . does not drink in company . . . seems completely unsuitable for our purposes . . . he might make a good teacher or perhaps a clerk . . . recommend he not be recruited and no further action be taken on him.'

I finished it quickly, without any show of particular interest. It was no more than I had heard in any tavern. Really, people are so shallow, it makes one despair. Like any other tavern sprawler, Higgins couldn't really be bothered to get beneath the surface of another man.

'All of it true, as far as it goes,' said Our Man, and looked at me quite kindly, 'but that is not very far is it? Which is exactly why you will always be a better agent than Higgins.'

I suppose it is. I went away, consoled.

10. Marvell Roma

. . . we must be ris'n,
And at our pleasant labour, to reform
Yon flow'ry Arbors, yonder Alleys green,
Our walk at noon, with branches overgrown,

Milton. *Paradise Lost*

On to Rome which I accomplished by flying across the Côte
d'Azur at top speed, the place is riddled with bandits, and
hugging the shore line on down past Livorno, past the Italian
Riviera and to Ostia, then inland from there. All roads lead to
Rome, except for the one I was on, which was a bit off-route.
It would have been much easier if I could have sailed straight
across the Med, but just looking at the sea makes me heave
these days.

In Rome I took lodgings at the top of the Spanish Steps,
near our offices which were down at the bottom of the steps,
and which used a banking operation as a front. From our
office I could easily walk to that Caffe in the via Condotti,
which suited me well as a meeting place and dropping off
point for letters and packets. The main coffee man behind
the bar is in our employ, and once worked for the Thurn and

Taxis family and so has good contacts in the postal service. He can be relied on, for he keeps packets in a small safe in his back office, which is not only sunk into the floor, but has a small gunpowder charge inside, which will explode if the door is improperly opened, thus destroying anything inside the safe, and quite possibly blowing off the miscreant's hand too. Teach him a lesson.

I was out strolling in the morning sun, heading for my eleven o'clock *ombra*, when who should I run into but Mr Milton, scurrying about the place, his countenance open, his thoughts reserved. Really, our office here is becoming most slack, for they surely should have informed me that John Milton was in town.

'No one knows I am in town,' said John. 'Please do not tell anyone I am here.'

I nodded gravely, to indicate assent, but also to beg him to continue by way of explanation.

'I am here on official business, from the Office in London,' he said, and that was all.

'Which way are you going, sir, I will walk with you if you like.'

'I would like that Mr Marvell,' he said, and so we walked off together, our heels ringing out in time on the cobbles of the Condotti, for we naturally fell in step. He was heading toward the Corso.

'Have you seen the Vatican, John?' I asked. 'They say the famous ceiling is worth a detour.'

'I have not, sir,' he said, without actually sniffing loudly. 'I will not go near the place.' Well, I know the Pope lives there and is surrounded on all sides by Catholic priests and other impedimenta of the devil, but the last I heard they weren't actually stopping sightseers and arresting them if they were Protestant, and I never heard of a Protestant turning to stone either, just because he let his eye fall on a surplice or an altar rail, let alone a painting by Michelangelo.

'And I will not,' he added in a voice of rusty iron. '*Idolatry.*' This time, though, he did clench his teeth to make the point. It made it hard for him to spit, but I swear he managed it. I nodded as if to say that I understood perfectly, and would suffer many nights of torment to my conscience simply for having thought of the idea, let alone suggested it.

'You are right, John,' I said. 'Even the simple act of going to see it would lend too much credence to it. It would increase its importance if only by swelling its audience. One does not need to go to the Pole to know that it is cold. And so likewise with the Vatican. I will rest content in the knowledge that it is wicked . . .' And Mr Milton went stumping along, muttering to himself all the while without listening to a word I said, for which I cannot entirely blame him, for I get long winded when hypocritical. I must guard against that.

'Have you been to see Flecknoe?' he asked. Flecknoe is a bit of a fixture in Rome, a renegade English priest long since defrocked, who fancies himself as a poet, and who lives in some squalor in a tiny attic. He seems to be a port of call for any Englishman passing through Rome.

'I have, John,' I said, and could think of nothing more to say.

'Crashing bore, isn't he?' he said.

'I fear he is,' I said, with some relief. Flecknoe is one of those figures who is no bleeding good at their job, and is a bore to be with, but somehow always ends up being discussed by everybody as the main topic of conversation. I do not know why, or even how he does it. No doubt someone will write a book about him eventually, and it will be quite a challenge. For how do you make a bore interesting to a reader? I may even have a shot at it myself, just as a technical exercise you understand.

We stumped on a bit, and eventually came to the square of Santa Maria del Popolo, just close to one of the city gates.

'Here, let me show you something,' said John, and drew me inside the church that was there. A Catholic church, I should remind you. I must say, for a man who won't go near the Vatican for fear of some of the Catholicism rubbing off on his arm and infecting his body with the devil's juices, he seems remarkably, um, how can I put this, *supple* in his views. Perhaps a humble local church doesn't carry quite the same freight of viciousness. It is a matter of scale, no doubt.

Inside was cool and dark. The only thing that Mr Milton seemed likely to be infected with from this den of Papacy was a mild chill. No service was in progress, and there were only a few of the faithful on their knees here and there. The altar was lit with candles, and also the nave and a couple of lady chapels. I saw Milton shudder slightly as he crossed the aisle, and very ostentatiously *not* cross himself or bend his knee.

He drew me to a side chapel and pointed at the wall. After a while my eyes became accustomed to the gloom and I could make out a painting hanging above the small altar. It was a crucifixion scene, except quite unlike any other I had ever seen before, for the crucifying was being done upside down, which obviously suggested to me that the man must be St Peter. You will recall that he was sentenced to this form of execution, but begged to have it done inverted because he was not worthy of dying in the same way as our Lord.

The painter has frozen a moment in time, when the three burly doing the execution are just in the act of pulling the cross upright. Peter has already been placed on his final plank, and is now being hoisted into an upright but inverted position. He hangs there at about 45 degrees, watching the progress of these three workmen, who are going about their business as if it were no more than, say, paving a street, or digging a trench. I am sure that is exactly how it was for the people doing the dreadful deed. Just another job of work to be done, and not thought about too much, just collect their wages at the end of the day and go home to the wife and children. They have filthy bare feet.

The thing that really haunts you about the picture is St

Peter's face. He is an old man, bald, and with a wrinkled face, but his expression is something that, once seen, you will never wipe from your mind. There is horror and fear there, of course, at what is being done to him. That much would be inescapable in anyone who was human, no matter that he was beatified later, but there is more, much more in that face. There is pain and humiliation and even a sort of bewilderment at what he is facing. All of these seem to co-exist and mingle in one old man's face, but, almost surmounting all of these – and I think the one expression of the emotion from the man which you take away with you from the painting and that haunts you down the years – is disgust. I never saw a man so disgusted at his condition. 'That it should come to this!' he is thinking. 'Me, the man that Jesus himself called his anchor, his foundation, his rock upon which the church is built; and now, to die in a field, hoisted upside down by three filthy labourers.'

I was lost in this painting for many minutes, it absorbed me to the point where I almost thought I was inside it, and could talk to Peter as he suffered, quite forgetting who I was with and where. The odd thing is that there is barely any landscape in the picture, so that it is very difficult to imagine where you might be standing if you were in there. The painter has lit the action as if it were a piece of theatre, concentrating on the centre of the drama, and leaving nothing around it but velvet blackness.

'That darkness is visible,' said Milton to me after a while. I swear he can read my mind.

'It is a rare and strange picture,' I said, 'do you know who painted it?'

'A Michel Angelo,' he said. 'Not the first one who did the Vatican, this man came later and just had the same name. He was usually called after his home town, Caravaggio, near Milan. He died not fifty years ago, murdered, so they say, by the Jesuits.' At this Milton pursed his lips and gave a knowing look.

'Was he then a Protestant?' I said.

'If you look at that painting, he might as well have been, mightn't he?' said Milton. 'But no he wasn't. He was a Catholic, like any other Italian. It was just that he refused to paint anything but what was in front of his gaze. Hence the dirty feet, and the very unsaintly Peter. Of course the Jesuits started shrieking blasphemy, and pretty soon it looked like they would burn him if he didn't start adding a few angels flying up to heaven with pious expressions on their chubby little faces, the way they wanted.

'He went on the run, all over the place, but they tracked him down, and killed him. There is no proof of course, only stories, but they silenced him as surely as they would silence all dissent against their practices. So in a way, he was a Protestant. He just didn't know it,' said Milton.

He thought a while and then said finally, 'And what better way to be a Protestant than within the ranks of the Catholic

Church? Much better to do it from the inside than by open rebellion. Burrow away at all that rotten wood like a termite. If we want Rome to fall, then we must infiltrate their congregations. Men who question, men with doubts, men with a taste for freedom. Eh, what do you think Mr Marvell?'

'An admirable idea, sir, and I am beginning to understand why you sent me around Europe like this on my travels. "Broaden the mind," you said. "Learn as many different languages as you can," you said. "Never know when you might need them."

' "Do some trifling services for us as a messenger," you said. Well, I understood you well enough at the time. A nod was as good as a wink to me. I had no trouble with my conscience about becoming a spy. After all it was for the good of my country. And if the spy is not well regarded by other men, well, I have little care what others think of me, and am so well removed from the company of most men as to make no difference.'

I paused here, just to let him know that, after all the positive arguments, the *non placet* was coming. 'But the downfall of another man's religion? Well, I had not expected that, sir. I hold no liking for Catholics, but they worship the same God as you and I, and are not heathens like Mahommetans or Jews. I wonder if I am the man to be involved with your plans.'

And he began to laugh.

'No, no, no, Mr Marvell, you take me too literally and too

much at face value. I was simply thinking aloud, and letting my thoughts wander. I have no plan of infiltrating the Vatican. At least I do, but it is only a thought and a whimsical one at that. It amuses me sir. It would be completely impractical. We can't cut the Pope's head off, can we? Eh? Much as I would love to see it. I mean, all hell would break loose, and we can't afford a war at the moment. No, no just dream on it awhile, sir.'

I may well go down in history as the man who made Milton laugh.

We walked out of the church, and I straightened up and stretched my back, for we had been in a huddle in the side chapel for fear of being overheard. The sun was now at its highest, and quite blinding. There were fizzing little blue spots across my vision for a while until my eyes adjusted. We walked on, thinking of the painting and saying nothing; for there was much to dwell on, but little to be said about it. In a way that is a little like my poems. Once you have understood them, there is very little more to be said about them. The trouble is that very few people seem to understand them.

Damn, there I go about my poems again, I have always sworn myself to silence on the subject, but did I say something aloud, or was I just thinking? I am not sure. Dear God, what is wrong with me? It must be the heat, for my brain is becoming a little strange these days. I want to go home. I miss the cool.

We found ourselves back at the Piazza Navona, an elegant

oblong with rounded ends to it, which the locals were busy flooding with water from somewhere, the river perhaps. They hold horse races and circuses here, and occasionally they like to stage water displays. I have never seen one but Milton assured me that they even stage mock sea battles with shallow barges and gunpowder flashes and soldiers in cardboard armour. They had a mock sea serpent once, made out of wire and painted paper. For the re-enaction of the battle of Lepanto, when the Christian Knights saw off the Mahommetan threat a hundred years ago, half the actors would black their faces to imitate the Turk. I wondered who bore the cost, for it would surely be a very expensive entertainment, rather like the court masques at home.

'Oh, the Pope of course,' said Milton. 'He will pay anything if it keeps the common herd happy and in their place. You know the old formula, bread and circuses. They burn men here too, and in the Campo Marzio just around the corner. They say that makes a fine spectacle.'

'What is that?' I said. We had paused in front of what appeared to be a bed of flowers in a curious design.

'It is a flower clock,' said Milton. 'It is from a design by Strada for the Aldobrandini family. It is pretty and it tells the time.'

'Ah.' I stood for a while in silent contemplation of the thing. It was large, some ten feet across, and was highly coloured in a rather florid, Italian sort of way. There was little greenery in it. 'Where does the mechanism go?' I asked finally.

'Under the flowers I dare say,' said Milton.

'And how do the flowers grow through the cogs and wheels? And how are they watered properly?' I am sorry but my mind is often keen on detail.

'No doubt there are subterranean *springs*,' said Milton.

'Springs, eh!' I said, slapping my thigh. 'Springs! By God I like that. Very good, sir, very good.'

Perhaps I will go down in history as the only man that heard Mr Milton make a joke?

That flower clock. I must, must, must use it some time in the future.

We walked on a little more and then he bid farewell of me, at the bridge over the Tiber, which has the isolation hospital upon it. He made no further comment on what his business might be, nor when we might meet again. Still, there was no need. I know where our offices are, and can arrange to meet him from there. Besides, I am busy enough. My boy needs tutoring (he is my cover story for being here, no more than a couple of hours a day), my letters and messages need delivering, and Italian must be learned for any possible future missions that Mr Milton may require of me. He will be a power in the land I am sure of it. And so will I if I play my cards right, for I will be attached to him – yet not so close that the ties might not be cut, for I fear for the future of our country. The King and Parliament are fighting, and both sides think their cause just. A man comes down too heavily on one side or the other, and he had best look to his head when his party falls. As it surely will. No system of human devising lasts forever, and it pleases the Lord to relieve His boredom and amuse us with change.

I may look like a Puritan, but I am not.

I am Mr Milton's man in the Foreign Office, but I distrust that Cromwell more than any foreigner.

I am of Parliament's frame of mind, but I would prefer a King *and* a Parliament, if only they could get along.

The poets I admire the most, and so share my time with, are all Royalist cavaliers to a man. And they think I am one too. I do not correct them, for so I *am*, when I am with them.

And when I am with Mr Milton, I am not. I dissemble, I know it, but what am I to do? For I do also admire Mr Milton in his way. He is so lofty, so far above us all, as to be nearer the divine. Yet there is something chilly about him, as if he were both more and less than human. I have a feeling that he might even ask me, some time in the future, to commit a murder for the good of the state. I would not put it past him. A man like he is could in time come to think he was above the law. And would I do it?

What do *you* think?

The flower clock found its way much later into 'The Garden'. I can always make use of the most unusual stuff. It just comes to me unbidden, years after I have seen it. All I have to do is be busy writing, and up it swims into my vision. It won't necessarily come when I am starting out, but once I am off and running, it just won't stop pushing its way in.

Something about a

> *. . . skilful gardener drew*
> *Of flowers and herbs this dial new,*
> *Where from above the milder sun*
> *Does through a fragrant zodiac run;*

Fragrant zodiac. I like that. What do you think?

11. Nature, Orderly and Near

Society is all but rude
To this delicious Solitude.

Marvell. 'Upon Appleton House'

Common beauties stay fifteen;
Such as yours should swifter move,
Whose fair blossoms are too green
Yet for lust, but not for love.

Marvell. 'Young Love.'

My Lord Fairfax was indeed a great soldier but he had no taste for killing. That is no paradox, as anyone who has ever been a soldier will tell you. Every battle won is a battle lost for the opposing side, and every soldier knows that he cannot win every time. Indeed my Lord Fairfax came to abhor the fight, and let it be known too, thus giving Cromwell good reason to complain against him, though I noticed that he was not slow to seize command of the army once Fairfax stepped down.

In point of fact it was Cromwell who manoeuvred him

into the corner from which he could not escape. Cromwell is too cunning ever to be well liked. Fairfax had been ordered to attack the Scots, as a pre-emptive strike, since they were well known to be bubbling for war – red-haired, bony-kneed, Presbyterian bores the lot of them – but he would not, saying that human probabilities were not a good enough reason to make war on a brother. It strikes me as good sense, but Cromwell started shooting flame from his nostrils, and I fear he is going to do to the Scots what he did to the Irish: kill the lot of them and come back dripping gore.

So we left, Fairfax and I, for his family manse, Appleton House in Yorkshire, and mighty nice it is too, what with two big rivers and a large enclosed garden and trees and such. It was once a nunnery, and retains an air of seclusion. It is seemly, civilized and serene.

And that is exactly what I want, no more and nothing less at the moment. We will retire from the stage a while. He needs a rest from war, and I from observing it. He has his coin and medal collection to keep him busy, not to mention the house and grounds, and he writes poetry too. Some of it is almost good. I will concentrate on my poetry too, though I will keep quiet about it, for it is better than his.

I will write something about the house and its grounds, I think. I have read something that Ben Jonson wrote on a country house, Penshurst I think it was, and while it is aimed at pleasing the rich owner, yet there is something there to emulate perhaps. My beloved Horace and also the scabrous

Martial wrote of country seats outside the city, but it was
Jonson who praised the way that such houses became an
ornament and a model of harmony for the rest of us all.

He hired me, for form's sake, as tutor to his daughter
Mary.

As I entered the kitchen of the house, there was a girl
standing across the room, looking out of the window. Her
golden hair was unpinned and curled, though not very long.
She wore a dress of lime colour, and over it a starched white
apron, stiff as snow-frost crackling. Her hands were on her
hips as she leaned forward slightly to see something outside.
The sun was shining through her pale hair, so that it all but
vanished into a bright halo of down. It was hard to tell her
age, for her full face was three parts turned away from me,
but she was still young I could see that, and I thought: let the
world cease turning, let time have a stop, before you turn
around.

But she turned and smiled and greeted me with some
words or other. My ears were ringing too loud to make them
out, but my tongue was not tied, it is never tied, and I made
the usual courtesies. I could feel her father's gaze upon me,
so I did not look at him, but busied myself with little Mary,
for it was she, his daughter and my charge. Dear Lord, what a
thing. She is twelve years old, I knew that before I arrived,
and that is why I did not immediately recognize her. She is
not yet a woman, but not very far off it either. I must guard

myself, for she will be destined for someone from a higher station in life than mine. She is very pretty, and most spirited too, for she is her father's only one, and so takes on the characteristics of the boy that he perhaps wanted. She strides about the place like a Tom, but then can melt like a candle placed too near the fire at the slightest upset.

What will I teach her? She does not look ready for Latin, nor is she the sort that would enjoy or even need it. Well, we will tick off the plants, and name the trees, and learn the different kinds of vegetable and fruit from the kitchen garden, and no doubt that will suit us both well enough. And she will play a little. I would like that, never having a notion of it at all. My sisters would often play together, but not with me. I never played as a child, and since they would not share a doll or a top or their knuckle-bones with me, then I affected contempt for playthings as being unworthy; and if you affect something long enough, it soon becomes sincerely held. So play was beneath me, and still is.

We walked the grass of the parterre, which fronted the house, and which was rolled smooth every day by one of the gardeners. The landscape had been cunningly done, for at the far end, just beyond a statue of a lion attacking a horse and sinking its teeth into its neck, a savage thing, the ground fell away downhill, in a sudden swoop which was invisible to anyone until they were almost upon it, like a ha-ha, but not so steep. The lawn continued but the ground rolled down to the reedy banks of the river, which was not so big or fast moving, but sluggish and pleasant.

Little Moll never failed to be pleased by the sudden drop in the surface of the ground, and would go tee-hee whenever we came to it, as if I might not notice and go tumbling down the slope. She laughs like an olive tree. I wondered if I might pretend to slip some time and perhaps roll down toward the river. It would amuse her, but I do not know I can do it. I am not a one to stand on my dignity, but I cannot seem to lose it somehow. I can dissemble almost anything in adult affairs and politics, but when it comes to play-acting, I am at a loss. It requires a greater sincerity than I am capable of showing. I have seen it in actors. No wonder Cromwell's grey men closed the theatres.

In fact the whole garden is constructed around a series of surprises. To the left of the parterre there is a gravelled walk with a box hedge on the other side. Here you may turn into a small opening in the hedge, over which hang weeping trees, all of which obscure any view beyond. The path winds a little way further, past a sculpture of a dying Gaul, and then you meet another gap in foliage and pass through this, and what then greets the eye never fails to make a stranger gasp.

A magical bower is laid out behind the fringed curtain of verdigris. Down below is a pond, full of golden carp, but this is only the middle pond of three. The one to the left is highest up, and surmounted by a lead statue of Venus. It cannot be seen from the entrance, but one must walk a little way toward it, through thick shrubbery and a gentle rise in the ground, and as you walk, so satyrs and fauns appear, leaping from the foliage and bluish-green leaves. When you reach the top-most pond, which is supplied by an underground spring, you may cast your gaze down the full length of the grassy slope, with the carp pond in the middle, followed by the briefest bump in the ground, then a further long grass-green swathe until it reaches the banks of the same river as I spoke of earlier.

On the plinth of the statue is carved a poem, not a very good one, to the memory of a most sagacious otter-hound called Ringwood. I have read it, and it is easy to learn by heart, for it is only doggerel, and has no more meaning than its surface. Little Moll could recite it complete when she was just three years old, and she did it for me just once, but got bored with it halfway through, and I never taxed her with it again. Perhaps I will teach her the art of good poetics.

Perhaps I will not. She is only a woman after all, and would never make good use of it.

Anyway, she did delight in showing me the surprises of the garden. For if you step lightly down the soft sward, it is most pleasant, pausing to take in the carp and the carp pond, which is fed, not just by the upper pond from underground, but also by a long trickling gutter to its left, placed centrally in the mid of a path and called The Watery Walk. Then you come to the hump in the ground, like an ancient burial mound, and skirt it without care or thought, and just as you are halfway around, it reveals itself to have no other half, but a great bite out of the lawn, and another rock pool down below it. It is a very great surprise and delight. Moll says that a servant got drunk one night and failed to notice the way the hump stopped suddenly; he fell in and drowned. I said it was unlikely, for the pool is not so deep.

'Ah,' she said, stroking her chin, as she has seen me do, cheeky minx, 'but the drop is a good double of your height, sir, say twelve feet (see I have done my sums as you taught), and he bashed in his head on the brick surrounding to the pool.'

'Well, that would do it, all right,' I said. 'That would kill the man. Though he didn't exactly drown did he?'

'Well, he was found face down in the water, and he never came up for air,' said Moll.

'Don't get pert with me young lady,' I said, but could not stop a smile. Moll went off, rocking her head from side to side, not back and fore, nor shaking it. I can see her expression, even though she has her back to me: resignation, even exasperation at the old fool, and a wicked smile at having put one over on me. Her father says I must teach her discipline. How can I? I cannot even raise my voice to her, let alone my hand. By God I would love her if she were a woman. As it is I must be content with letting her keep my heart young. She is good at that, and she knows it, the flirt.

Around the pond, the lawn slopes away once more to the river, as I said, and here we once made little boats from reeds and mud and greengrass cuttings and floated them out, and I told her of the sea and naval engagements which I recalled from my travels, and she sat and marvelled. She made great play on the last word, playing a joke upon my name.

I hate jokes about names. If there is a golden rule in this life, it is that you should never make a joke about someone's name. For two good reasons. First, they will have heard it already a thousand times before, and second, it is offensive, for your name has a private meaning to you. It is close to your soul. When I was at school, I endured a pun upon marvel twice, but then upon the third time, I broke the boy's nose with the edge of my hand. After that there were no more jokes on my name. Or none that I heard at any rate

Moll jokes about my name all the time, and it never fails to make me smile. And I smile without strain, which is unlike me.

Looking upstream a little, there are the woods, which border the lawn all the way down the slope, and as you descend the slope, every so often the dense Brunswick trees part dramatically to reveal a vista, paved with lawn. Three times, your gaze is diverted in surprise along a straight path through the trees, and at the end of each vista is a different thing. At the far reach of one is a statute of a naked Apollo, with his back to you. How it has survived the Puritans I do not know, although its privities have been knocked off with a hammer. I once saw Moll stroking its buttocks, which have gone a coppery green due to oxidization but are still smooth.

I said nothing, since I was hid in the trees, but she had a most dreamy smile upon her face, as she looked up at him, and gently stroked the small of his back and down his fesses to the back of his narrow thighs. She was clearly enjoying herself, and that pleased me. She never even glanced around the front of the naked boy, and so I cannot help but think her innocent.

No she is not. No one is innocent, not even from birth.

And so I was lying when I wrote that she was 'too green yet for lust'. It was in the first poem I wrote at Appleton House, and I called it 'Young Love'. I wrote it out quite quick in the library, before embarking on a longer one about the House itself, which I did not finish for some years. There's something in it of the *carpe diem* theme, which I like, and will certainly return to later, for it is in Horace too.

> *Come little infant, love me now,*
> *While thine unsuspected years*
> *Clear thine aged father's brow*
> *From cold jealousie and fears.*

I had written it with the express intention of showing it to Fairfax, since we were whiling away our sabbatical from the world with many distractions, and writing poetry was one of them. I also wanted to help him improve his own attempts, which were passing good for a soldier, but of a lower rate than Sir Philip Sidney's. I was pleased with the verses too for they came out quite neatly, and have an ease about them. The message to Fairfax is clear enough: don't worry about your twelve-year-old daughter. She is quite safe with me:

> *Pretty surely 'twere to see*
> *By young love old time beguil'd:*
> *While our sportings are as free*
> *As the nurses with the child.*

Hmm, me as a nurse eh? I don't quite see that, and, besides, what nurses get up to with children is not quite so innocent as fathers would like to hope. Still, as I said, it later goes on about the way she is 'too green yet for lust', and that seemed to satisfy the General well enough. It is not yet time for him to learn that all poetry is lying.

Anyway, it is a sporting little thing, and I will do more of them. I haven't much time for shepherdesses and Dorindas and so on, but still I do like some elements of the pastoral. Thwarted love is a good theme, and one which comes all too easily to me, alas for my frailty. I must work myself up to the point where my wheels are turning fast enough for me to attack the long House poem that I plan for Appleton, and a few little love tunes first will oil my axles admirably.

Where was I? Sorry, that is how it is with writers of any sort. They are staring at a statue for a few minutes, and then you find them half an hour later still in the same spot, but staring at the grass, muttering wildly to themselves. It looks like they have deranged their brains somehow, but all they are doing is trying to find the right rhyme for a couple of lines they have just thought up, and if you interrupt, they will look up with a wild stare in their eye, and go half mad with rage at being deflected off course when they were just half an inch from *le mot juste*. I have done it time and again. 'See' and 'free' came so easily that I knew I would have to work up something more difficult just to make the poem worthwhile. And I knew I had to end on 'child', just for the sense of the thing, and the problem is that there aren't that many good rhyming words in English, so I did well to find 'beguil'd' and it only took me a whole afternoon of talking to the grass.

When I was recently in Rome, I found that rhymes are easier in Italian, for they have so many words that end in stock syllables like 'iente'. Which is probably why their poetry lacks toughness. The rhymes, and indeed all the rest of the poem by extension, are too easily won for them, and anyway their language sounds to me like a perfect correlative to the way they behave. They are a conceited and futile race, and they sound it.

Poor old John Milton, whom I met the last time I was there, I think I told you, he was in such close proximity to so many Catholics that his trousers all but caught fire from rage.

Where was I? Off again on another byway, I do apologize. When I am composing or even recalling my compositions, my brain becomes crammed with images and ideas, and memories too, which are nothing but imagination, as Hobbes tells us. Ah yes . . . the garden, and here we are, in it.

At the end of another vista is a little summer house, constructed like a Greek temple in the round, with pillars and a domed top. The back half of it is walled, and has a stone seat, and in the middle is a small stone table, like an altar. We sat there one day, as the summer sun was declining and the shadows lengthened on the grass, eating bread and a cucumber, which the butler had brought us, and we heard a creaky noise coming from the table. There was a crack off the corner of the flat top and below it a niche in the pedestal, and a small bird's nest was in there, with six little ones, all craning their necks upwards, and their mouths agape, and squawking for food. With a little cry of sorrow, Moll scampered out to the edge of the lawn, and dug it with her fingernails until she found a worm, and brought it back and fed it to the greedy little mouths. She has a large and tender heart, and is so easily moved to tears at the plight of the smallest thing. I fear for her in the wide world, outside this garden.

For *her*? Christ protect her, but I fear for even myself these days, what with the grey ones in charge now. They'd lock her up just for smiling. And me for encouraging her.

Just as I had that thought there was a commotion at the main gate in the far distance out of sight. I had heard many horses approaching and wondered what it was, but said nothing for I did not want to frighten Moll. Then came the clear sound of a pistol shot.

12. Trouble in Paradise

The wanton troopers riding by
Have shot my fawn, and it will die.

Marvell. 'The Nymph Complaining
for the death of her Fawn'

There was a back-gate in the wall, half hidden by foliage, not
far from where we were sitting. I went through it on to the
outside lane that ran beside the wall, and stole down
the length of the wall until I had the main gate in sight. There
was a squad of troopers, I counted ten in all, with their
Sergeant. They had dismounted and were standing confer-
ring on a plan, I could see that much, and they looked shifty.
Their pistols were still in their saddle-holsters, and they were
armed only with swords, except for two troopers who
were unarmed and struggling to lift a dead deer on to one of
the horses, behind the saddle. The deer's tongue was lolling
from the corner of its mouth and its teeth were bared. Small
flecks of blood were spattered on its coat from a wound in its
chest, where I would guess they shot it. The little thing was
steaming.

The main gates were open as usual, so they must have stepped inside the park for their kill.

I stepped out of the shrubs, squared my shoulders, and strode up the road, my heels ringing loud enough on the stones of the path to beat my approach. They paused and turned and looked at me, and the Sergeant stepped forward and opened his mouth to speak. 'Stand away,' he said but without too much conviction. 'We go about our duties, and we are here to gather . . .'

'Who is your commanding officer?' I barked at him. Always deliver the first blow. His mouth stayed open though his initial bluster had changed to slight wariness.

'Captain Harrington is currently . . .' he began.

'Then go and tell Captain Harrington that you have just killed one of the deer belonging to General Fairfax, his former commanding officer,' I said.

His mouth stayed open for a moment, then he swallowed loudly, with it still open, and gagged slightly. One of his troopers spoke up. 'Soldiers defend the likes of you and soldiers must eat,' he muttered, 'always the same story, as-cendancy defending its privilege . . .' So they are Levellers, I thought. The army is riddled with them. They march around doing as they please and killing whomsoever and demanding that all land be made common property, and all because they claim some special dispensation from God.

Why, any man might do that, with no more authority than a fool. Fuck that attitude. I had heard that there had been courts martial of his kind for attempted rebellions within the ranks.

'Any more talk like that,' I shouted at him, my voice rising to full pitch, 'and I'll see you hanged for a mutineer.' It was wondrous the sudden quiet which descended after my rant. They fiddled about with their fingers and looked at the ground and the sky and the trees, anywhere but at me in fact. Then one of them started to mount up again, and the others followed suit quite quickly and with some guilty relief. The two troopers who had been tying the deer up, threw it to the ground with a dismissive gesture as if to say it was nothing to them, and they got on their horses. I noticed that the soldiers at the rear were resting their hands inside their saddle-holsters, and even the ones closer to me had their hands on the pommels of their swords. I did not think that things would get ugly, but I was unarmed and so I did not want to provoke them further.

I turned my back on them and walked toward the house with firm tread and squared jaw, as if I were about to take the news to my Lord Fairfax. That seemed the best way of deterring them, for it is hard to shoot a man in the back, unless your blood is up. Mind you, I wouldn't put murder past those Leveller scum. They would turn the world on its head for no better reason than a boy might destroy a bird's nest. They have that evangelical zeal about them that suggests they know they will fly straight to the arms of the Lord after they have killed and raped their way through the entire aristocracy and middle classes of England. And Scotland too for good measure and the fun of it.

I knew that Fairfax was not in the house, but I didn't stop as I crunched up the gravel drive. As I neared the great oak door, I could see a musket poking through one of the gun-ports set into it, though it was pointed past my shoulder and not at me. It was very steady. It took a supreme effort of will on my part not to look back over my shoulder, but I thought that if one of them were coming after me, I would hear him soon enough, and anyway I would have to trust to the good aim of whoever had the musket. It was probably one of the gardeners, all of whom are fair shots, since I have seen them scaring away rooks and shooting pigeons for the kitchen. Besides I wasn't going to let those troopers have the satisfaction of seeing me checking over my shoulder.

I seized the iron latch and lifted it and swung in the door with a sharp cry of 'Coming through,' and the musket also swung off target since the gun-port was narrow and would not permit too much lateral travel. It was dark in the hall, for the candles had been extinguished; I could smell the smoke of the trimmed wicks. Then I made out a figure in a pale dress wresting the gun from the port and uncocking the flint. It was Moll.

'Mary,' I said, 'what are you doing, be careful, put it down, that thing is dangerous, put it down immediately.'

'Of course it's dangerous,' she said, raising her chin at me, with that defiance I am coming to see more and more from her. 'It's supposed to be.'

'But you know that you must not use those things. They are not for children,' I said. 'Or for women,' I added.

'You're always telling me I am not yet a woman,' she said. 'So that's all right then, isn't it?'

'It is not,' I said. and I was losing my temper badly, 'I will not have it. I will tell your father.'

'Do so,' she said, rather too sharply for my liking.

'And not just for the musket,' I said. I took it from her, and checked the uncocked flint and lowered it to the pan. She had known how it worked all right. 'But for your unconscionable rudeness also. You know he will not abide that.'

'And will you tell him I was covering your retreat from the soldiers too?' she said, defiant now, 'And would have saved your *silly* life if they had come after you, which they nearly did.'

I reached over and slapped her face.

And regretted raising my arm even as I stretched it to do the deed. She went to speak but could say nothing, and her face coloured a deep crimson, as if she had been shouting. She ran off across the hall and out through the door to the servants' quarters and the kitchen. But she did not weep.

I went to my room, and paced, for I was too distraught to be able to think clearly. First the troopers and then Moll: they had unhinged me quite and I was not in a fit state for anything. I steadied my breathing and slowly mastered myself, as I have taught myself to do. My brain was hurtling hither and yon, but my body must never betray it. I looked in the glass, and saw I was quite sober and steady. My colour was up slightly, but I was otherwise quiet and without expression. I knew that I must do one thing, and one thing only.

I went first to the kitchen and the servants' quarters but found nothing, so I returned to the Greek temple and there she was, close by. I felt enormous relief wash over me, but also slight apprehension. She was squatting over the first out-fall of water which comes up from a spring and feeds the rill down the centre of the Watery Walk. The Walk is framed by trees whose boughs touch at the top, and the trees begin just at the spring.

I like the beginning of a path. It is like the beginning of a narrative – a reassuring and exciting sign of former human presence.

I thought at first she might be relieving herself, but she was just staring at the water intently, as children do. The business with the troopers was still heavily on my mind, but I thought that I should approach her by indirections.

'Time for a game,' I said.

'Which game?' she said.

'I will teach you one,' I said.

'Goody, I like to learn from you. I am sorry,' she continued, quiet but confident now. 'I know that you were concerned only for me. That is why you lost your temper. My mother is the same when I am lost and she cannot find me. When she finally sees me, relief gives way to anger.'

Oh, she was mine. How could she be so young and yet know so much?

'It is not so much that relief gives way,' I said, 'but I do believe that the relief often causes the rise of anger. Emotion moves quite fast upon us, and it is like any motion, it causes commotion in its wake. The one can cause the other, without any reason.'

'You can't explain everything,' she said, looking very serious, in a tone that robbed the phrase of all offence.

I got a twig and broke it into two short pieces about three inches each, and made each as close to the other as I could with my pen-knife. Into one I carved a notch and gave it to her. 'Yours will be the nicked one,' I said. 'Now, we'll start right here at the spring. Place your stick next to mine, drop it in the water, and we will watch the race, to see whose stick is the fastest.'

'The *faster*,' she said. 'It is a comparative of two.' Cheeky little minx. It is amazing how fast she can change her mood. And mine too.

We dropped our twigs in together and watched as the slow current took them up, and swung them around, and took them away down the little gutter of bubbling clear water. We followed them, our cries of encouragement getting louder all the while. Little Moll's twig got stuck in some leaves at one point, and she became almost hysterical in her vexation, jumping up and down, and half-reaching to the twig to free it, and catching my stern eye and pulling back. Finally, the twig broke free and continued its path scudding along the rill, until, just behind mine, it entered the bath, a square pond halfway along the Watery Walk.

The bath was built in front of a small hermitage, which was no more than a conceit. It was a red-brick square room with a roof so low the inhabitant could not stand. The idea was that a hermit in rags would be imported for any rout that the owner cared to throw. There had been no parties since my sojourn here with Lord Fairfax, nor did I think there ever would be. The hermitage was crumbling, for want of attention.

I reached down and grasped both sticks and lifted them out, to cries of 'Oooh, cheating,' from Moll. 'No, no,' I said, 'they were both stalled in the bath, let us begin again on the other side, and I will not take the advantage that I had over you.'

Moll clapped her hands, and I put the sticks down again at the start of the final length of rill. I looked down the rest of the vista of the Watery Walk, and could see a faint blue crepuscular light settling on the bezique-green foliage round the carp pond. There was a mist rising from the waters, shrouding the plants in blue-white swathes, and a faun was rising, erect, priapic, from the undergrowth, his sinister grin looking like a boy who had just fled the scene of a crime undetected.

She looked in the same direction and gave a little jump and shiver, saying, 'I thought he was real for a moment.'

'Oh, but he is,' I said, 'most real. The world is full of him.' She looked at me in full belief, but with no understanding I think, so I continued: 'And when the night has come and the stars are young and green, then he and all his friends come alive and dance in the garden under the moon.'

'What do they dance?' she said.

'The coranto,' I said, 'and others, I do not know dancing well. Oh, and they play pell mell, I know that, and search for young girls to seduce.'

'They do not,' said Moll, stamping her foot, 'you are making it up to tease me.'

She flew into tears of rage or vexation, I knew not which, and I rushed to her, and petted her, and said I was sorry, and said that it was only a game, but she would not be consoled. I think the problem was that she fell for the magic of it, all which made the deceit more unbearable.

Or perhaps the world did not go the way she wanted. They do that, women. Throw a tantrum, I mean, when they can't win; or when they can't change the rules so that they can win; or when they are caught out in a cheat; or when they are facing disappointment. I was proud of her though, proud of that business with the musket. By God, she is nearly a woman already.

13. Some Trees

So architects do square and hew,
Green trees that in the forest grew.

Marvell. 'A Dialogue between the Soul and Body'

Here there is the Balsamea prostrata, a low prostrate dwarf bush of dark green. And there an Obtusa coralliformis, with cord-like twisted branches, and green pyramid-shaped foliage. And here Thyoides andelyensis, which is dark green with red male flowers in spring, which dislikes chalk. Japonica globosa Nana with its slightly pendulous green globe.

Lanceolata, a glossy-green prickly leaf, which dislikes strong wind.

A Communis Horstman's Pendula, very prickly weeping green tree.

The semi-fastigiate Kaempferi Jakobsen's Pyramid.

And the country park fire Podocarpus, an attractive female form, low-spreading, young growth is creamy-yellow in May, becoming salmon-pink then green in summer. In winter the foliage is purple-bronze. In late summer all these colours will appear at the same time. Totally hardy in the country.

Plicata Irish Gold, of the Thuja variety, note the yellow variegation.

I like lists, there is something very soothing about them. They have a ring to them, and often read well aloud. Having dispensed with every fanciful term and artifice, and being just the barest of facts, they become a form of poetry, stripped like a bride awaiting nothing but one acknowledged act. Also they take a while to compile here, around this garden, and I do need much distraction at the moment. What is happening to me over Moll, I dare not name, let alone contemplate. I have been here nearly two years now, and all of it divine solitude. Now I find Moll's teasing is beginning to work upon me. What was once a little tiresome is now a daily necessity for me. If I do not have her eyes catch mine, even for a little, I feel my day is wasted. Must there always be a snake in the garden?

You might think that my poem 'The Garden' dates from this period of seclusion at Appleton House, and indeed many of the people to whom I have shown it have made this mistake. It is not so. Read it for what it is, and you will see that I am not describing one particular garden at all, but my state of mind. The poem came to me later, when I was embroiled in the political life, and yearning for a little quiet and ease. Bear with me a while, I will relate the occasion of it later.

14. Appleton House

But now the salmon-fishers moist
Their leathern boats begin to hoist,
And like Antipodes in shoes,
Have shod their heads in their canoes.
How tortoise-like, but not so slow,
These rational amphibii go!
Let's in: for the dark hemisphere
Does now like one of them appear.

Marvell. The final verse of 'Upon Appleton House'

It was not until after I had left the House that I could bring myself to write a poem to its great qualities, which was a shame in one way for my Lord Fairfax would have enjoyed it while we were there in our seclusion. It just would not happen. I needed sufficient distance from the place in order to get my perspective right. *Ut pictura poesis*, says the Roman, and indeed there are many ways in which a poem is a kind of picture in words, but sometimes it cannot be drawn from life. It must wait, gestating in the memory. Moll would have liked it too, for I used plain language such as she would understand, and she was advanced for her years anyway, as I told you.

I put her in the poem, and she liked that, when I showed it to her later. I referred to her as the sprig of mistletoe, which 'on the Fairfacian oak does grow'. She was their only child, alas, and so they pinned all of their hopes on her. As far as they were concerned she was

> *Heaven's centre, nature's lap,*
> *and paradise's only map.*

As I am sure you have guessed by now, that is not what she was for her parents, that is what she was for me.

I finished it all with a joke, just for her, which she later told me she also liked very much, and made her laugh. I had already compared myself to a nurse for the young girl, and I had seen nurses call their charges indoors from play in the late afternoon, when it begins to get dark, for the night air is considered bad for growing children.

It came to me, what I should compare the darkening sky to, quite quickly. Normally I do not like to explain how my poetry comes about, but this is really very simple, and something of a good conceit too. I had watched the fishermen at Hull, ending their day's work by dragging their leather coracles from the water, through the mud on the bank, and then hoisting them over their heads, and trudging their way home.

Moll had a little tortoise in the kitchen garden at Appleton. She kept it near the dovecot, where it had a warm box of straw for sleeping in. One of the gardeners had drilled a small hole at the back of its shell, and passed a string through it, which was attached to a stake, so it could not wander off too far.

Moll and I would spend hours watching its slow progress towards the lettuce patch, while we talked of the plants and how they grew, and the trees in the distance down to the river. She marvelled at its patience, and we discussed what a virtue patience was. I found a volume of Marcus Aurelius in her father's library, which helped me greatly in expanding upon the subject of patience, for the man was a true and great stoic.

Every time she saw that tortoise she laughed and clapped her hands together, and then would settle with a look of great and solemn gravity to watch its progress, her chin cupped in her hand, while pretending to concentrate upon my talk. I would pretend to lecture her very seriously, but after a while would talk the most stupid nonsense, and she would carry on nodding gravely, and watching the tortoise grind ever forward towards his evening greens. Before I even knew it, I was acquiring a sense of humour.

I told her one day that the tortoise looked exactly like those old fishermen, with the leather boats on their heads.

'*Leather* boats?' she had said. 'But boats are wood. Only shoes are leather.'

'Not these boats,' I said, 'but they are very like shoes, it is true. The men who use them must be Antipodeans, because they wear their shoes upon their heads.'

It was not the funniest joke in the wide world, but it hit a nerve. Now that I reflect upon it, it makes me think of the man who pulled himself up by his own bootstraps. Pulling oneself up by one's own boots is an impossibility, but one only recognizes that after one has blinked at the suggestion. Before the blink it seemed reasonable, and amusing. I also had in mind my friend Richard Lovelace's very pleasing poem about 'The Snail', in which he makes the conceit that the snail is an animal who is his own house. It blends two separate things – a house, a snail – into one improbable thing by folding them in on themselves, like sheets of paper.

The idea of a man wearing shoes upon his head was too much for Moll, and she got the giggles and then could not stop and finally she fell to the Brunswick green lawn clutching her stomach, doubled up, and fairly hysterical with laughing. Her laughter was infectious for I could not stop myself either. We were both quite enfolded together. I think it was the happiest day of her life. It certainly was mine.

The busy world of men was to call me back from that garden, and I could not help but go, for it was my duty, but I always think of those days with Moll, and know that it is not given to mortal man to be so happy ever again. God gave me a glimpse of paradise, and then took it back. How can I ever find a way to forgive Him?

15. An Axe Brought It In

He nothing common did or mean
Upon that memorable Scene;
But with his keener Eye
The Axe's edge did try:
Nor call'd the Gods with vulgar spite
To vindicate his helpless Right,
But bow'd his comely Head,
Down as upon a Bed.

Marvell. 'An Horatian Ode upon Cromwell's
Return from Ireland'

They killed my King, and I saw it. It was a cold afternoon on
a Tuesday, late in January. I had been with Cromwell when he
had frightened so many into signing the death warrant, and I
was sure that he would want to witness the act itself, but
he was more cunning than I took him for. Fuck me, that is
not saying much, is it? All right, he is more cunning than me,
and that is saying something. He decided to stay away, and let
it be known he was with his commanders in a house nearby,
praying for God's good guidance. I wish I could say that he
was celebrating with a little carousal, but as you know, that is

hardly the style of the man. Still he did sit with his feet up, staring out the window and occasionally talking to his men, although brooding rather more.

'Do you pray for guidance?' I asked him after one long silence.

'By God no. I'm wondering all the possible outcomes of this event. It is too late to stop it now, but blame in the future must not fall too close to me. I have over fifty signatories on the warrant, but still I feel the people who will cleave to the King's memory will see me as the chief instigator. I must keep my distance.' Actually there were fifty-nine that he had brow-beaten into signing, including himself.

'Is there no hope of a reprieve?' I said.

'Shall we see if God wills it?' he said, and I swear I saw him smile.

They cut his head off at two o'clock. Cromwell had been most clear in his commands as to the scaffold. It was to be built outside the Banqueting House in Whitehall, a place the King had loved and spared no expense in maintaining. It was here that he had staged some of his most elaborate masques, in which even he and his Queen had taken part. It was designed by Inigo Jones, a Catholic and therefore hated. Also it was a place where the King's cavalry had once dispersed some protestors very early in the war, so it was symbolic for Oliver, though I suspect the King was indifferent to such signs. There is a painting by Rubens on the ceiling, and he glanced up at it upon that last walk, and then sauntered in at his usual pace, for all the world as if he were going to see a play of an evening, especially written just for him. Which in a dreadful way was true.

I was at an upstairs window opposite, and so had a better view than the common population, for the scaffold platform was shrouded in black curtains to chest height. They were old and had a greenish tinge to them. The King appeared from a second storey window and walked very calmly forward, still glancing casually about him as if he were at the theatre. Dignified, erect, calm, yet with an almost pleasurable expectation on his face. Cromwell will talk forever about his God, and wonder what He wills. My King was on easier terms with Him, and now nearer to Him too.

He addressed the crowd from the rail, but his words were lost on the wind, and he was brief. He turned and had words with the axe-man, begging leave, I later heard, to pray briefly on the block, and also pardoning the man for his crime. He looked at the axe. There was a mattress on the platform.

Then he laid his head down, as quietly as a maid upon a pillow. I had half closed my eyes up to slits, for I could hardly bare to watch. Yet I did not turn away, as I often do.

Suddenly he extended his arms sideways, as if bestowing a benediction upon the crowd below, although none could see him. I was wondering what it could mean, but the answer was brought home to me quickly. It was the signal, and the axe-man did his office, in one stroke thank God. He lifted the head and showed it, over the top of the rail, to the crowd, but he did not say the usual words. He was wearing a full-face mask, but I do believe that he was fearful that someone might recognize his voice. Cutting a king's head off is not something you do every day, and you had best hedge your bets for the future, in case the Royalists get back in power.

I did hear a groan from the crowd such as I never heard before, and desire I may never hear again.

The Bishop had arranged for the body to be taken and for a chirurgeon to sew the head back on the trunk. This was so that he might rise again at the latter day when the trumpet shall sound, and the earth shall part and yield up the dead, and he will be youthful and fair in the fullness of his being. This at least is what the Bishop and all his flock in the established church believe, but all of that veers a bit too close to Rome for some of England's church-goers and I am not just talking about the Anabaptists and the Quakers and all those other freaks of nature. No, the Puritan wing of the C of E believed that this business of the dead rising was all so much rot, that a decent burial and proper mourning were simply there for the benefit of the mourners and not for the corpse. As far as they were concerned, the soul went flying straight to the arms of the Lord (or not, as the case might be), and what was left was just so much corrupted meat. Let it lie wheresoever it fall.

I can see that they have a point. Indeed I incline to their

way of thinking. I have seen enough dead bodies now to realize that the soul has gone. Whatever it was that animated the person has departed, and the rest is just a loathsome carcass.

However, when I think of my King, I must say that it seemed the right thing to do. I listened to the Bishop arguing that the body must be whole and entire for the last trump, and I appreciate all that, but, myself, I thought it just a common decency, and the very least that might be done for a man. The corpse was then spirited away to Windsor, to be away from fanatic parties who might dig it up for their own ends.

And it was there that Cromwell confronted the man, to his face, for the only time in his life.

And reached into the coffin, with his bare hands, and tore the King's head from its body. He sank his fingers up to their knuckles in the wound about the neck, and wrenched as if he were tearing a sheet. There was no blood, but still . . .

The Archbishop swore so strong that people at prayer fled the building. 'You are an animal, no, not even a beast would have done this. God strike you dead for this profanity.'

'Animal? No, worse. Human,' said Cromwell, his fingers dripping with corrupted meat. It was a blasphemous and shocking thing. I know that the dead body has no meaning to a Puritan, and that it is only the soul that they worry about, but still. There are common decencies which should be observed. There was also the symbol of the thing, of which I am certain Cromwell was aware. Here was a usurper, destroying twice over the man whose power he had taken. It was not enough to kill him once and take his life. He must then dishonour the corpse.

It will rebound against him, I am sure of it. It will do him no good at all. The high church people, the bishops, the established church and any good hearted royalist will be profoundly shocked at the indecency of it. The rest – the Puritans, the zealots, the Levellers, the Shakers, and even the middling sort of gentlemen like me, who don't care very much either one way or the other – they will be indifferent, for they care nothing for a corpse; it is but the empty husk which once God used to house the soul, and is now discarded.

Still, he was raising a fist to heaven. I did wonder if the man thought he had divine powers that would protect him. Perhaps he had, for here he was, our ruler. The King was divinely appointed. Who is to say that Oliver is not also? Here he is, in charge, and there is no denying it. It is not my business to criticize whoever rules.

I mean that most sincerely. It is *none* of my business. Within ten years I would walk at his funeral with Mr Dryden the play writer and Mr Milton the poet, who took my arm for guidance, and Nat Sterry. John Milton was given nine shillings and sixpence, as was I, for mourning cloth, but John Dryden was given nine shillings. I do not know why the difference. He still had the full nine yards of black which custom dictates. We walked in step to the drum like soldiers, and we felt most martial, even blind John, and I felt that showed great respect to Cromwell who would have liked us for it.

I am not so sure he would have liked the trappings of the funeral. There was much pomp in it, almost, no I have to say even more than, had he been a King. The body was embalmed and was removed to Somerset House, where it lay in state, arrayed in purple, which was the colour of the Roman Emperors. Worse, his head was garlanded with a golden crown and in the crook of his arm was placed a gold sceptre. This for a man who had refused the crown! The guard that lined the route were girded in new red coats with black buttons and mighty fine they looked. It was certainly a more lavish send-off than the last King got, poor man.

Cromwell would not have been amused. His son made a brief protest, but he is not a strong man, and was ignored. I do not think he will make a successor; I think he will retire. He is a good enough man in his way, pious and even-handed, but no ruler, and I thank God for him, that he is not ambitious to rule. That is a hard and lonely path and I would never condemn any man who chose not to tread it.

As to Cromwell's death, I will tell you how it came about and how I had a hand in it, later. Indeed I brought it about.

16. Stygian, Plutonian, infernal is desire

Such was that happy garden-state,
While man there walked without a mate:

Marvell. 'The Garden'

The night of the execution, I took myself back to Clerkenwell, and, in one of the neighbouring stews, indulged myself in my favoured carnal pursuit. I live not far from Mrs Creswell's famous establishment, and indeed I had been there once, but I had left without corporal relief, for it was altogether too public for my liking. All sorts of men congregate there, especially the Cavaliers, and hang around in the lobby, greeting each other like long lost friends as if they had just bumped into each other in the park. It is all very jolly, and I suppose many men like that kind of convivial atmosphere, drinking and singing in the parlour over a bottle or two, watching the half-clad whores caressing each other, and then retiring with the girl of their choice.

Myself, I am embarrassed. Mrs Creswell prided herself on getting to know her clients and their tastes, and that is what scared me off. I don't want anyone knowing my tastes, except most briefly, and after that I want them to forget me. To this end I will never seek out the same whore twice.

Likewise, I prefer to eat alone. Why men must shovel food into their mouths and chew while in the company of their fellow stuffers I do not know. You would not share a room with several others for the elimination of the meal, would you? Why then its ingestion? Both strike me as equally a matter for privacy. Besides, any intimate knowledge of a man may be used by his enemies, as I know well enough, for I can blackmail with the best of them.

And so I tried a woman of some quality I found walking in Lincoln's Inn Fields. She was a jilt, rather than a common street whore, and no doubt she was climbing her way up by degrees to being a Miss of one of the courtiers in St James's Park. She certainly looked a frigate-well-rigged. I encountered her just before dusk, out with a maid, but eyeing me with obvious intention from behind her fan. I happened to be carrying a book with me and she inquired as to what it was. I explained that it was by John Milton (she might have guessed, it was very long), but she looked mystified. She said that she had a book at home by Aretino called *The Postures*, which was most umm . . . *instructive*, and here she slapped her fan shut with a snap, and tapped me on the upper arm with it, and asked whether I would like to see it.

'Why not?' I said, though I could think of several reasons

why not, at least one being a healthy prison sentence for being caught in possession of lewd books. Still, my blood was up, I think because of seeing the execution, and so was my prick, and when the prick stands up, the brain stands down, as Rochester always says to me.

What is it about women with fans? They shake them, they flutter them, they snap them shut to make a point, they snap them open to make another, they tap you on the arm to flirt with you, and then hide their face behind, so that only the eyes can be seen, and then they flutter their lashes as well as their fans. In fact they do everything with a fan except fan themselves.

Typical female behaviour. They think it attractive, alluring, coquettish, disarming, flirtatious, lascivious, charming etc, etc, when in fact they are just being damned obvious. They might as well jump out from behind a doorway, lift up their skirts and go: 'Wey, hey, look at me big boy.' Christ's blood, but they can be an irritation.

Why do I put up with all of their little ways? Because I am heterosexual is the answer. If I get an erection then I have to pay a tax on it, and the tax on my prick is having to put up with a woman's little ways.

Do you know why I pay for a whore? Women think I am paying to have sex with them, but I am not. I pay them so they will go away afterwards.

That is enough of thinking, first I must get this green monkey off my back.

Her house was of middling size and well appointed, so she was doing well in the trade or else she had a protector. There was no sign downstairs of a pimp, which was good, for if there had been I would have fled. I would not risk another man having a hold over me in the future. We went upstairs to her chamber, which was one of two at the top of the stair. I did not know what the other room was for, because the maid had slipped off to her home elsewhere, and there was no other sign of life in the house, even though it was warm and well lit inside.

'And what would you like, my boy?' she said, in a most business-like voice, which I liked. It was a long time since anyone had called me a boy, but there was no false charm in her voice, and we were getting down to the business. So I told her, and she asked for a few shillings and I agreed and laid the money out on the table, which she scooped into a small linen bag and placed across the room in a chest with a lock on it. She is clearly saving her money carefully, so that when she is old, she may buy back the love she sold when young.

I retired to a corner and sat upon a hard chair.

She slipped the sleeves of her gown over her shoulders, and it fell to the floor and she stepped lightly out of it. Her shoes were white damask, decorated with a sage green leaf motif, and had the slightest of heels so that she stood not so tall. She began to unlace her bodice behind her, which was most tight and had strapped her breasts up so that there was an inviting valley between them. I do love that valley, and often wish I were only six inches tall so that I might sled down it. Now, there's a thought for a satire: the world as seen by a tiny homunculus.

She even had a small patch of black velvet on her left breast as a beauty spot, which she picked off carefully and placed on her table. She had moved across the room to do that, and I must say that seeing a half-naked woman walk across the floor doubled my pleasure.

She continued with the unlacing, all the while chatting in a low voice about this and that. The blood was pounding in my ears like a stampeding herd, so that I did not hear what she was prattling about. After a moment I realized that she was whispering lewd suggestions as to what I might like to do to her, but in such a wheedling whisper that you would have thought she was addressing a sleeping child.

At last, after some minutes and much wrestling with her arms bent up behind her back, she finally unloosed the last of her laces and her bodice fell away, and her breasts swayed slightly as she bent to drop it on the floor. She was now only in her under-skirts of white linen, with a little border of embroidered flowers about the hem, and her shoes. She leaned against the bedpost and arched her back and placed one hand behind her head so that her breasts lifted a little. They were larger than most, and in the candle light I could see her nipples were pale rose and very large. She swung from side to side a little and asked how I liked her?

'Oh, very much,' was all I could manage, and it was in a hoarse whisper, for I did not want to speak for fear of breaking the spell she had over me. Indeed I wanted her to ignore me altogether. In fact, it was not even a matter of ignoring me, I wanted her to think I was not there at all. I wanted her to behave as if she was entirely on her own in the room and enjoying a purely private moment. Not that there was anything pure about what I wanted her to do. I wondered if she would.

She sensed my mood because she ceased talking, and half closed her eyes in a dreamy sort of way, and let her hand slip inside the waistband of her under-skirts. At first it lay flat against her belly, just up to the wrist inside the white linen, but slowly she forced it down and further down, until she was nearly up to her elbow, and I could make out the rise and fall of the linen, as she worked upon herself.

I still sat in my corner, in the shadow, almost unseen, and watched and watched. Her face now was clouded with desire. Her half-closed, heavy lidded eyes had that glassy expression, and bulged slightly in their sockets. Her cheeks and the skin of her slender neck were slowly tinting a deep pink, and the nipples of her breasts were even larger than they were, and puffy. She was well away now, and sufficiently gripped by lust to be shameless. She grasped the waist of her petticoat and rotated it about her slender middle, until the fastening button was at the front, and with a quick fumble of her fingers, unbuttoned and pushed it to the floor.

She stepped out of it, and pushed it aside with her foot, and stood there before me quite naked. She looked at me quite boldly, and licked her lips, but then, remembering my instructions, she looked away again and resumed her strumming with her left hand, and again a dreamy faraway look stole over her face.

She was still standing up, leaning one arm against the bedpost, so then she turned one leg outward slightly and jutted her hips forward, the better to show me her cunt. Still she beavered away with her fingers, foraging in the thicket, and now I could hear her breathing, for it was increasing and sounded louder and scratchy. After a while, she smoothed the bed beside her, and sat on the edge with her legs very wide apart, and placed both hands between her legs, the better to draw herself open and work upon herself, harder and faster.

I sat there watching, unable to tear my face away from the sight, my body singing with blood and painfully erect. Then she began to hum a small tune. I recognized it vaguely, though I could not put a name to it, but she carried on humming it under her breath. It was not for my benefit; I think that she really was just humming to herself for her own pleasure. Perhaps it was something she always did when aroused, I do not know.

As I listened, I felt as though a heavy curtain or shroud was falling over me. My eyesight dimmed, the room seemed darker than before and the pounding of my blood in my ears quite faded away to silence. Indeed I became near deaf to everything, so that her sweet humming faded too.

She saw that I was close to fainting dead away, but mistook my symptoms, and thought perhaps that my interest was flagging. So she got up and came over to me and with a cooing smile, began to fumble with my breeches and try to undo them.

My mood was shattered, and I was left completely unmanned. I stood up immediately, and went to speak, but found the words coming out in a shout: 'Do not touch me, never touch me, whore.' She shrank back with a surprised and fearful look on her face, which she quickly covered with her hand, but still she looked startled. I notice that she did not cover her naked body, but rather her face. That is interesting. I will wonder why later.

I gathered my self, swallowed hard, and tried to breathe more carefully. 'I . . .' I said, and was about to explain myself, but realized that she would never understand, and anyway I am damned if I will explain myself to a whore. So I lurched out of the room, and down the stairs and out of the door into the welcome of the cool night and walked my way home, fuming a little about it all, but calming all the while as I walked.

Never would I go again to a whore. Not because I was ashamed, but because they can never get it quite right. But then I am not sure even myself about exactly what I want. I must unravel the mystery and then give clearer orders to her when I next go. Except I shall not be going to her again. I will choose a different whore. Or rather no, as I just said, I do not want to go to them at all. Nor any other woman. They are a poor substitute. A substitute for what, you ask? I do not know. My own thoughts perhaps.

One woman's body looks much like another's. Have you ever seen a naked woman? They are like a malformed boy with udders on the chest. That is why she covered her face and not her body. The body might have belonged to anyone. The face is where the soul is limned and it is where shame shows. No wonder the Mahommetan woman wears a veil.

I encountered one once on my travels in Muscovy. She wore a veil and was therefore much more brazen with her body which was entirely shaved of hair, as is the custom with the followers of Allah, I do believe. Or so she told me. I will tell you of her some other time. Or did I already? I forget.

When I got home, tired and aching in my joints but unrelieved of my desires, I broke the wax seal on my glass box and took out some of my mother's cloth and lay back with it placed over my mouth and nose. Her body and her warmth came back to me in a flood of feeling, so that she lay next to me on the bed, and held my head to her bosom and patted the back of my neck. The earthy scent of new-plucked flowers, and the sweetness of a moss-green lawn after rain came back to me too. It was delicious, and calmed my feverish desires. Soon I was asleep and not dreaming, which is the state I desire above all others.

It was not a happy episode, but then that sort never are for me. Never mind, I will get a piece of poetry out of it.

17. The Job

'On the victory obtained by Blake over the Spaniards, in the bay of Sanctacruze, in the Island of
Teneriff.'

By Andrew Marvell

For three years Sir Robert Blake had been blockading ships
coming in and out of the Spanish coast, and plundering
their treasure which they in turn had plundered from the
Americas. He reckoned it fair game, since they were busy
destroying whole races of men for their gold, and he, a more
modest man, was destroying only a few ships. Besides, he
hated the Spanish, like everyone else.

Sea traffic had become light and with little to do he set
out for the Azores, to see what he could find by way of
passing trade, but got blown south to the Canaries. Thinking
that he would water his ships and take on some provisions,
he sailed through the narrow neck of Sanctacruze harbour,
smack into sixteen Spanish treasure vessels. And stap me if
he didn't destroy every one of them, with no loss to his own
fleet, in spite of the shore batteries being very close and

crawling with Spanish sharp shooters. Alas, poor Admiral Blake died before he arrived back in England, from a wound he got while fighting, but none the less it was a very great victory. I felt that I must do something about it, especially as I had nothing much better to fill my time, for at that period I was out of work, and desperately looking for employment.

The Canary Islands lack nothing that heaven can afford, unless it be having Cromwell for a Lord.

Which is rubbish I know, but was exactly what I put in my poem, along with a load of other arse-creeping stuff about Oliver's great renown, and his restless genius, and ended on the couplet:

> *Whilst fame in every place, her trumpet blows,*
> *And tells the world, how much to you it owes.*

It was a shameless in its *courtisanerie*. Christ, I all but coated Oliver in honey then licked it off, I held his jaws open while I pelted him with sugared almonds, and I knew exactly how a strumpet felt after writing it, for he made me the Latin Secretary. I had sold myself quite cheaply. Still, no more tutoring for me. I cannot help but think the less of Cromwell for falling so easily for flattery. I know that all men like praise, but you would think that he might be above all that.

That is all I want to say about Admiral Blake. He got me a job, and there's an end on him.

18. Cromwell's last days

I saw him dead.

Marvell. 'A Poem upon the Death of O.C.'

I found an entry in my diary for 1657, exactly one year before Cromwell's death, and I tore it out and destroyed it. Yet I can remember the conversation verbatim.

I didn't tell you that I kept a diary, and I did not mean to. It is very private and I employ a code. I will destroy it before I die; or if my powers are failing in old age, I will instruct a servant to do so, under my guidance. It must be torn apart then burned. I don't want posterity reading my mind. Let my poetry and my few friends speak for me. Though they won't, for my friends don't speak much.

'Could you kill a man, Andrew?'

'How do you know I have not done so?'

'I can tell.'

'No you cannot. For nothing is written on my brow which speaks of what is inside. I am known for it. All say that none can read me.'

'But a man who has killed takes on a certain look. They call it the mark of Cain. It is not a mark, but a certain look.'

'Then you know I have not.'

'But could you?'

'Let me think on it, and I will reply to you sometime later. Yes, I think I could, but I am not sure. I could say that it would depend upon circumstance, as indeed everything does, but that would be a cheap answer and I see you are in earnest. I will reply. Until then . . .'

'Not in cold blood, is my answer. I have seen the heat of battle as an observer, and I have seen the fury that makes men go berserk, and can easily imagine that I would so behave in battle. But in cold blood, with having plotted it beforehand, no I could not.'

'Why not?'

'I knew you would ask that, and that is what I have chiefly been thinking of. For many of my problems, both personal and professional and most especially ones stemming from the House, could best be solved by a dagger on a dark night. But I cannot do it, nor can I conspire and get others to do it for me. The reason is this: my life after the murder would never be the same as it was before.

'Oh, there are always changes in one's life. One learns something new, or a friend turns to an enemy, or one falls in love. I know of such things and they change your life, but I think that nothing could change your life so radical as if you killed a man.'

'Suppose you were threatened.'

'I have been, and I defended myself as far as was necessary, no more. I believe if you fight prudently, rather than intemperately, you will prevail.'

'Suppose a loved one were threatened? Suppose someone held a knife to your wife.'

'I have no wife and no children.'

'But suppose you did.'

'I cannot.'

'A betrothed then, a woman that you love.'

'There is none.'

'A friend, a man who favoured you, someone of whom you are fond?'

'No.'

'You say you would be different. How so?'

'I cannot tell, never having done it, but I know that I would be.'

'Your conscience would trouble you?'

'No, I do not think so. I have many things upon my conscience, but I do not brood.'

19. At the Exiled Court of Charles. 1658

How vainly men themselves amaze
To win the palm, the oak, or bays.

Marvell. 'The Garden'

We looked across the channel at England and we saw a place grown dull and livid. I was only over here on the briefest of trips, mainly some business for Cromwell's Secretary Thurloe in The Hague (the delivery of a secret packet of letters – spying is mostly dull business), but also a quick excursion to Charles's court in exile. He always welcomed me, partly because I never spoke to him of what was on Thurloe's mind. Charles knew well enough I was on Foreign Office business, but he did not mind. If you are going to spy, you must only do it in one direction. No one trusts a double agent at all, and right now it was Charles's trust I wanted, not Thurloe's.

We gazed across the grey expanse of water, and mused upon our country. On the one hand there were no Popish practices, and most people throughout the land had reached a peaceable accommodation with the Protector and his ilk, as well they might if they wished to continue in any form of employment or prosperity, but on the other, there was no dancing on the green, no maypoles, the theatres were locked, and everyone seemed to be wearing black wool, unrelieved by silk, or even the lightest hint of charcoal grey. Every citizen bore a look either pious or serious and universal dullness ruled the land. I don't actually recall an edict forbidding laughter or the making of jokes, but there might as well have been one for all the joking I had heard.

It looked like dullness might blanket the land unabated for a good long time, until the very country itself muffled, turned to the wall and died. Cromwell was late into his sixth decade, but was still striding about the place full of vulgar energy, brow-beating people into piety and seriousness. He wasn't nearly at death's door yet, nor for a long time. His eldest son was feeble, though harmless, but any one of his other sons could stand in that place well enough. True, Oliver had refused the crown, but only out of false modesty, and some craftier political reason. Any of his sons like as not would be happy to sit it on his warty head, and call himself King Jack the first.

From where Charles and his émigré court stood, gazing across the channel, the view did not look encouraging. Oliver could set up a dynasty of *stadtholders*, or stakeholders, along the lines of the Dutch republic, and the longer the émigré court stayed abroad, then the longer it would be likely to do so. Charles could die twenty years hence in poverty, mourned only by the handful of English courtiers who had stayed loyally abroad with him, and helped him bide his time in penury and exile.

'Something must be done, Mr Marvell,' said Charles, as he paced along the shore. 'Can't sit here forever you know.'

'I was thinking just the same, Majesty,' I said. 'I must think harder upon the subject.'

'You do that; and don't you worry if you are making my courtiers a bit nervous. It's always the same problem with having you intellectuals around the place. It unnerves people you know. People can't quite keep up with you brainy types. They can't tell what you are thinking, and even if you tell them what you are thinking, they still can't keep up. So they think you must be plotting something dark and dangerous.'

'I usually am plotting something dark, your Majesty,' I said, half in jest, and half letting him know what I might get up to, if given the green light.

'I know, I know, and I can't say I like it, or that I altogether approve. Give me an open man any day. But,' he said with a weary sigh, 'that is why I must have you on my side and not on theirs.'

He is honest about such matters of practical policies, and he is world-weary, but he has a secret weapon which Cromwell will never have and which will always work in Charles's favour. It is charm. When Charles speaks to you, he gives you the impression that you are the one and only thing that matters to him in the whole wide world, that the world could stop spinning on its axis if you did not tell him your true thoughts and feelings on the matter in hand, and that whatever you confided was of the deepest and utmost weight to the man. All this he did with the lightest and easiest of touches. Oliver talks at you and wears you down till you agree with him. Charles listens carefully to you, and you find yourself wishing to please him. No wonder he was such a success with the ladies. Whenever I had finished speaking with him, I always felt I had been seduced.

'Think upon it, sir, in the way that only you can,' he said. 'Think upon it long and hard. Bring that elegant mind of yours to bear upon it. Look for precedents in your Classics. Look for a delightful solution from your Lyrics. Look for a bloody solution from your Seneca. Look for a realistic solution from your days in office and your know-ledge of the ways of politicians. Look into the heart of Cromwell, if he has one,' he said with a shudder, 'and then bring all of your crafty nature to bear on it too. There must be a way. And soon. Were Mr Oliver to meet with . . . what can we say? An *accident*? . . . well, I for one would not die of a broken heart. Come to that, I might be very generous to the man who had perhaps *brought about* that dreadful stroke of fate. I am not asking for a murder at dead of night or any-thing, no, no, no. But should he fall from his horse and . . .

well . . . And I do believe the people of England would be grateful too. The place will die of dullness if we do not do *something,* and I would hate that.'

20. The Fly Trap

The same arts that did gain
A power, must it maintain.

Marvell. 'An Horatian Ode upon Cromwell's
Return from Ireland'

There is nothing like the threat of a king's hatred to get you up first thing at dawn to make a cracking start on what he wanted done. I do not think there is very much hatred in the man to tell the truth, but I would not want to test that theory.

I took the very first ship out, caught a good tide and a ripping breeze, was back at Dover before the day was done, was in London the next day, and by the end of the week, I had an inkling of what might be done. Nothing more, just an inkling, and it came to me from Mr Thurloe, who is Cromwell's very private Secretary, and a man I know well, as I have told you, for I work for him. It is amazing what you can accomplish when your brain is at full trot.

I returned to my house in Clerkenwell, and got a woman in to dust the place down and then dismissed her. As usual, I do not like servants about me. I went to bed and pulled the covers over my head, and slowly drank down two pints of wine and plotted. By the end of the wine I had my solution.

The problem was that when I woke the next day I could not remember what my solution was. As a matter of fact I had anticipated my usual brain-deadness which I get after drinking long and hard, and so had written a few notes on a scrapbook that I kept near the bed for that purpose. I rolled over out of my bed and sat on the edge, cradling my head in my hands, wishing that the small rat that had nested in my mouth overnight would scuttle off and die somewhere else. I picked up my scrap of paper and looked at it; scribbled in a very shaky hand it said: 'Kill C.'

Well, there's a thing. Did I think of that all by myself? My word, I must have been really going at the problem full tilt last night.

Yet the more I think about it, the more I realize that it is the only way. It is as elegant as a neat equation, and like all elegant proofs in mathematics, it may prove true, but the main thing about it is this: it is appealing.

What is it the Chinese say? Any problem may be solved by a bag of gold, suicide or pushing your enemy off a roof – and if in any doubt about it, oh, take to the roof, sir, every time. Save your money and save yourself. A man's death is neither here nor there in the general, and certainly not with England's earth soiled with so much of its own men's blood in the last twenty years. Let the man who brought it in, bear it out, and let him go where he will to the next world. Though I think he will end up below.

I will think on how to bring it about. Actually, I am sorry, let me be honest with you, I have already thought about that. It is simple.

But which C did I mean last night? And which C do I mean this morning? I am not sure. Dear God help me, I cannot remember which I meant. Am I working for Cromwell or Charles, here? And which do I mean to dispose of? It seems that I dissemble even when dead drunk. It is in my nature, and I cannot help my nature.

For what I had in mind, Mr Carteret would not do at all. He is one of the chief doctors that Cromwell allowed near him. As far as physicians go he is quite a good one. He does not bleed the patient at every opportunity, but takes his cue from the ancient doctor Galen in that, above all else, the patient must not be harmed. In fact what he mainly does is let nature take its course and then pocket an enormous fee. Whenever I get outraged about this, I calm myself by musing that in fact it is no more than a farmer does. By God's good bounty his crops do grow and he then sells for a profit that which has cost him nothing but a little sweat. Fair enough.

So Carteret is no butcher and besides is a good man, and so I will be unlikely to suborn him to my cause.

Bate though is a different matter. He is a nasty little figure, forever sounding off some spurious bit of knowledge about the bile and the spleen and the humours and all of that. Which may well all be true, for all I know, but he has about him the air of a man who is trying to blind you with science. He declaims, and I mistrust that in a man. Also he is effeminate. He is always flapping his hands around and saying in a loud voice that he is 'Cromwell's man', and then giggling behind his palm.

So I followed him about a bit, the way that I have learned to follow a man. He never suspected. He scurries from one house to another, plying his trade in human misery and hastening the end of many a poor soul who was on the mend and would have recovered had they been left in peace. My reasons for singling him out are that he is part of the vast medical team that tends on Oliver. C employs a lot of medical men. Indeed, that is his policy on almost all counts, to employ as many different opinions as he possibly can on any one subject, thereby believing that he can get at the truth. He cannot, and it will be the death of him.

After a couple of days, I began to despair of Mr Bate, thinking perhaps to turn my attention to some other quack, for he simply did his rounds and went to bed, and did nothing at all that I could use for my own vile ends. For what I had in mind, I needed some hold over the man. He would not do my bidding just for the sake of pleasing me, nor for a large sum of money, no matter that Charles said he would be generous to any who helped him out. I think Mr Bate probably earns quite enough already. No, for what I have in mind,

I will tempt the man by offering him advancement, for every man is fool enough to think he is worthy of higher office. Very few know their place. He is close to Cromwell, but very far down the ladder.

First, I must have my man in a headlock. I must have my arm firmly around his neck, so that if he so much as squeak, if he so much as demur from what I demand, if he even raise an eyebrow, I can throttle the life from him. Hobbes is right on that score. There are certain people who must do as they are told. And those certain people are 99 in 100 of the population.

Under my King, I will do as he bids, but as far as the rest of men go, I will do the telling. And you can wipe that smirk from your face.

On the third day, darkness was falling and I was about to return to my lodgings in Clerkenwell, when Bate began to act like a man in the grip of strange urgings. He looked about him left and right, and behind him to see if anyone was following. He never saw me though. No one ever sees me, when I sink my thoughts deep down inside myself and never think about my quarry. He hunched his shoulders a little and began to scuttle. I do believe he pulled his hat a little lower on his brow to shade his eyes. If someone had given him a special cloak with the word 'thief' or 'adulterer' embroidered in huge scarlet letters on the back, he could hardly have cut a more convincing picture of a man going out of an evening up to no good.

He did not head for his house, but began to weave his way northward, indeed toward Clerkenwell, not far from where I live. He turned down Old Street where there were still a few torches burning and then crossed diagonal-wise toward Shepherdess Walk, and it was then I had a notion of where he was going. The place is full of stews, as you know, but I do not think it was a run-o'the-mill bawdy house our man was skulking about looking for, if I know my man at all. His step was sure and had a purpose in it. He looked a good deal more perky as he went along, and he got a spring in his stride. Oh yes, he was out on the razzle all right, and, if my instincts were right, he was heading for one place only.

Sure enough he arrived at the very house I expected. He looked about him, but the street was deserted and there were no lights to be seen, and he rapped upon the door. A spy-hole opened, with a brief gleam of light, which was quickly blotted out by the head of the person looking out. Then it closed again, a curtain was drawn about the door on the inside, and it was opened with only the barest of light spilling out, certainly not enough to illumine Mr Bate's face. In he bolted, as fast as he could.

The house stood alone, with a small garden about it, which was rare in this part of town, but it had about it an air that was at once both anonymous and sinister. Perhaps houses take on an appearance slowly over the years which is reflective of what goes on inside them. I do think so, from my wanderings and from what I have observed. A few minutes' contemplation of a house, and I can tell you its history and what goes on inside. Some houses have a pleasant face with which to greet the world, some have an ugly one, but are still friendly, and some, a very few, are so downright vicious that you cross the road rather than pass them. This house was one of those.

I went around the back, and strangely there was no back door. From what I know of this house's business, I was surprised, for the occupants might have to flee in short order if ever the watch came round and knocked the front door off its hinges. Which it might well one day, if ever I have anything to do with it.

I found a barrel that was empty and was being used as a rubbish container, and dragged it over to the back wall and placed it beneath a window. The house was built upon a slope and the back windows were curiously much higher than the ones at the front. It was quite crooked, the way it was built, but there was a top storey to it, and a central staircase, that much I could divine, and so I would guess about nine or ten rooms in all. A fair size house, then, and one which would work well enough as a tavern or a town house for a well-off merchant with a large family.

The window was open a crack and so I pushed my fingers in and gently heaved. It moved an inch without a squeak or a groan. The weather was dry enough, and so the frame would not be warped, but I needed to test it. No light came from inside, but I stood awhile, my ear to the window crack. There was no sound of movement, and none of breathing either. The room was empty. I opened the window in one swift clean movement, and only at the end of its travel did the wood groan slightly. I stopped dead without moving. Two streets over a dog began to bark and would not stop. There was no moon, and clouds covered the stars. Only the faintly hellish orange light of link-boys' torches flickered over London, colouring the air but hardly lighting anything. I resumed my breathing, which had held a while.

The feeling was delicious. That I was about to invade another's house without their permission, without their even knowing, filled me with a secret joy such as I rarely feel these days. I noticed I had an erection. I would have to deal with that later, in a house I knew of, not far from here either.

With a brief motion, which I had practised often enough before, I swung my legs over the sill, and ducked my shoulders and head through, dropping my legs inside and sitting on the sill a while without letting my feet touch the floor. The room was empty all right, as I had already suspected, but I found by gently lowering my right toe that there was no rug below the window, only bare boards. I crept my toe forward, and found the edge of some floor covering about a foot away. Gingerly, I jumped from the sill to it, and made no more sound than a cat. I even had my hat still on, so I took it off, and then felt rather foolish, for there was no one in the room. Still, I cannot keep my hat on indoors. Well, there was no place to hang it, and anyway I will be making a sharpish exit soon, so, no time for nicety, I clamped it back on my head and squared the hatband firmly across my brow and went on to do my business.

The door handle was well oiled and so were the hinges and I had opened it wide in the matter of five minutes or so. I had learned patience in my craft, which is the hardest thing to do when house breaking. In the dark, time crawls very slowly, and when you are engaged in something nefarious, it practically stops. I patted the pistol I keep in my waistcoat pocket – that always calms me a little – and the dagger inside my shirt. My eyes were now well accustomed to the dark.

I looked around the door first to get the lie of the land, and could see faint flickering candle light coming from under the crack of one door, just across from me. Other than that, there was some light coming up the staircase from below, giving a warm glow to that end of the corridor. Good, I can use that for what I have in mind.

I tiptoed across to the door and pressed my ears to the wood. There was movement from inside and soft whisperings and some heavy breathing. I think Mr Bate had found what he came for. I tried the handle. It gave all right and the door began to open but then stopped abruptly. I thought perhaps that the occupants had placed a heavy object, a chair or a settle, up against it, but then I looked down and just spotted the haft of a cabin-hook with which they had fastened it.

I slipped my dagger from under my shirt and slid the blade gingerly under the brass lever, pulling the door slightly toward me, and levered upwards. The latch lifted slightly, and I could feel no more resistance was likely, but if I lifted it all the way up so it unhooked, it would fall with a clink, and I would be discovered. Well fine, that is the best course of action I think. I pulled my collar up to cover the lower part of my face, and pulled my hat well down. The main light source would be behind me too, so I would present nothing but a black outline.

I flipped the latch up, pushed the door open with a bang, and stood there in the frame. And what a thing I saw there!

A small candle flickering in the draught showed the naked Mr Bate there on the bed, kneeling on all fours. His face turned toward me, and, by the light, I read in it first annoyance, then surprise and finally horror. He was panting heavily and sweating and I think I could see he was red-faced, though that might have been a trick of the light. Behind him, quite oblivious of my entrance for he was facing away and, I think, coming to the end of his labours, a huge man was engaged in the act of darkness upon my man. He was bearded, and so I suppose a sailor.

Ah well, worse things happen at sea.

I let out a laugh, which I made sure was quite low and completely mirthless, and then said in as rasping a voice as I could manage, 'Ah, Mr Bate.' The horror on his face intensified. He pushed the man behind him away, gathered up the sheet to cover himself and was, I think, about to struggle from the bed and perhaps close with me, but after my dramatic entrance, I turned upon my heel and swept out of the door, slamming it behind me.

He will not be able to identify me initially, but he will be perplexed, for he has heard my voice on occasions, though we have hardly met for some time now. So he will be thinking that he knows my voice from somewhere but cannot immediately remember where. And he will rack his brains on it. And eventually remember.

I wondered whether to go downstairs and leave via the front door, thus making myself known to the people loitering in the parlour. The owner of this place knows who I am, and so word would reach Mr Bate that much more quickly, but I decided against it, as I was not short of time in this venture. I will play the long game. Besides, let Mr Bate sweat while he thinks upon who I might be, and all the possibilities that might ensue. Could I be simply one of the watch? No, I would have arrested the lot of them, along with him. Could I be a spy from one of his patients? Possibly, for patients are notoriously fussy about their doctors. Could I be an agent for that patient who was demanding a return of a fee? Could I be a spy for . . . oh, the list is endless and it will all be the worse for him because he is a scoundrel and his conscience contains so much sin he will burn in anguish for months until he can recall who that voice belongs to.

When he does, he will be mine. As I left by the same window, out the back, on to the barrel, and quickly down the dark side alley into Shepherdess Walk, I allowed myself a small smile of satisfaction. One word in the right ear, and I can get Mr Bate hanged for what he was up to. And he knows it, the silly little Molly-puff! I could have recommended a far more discreet establishment, where he could have had a much better john-and-john, got buggered senseless by whole teams of horny young stable lads, and all of it not half a mile from here. You'd think the man half-wanted to get caught. Let the fool sweat on it a few days, as I say, he is mine and I have time enough to toy with him. What's that I hear you say? Blackmail? Well, of course it is. Hypocrisy? Yes, that too.

As it was, it took him less than a couple of days to remember my voice, and he was round at my office tugging on my sleeve, looking pale and all but blubbering on my coat collar. I affected a stern air, but he must know that there is something that I want from him, otherwise why would I have followed him and surprised him as I did? He knows well enough that I work here as the Latin Secretary in the Foreign Office, under Mr Milton, and also am an MP, and that I am well acquainted with Mr Thurloe, always being in and out of his office, indeed that being the very place I had previously encountered Mr Bate, since he was 'Cromwell's man' (tee hee). And therefore I was like as not to be engaged in clandestine activity. So he should have twigged by now that I am about to blackmail him. All he has to worry about is the exact nature of my demands, and whether he can fulfil them without endangering himself too much.

That much can be thought through with a little reasoning, surely? Well, he may well have reasoned it all through, but it didn't stop him going green about the gills when he saw me. I can't say I blame him. All my life I have been careful never to let another man have the balance of my life in his palm. No one ever gets anything over on me, you can depend upon it. Always strike the first blow.

I wondered whether to affect a mateyness with him, perhaps to reassure him that our little secret was safe with me; all lads together, what? That ploy can work well with the nervous, for then you can pull the rug from under them later, and get them to do almost anything, for they thought you were their friend.

But no. I will keep up the air of an appalled Puritan, albeit one who will do nothing as yet until he has considered long and hard on the dreadful sin, and perhaps consulted his masters as to a course of action. Which, if I ever do, will of course mean a short trip to the hangman for Mr Bate, before his four quarters are displayed on spikes around the city wall as a warning to anyone else who might fancy having a matelot ream out his arse.

'Mr Bate,' I said coolly, 'what may I do for you?' With just a shade too much emphasis upon the 'you', as if to say, 'What are you doing in my office, you jumped-up, fairy-featured, little nance?'

He swallowed heavily and said, 'I have a friend who . . .'

'Has a taste for sailors?' I said, and raised my hand to silence him. 'The answer is that I may do nothing for you. I will sit long and hard considering your sin, before I decide upon a course of appropriate action. And I may consult with my superiors, of course.'

He looked about him briefly, just to confirm we could not be heard, and one brief spark of defiance lit in his eyes.

'You have no proof,' he said. 'No witnesses. Nothing would stand up . . .'

My laugh was mirthless again. 'I have all the witness need,' I said. 'You were at the house belonging to one Josiah Spode.' I passed him a blank sheet of paper with Spode's signature at the bottom. 'He is in my employ, indeed I set him up in this very house for my own purposes. He will sign any witness document if it means he will be immune from the courts. That is part of our deal together.'

'But, but, but,' Bate was spluttering, 'what on earth do you need that place for?'

'It is what we call a honey trap, sir,' I said, 'to catch greedy little flies like you. It is of some use to my office, when I have need of an agent.'

He looked a little happier at all this, for he could see a way out of his predicament now.

'Oh, I can spy with the best of them, sir, I am very well placed for all of that, going in and out of people's houses and inspecting their health, you would be amazed at what I see, and I can be out at all hours too with no need of a reason . . .' The poor fool was now bursting over to help. I raised my hand again to silence him.

'Go about your proper business for a few days. As I said, I will consider what to do about your future. I will find you if I have need of your talents. And if I have no need of them, then look to your soul, for you will swing for your crime. Now, not one more word. You may leave.'

He stopped kneading his hat between his fingers, plonked it back on his greasy head, and turned for the door as if in a daze.

'Oh, and Bate,' I said. He paused and looked at me like a whipped spaniel. 'Antimony,' I said.

'Antimony?' he said.

'Think upon that. You may go now.'

Antimony. A brittle, silvery-white metallic substance, often used in alloys with lead. From the medieval Latin *antimonium* (eleventh century) of unknown origin. Not to be confused with antinomy, which is a contradiction between two beliefs that are in themselves reasonable, and gave a name to the Antinomians, a heretical sect in Germany who believed that

Christians were released from obeying the moral law, the cunning buggers.

Antimony is very poisonous.

After three days, long enough to let him suffer before jerking in his leash, I sent a boy to fetch Bate, and he duly turned up at my office.

'Did you think on what I said?' I asked. He looked all sly.

'Ho, yes. I do keep antimony among my remedies. It is a useful purge, but it is very poisonous.'

'I know that. The Romans used to induce vomiting by drinking wine from a cup made of antimony. Tell me of its properties,' I said.

'If it is absorbed slowly, it will produce an irritation in the abdomen. The patient may exhibit gastro-intestinal distress and other distempers. Long term usage can produce heart murmurs and skin discolouration.'

'And how would you poison someone with it?' I said.

'Well, *poisoners* . . .' he said unctuously, as if he had heard of their devious ways but never actually known one, 'are said to employ one of two methods. There is the acute poisoning, or a high concentration over a short term, and there is the chronic poisoning, or the low concentration over a long term. The acute sort can be effective, but it leads to suspicions on the part of other observers. It is too sudden a death, and can cause convulsions and other signs. Chronic poisoning though is insidious and creeps about a person's veins like a thief in the night. It will take a while, but none will notice it.'

'How long would small doses of antimony take to act?' I said.

'Well,' he said, warming to his subject, for he could not resist showing off his knowledge. 'I am not sure that I would use antimony solely. It can all too easily be expelled violently from the body, which does not like to store it. True it can be deadly, but for a long term effect I would perhaps use a mixture of it with mercury. Now, mercury is a friend that can flatter or lie. It can heal when administered judiciously, but it can be a wicked murderer. It is produced in Venice where they mix quicksilver with salt, and it is distributed all over the continent, where I often go to get my supplies.

'When taken in large doses it produces violent gripping, distension of the belly, vomiting of slime and froth, blood in the stools, and intolerable heat and thirst, tremblings and convulsions unto death. It has a malignant quality, which leaves the patient feeling as if knives and daggers were working their way through his stomach, and causing abrasion to the natural mucus. It is most violent and should be administered ah . . . slowly.'

'Good, I said. 'That is more than I wished to know. Incidentally I will introduce you to a Venetian of my acquaintance. He is their foreign secretary here in London, and may be able to procure Venetian *things* quite easily for you. His office regularly send him all sorts of supplies in a diplomat's trunk. You may go now.'

But little Bate was off and running. 'There is also arsenic,' he continued and was all set to give me the gory symptoms of a good arsenic poisoning.

'Enough for one day,' I said, 'I will call upon your skills soon.' He crossed the room with a little more spring in his step, for he does like to show off. 'Why not go down to Spode's establishment? Give yourself a treat. The fleet is in I believe,' I added, without a hint of irony, though with a steel in my voice.

He stopped dead on his way to the door, but did not turn around before continuing on his way. I could practically see the scowl on the back of his head. Well, I am not going to let him forget my stranglehold. Wriggle away Mr Bate, you are still mine, and, though you do not yet know it, no longer Cromwell's.

21. A Period to His Life

He without noise still travell'd to his end,
As silent suns to meet the night descend.

Marvell. 'A Poem upon the Death of O.C.'

Sometime after the last day of July, Cromwell met with the Dutch ambassador to London, Willem Nieuport. After he had left the Dutch office, he came down almost immediately with a bad attack of the gout. This was not unusual for him, for he frequently suffered the plagues of gout, even though he hardly drank strong liquor at all, but it was followed by worse. As he lay in a chair nursing his foot, the pain spread to his lower guts and he was forced to run very quickly to a stool and relieve himself several times over. This brought no relief however and he succumbed to very bad colic of the abdomen. He lay in bed some four or five days with this attack, and also a general distemper. He could hold down little food, and sometimes even vomited the water that he drank. His skin became pale and took on a pinched look due to dehydration.

It was a nasty illness and worse than he commonly

suffered, and so his Secretary, Thurloe, took careful note of the symptoms and relayed them to Cromwell's doctor, in great detail, keeping the man informed throughout the day and much of the night too, of the patient's state.

Needless to say, many people attributed the whole thing to his visit to the Dutchman, since it was well known that the Dutch, a perfidious race still vengeful over historic grievances, carried poisons about them in order to slip into any food they might share with an Englishman, especially an important Englishman. I dare say they also have cloven feet and eat babies. Still, it suits my purposes very nicely, and so if anyone mentions Cromwell's illness, I always remind them of his visit to the Dutchman. I don't actually tap the side of my nose, but the implication is clear enough.

I do believe that Cromwell would have recovered from this first bout of illness quite well, and many more too, for he was built as strong as an ox, and all his forebears lived to a mighty old age. It is often the way with those who seize power I have noted. They have an iron constitution. They are like those vines which seem to need a long life in order to survive the worst of winter's rages. Except perhaps for that Frenchman, who had a permanently green expression from indigestion. I digress.

Early in August, his beloved daughter Elizabeth finally died. She had been very ill for some time with a cancer of the uterus. The doctors had proved useless as they always do in such cases, one of them even suggesting that she try the waters in Tunbridge, as if that would have made a blind bit of difference. The sad truth is that few of them understood her case, and the ones that did realized there was nothing to be done.

Doctor Bate had advised Cromwell about his daughter's condition some months earlier. While that sort of news can do down even the strongest of men, yet it did not dismay Oliver. So strong is he in his convictions of the Lord's personal attention to him and his family, that he must have thought that either He would personally intervene with a remedy, or else, if she succumbed, then that too was simply because He wanted Elizabeth by His side. Well, you or I may snort a little at this sort of thing, but pause a moment. It is little more than our priests tell children to calm their fears of the dark.

Then she died, and it broke the poor man. He was utterly inconsolable. I have seen it before, this thing. A man may be prepared for the death of a loved one for a long time, and he may seem well rehearsed for the event, so that friends and relatives do not fear too much for him. He seems to have drawn the coming dread well into himself and become reconciled to the inevitable end. Then it finally happens, and he goes to pieces.

Believe me, friend, you cannot prepare for death. Not your own, and, even more certainly, not for anyone else's.

Death will take your loved one when It pleases, and there is no knowing how that will leave you.

One minute she is there and quietly bathed in a love which has been growing for half a lifetime. Then everything that she did, everything that she loved, all that she laboured over, and all the children she raised, any thing she cast a kind glance upon, every man she raised up a little, every dumb beast she fed, every happy day that made her smile, yea even the dark days that she endured with fortitude because she was safe in the knowledge of your arms; this, all of this, every last thing, that lightened your heart and made your step less weary, is over and gone for nothing.

He had loved her and she was dead.

He said nothing about it. He did not seem to grieve. He did not howl at his affliction. No one saw him weep. Aside from the increasing discomforts of his illness, there was no change to him, but in those fearful hours of the night, at the mid-point between midnight and dawn, when the earth becomes most utterly silent, and the very spirit of life sinks deep below the world's surface, then he turned his face to the wall and succumbed.

A man who had never surrendered in his life, finally gave in – a man who had charged down cannon armed with no more than a sword, a man who had waged war on his own countrymen safe in the conviction that it was God's will so to do, a man who had cut the head off his own King, and then ruled the kingdom not by divine right but by will alone, a man who had raised his fist to God himself and defied Him to bring down His wrath just to prove his very existence. This was a man who did not know the meaning of the word retreat. This was a man who thought that being outnumbered two to one was the beginning of an interesting day. This was a man, oh . . .

His daughter died, and he gave up. Wherever it was she went, she took him with her. Not immediately, perhaps, but some part of him died along with her and departed his body and left him a husk. Nothing could distract him and little could claim his attention. The body endured, the man was gone.

I think I liked him for it more than any other time in his life. He had always been a stickler for his duties toward his wife and family, and never was he remiss or unkind, but I never thought to see such a depth of love in the man.

Still, it did not deflect me.

He should have travelled to Westminster Abbey by barge to attend his daughter's funeral but he could not. It would have been a gentle journey, just a float downriver from Hampton with the tide, but his body was racked by worse and worse pains and distempers. The intestinal pains were terrible. News of his health was not put about, for it was always kept secret from the population, but Thurloe went so far as to prepare a notice of his death, so badly was it feared. He stayed in his bed and looked fit to give up the ghost.

Bate ceased to attend on him. Then, after a week, he became better without apparent reason.

An evangelist was out riding in the park at Hampton, and was astonished to see Cromwell canter past at the head of his life guard. He thought that Cromwell had the distinct waft of death about him, yet they stopped and spoke awhile, mainly about the way the Quakers had been oppressed lately, and Cromwell suggested to the man that he come to the Palace for further discussion on the next day. Clearly the man was feeling better and had hopes of improvement.

I read Doctor Bate's report from the next day when he made a brief medical examination of the man. It seems he was still deathly pale, but was well recovered from the vomiting and diarrhoea. His pulse was intermittent, however, and he was sweating badly. Bate assured him that he was well on the road to recovery, and made out a prescription for more mercury. Cromwell went to bed and promptly made out his will. He called Bate as a witness, and Bate administered a late cordial, 'to enable him to sleep'.

Apparently some ministers prayed through the night for his safety, but Bate dismissed them as a nuisance, saying that his doctors were good enough to get him through this bad patch. Then he returned to Cromwell's bedside to ensure he slept soundly. Which he did.

I met with Bates once more a day later and told him to

break off his ministrations for a while. There was no need of rush now for the thing we intended. Indeed it might happen of its own accord should the melancholy continue. I have known men die from the black dog.

But he did not. He got better in his body again, but his brow did not lift. Every night the Chaplains all got together on their knees and expended much hot air in beseeching for his good health. He told me that he could do without it, for 'God, not the doctors, guards my grave.' I would say that he has got that right, in the general scheme of things. He would certainly do better for his health trusting to God than to his doctor.

Then on the twenty-first he came down again, this time with what was reported as an ague, and he suffered malarial fits on successive nights, some three or four times over. Four days later he thought that he was enjoying what his doctors called an 'interval' day from his ague, and he rode down to Hampton for a change of air. He even took off the body armour that he wears beneath his shirt at all times. That was a mistake, for he had another fit that night.

On the twenty-sixth I brought my old friend General Fairfax to see him, about the matter of Buckingham. The wretched man was in the Tower, and as far as I and everyone else was concerned, he deserved to be there and could rot in his cell till the trump of doom. Fairfax felt much the same, but of course his daughter, poor little Moll, the one I tutored, of whom I told you, had gone and succumbed to the man's advances. Being married to her was all part of Buckingham's overall plan at regaining his estates, which had been confiscated by Parliament, and now he was in the Tower, well, Fairfax felt obliged just for form's sake to try and intercede with Oliver to get his son-in-law freed.

The interview was a disagreeable one, and nothing was resolved. My good friend returned to Yorkshire, not altogether entirely disappointed, for I do not think he wanted to see the scoundrel released, son-in-law or not. Mary though was out of sorts. She did not know where she stood.

I managed to get her in private just before she returned with her father, and whispered a few words in her ear, the way she used to like when she was twelve years old. She even giggled a little, just as she used to. Oh, Moll, how I did adore you and your girly ways. I told her that she was not to worry too much about her husband's future, for it was widely thought that Oliver had his doctors in a state of nonplus, and they thought that he was not long for this world, and after that, well, who knows whom God would see fit to rule the kingdom. Who knows?

Well, I do for one.

'He has a son, Richard,' said Moll, with her usual look of knowledgeable wit, 'and he is a good enough man in his way, but I do not think that he would have a taste for power.'

'Nor would anyone seek to press power upon him, I think,' I said. 'Do not tell your father, but I think we are for a King in the future, and then, well, who knows, but your husband will at least be released if not restored.' She nodded and looked sad. She would like to have her lands and her house restored, but perhaps not at the price of enduring life with that beast of a man any more. Mr Milton had long been campaigning for more rational measures of divorce, but she would never avail herself of that I think. We parted, once more with our hearts warm for each other, in spite of the long gap between our meetings, and I often wonder how things might have worked out if I had not been so averse to sharing my life with a woman. I would probably have been worse for her than Buckingham, though, and I think she senses that, even though I have such a *tendresse* for her still.

The army officers met, telling everyone that it was in order for them to pray for Oliver's condition. They may well have started to pray, but within the hour they were at each other's throats about the state of the nation and who should seize power. If anything they are worse than their men, who at least have the excuse of being Ranters or Levellers, or what-ever enthusiasm is currently sweeping through the rabble.

The Cavaliers began to gather at inns, and drink a little more than they used to, and carouse a little louder, and cautiously congratulate themselves a little more openly. The watch, which once would have seen them off with Puritan relish, can now only look on with a surly resentment.

Everywhere people are wondering about a successor.

Thurloe said to me in private that Oliver told him he had

written him a letter naming a successor, and had thought he had sent it, but because of his recurring malarial fits could not remember for sure whether he had sent it or not, or indeed where he might have left it. Barrington, the Clerk of the Green Cloth, was despatched quickly to Whitehall to search Cromwell's desk, but returned empty handed.

This did not surprise me, for the good doctor Bate had overheard the conversation between Cromwell and Thurloe, and wisely, on his own initiative, for he could not find me in time, had gone ahead to Whitehall and found the letter. He passed it to me, and I burned it. It did no more than name his son Richard successor. Well, that may come to pass, but even if it does, he will not last five minutes in power, and it won't be the Cavaliers that throw him out either, it will be the warring factions in the army. They are like dogs that will foul their own kennel sooner than shit outside, just to be bloody minded. Still, no point in helping them rather than hindering. Mayhem is better than order for my purposes.

There was a storm on the penultimate day of August, which was very handy for my plans.

I do not know if there had been a great storm on the night when Cromwell was born – no doubt the astrologers will cast his charts and claim such a thing as a presage for the coming of a great conqueror – but there was a mighty raging tempest on the night of the thirtieth. I slept through the whole thing as a matter of fact, having gone as far as three bottles the evening before, and practised my usual perversion. When I woke up the next morning and stepped out, with a hangover like a dead cat in my mouth, the streets were littered with branches broken from their trees by the wind. Folk were gathering them up for fires, even though the wind was still high and tearing the leafier twigs from their hands. Horses were hardly about the place, and the ones that were still looked fearful, as they do in storms. I was told that the wind was so high last night that no horse could draw against it nor move. It was a very raging tempest, and it was surely an omen.

In a letter to his office in Venice, Giavarini, the Venetian Ambassador to London, wrote: 'On Tuesday eve he was given up by his doctors.'

Not quite he wasn't, but it was close. I had read that letter. In fact I read all of Giavarini's letters. Secretary Thurloe has the postal service neatly tied up, and they give him whatever he wants.

I had managed to catch Bate before he went to Oliver the next day, and told him to redouble his efforts, for the storm had surely been a sign. Bate said that this was not at all easy, for Cromwell had always changed the room where he slept, for fear of plots against him. This much I knew, for he also used to change the route that his coach took, giving instruction to the driver after the journey had begun. He also kept a breastplate of metal under his shirt, and his life guard always surrounded the coach wherever he went. He was a fearful man, and he was right to be, but it was worse now according to Bate. Apparently Oliver would only choose rooms which had a separate exit from their entrance, in case he had to make a hurried departure in the night. 'Ho, ho,' I thought, 'just like an adulterer caught *in flagrante*. Fat chance of that with Oliver.' Bate said that he posted armed sentries at every door.

'Take no notice. Sweep in as if you own the place. A doctor can always gain entry where even a senior courtier cannot.' Bate carried on looking miserable, and whining and moaning about not getting enough money, so I put on my stern look, and did not even have to remind him about our little secret concerning the matelots and how he liked them sniffing round his coal-hole. He went back to work quietly.

And so Oliver worsened. Then, damn me, if he didn't get better again. Christ almighty, what does a man have to do to get rid of a tyrant? He must have absorbed enough poison by now to rid London of all its rats. It hardly seems possible that the Venetian can keep it coming. We must have used up a year's supply of the stuff at least by now. Still, the heads of the top men in the Serenissima will rest a little easier for a while. No one will assassinate them for a few years because Venice will have run out of poisons.

Thurloe intercepted the Venetian's daily reports as usual and the next one read: 'All of a sudden he became better, slept well . . . The improvement has been sudden, unexpected and extraordinary.' Well I knew that, but it's nice to know that others have their close sources, and Thurloe is still apprised of every letter that leaves the country.

So Bate went at it again, and finally brought the man down. On the Thursday morn Cromwell drew near to the gate of death, and by evening, it pleased God to put a period to his life.

So that was done, and I, for one, took my hat off, wiped my brow and breathed a heavy sigh. I had already rustled up a poem for the occasion, something about silent suns descending to meet the night, that sort of thing. It was duly posted around the place among interested parties, Royalist Cavaliers and the like; they have a taste for my stuff, unlike the Puritans who are philistines to a man and don't like poetry. Secretary Thurloe posted the official announcement on the palace gates, which read: 'A great man is fallen in Israel.'

When I looked at my poem later I liked it less. Silent suns? What in hell was I thinking? All suns are silent aren't they? And as opposed to what? Talkative suns? Raucous suns? Suns who form clubs with their friends? Ah well, no one noticed. Some born fool wrote that he had been hurried away by the devil, which had lived in the mighty storm of a few nights previous. Let them think so, if they wish.

Venetian Ambassador Giavarini wrote a final letter back

to his people in Venice, saying: 'The death of Oliver came, we may say, unexpectedly.'

Oh, *we may say*, may we? I can just see him pursing his prissy little lips as he wrote that, going as far as he dare to suggest that there was something fishy about the death. I must have words with the little fairy, he is getting loose-lipped, in the way that his kind always do. Let him talk to his confessor about his role in securing poison for Bate, and *no one else*. If I get so much as a whiff of suspicion from anyone else as to his role in all this, I will personally see that he disappears, and not just back home either. He will find himself being posted to a consular office somewhere very unexpected, like the bottom of the North Sea. Besides if Bate or I are exposed, then he will swing for it too, the fool.

I did not send word to Charles's court in Holland, for obviously they will hear the news soon enough. Besides, I wouldn't want Thurloe intercepting that letter. He knows well enough about my spying activities, and how shifty I have been, what with my talks with Charles in Holland and my carrying messages from Oliver to the King and so on, but let that be all he knows. I have taken pains to stay a single agent, even though I have spoke often with my King in exile. I seem not entirely trustworthy I know, but in the world of espionage, I am the leper with the most fingers. And Thurloe knows that too.

Richard Cromwell was put in power, as we all knew he would

be, and already the army started up an enormous row, just like a bunch of women, about how each and every other General among them should be ruler instead. The problem is that Richard never has been an army commander, so they don't respect him, and he can't control them.

The answer is simple: disband the army. We have no use of them and they are nothing but a confounded nuisance. I'd strip the armour off the back of every mother's son and send him back to his home town and tell him to get on with an honest day's work, but Richard lacks the will to do it. He is a nice man, but *nice* just won't be enough, when you have a country to run. What's worse, the army hasn't been paid for a long time now, and there are signs of mutiny. If the officers harness that rage toward the common enemy of Parliament we could see another revolution if we are not careful, with martial law replacing Oliver's. Oh dear God, what a prospect. The idea of some iron-arsed blimp like Monck ruling us all is too much to bear. What have I done?

I wrote a letter to my good burghers of Hull, telling them some of the more intimate details of Oliver's last days on earth so they could disseminate it in their news sheets, and asking what the people of Hull felt about it all. They wrote back saying that people were not much minded about Oliver's death one way or the other. So much for earth-changing news from London. The provincials carry on croaking in their swamp undisturbed.

Bate described to me later how the body was laid out and disembowelled. The cavity was then lined with sweet smelling spices, the carcass wrapped in a cerecloth, then wrapped once more in thin lead sheet, and laid in a wooden coffin, very plain as the man himself had expressly wished.

I told you that I walked at his funeral, and so I did, and wondered very much at the pomp on display. It was more than my previous King had got, and was altogether too much for the occasion. I took John Milton's arm and steadied him, for he was very sad.

But the funeral took place some time after Oliver had been buried.

Crowds gathered around at Somerset House to see the body and to pay their last respects. What they did not know was that they were looking at an effigy. The light inside the house was saffron-gold from the candles, but made dim on purpose by a man named Bone, who had formerly been stage manager in one of the theatres before Cromwell closed them all down. They hired him to dress the room for the occasion, thinking that he would be well versed in putting on a show and a pageant. Oh, I do not think anyone saw the irony. For he did indeed give this Puritan man the most theatrical of send-offs.

They had had to use an effigy, because Oliver's corpse had exploded. I think it was because the doctors had failed to embalm him properly, rather than any comment from the dead man on having to endure the attentions of a stage manager from one of the cursed theatres. Apparently, it was lying there on the catafalque, its lead sheet all soldered up, being adored by a group of divines, when suddenly there was a sound like a noisy wet fart, the lead sheet burst open and the divines were showered with putrefied meat. This did not do much for their devotions.

What little they could scrape up from the floor they added to whatever remained in the burst lead envelope and hustled it off to the Abbey to be buried quickly and quietly. We didn't want *hoi polloi* knowing about Oliver's final eruption, though I must say it seemed a fit end for a man who spent his whole life exploding over one damn thing or another. Still, he had the final word as usual.

The funeral came later, and they used the effigy in the coffin for want of a corpse. There was some row with the Ambassador of Sweden over the order of precedence at the ceremony. Typical diplomatic behaviour. They are worse than women when it comes to snobbery. I wouldn't have expected it of a Swede though. Most of them are too thick by half to even notice.

Much was noticed about the pomp and ceremony: much noise, much tumult, more expense, too much magnificence, all of it vain-glory. 'A great show, but an ill sight,' was Mr Evelyn's summation of the whole thing, though I think he was busy trimming his former enthusiasm for Cromwell at the prospect of a new monarch, as was everyone else in town who had once kissed the Protector's arse. It will do them no good. No one trusts a man who shifts his allegiance where the wind takes it. Better by far is to never declare it, but rather keep your head down and work hard for whosoever gives you employment. As I do.

There were rumours that the corpse was sunk in the Thames, buried at the fighting field at Naseby, even that he had been taken to Windsor and displaced the body of the First Charles. I do not know why these rumours sprang up, but perhaps some people had got wind of the wax effigy. No, Oliver was definitely put in the ground at the Abbey, among the kings in Henry the Eighth's chapel. At least, to start with. How, and why, I dug him up, I will now relate.

22. First Instructions to a Painter. 1660

Lord, dost thou not care that my sister hath left
me to serve alone?

Luke 10:40

No I won't. I will postpone that story and tell you of it later, for my King now waits in the wings for his entrance on to the grand stage.

I was in Holland, at The Hague, doing my usual business there (i.e. spying, nothing very exciting, just doing the rounds of the intelligencers, under orders from Ewbank, late of the Oslo office) when the joyous offer came. So, while Charles's advisers dithered around, offering him ten kinds of different reasons why he should get back immediately to his Kingdom under any circumstances, or why he should delay and sue for better terms, I took myself off to Willem van de Velde. There are two of them apparently; one is called The Elder, the other The Younger. Which one I deal with, I do not know. He looks pretty gnarled to me, but then so does the other one.

I secured his services to do me another *Penschileringen* as they call them here, or pen drawing of ships, at which he is a master.

'My king will be returning to his country to take his right and true estate under God upon the throne,' I told him. He nodded and chewed the end of his pipe. He did not exactly burst into song and dance at the good news, but then why should he? The Dutch are not for dancing measures. Indeed, it is hard to say what they *are* for. Or indeed, what they are *for*.

However, most people do have a sneaking fondness for the Dutch, and it is hard to say why. They are plain, and not very witty, they love wealth but not display. Their dress is seemly, and not ostentatious. Work and making money are their watchwords, and they have fifteen different terms for 'bourgeois', each with a different shade of meaning, though none of which quite conveys the true esteem in which they hold the word.

He seems a little slow at times, but that is only what he affects, for his mind and his eye are both as sharp as a serpent's tooth.

'He will embark his fleet at Scheveningen, not far from here, and it will be a great occasion. If you could set up shop on the shore line and do one of your little sketches, or even a big one, for I suspect the crowds will be huge, then I will happily pay you more than your going rate.'

He nodded and said nothing. I could not say whether he was nodding to say he understood, or nodding to say he agreed to the whole plan. 'And perhaps, from your sketch, you could produce an oil painting of the great scene,' I said. 'It would please me greatly, and it may well please my King, for he is a man much given to the arts. His father before him kept Gentileschi and also Van Dyke at the court as his painters.'

'And they cut his head orff,' said Van de Velde, in that curious accent that the Dutch have, wherein it is impossible to say where the meaning lies because there is no tone to it. Is he saying, 'No wonder they cut his head off'? Or, 'They did the right thing to cut his head off'? Or 'His taste in painters was so bad, beheading was too good for him'? I don't know, I am getting tired of trying to understand foreigners.

'Will you do it?' I said with some impatience.

'Oh, yersh,' he said, after some time spent gazing at the end of his pipe, tamping it down with a horny brown thumbnail, sucking the stem with a filthy gurgling noise and generally annoying me in the way that only pipe smokers can do. 'I am good at the sea.'

It all went off all right, though my King did look a mite shabby. He is very short of money, in spite of the large sum sent over by the City to help speed his way back. He did insist on knighting every single one of the envoys who brought the money, and then he gave five hundred pounds to the crew of the boat. He may not have much money, but all six-and-a-half feet of him is generous to a fault. By God he is every inch a King.

The fleet came in, and his young brother James proclaimed himself Admiral, which I suppose he has the right to do, though it struck me as a bit previous. There was no barge, so some local oik with a name like van Pryck or de Hogspew – no doubt they will knight him now – carried the King upon his back through the bottle-green surf, although the tips of his toes still trailed in the water. He complained as usual about his shoes, for it is nigh impossible to find boots for such huge feet, and the toes pinch.

Then he was aboard, and striding back and forth on the deck, declaiming and holding forth and waving his arms even above his heart to make a point. He was so happy. Well you would be too wouldn't you? Even in my happiness for him, however, there was a faint worm of worry. I think of what they did to his father, and I wonder if that shadow might still hang over the throne.

I think not on balance. Those days are long gone, and while the grey men are still all over the place, hiding in corners and frightening children, the people are weary. They got their peace all right, eleven years ago, but it has been a great long streak of piss of a peace, a decade of bible-thumping and God-bothering and general all-round sniffiness. Now they want their fun.

And if fun is what you want, then, by God, Charles is the man to give it to you. He will give you back your maypoles and your dancing on the green and your playhouses and your heavy drinking and your whoring and your bastards; and, if he could, he would invent a new pleasure and give you that too. They say he has an enormous prick, almost as big as his sceptre. He will give you fun till you beg for mercy.

I watched the boat, the *Naseby* as it was, scud away over the horizon at a steady pace for the wind was good, and he should be at the white cliffs by tomorrow eve, God willing. They renamed the vessel the *Royal Sovereign* in no time, the sailors knowing a good thing when they are on to it, what with Charles scattering gold coins hither and yon as he paced up and down telling stories about his hair's-breadth escapes when he was last in England. The crew were all nodding furiously and trying to creep off about their duties, but he just went blasting on fit to bust.

When he was finally gone down over the blue horizon line, I turned on the sand to go back to my lodgings. The crowd had mostly dispersed, but there was a woman, still looking out to sea, weeping. She had a small entourage about her of maids and attendants, all tutting away, but they could none of them comfort her.

It was his sister, Minette.

By God it touched my heart to see her so, to see her in such distress, for she loves her brother so much, more even than her father or her mother or any of her family, more even I dare think than her own husband. And that, as much as anything else, persuades me that Charles is a good man.

He is a powerful man, yet I never saw him treat a woman badly. He knows his kingly duties, and he knows that they must drag him away from her, but his heart is soft, and his sister has a most special place in it. That may not seem like very much to you, in the general scheme of things, but if all men were like Charles in that respect, then the world would shine with love as bright as the moon.

It is his birthday in a couple of days. They should allow him a triumphal entry into London on that day. What a fine present that would make for a man.

23. Last Instructions to a Painter

Imagination and Memory are but one thing.

Thomas Hobbes. *Leviathan*

After a few days I went back to old van de Velde, or perhaps it was young van de Velde, and without any folderol he threw off a length of sacking from his easel to reveal this oil painting for me.

Well, I could see that it was the sea all right, and the sky with some nice puffy clouds, and a few ships, but I could not make it out at all. It was *nothing* like the scene that I had witnessed on the sea shore. I hardly knew where to begin.

'But there were crowds, all over the shore,' I said, 'all about to see him off, hundreds of them.'

'I don't like crowds,' he said, as if that were the end of the matter.

'And what of the King?' I said. 'Where is he in all this?'

'He is aboard,' he said, 'out of harm's way.'

'But he was lifted aboard and he walked the quarter-deck, I could see him,' I said. 'Surely he should be the subject of the painting. The hero of the hour, the prodigal son . . . all that sort of stuff.'

'Yes, yes,' he said, 'I saw him too, but I don't know how to paint a king. We do not have them.'

'But he is a man almost like any other,' I insisted. 'He may be a little taller, but he is not hunch-backed or winged or with a halo.'

'Oh, I know he may look like a man, but he is not. He is a king. Anyway, the action is all over, he is aboard and that is that. I do not know how to paint one.'

'This is nonsense.'

'To you perhaps, but you aren't a painter.'

'I am a poet, sir,' I said, forgetting in my vexation that I rarely reveal it to anyone. 'It is much the same.'

'Maybe it is, and maybe it isn't,' he said, 'perhaps what I should have said is: you are not me.'

'But I wanted a record of what happened,' I said.

'And you have got one,' he said. 'There you are, this happened.' He tapped the canvas with the end of his pipe.

'I wanted the King, and the crowds and the drama,' I said. 'This could be anything.'

'Then you should have painted it yourself.'

'I will do so, I will. I am not a painter, but I will paint you a picture in words. For that is all a poem is, it is a picture in words. It is the very simulacrum; no, it is more

258

than that, it is the thing itself, just as a good painting is the thing itself. *Ut pictura poesis* to you, my good man.'

He nodded and sucked his pipe. I will ram it down his throat soon. I will make him swallow it till his arse gives off puffs of tobacco smoke.

'Look,' I said. 'The warships came thundering over the horizon and hove to about a mile out, and sent in their smaller boats whatever they are called, barges or cutters, and there was my King standing watching on the shore, surrounded by his court and advisers, and he was complaining of his boots, just as he always has been ever since he was on the run in England, his feet give him a lot of trouble, and cobblers are not so good at making comfy boots for his size feet, they haven't the right lasts, and so a humbler man, a fisher I think, offered half in jest to give him a pick-a-back through the waves to keep his feet dry, and the King was in such a good humour that he was tickled by the offer and gave a run at the man and jumped on his back there and then, and together they rode around on the beach like a frisky horse and rider, the King waving his hat all the while and everyone laughing, and then the pinnace arrived with the royal ensign snapping in the breeze, and the man waded out and most gently lifted the King over the gunwale and the King thanked him most kindly and gave him some money, then stood, somewhat shakily, for the boat was not so big that a man might not upset it, and bowed to him, then he turned toward the shore, and bowed most deeply to us all, and we, as one, bent low in a bow, and I will never forget the faint swishing noise made in the air as a hundred caps were lifted from a hundred heads and swept down to the ground, it was a ghostly sound and audible above the waves, and made the short hairs upon the nape stand on end, and then the oars-men, sitting well in order, smote the sounding furrows, and their purpose held, for they were out at the tall ships within the hour and my King but a speck in the distance, though I could still tell that he was happy, even though so far away, it was something to do with the stance of the distant figure, like a man when he dances, the way he held himself spoke of joy and love. And that is how it was.'

'And here in my painting,' said the dauber, 'there is indeed a man on the back of another, but it is not your King, for he is safe on board now and gone and near invisible, it is just some hairy old ostler, who saw the piggyback ride and wanted to try it for himself, and the fisherman is happy to take others on his back so they may sit where a King once sat, his back is become a throne, and, look here, there are two horsemen standing in the surf, both looking in the same direction out to sea, in the direction that your King has since vanished, and look here, there's a small boat that might capsize in the swell, but no one is paying it much attention, and there are plenty of other boats with loads of other sailors, all being busy at their usual business, and the sky is blue as usual, and the clouds are here and there as usual, with just a hint of darkness about them threatening rain later perhaps, but do not, I beg you, take that as a symbol about any forthcoming doom for your King, I do not paint prophecies or symbols.'

'But neither do you paint what is in front of you.'

'Oh, but I do.'

'But all this is after the event.'

'So?'

'And it is from your imagination.'

'So?'

'But it was an important occasion,' I wailed in frustration.

'Of course it was,' he said, 'and like all important occasions, it was soon over, and most people just missed seeing it, for they had no idea that an occasion was about to take place, nor even that it might be important, but that does not matter in the slightest for life goes on, whether or no they saw it. The wind bloweth where it listeth, my friend. Besides they will soon enough imagine they saw it well, and tell their grandchildren all about seeing it, clear as day, right here before their noses, and mighty bored their grandchildren will be too.' He went back to sucking on his pipe.

'I do not want it,' I said, as fierce as I could.

'Very well, I will throw it away,' he said with perfect equanimity.

I could not restrain myself, but snatched the canvas from the easel and hugged it to my chest, and almost ran from the studio. He looked at me without astonishment. All things seem to be as one to him. He is a most calm man. Or else he saw through me too easily. And that cannot be, for men always say that I am opaque.

24. An Audience

Paint him in a Golden Gown.

Marvell. 'Last Instructions to a Painter'

'Majesty, may I speak honestly?'

'I would want nothing else from you, sir.'

'It is, I think, a masterpiece, for it shows what you would least expect. He might have concentrated on your embarkation and the cheering crowds, and the glorious pennants and so on, but had he done so, then the painting would simply be like a hundred others that have gone before: vain, empty pieces of trumpery that people would say was just a piece of propaganda for your Majesty and his court. Instead, what the man has done, and here he has been most subtle I think you will agree, is to capture the moments after you are safely on board. Once the peril of the thing is over, and you are well ensconced and on your way to regain the throne that is rightfully yours, then the painter and all the other people too can relax slightly, in the sure knowledge of your assured future and good fortune. They can return to that happy state when they had a king, and not some zealot, to look up to;

and the nation once more has a man concerned for their happiness as well as their safety. So they go about their daily business with a lighter heart. See, here in the foreground, a man trying out a pick-a-back, just like the one you enjoyed. A minor piece of *lèse-majesté* to be sure, but surely a harmless one, and done in jest. Even the sea seems boisterous and happy at your newly begun safe voyage, and two men on horse watch out to sea, not agitated, but with a keen desire for your homeward passage. See, it is a calm painting, and most beautiful, Majesty.'

'It is sir, it is, and you defend it most eloquently. I might never have seen so much in it had you not told me what to look for.'

Did I see him smile? I think so, very slightly. He has his own quaint humour, and not every man can follow it.

'About the matter of acquiring another court painter, Majesty . . .'

'Yes, yes, yes, bring him to us, if he will come, I like pictures of boats and stuff. We can put him up in Greenwich, loads of boats down there. Should keep him happy. Say £100 per annum?'

'I am sure he would be honoured, Majesty.'

'Very good, get it done then, sir, with your usual speed and efficacy. Oh, and no need to talk things up quite so much in future, eh? I know artistic temperament when I see it. It always strikes me that they are demanding the sort of tolerance such as one would only give to a toddler who just shat on your carpet.'

I bowed low, to hide my grin. 'Your Majesty is most . . .'

'Yes, yes, yes, get about your business . . . ah, hello my dear!'

I left as some woman or other entered. She was most pretty. Not that he cares either way so long as she is putting it about.

He later passed a law which was 'Liberty to tender consciences and that no man shall be disquieted or called in question for differences of opinion in matter of religion, which do not disturb the peace of the Kingdom.'

The Presbyterian divines from Scotland, who had made his life such a bore, tried to make Charles promise that he would suppress the Book of Common Prayer and the use of surplices in his own chapel and elsewhere. He muttered an aside to me, 'This sort of thing has been steadily getting on my nerves for years.' Then he said very loudly, 'In giving liberty to others, I do not intend to renounce my own.'

I am moved to say that that is just about the best reply I have ever heard to give to a zealot. I made a note of it later, for my future use in argument, should I ever be stuck in a similar bind. Charles thought of it off the top of his head. For such a lazy man, he is fast.

25. Bare Bones

A secret cause does sure those signs ordain
Fore boding Prince's falls, and seldom vain.
Whether some kinder pow'rs, that wish us well,
What they above cannot prevent, foretell.

Marvell. 'A Poem upon the Death of O.C.'

Now where was I with Cromwell's corpse?

After the King got back, there was much ado about revenge on those who had chopped his father's head off. As a matter of fact he was much against it, for as I have said many times, he is an easy man, and not given to avenging slights. No two persons could be less alike than he and his father, and the young Charles had his father's measure pretty well, for he had more understanding of all his fellow men than his father did. I do believe that secretly he thought that his father got what was coming to him. Never did he say so of course, but he was not at all exercised about catching the fifty-odd people who signed the death warrant, including the judges – poor stupid men, what a mistaken judgement they had made.

That didn't stop the courtiers and dignitaries and anyone else around the place, who wanted to start climbing up the seams of Charles's stockings to preferment. They were all for searching out the wretches and dragging them back from their hidey-holes on the continent and stringing them up as a lesson for anyone else who might get it in their heads they didn't like the King that God had given them. London is suddenly devoid of Republicans.

Christ, they even threatened to do something frightful with John Milton, just because he had been close to Oliver, and had written anti-Royalist pamphlets. As a matter of fact, now I think about it, the man was stupid enough to write reams of the stuff suggesting that it was not at all illegal to cut the head of a King. In fact it was the common duty. Well, that will fire up the mob all right. I managed to get poor John out of his house in Holborn, near the Red Lion Inn, which opened at the back on to Lincoln's Inn Fields, and spirited him away up to my secret place in Highgate – which I have not told you about, nor will I. I go there to get away from the world of busy men, and recover my self.

He stayed there a fortnight, while I asked questions in Parliament about the legality of it all, and generally persuaded people that it was a very unsporting gesture to go harassing a man like poor blind John; and anyway he was a great poet and therefore exempt from the usual rules, on account of being an artist.

Artists are special people. They have a special dispensation from the muses, which allows them to get out of nasty things. You want to get out of your social obligations? You want to be horrible to your wife? You want not to be held to account later for your former *bêtises*? Become an artist. People will then say, oh, you can't hold it against him, he is an artist. It's like being given a free entry ticket to the best play in town. Milton was back in circulation in no time, though that didn't stop the Sergeant at Arms, a man called Norfolk, trying to bang him up in prison. Nasty little fellow he is, Norfolk. I will have later dealings with him I think.

Anyway, the King was set against too much vengeance, but the people were not. So, being a very wise and sagacious sort of monarch, he said, well, let's dig up a few of the chief offenders' corpses and put them on trial, *in absentia* as it were, and then hang them for their offences. It will all be very symbolic, and a lesson to all who might be watching – and no one gets hurt, he thought to himself without saying so, which generally is how he likes it. He is not at all a violent man. He walks about the place without so much as a life guard.

So they dug up Oliver, and also Ireton and a couple of others. The corpses were wrapped in cerecloth, but were glaucous green and stank. They were dragged in their coffins to Tyburn, and there they were hung up on the gallows until the setting of the sun. Apprentices gathered around and cut off the toes for souvenirs. I believe Oliver's big toe fetched a tidy sum from the collector of curiosities at the Museum. Then they were cut down, the heads removed and shown on pikes, and the remains thrown in the ground under the gallows. So perish all traitors. I must say that I am sure they have learned their lesson, and will never do it again.

Their heads travelled to Westminster Hall, and the official hangman put them on poles all in a row, as brand marks to their posterity and the expiatory remains of their accursed crime.

Which was very funny, because the heads were not the heads that people thought they were.

Not that that would make much difference you might think, one corpse's head is much like another, especially when it is wrapped in several layers of mummy-cloth; surely it is the gesture that counts, it is the symbol of the thing. Well, yes and no. People thought that that was Oliver's body and that is how they wanted it. They wanted the poor man's corpse up there to be jeered and kicked and have its toes cut off, and they wanted that head of his on a pole so they could look at it and sneer and frown and shake a fist. It was important to them that it be Oliver's body and no one else's. They had suffered under him, or else had not gained prefer-ment or prospered, which they now did under the King. Or they had been true Royalists all along. Or else they just wanted a bit of fun in their lives, and had not got it till now. So it was personal.

I had the last laugh, because I and Mr Milton had swapped the body around. Why would I do that for the man I had had killed? Well, it was a personal matter too.

On the way from the burial place in the vaults at

Westminster Abbey, the cart carrying the bodies stopped overnight at the Red Lion Inn, at Holborn, near the Fields of Lincoln's Inn. An odd place to stop you might think, for it is not on the route to Tyburn. Indeed it is well out of the way. I had suborned the Sergeant at Arms of Parliament who I mentioned before. His name was Norfolk, and he had been charged by the House with this whole stinking mission.

I had had occasion to remonstrate with Mr Norfolk before, for it was he who had imprisoned John Milton briefly and quite against the legal orders of the time. Then he had demanded extortionate fees from John, after his release, for board and lodging. I raised this matter in the House and got them quashed. So Mr Norfolk was more than resentful of Mr Milton and Mr Marvell for undoing his nasty plans, but he was a greedy man, and would do anything for gold. He was, in other words, the very easiest sort of man to recruit, having no need of ideological persuasion, nor blackmail. Just pay him a fee and watch him dance to your jig. An odious little creature.

We also recruited a good man called Barbon, or Barebones as he was more commonly called. He was useful to our plan for he was the son of a famous Puritan who had been a staunch supporter of Oliver, and also because he was a medical student, in training to be a doctor. He thus had the motive and the means for our plan.

Norfolk had been despatched to the Abbey to dig out the bodies. Once done, he stripped Oliver's corpse of a brilliant gold gorget, which had hung around the neck, and he kept it for himself. As if grave robbing were not enough, he then charged any tourist who was passing sixpence to see the body; so this once-great man had become nothing but a raree-show.

Dear God, the man was a howling shit. Still we needed him, so we let it all pass with no more than a disapproving look between us. I think Mr Norfolk saw the look, because he became truculent after that, and started demanding his 'rights'. I am beginning to wish I had used blackmail after all. At least it would give the pleasure of being able to squash the little bug if I wished, and it would give me power over him. I will work upon it, once this business is done.

In the middle of that night in the field out at the back of the Red Lion Inn, in Holborn, we all met.

Mr Barbon had with him a fearful looking rogue in a ragged coat, with a patch over one eye, and breathing fumes of heavy liquor. He did not introduce the man, not from rudeness, but because I think the man would not want his name known. He was oily in manner and presumptuous of a friendship with us, for he knew that he had done us a considerable service, and one which was illegal to boot, and so he addressed us as if we were co-conspirators in crime.

'I have what you need here, sirs,' he said, wiping his mouth with his sleeve, and sniffing hard. I could smell something rank and decayed upon the evening breeze. 'If you will give me a hand with the cart, then we may get the job done as quick as we can, and I will be on my way. After you have recompensed me of course,' he said, and he wheezed with mirthless laughter as he began wheeling a small handcart towards us. We walked alongside, without lending him a hand. Let the oaf handle his own nasty wares. He was a 'resurrection' man. Barbon had need of them from time to time, and a blind eye was turned to their trade with medical men.

He stopped the cart alongside the carriage on which rested Oliver's coffin. I had drugged the sentry's drink and he was snoring loudly in a mound of hay, some way off. We took off the lid of the coffin, from which Norfolk had already prised the nails, and we took what we could of Oliver Cromwell's body, for it was pretty much in pieces. Barbon and old Cyclops lifted the more entire corpse from their handcart, and we swapped them over.

That was all there was to it. We bid Mr Milton good night and saw him back to his nearby house. Barbon and his odious crony disappeared with the handcart and Oliver's few remains, and our anonymous dead friend, may he rest in peace, was strung up and endured the jeers and indignities of the ignorant mob for a good few years. He did not deserve it, but he did not complain.

I went home and, as I was undressing, noticed a piece of burial cloth, hanging from my sleeve near the elbow. I was about to brush it off to the floor, but I did not, and lifted it to my nose. It had a strong earthy smell to it, and strangely was not at all rank. Beneath the earthy smell, I could detect something more. I was not sure what it was, and so I finished my ablution, and brushed the dry earth from my outer coat, and while I was doing all this drank down a bottle of red wine, and then another. All the time I was careful to keep composing something in my head, a tricky translation of something from Ovid as it happens, for I was cunningly diverting my mind from wandering too close to the subject that I wanted.

I finally lay on the bed and carefully placed the pillows to one side so my head was flat in the mattress. I had shut the window carefully, for night air has noxious vapours, and I lay back and placed the cloth over my nose and crossed my hands upon my chest and lay there inhaling the while. Slowly across the years the smell returned to me. There was earth, and there was that deadening smell of geraniums, which is so close to a graveyard's smell. Finally it came to me, and I began to weep gently, for I could smell Moll. It was not exactly her smell, for she smelled sweetly of a fresh world of newness and light. No this was dank and old, but still it was Moll and no one else that this smell reminded me of. She is dead to me. Presently I fell asleep. When I woke I felt no better. As I shaved myself I could hear my mother's voice: 'Just who do you think you are, Andrew?'

Mr Barbon buried Oliver in Red Lion Square, where he stays to this day, beneath an obelisk, which is not marked with a name, but whose special nature is passed on to those in the know. It is much visited by liberty-minded people from all over the world. You know the sort of men: ill-barbered folk, who will eat no meat, and build barricades in the streets and preach overthrow. They even hold meetings and lectures in a nearby hall. I went to one once, and dear God but they were crashing bores to a man.

Why did I do it? Take part in the transposal of the corpses I mean, and the spiriting away of a man for whom I did not much care, and against whom I would have been happy to see the mob throwing stones. A matter of common civility perhaps? I wish I could say, but I do not know. I truly do not know.

26. No Instructions to this Painter. 1661

What but a soul could have the wit
To build me up for sin so fit?

Marvell. 'A Dialogue Between the Soul and Body'

Sat all morning for my portrait to be done by Mr Lely. He is a mighty proud man, and full of state. He was working on my face, having left the shoulders and clothing to an apprentice to be done later. It will be a bust only, for I cannot be bothered with a full-length portrait, and nor do I want my hands in it. My hands are long and thin, with narrow wrists and knuckles, and slender, tapering fingers, and I am not sure that I like them at all. Women have often remarked how fine they are, and not like their husband's big, spatulate hands, but as usual with women, their admiration is simply a form of vanity; what they are admiring is something they would like to have for themselves.

Indeed I do think there is something unmanly in my hands. They are not very strong in their grip, and quite unsuited for work of any kind except with a pen. I told you that my gardener taught me to mow a field when I was young, and indeed I was very dextrous at it, and picked up the rhythms and motions quite quick, but I lacked the stamina in my wrists, and also the pads on my palms were soon blistered and bleeding. I could do it all right, but not for long.

So too with a sword, as I have told you. It is always best for me to strike the first blow. That way I can win without having to test my wrists too far. In a fight, it is near fatal for me to punch with my fist bunched, for I have often broken a knuckle when I do. I tend to use the heel of my hand, or else the edge, and then I can break a nose with the best of them.

A music master once said that my hands were like a gift from God, and would be very good for playing the viol, or indeed any stringed instrument, or even any keyboard, for I have a good span, and the fingers are very long and supple, being almost double jointed in their knuckles, most especially the thumbs, which I can bend backwards. However, I have a tin ear, which is music's loss. So what could I do but pick up my pen and be a civil servant? It's all I can do, and that is a great regret to me. For I do not like people knowing about me. The soul is best known only to God, and kept in His cabinet intire.

Sorry, where was I? Ah yes, my hands. I have noticed that when I play at cards, I am expert at deceiving my opponents, I can lie with an absolutely bare face, but once, I found myself up against a flair player, and he could spot whenever I was bluffing, and I did not know how he could tell, for I have no tics or stutters which give me away. Then I saw that he was looking at my hands, and I noticed that they do indeed sometimes flutter when I am prevaricating. It is not like a shaking, such as when one is frightened, but more like a casual flick of the wrist, as if to dismiss what I am saying as unworthy. It is a nasty give-away, and I am glad that I learned of it. Not that I play cards much, I do not approve of gambling.

I'll not have my hands in the portrait. Needless to say, Lely was disappointed, he wanted me pointing at some little object which was symbolic of my taste or thought or political leaning. Forget that; since I'm paying him, I will call the shots.

My nose is large, thanks to my father, and bulbous at the end just like his. The face is broad, somewhat like a bear's as one woman told me, and the cheeks have gone puddingy with the years. My lips are full, especially the lower, and when I am enamoured, they swell and go red quite like a woman's. They are built for kissing, though I am choosy where I put them.

It is my eyes that are my best feature and for them I must thank my mother. They are large and deep hazel, flecked with gold. They are set beneath narrow but well-arched brows, which nearly meet above my nose, and they are set wide apart, so that I look as though I had a trusting and open nature. They say that the eyes are the window of the soul. My, how our features can lie! I can cheat, lie and dissemble, and none of it shows.

I have a lazy eye, my right one, which does not always swivel in time to the left, and the painter has toned it down a bit to flatter me, but still hinted at it. It unnerves men, I know, for when they look me in the eyes, they cannot decide which to focus on, one or the other. Also it gives me a faraway look, as if I were musing on something impenetrable. I am short sighted, but cannot be bothered with spectacles, for I can read if the page is close enough, and I prefer to see the rest of the world in a blur.

My hair is my own. It is somewhat too long for the fashion, but I will not have it off just to please the Puritans. Later in my life, wigs became the thing, but I never had need of one, for baldness is not a Marvell affliction. It is greying at the edge, though Lely did not put that in. He likes to flatter a little.

I was wearing my plain brown, and my neck was banded, and the band-strings are white with artful knots at the end. It looks like a Puritan garb, until you notice the decorative band-strings, which are quite Cavalier. Very telling.

So I sat patiently, and he kept darting looks around the corner of the easel, and sucking his teeth and sticking his tongue out, and scrubbing away furiously with his brush. It is such a terribly physical occupation, as I had noticed in my dealing with old van der Velde.

Presently I was allowed to look, and I must say that I have

absolutely no idea whether it is a good likeness or not. Friends have told me it is, and so I suppose I must take their word for it. I look at it and can see that it looks roughly like me, the features are all in place and they are demonstrably my features, yet nowhere can I see my self in it.

It is very strange, but I do not think I have a very good idea of what I look like. So perhaps you should ignore my descriptions above. Or perhaps just check my hands. There is no blood on them, yet they have been up to their wrists in gore. Strange, how easy it is to wash one's sins away.

I had another portrait done later, and then later still a reworking of Mr Lely's into an historical panorama, in which I survey the main public events that have taken place in my span of years. Of course the years have taken their toll on me in that one. It has been re-touched to be altogether more sagged and wrinkly than the first one, but I would say that if the expression says anything at all to the viewer, it says this: 'Disappointment'.

Which is hardly surprising after all that I have seen. I have finally come to the conclusion that whatever we do, it will make no difference in the long run. The good Lord disposes of events as He will, and we might as well let history take its own course as try to influence events. It doesn't stop us trying though, does it?

The Cause was too good to fight for. And you can make of that statement what you will.

27. Ordeal by Fire

And he looked toward Sodom and Gomorrah, and
toward all the land of the plain, and beheld, and, lo,
the smoke of the country went up as the smoke of a
furnace.

And Abraham drew near, and said, Wilt thou destroy
the righteous with the wicked?

Escape for thy life; look not behind thee, neither stay
thou in all the plain; escape to the mountain lest thou
be consumed.

Genesis 18 and 19

An entire arch of fire . . . a most horrid malicious
flame . . . not like the fine flame of an ordinary fire.

Samuel Pepys. *The Diary*

Assuredly the Lord visited himself upon this great city in this
year. For no other explanation can be possible after the most
horrid and dreadful plague of the previous year. The story
put about tells that it all began in Pudding Lane, at the house
of a baker who was foolish enough not to check his ovens
before going to bed. It's a good enough story: both believ-
able and also a mite too simple, as if so great a horror

could not possibly have so simple an explanation, so that the rumours about who had truly started it, which I put about later, could be stoked up without trouble. In fact the fire did start where the story would have it, in that baker's in Pudding Lane, though it was not carelessness on his part.

The baker got away with his life by shinning up and along the roof to a next-door house, but his maid was too silly and returned to her own room and stayed there, and was burned up so that nothing of her was left, not even a puddle of cooking grease. This left the baker feeling somewhat guilty, which was good for my purposes. He is happy to accept the guilt for starting the blaze. He has become universally reviled; the poor man can hardly go outdoor for the shame, and would do well to move to another town and change his name. And his profession too, since he did not prove so good as a baker. Something more simple for him in future I think. Such as a night-soil man.

After my initial visit to Pudding Lane, I retired into the shadows with my cloak about me. It was after midnight, and no tavern was open, nor any light to be seen, for the watch was much diminished that night and hardly a lantern could be seen in the area. The fire took hold quite quick after I had lit it from a smouldering fuse I had kept beneath my cloak, and was fanned by a sharp Nor' Nor' Easterly, but it was not progressing as I would like. So I went across the way, to where there was a coach yard of an inn which suited my purpose to perfection. I loaded some bales of straw and loose hay on to a small cart, which was used to take feed to the horses, and as quietly as I could, pushed it a little way out into the entrance. Showers of sparks like little glow-worms were flying on the night air. Some caught on the lower part of my hair and singed it with that strange bitter smell which always makes me think of poison, but my purpose held and soon the straw and hay were alight and burning merrily. It was then the alarm were raised, for there was quite a roaring noise by now, as well as the light and heat. I retreated into the night.

Two or three of the watch had arrived and were standing looking at it all stupidly. They were old men and not given to quick thought, and I think they liked the prospect of a little blaze, for it warmed their old bones and gave them a little thrill too. They hadn't had so much fun since running around shouting 'Bring out your dead'. Then one of them came to, and cried that they had better do something about it all, and he went to fetch the mayor, who lived not far away in upper Maiden Lane.

The mayor Bloodworth arrived in his nightshirt and hat, rubbing his eyes and looking cross. 'God's teeth man,' he shouted, 'is this what all the fuss is about? A maid could piss it out.' With that he went back to bed. He couldn't have played his part better if I had paid him large sums of money.

Now there's a thought for the future.

The two remaining of the watch had been quite brave and

tried to wheel the blazing cart out of the way, but the fire was picking up a treat and was too fierce for them and beat them back. They were coughing and roaring and batting at their hair and clothes, which were smutted. Then, having felt that they had done their bit, they staggered off and left it to others, for a small crowd was now forming of bleary men and women, hastily pulling on their day clothes and looking frightened. One man suggested buckets, another that they find a water pipe, but the problem was one of leadership. There was none to take charge. So up I stepped.

'You there,' I barked, 'run to the back of the inn here and fetch buckets, he will have plenty for his own purposes. And you,' I pointed at a couple of others, 'go back to Thames Street. There is a pipe there. Open it, and begin a chain.'

They did as I bid them, although it took a little while for the men to return with leathern buckets from the inn, for the fire was creeping fast now. It had almost finished its work on the baker's shop and was now roaring on to Fish Street. It would soon be up close to the Thames Side.

A chain was formed and I took my place at the head of it, taking bucket after bucket in hand and throwing the contents on to the fire, and making a great business of getting myself close to the fire so that I was sweating profusely and soon grimy. I took care to throw the water at the height of the fire and not at the base of the flames. The fire prospered and grew.

Soon, the buckets were arriving in my hands only half full.

I flew back along the line and shouted, 'Where is the water? Why so little?'

'The pipe is running dry,' said one of the men. 'It has been a hot summer and little rain. I think it is running out.'

'It's true, we must be short of water,' I said loudly above the increasing roar, though I didn't tell him what was also true about the pipe. It was a very old wooden one, which dated as far back as the Romans for all I knew, but it was badly crusted and would not yield half the water we would need. I knew that, which is why I had suggested the pipe in the first place.

So back to the head of the queue I went, and saw that the chain had ceased and people were standing idly by, empty leathern buckets in their hands, with a glazed look of hope-lessness on their grimy faces. The fire had spread the length of the street at least, and would not be stopped.

Someone with great courage must have summoned the mayor Bloodworth again, for he re-appeared looking even more cross than before, but that quickly changed when he saw the extent of the fire which he had thought could be pissed out. Nearly the whole of Billingsgate was under flame. A great arc of gold-white flame soared across the sky, from the nearest end of one rooftop to the far end of the street, and beyond my range of sight. Men ran from it in horror, but I could only stand as close as I could bear, and wonder at its beauty. It was a living thing, moving forward and licking and devouring and growing as it went, and I marvelled that anything so powerful and so destructive could be so bewitching. Truly, evil is more spiritually attractive than good. The flames were like a glass, and in them I could see my likeness. So bright was the fire, that it made the edge of the sky far blacker than usual, a deep, and fathomless black, like darkness visible, and at its edges the black was banded with the very deepest green.

There was a general panic. Men and women were abandoning their homes as the fire closed in on them, and it was pathetic to see what they tried to save. One woman ran past me with a spinning wheel, which struck me as very sensible, for it may have been her only way of earning a living, but elsewhere men were bowed down with sacks of cutlery, and useless old chairs, and even mattresses. It is amazing what people become attached to. As I watched the rout, I pondered on what I might save, if the fire threatened my house. I finally decided upon nothing. Indeed, it would be pleasant to have everything that I once thought important swept away. I would feel clean.

In the scurry, I ran into Sam Pepys, being his usual busy, flustered little self. I must say I do quite like him, in spite of his hypocrisy, he is so full of himself, but quite aware of it, and therefore not so puffed up or vain. He can always see the funny side of things, but also, more important, of himself.

'Is your house under threat, sir?' I shouted at the top of my voice, though we were only feet apart, for we were both close to Thames Side, and the roar was deafening. People were hurrying past us to get into boats. 'Not, yet, not yet,' he answered, 'and I pray God will not be, but I hold out little hope, for it is spreading like the devil.'

'What will you save, sir, should it come to it?' I said.

'Oh my,' said Pepys, 'I had not thought of it, sir, it is a big question.' And he fell to musing, in the midst of all the terror.

'Your music perhaps?' I suggested. 'You do so love your music. Your virginals would be too heavy and, besides, easily replaced, but your writings and your music sheets, you have spent years over them.'

'I do love my music, I do,' he said with that note of dubiety of one who knows almost instantly in his heart that he can do without it. 'But, do you know . . .'

'You could live without it,' I said.

'You always could read my mind, sir,' he said. 'Do you know what I will do? I will dig a little hole in the garden, and in it I will put my parmazan cheeses, and a little wine, a few of the very best bottles.'

'A good reply, sir,' I said. 'Art is all very well, but we must eat and drink, and what is life without a little treat to come home to after a long day?'

'You teach me well, sir.' he said. 'You are more than the poet I took you for, you are profound too.'

The pair of us bowed low with a flourish, as if the fire was but a cold stage backdrop, instead of something that was showering the both of us with sparks so big that out coats were smouldering here and there, and the fabric quite burned through with holes so that our linen showed through, charred and browned.

As we parted, I shouted something about the mayor. 'He must pull down houses,' I said, 'to make a fire break. It will stop the fire spreading. Will you speak to him?'

'Very wise,' said Pepys. 'I will speak and try to persuade him, though he is a stubborn man, and not one to make hard decisions. It would not earn him love from the people, and it will cost the city much to have to rebuild them.'

'But it must surely be done,' I cried.

'Better to try the King,' said Pepys, and then looked a mite fearful. He nodded as if he had convinced himself, and turned upon his heel. 'Surely, it must, it must be done,' he said over his shoulder, and he trotted off at his usual quick clip, like a little pony, and waved a goodbye. Busy, busy Mr Pepys.

I went back down Thames Street, and the fire was increasing. Its great arc of bloody flame was now reflected in the waters, and even the far bank was taking on a hellish glow. The sky was brightly lit, though not as if it were day, but as if there had been an eclipse and something infernal ruled the earth. Men were rushing everywhere, but it was the poor animals who were worst afflicted. I had pointed out to Sam the pigeons who flew too close to the flames and singed their wings and fell down, and in a niche I saw a little cat with its fur quite burned away, crying piteously like a baby. Men were trying to harness their horses to carts in order to drag away what goods they could, but the horses reared up on their hind hooves and broke their traces and bolted through the streets, their eyes turned up in the sockets so the whites were all visible around the balls. Everywhere, dogs howling.

On the river, barges and lighters were swarming to the nearest landing stages, and furious bartering was going on with the boatmen, who were charging ten times what they would normally. One family I could see had simply taken a wherry, I think one that they owned, and rowed into the middle of the river, and there they sat looking fearful but safe. At least the fire could not walk upon the water, although when I looked again at the speed at which it was now spreading, I began to think it might. The flames were now higher than the tallest of houses, even halfway up the height of St Paul's, and the fearsome thing looked like it could clear the river in a single leap. It would walk the bridge if it wanted, with no trouble.

So I turned and went home, my work done. Soon there would be recriminations, and attempts to find the guilty party. It can only have been the Catholics, of course, which is exactly why I started the thing in the first place, and now I must very carefully disseminate that libel, so that it spreads amongst the population.

I will do my bit, in that line.

My bit? Dear Christ, I will have a field day. The Papist bastards have been getting way above themselves lately, and the mob have been worried that Charles has been doing secret deals with the French king, who has offered to pay off all his debts and give him a handsome bonus, if only he will convert to Rome. Everyone pooh-poohs this idea of course, and says it is just a nasty rumour, because everyone believes Charles is a true Englishman through and through, and would never do such a thing.

The only slight problem is that it is all true. Charles has indeed been having secret talks with King Louis and will convert to Catholicism if the French would give him enough money to do so. He would probably convert to Witchcraft for the right price. I know all of this because I have been to-ing and fro-ing to the French court, making representations to Louis on Charles's behalf.

So it is time to do the left-footers down. Setting all of London on fire might seem a bit extreme, but I never did intend for it to spread so far. And anyway, hardly anyone was killed. Though they'll be lynching Catholics before the week is out. Ah, mischief.

I was wrong about that. They started killing Papists within the day. I myself was passing a mob only twenty-four hours later, when they were setting about a Walloon. Never mind that the man had lived in London these ten years, was well known as a trader, and was a Protestant to boot. The bunch of drunken louts didn't mind about any of that as they gave the man a good what for with their sticks. He had a suspicious-looking bag on him, which I picked up and looked inside. 'Hmm, fireballs?' I said.

The mob soon picked it up. 'Fireballs! Fireballs!' they all howled and quickly looped a noose about the damned Froggie's neck and dragged him off in search of a lamp post. I resumed my meander, musing upon your average Englishman's terrible sense of geography, and once around a corner drew one of the objects from the man's bag and lobbed it high against a nearby wall. It rebounded smartly and whizzed back at me and I caught it smack in my left hand. It was a tennis ball.

Oh well, one less Walloon in the world is Flanders' loss not mine. There was also an orange in the sack, which I peeled and quartered and ate. I do not like the taste of orange, being too acid, but it has a nice colour and goes well with the green of its leaf.

Hmm, orange and green. Not a combination that you would think would work at all, but if they are the right shade then they are certainly very harmonious. I kept thinking of the flames which had a greenish tinge at their edges.

I later sat on the Parliamentary committee which was convened to investigate the causes of the late fire. After much questioning of all concerned, listening to interminable tittle-tattle and denunciations from men who had a grievance, and many weeks of due deliberation, we finally came to the conclusion that it probably was not the Catholics who caused the fire after all, though that didn't stop me from circulating anonymous pamphlets claiming that they did.

James Shirley died in the blaze. His plays were lifeless and his poetry wet, so perhaps there is some justice in the world.

28. Highgate and 'The Garden'

What wondrous life is this I lead!
Ripe apples drop about my head;
The luscious clusters of the vine
Upon my mouth do crush their wine;
The nectarine and curious peach,
Into my hands themselves do reach;
Stumbling on melons, as I pass,
Ensnared with flowers, I fall on grass.

Marvell. 'The Garden'

I should tell you about 'The Garden', not because it comes now chronologically, but it represents as good a curtain as any to the first part of my reminiscences of lost time – and the combination of green and orange prompts me to do so. I wrote it a little while after the Restoration of the King, when I was heavily involved in politicking and becoming heart-sick of it all. I cannot recall one thing that set it off; it may have been the failure of the King to keep his word on so many of his financial promises; it may have been the doing-down of Clarendon, which I missed because I was out of the country, beyond the sea; it may have been dismay at the plague. As I say, I cannot now remember.

I wrote it in a kind of inert fever, while I was staying at Highgate.

Did I tell you of my house at Highgate? Please do not be alarmed; I have told no one of my house at Highgate. It is an utter secret. But yes, I think I mentioned that I hid John Milton there for a while so that he might escape prison and trial for regicide, which the King's supporters were screaming for, though the King was not. So it is not quite the complete secret that I would like, for Mr Milton knows about it now, and so do a few others of the grateful wretched who might now be decorating a spike with their heads had they not hid there, and people will talk.

It is halfway up the hill at Highgate, well outside London, though commanding a good view of the city from its upper windows. It is well surrounded by its garden and, but for a tiny gate, through which only an overgrown winding path can be seen, it is all but invisible. Few people pass it, and none remark upon it. It is quite without any character or style, and could have been built in any era, which is exactly the reason why I chose it.

I do not always know exactly whether a poem works or not, and I certainly don't always know why, but this one is special. I have not yet had any one person who has read it who can manage to find more in it than I can, and that is not always the case, believe me. I have had my eyes opened several times by scholarly men who point out a parallel between one of my phrases and the classical original – something which once I had learned when young, but had long since forgotten or rather put to the back of my mind, whence it had thrust itself forward under the press of my writing. They have often pointed out things to me that have made me jump out of my boots.

There *is* a garden at Highgate, and there is even a curious peach tree in it, but both are in some state of neglect. True, there is also an apple tree from which 'ripe apples drop about my head', but there are no nectarines, nor melons to stumble over. There are flowers, by which it would be possible to become ensnared, and I could go on, but the point is that nothing in the garden has anything to do with my poem 'The Garden'.

I had retired there by myself as usual. I take no servant, and stable the horse a mile away from the house and approach on foot. I light my own fire and prepare my own food, and I do nothing here. Nothing at all. I might have a book in my wallet, or I might write the occasional letter, and I eat, but other than that I do nothing.

It is hard to do nothing. You should try it some time. The urge to move is continual, and fidgeting occurs whether one wishes it or not. A sudden noise will urge you to the window, the sight of an unmown lawn might spur you to oiling the scythe, a man delivering a letter will occasion much pacing up and down, but to sit quietly in one's room is the hardest of all disciplines to follow and one of the most rewarding. It induces in me a delicious kind of torpor, such as I have only known when taking opium from a doctor. My brain runs free and what it thinks is impossible to visualize for it is wholly abstract. I become ensnared in the brambly thickets of the mind, immobilized by the thorns of my thoughts, held fast by imagination's vines. I see visions that have no earthly counterpart.

I am sorry, this is no more than a prosaic explanation of my poem. You may read it all there, if it is ever published after my death. Or you may ask Wilmot for a copy; he will certainly oblige, for he likes me more than most.

Wilmot?

I am sorry, my mind is breaking free of its moorings again. John Wilmot, the Earl of Rochester, I have not got to him yet, but I will do shortly for he plays a large part in my story and, though a bad man, is a good poet. Until then let this stanza do for you:

> *Meanwhile the mind, from pleasures less,*
> *Withdraws into its happiness:*
> *The mind, that ocean where each kind*
> *Does straight its own resemblance find;*

Ah, you look puzzled. That is a learned reference. There is a scientific belief that the ocean once held mirror images of all the flora and fauna on land. Like all science, it is nonsense, but many do believe it, and it fits the lines.

> *Yet it creates, transcending these,*
> *Far other worlds, and other seas;*
> *Annihilating all that's made*
> *To a green thought in a green shade.*

Green means something special to me. I cannot, I will not explain it to you. You would only understand if you entered my own mind.

Upon writing it out again, I realize I have fallen into a crass error by trying to spell out whatever it was went into the making of this poem. I often wish it were more like a painting. A picture can at least be adequately described, but a poem is more like music, which cannot.

I have often written occasional poetry in the past, such as 'An Horatian Ode upon Cromwell's return from Ireland', and duly spelled out the facts in the title and verses for its audience. But not here. I go to Highgate to write it, but it has nothing to do with what is at Highgate.

This poem is it's own occasion. That is all.

As to why I write poetry, I can no more tell you that than I can tell you why my hair is dark brown or my conscience flexible. It is natural to me, and we cannot help what is in our nature. What I can say is that it came about quite without ambition. One moment I was translating my Horace, the next I was trying my own versions of his poems, slipping them into more modern English in the hope that he might not notice, and then I was writing my own, having slipped the chains of translation, but still modelling myself upon the great masters. The one thing led to the other without clear line or division. I did not set out to write poetry, nor did I resist it when I found myself doing it. I slipped into it as easy as dreaming.

But I tell you one thing. There is no better way of making time run through your fingers. There is no greater pleasure than wrestling with a line for hours, then dashing the paper on the floor in anger and frustration and then, quite suddenly, without strain, a new line seems to write itself and is perfection just this side of heaven.

Where that line, that rightness, that justness comes from I do not know, but I do know that it will not come without having put in the labour first. You must wrestle with your angel for hours, days, even years. A poem will not be hurried. Like the statue that lurks inside the marble block waiting for the sculptor to release it, the right poem is in there somewhere, biding its time until the writer springs it from its gaol.

A sculptor once told me of that idea, that the statue lurks inside the block, and I was much taken with the notion, but in fact for a poet it is not quite like that. The poetic task is more like that of the potter, judiciously adding or taking away clay from his wheel, a process of assembly and due trimming, but, however you figure the process, it will not be hurried and it will take its own time. And you must labour. You must sweat more than an indentured slave. You must work long and hard into the night, shovelling words, hammering phrases together, chiselling away in the word-mine until your back is bent double for all time, your eyesight ruined and your fingers permanently ink-stained. It is the toughest work I know. It has driven men mad and will kill the weak.

It will not turn out quite how you wished it to, but will have its own form waiting for you to unwrap. That is as it should be. Let the thing catch you unawares, but only after you have wrestled with it to your satisfaction and exhaustion. As to the rightness of the finished thing, you will know it when you see it. And if you do not see it, then never show it to anyone. Shred the paper to ribbons, throw it in the fire and let your scribblings finally be put to honourable use, if not in delighting your fellow man, then at least in keeping him warm.

One final piece of advice if you seek to become a poet. Resist the temptation.

Writers are moved to write either by ambition or charity: if the former, they seek fame and advancement; if the latter they seek to delight and profit their fellow men. But most writers assume that they are superior to the reader if only because they have a gift of learning to bestow upon the ignorant, which makes it an envious and dangerous employment. And so not to write at all is by far the safest course in life.

But if fate or genius cannot be resisted, then three things are necessary: he must be copious in matter; solid in reason; methodical in the order of his work. After that, then he must choose the subject well. For whoever bursts into print either makes a treat or a challenge to all his readers. In the first case he must not be short of provisions. In the second, he must be completely armed. For if he is deficient in either case, then his readers will laugh at the meanness of the entertainment or at the weakness of the attack.

Do not content yourself with a tiny amount of writing, published only in thin volumes. For geniuses vary widely in their style, but there is one thing, and one thing only, that they have in common, and that is fecundity. If you are going to write, then write a lot. And never complain of writer's block. There is no such thing, except for the second rate.

Outside it had begun to rain, and was getting dark. I lowered the flame in my lamp and sat quietly listening to the clicking of the drops on the ivy. Then I turned it out completely and smelled the silky smoke for a while, which filled my nostrils with the memory of tamped-down candles, that day when Moll extinguished the lights in the hall at Appleton, before taking up the gun and covering my back against the troopers. It was the smell of untrimmed wicks that brought it back to me. By God, what a thing in a thirteen-year-old girl. She was more bold than I, at less than half my age.

Then I relit the lamp and went to the kitchen and cut a loaf that I had bought on my way here. There was some cheese too, and an apple that was going soft and wrinkled, and on the turn from green to brown so I ate it quick. It was drying out and had little juice and tasted slightly of sulphur, a taste which put me in mind of something else I could not quite pin down. No doubt Mr Milton would have said it was the Devil, but never did I ever come across anything infernal in my whole life, no matter the outbreak of witch hunting in the Fens when Oliver was in charge. That was mass hysteria, I am sure of it, brought on by religious mania. The witchcraft was put down with official savagery by a Witch-finder General, with much torture and burning, which I ascribe to an excess of public zeal, and private sadism, neither of them worthy habits in a man.

The apple, that apple-taste, I cannot quite place it.

I saw a pine-apple once. It was at Hampton Court and had been grown by the King's gardener under a small glass house which focused the rays of the sun on to the plant so that it grew as if it were still in the tropical Bermudas, beyond the Mexique bay. There is a painting there, of the gardener down on one knee, presenting the strange, gnarly fruit with its green spiked crest to the King for the first time. It is said he ate it all in one sitting at supper and was up all night at stool. The experiment was not repeated.

I remember now about the Bermudas. I wrote that poem about them that I mentioned before. Looking back on it now, I do not think it was one of my best, but only a good poem, but it does contain two couplets of which I am proud. No, more than that; I love them for they are close to my heart and pleasing to my ear. They are:

> *He gave us this eternal spring,*
> *Which here enamels everything.*

'He' in this context being God, and what He gave us was a sort of Utopia of eternal spring, if you want a prosaic description of it all.

And the other couplet goes:

> *He hangs in shades the orange bright,*
> *Like golden lamps in a green night.*

I refuse to give you any explication whatsoever as to those two lines. All I will say is that if you like them, then you will like me. And if you love them, then I will love you.

They are two great couplets in a poem which is otherwise no better than middling. I know that at least, if I know anything at all about my own work. I sometimes fall to thinking that I should have saved those couplets for a better poem, one closer to my heart, but on reflection, I could not. Firstly they would not fit any other poem. Or rather they would not fit the occasion of any other poem, for I would not be of a mind to use that couplet at some different time in my life, other than when I thought of it.

Secondly, they shine so well because they are surrounded by the second-rate. It is like finding a diamond in a midden, blazing all the more bright than in a filigree setting. Thirdly, if they were in a better poem, they might be swamped. A great poem can only hit you hard with one or two of its lines, or it becomes too much of a deluge.

So take 'Bermudas' for what it is: a competent poem, with some nice rhythms. See the last line – 'With falling oars they kept the time' – quite good that, for a young man, if a little pat. Also it is a lying poem, in that it does not record the horrors that awaited the would-be colonists in the Bermudas, and those horrors were, of course, no more than what was in their own natures: greed and aggression.

Finally, no matter. It has a few great lines, and no more than that, and all of this I can now admit, with the years that passed between me and the making of it. At the time, I would have hit any man who said it was less than worthy of Dante. Ah, the passing of the years and the consolation that age brings.

Consolation strikes me as one of the greatest of virtues that God placed here for man. I often think back to that time when I was nearly killed in Ronda, and I reflect that I was not, and so every day since then is a kind of bonus, a free gift, which I would be a fool not to enjoy, and which to refuse would be the basest ingratitude.

However, my thoughts in middling age turn more and more sombre. I cannot help it, especially if I dwell too long on the wars and what they did to this country's men. There was no honour to be found in it, as can be earned when defending one's motherland against a common foe, such as the Dutch. No, this was brother killing brother, father killing son.

I resort to the consolation of my near-death more and more, but, like the Jesuit's Powder, the medicine the doctors give me for malaria, it becomes less effective with overuse.

The taste of that apple will come to me, if I sit long and wait upon the problem, but it is best to distract my mind in some other direction. Then it will take me by surprise.

From consolation, I turn to cheese. The cheese on the kitchen table had a hard rind, which I ate also. Its flavour put me in mind of . . . mmm, here I go again, but the taste is something very evocative, though in the case of this cheese, what it reminds me of is other cheeses. The cheese in Spain is very bad and of no interest. In France though it is a culture to itself, a country with its own rules, a kingdom of a million different citizens, all yoked together under the sovereign name *fromage*. They have as many different cheeses as they have men, and each varies according to the type of cow's or goat's milk and the spring water and the local method of making and ageing it.

This cheese was English however, and therefore only of one kind, though good. English cheese is yellow and comes in a large wheel, with a white crust like a skin disease, and it sweats in the heat, then cracks with age. It is impossible to eat without drinking water. It tastes of old wardrobes.

I have it by God, yes, at last I have it. It was Rochester. He smelt of apples. Or so Nell, the King's mistress, told me, and she also said that was one reason why she liked him. The fact that there were other reasons that she liked him, inclines me to think that he is perhaps not quite so wicked a man as they say. She didn't tell me what his taste was like, though I would lay odds she had tasted him once or twice. He is a fatally attractive man, but vicious.

two

THE GOLD

29. The Earl of Rochester at Sea

He was very early inclined to intemperance . . .

Dr Johnson. *Lives of the Poets*

10th August 1665
The Revenge
Captain Teddiman's log
Hove to at dawn outside the mouth at the fjord and
heading for Bergen, Norway. Already there are
some of the Dutch fleet in the harbour, awaiting
the arrival of their Indiamen. So do we. But we
cannot easily enter the narrow harbour and need
the assurance of help from the Danish governor.
My messenger Mr Hardiman rowed ashore but met
with no success with the Dane, who is most
suspicious. We have offered him half the booty
from the Dutch fleet if we are allowed to attack
without hindrance. He visibly brightened at the
prospect, but I do not trust him.

'What in hell was that?' shouted Rochester, as the seaman
plummeted through the air and landed with a smack on the

deck not ten feet from where he stood. The ship was other-wise quiet.

'He was shot, my Lord, I think,' said Wyndham.

'I am sure he was, though it will be hard to tell for sure now,' said Rochester, looking at the broken lump, from which blood was seeping slowly over the deck in a thick dark-red cloud. 'I heard the shot all right, but where did it come from?'

A man higher up the mast called out, 'It was from the shore garrison, sir, I saw the puff of powder, up there on the ramparts.'

'Bloody outrage,' said Rochester, turning to Teddiman. 'Captain, we should send again to that Danish bastard, an armed piquet this time I think, and raise merry hell. Get that wretched sentry who fired the shot hanged, and maybe demand some reparations too. Something in the nature of a little of his good will, perhaps; a blind eye turned at the right moment would be appropriate, you know the sort of thing. Bloody Danes, I hate them more than the Dutch.'

'Thank you, my Lord, for the suggestion, but I will do the sending while I command this vessel. We failed to strike the topsail and flags when we entered the harbour, and I suspect the locals were outraged. Quite right too. One should observe the courtesies.'

Rochester lifted his chin in the direction of the dead man, who was being scraped off the deck by some sailors, 'I hope he appreciates the courtesies.'

'He appreciates, and so do all his mates, that he is paid to take the risk of a musket ball,' said the Captain, and turned on his heel.

'He does not,' said Rochester to Wyndham, who was looking at the scene and turning very pale. 'Wherever he is now, he does not appreciate anything.'

'But where is he?' said Wyndham.

'Nowhere,' said Rochester, 'he is gone, quite extinct, there is nothing there any more, and he has gone to nowhere. There is nothing out there beyond this life. I know it. I have read my Hobbes, sir. It is like total dark in the forest at dead of night, or like utter silence in the desert.'

'Hobbes may tell you that, but you cannot know, any more than he can.'

'Or any more than you can know there is a heaven after all.'

Wyndham shook his head at this, though not strongly. Rochester glanced over at him and could see sweat running down his neck behind his ear. The skin had an olive, greenish-yellow pallor. 'I will not survive this encounter, I know it,' said Wyndham.

'Nonsense, you cannot know the future, it is yet to come, and therefore does not exist. What you feel is an indigestion, or an imagination, what Hobbes calls a decayed sense impression. It is a flight, a fancy, a faerie, no more than that.

'Look, here is a thought,' he continued, raising his right hand in a solemn manner. 'If I am killed in the fight, then I promise to appear to my friend Mr Wyndham afterwards and report on the existence or no of a heaven. And if indeed I am killed and do not come back as a revenant, then you may safely take it that there is no heaven and no afterlife.'

Wyndham was clearly moved even though the whole thing was more than a little mocking. He too raised his hand and said, 'And I likewise promise that if I die, I will also appear to my good friend John Wilmot, and inform him of the state of the hereafter.'

They both smiled and shook hands.

'But what if we both die?' said Wyndham.

'Then,' said Montagu, who had witnessed the whole ceremony and was now moving towards them, 'you can both sit on a cloud and discuss the sense impression that the cloud makes upon your arses.' Wyndham actually raised a laugh at this, and Rochester did so too, to help him along more than anything. 'What about you Montagu,' he said, 'any premonitions?'

'No my lord, not because I am an atheist, but rather because I do not seek to know the ways of the Lord. And I am, well, I am shocked by your suggestions. You may not believe, that is one thing, but I beg you do not mock my own beliefs.'

'Please believe me Montagu, I do not mock you, and never would, for you are not a fool, and you are my friend. Now, won't you join us in our pact? It is only a sport, a little prank, but it has a serious intent to it. It is a metaphysical inquiry, if you like. I do not think that God is much bothered by it.'

'My Lord, I will not. And I do most sincerely wish that you both survive this thing tomorrow and come through it a little more penitent and a little more humble for your behaviour.'

'And if we do not, we will certainly visit you Mr Montagu. You will be haunted by us. Woo, woo.'

Montagu went below to his hammock, shaking his head but smiling.

Battle was joined at dawn, after the men had hung yards of red cloth from the spars and about the ship wherever they could. The bunting looked gay, but was there to cover the men's movements rather than improve the ship, and give them the impression of concealment. At five, the *Revenge* let fly the first broadside. The Dutch replied with chain shot, which tore through the rigging and dismounted a spar.

Rochester spotted Dutch sailors ashore running about the ramparts of the castle, and shouted a warning to the Captain, but the ship was facing the wrong way to respond with a broadside. Soon, the shore batteries were firing upon the English fleet. Over three hundred guns in all were trained on Teddiman's ships, but what was worse initially was the gunpowder, carried by a light offshore wind, which came both from the Dutch vessels and from the shore cannon, and hung about the English boats in a great black choking cloud.

Rochester and his friends could only stand there in the dark, gagging for breath, while random shot and shell flew about them, tearing at the wood and shrouds and killing men with no warning. It was like being at the mercy of night-time demons, striking unseen out of the dark and carrying men off.

The gun smoke cleared, leaving all the sailors covered in black smuts. The *Revenge* had backed a little and Wyndham found that he had a clear shot at the ramparts of the castle. With his own and then with Montagu's musket he shot two of the Dutch gun crew and watched while the rest retreated from the wall. Rochester then called him over to the other side, where men were fending off a burning ship with fire-booms. The noise was appalling, and not just from the continuous cannon fire, but from the shrieking of all the men. The cries of the wounded were mingled with the war-cries of the living, shouting to keep their blood-lust up. After three hours of exchanging shot and with no clear end in view, Teddiman ordered the *Revenge* to pull back at about eight o'clock.

As the firing slowed, and the noise abated, Montagu and Wyndham reversed their muskets and leaned on them, even though the fighting was still continuing sporadically. The wind had died down and the sails hung like empty sacks. The careless slap of cross-currents was now audible over the gunnery.

Commander Langhorne was just crossing the deck

toward them when he was cut in two by a cannonball and spattered them with blood and rags.

Montagu staggered to the rail on trembling legs to be sick over the side. Wyndham went to support him, and told him a joke about the Dutch. Rochester saw them laugh weakly. A second cannonball hit both of them, flinging the dead Wyndham at Rochester's feet, and tearing away Montagu's stomach and intestines. He lay on the deck screaming and trying to pack a long rope of his guts back into his open abdomen.

After enduring the screams for some time, a boatswain despatched Montagu with a shot from Rochester's pistol; Rochester having drawn it first, with that intention, but having been unable to do the deed himself.

No ghost ever appeared to Lord Rochester. His atheism was finally proved to his own satisfaction from that moment forward. Four hundred men were killed that day, though the outcome of the engagement was indecisive. There was no booty.

When Rochester returned to London, it was in the grip of the plague. Seven thousand people had died in the previous week alone. 'So much death,' wrote Rochester to his wife, 'and so little money to show for it.' He went to Oxford, where the court was sheltering from the plague, and the King awarded him £750 per annum for his part in the war. It was not paid.

Rochester returned to Putney, which was considered safe from the plague's scourge, and there met Mr Marvell, who was admiring the remains of one of Cromwell's trained bands, drilling in a field next to the river. There was talk of maintaining the New Model Army as a good thing to have, but no one would pay for them and, being mainly Levellers, they would mutiny at the drop of a hat, so it seemed unlikely they would continue.

30. A Year Later. 25 July 1666

Heaven is just, and can bestow Mercy on none but
those that mercy show.

John Wilmot, Lord Rochester. 'After Malherbe'

Why he went to sea again was a mystery, but he did so, like a
gambler pushing his luck.

The Dutch were sighted on this day, making for the
mouth of the Thames.

Spragge shouted, 'Where in Hell is the *Loyal London*? I
must inform Smith of our position. Someone must go in the
ship's longboat and inform Sir Jeremiah that we cannot
return to our station, and we are heavily into the fighting
with van Tromp's ship over there.'

There was a silence on the deck while everyone looked at
their feet or the far horizon. 'I'll go,' said Rochester, and he
never later knew why he had spoken up.

He refused the offer of four oars-men and the longboat,
contenting himself with a smaller skiff. 'Lighter, quicker, less
of a target,' he thought. He had rowed the river, but it never

occurred to him that he had not rowed at sea before. He assumed it would be the same. There was only a light swell.

He set out in the shadow of the *Victory*, which hid him from the line of sight of the Dutch vessel, but within minutes he was in open sea, and already his arms were tiring from the heavy oars, and the weight of his cuirass was leaving him breathless. The first cannon shot soared past his head, with a high-pitched roar of wind, and he never saw where it landed. The second was short and blew a great fountain of water, which left him drenched, though cooler. His wet hands soon developed blisters, which he did not notice. The third was well to the south of his bows, and that was the last time that the Dutch deployed their cannon on him.

Musket balls zipped past his head and took splinters out of the gunwales of his skiff. One hit him on the breastplate, but was at a sufficient angle to glance off and buzz away, 'like an angry bee,' he thought. He looked down at the gash in his tunic and saw an inch-long furrow in the steel cuirass. Another ball nicked the padding at his shoulder, a third tore a splinter from the button of his oar which in turn ripped a sliver of skin from his forearm. Strangely it hardly bled, but stayed a livid white. He had seen this before in battle: when a man's blood was up it stopped the veins, so that they often did not bleed when wounded slightly. More often they bled like pigs though.

He carried on rowing, trying to gain speed, but unable to work his arms any faster. His feet kept getting dislodged from the stretcher and he would flounder on his back. Once he caught a crab with his oar and was nearly catapulted from the boat, but managed to duck under the oar as it rounded above his head. That alone saved his life, as another shot struck the oar handle where his head might have been.

After five more minutes, the musket balls began to die down, though one bounced off the surface of the water and went through the brim of his hat, knocking it backwards into the boat. He let it lie there. 'Less of a target,' he thought, 'but I will put it on when I arrive. One must observe the courtesies.' The sun was now high, and he was sweating furiously, his shirt and tunic drenched and his cuirass rubbing his collar bones raw, and the lower edge digging into his guts. Still he beat on, thinking his thoughts while the long range musketeers high in the Dutch rigging kept adjusting their sights and laying off for wind, and potting away in fury, quite unable to nail him with a decent shot.

When the sailors of the *Loyal London* examined the skiff, they counted more than forty holes and scars from musket fire on it, and another ten rips to his clothing and wig. Even a heel had been knocked off one of his boots. They bandaged the sores on his shoulders, but the hat was soaked and ruined.

'You did well, my Lord,' said Smith, upon receipt of the news.

'Nothing to it,' said Rochester, very plainly it seemed to those listening, without a hint of false modesty or braggadocio to it. Every other sentence that he had ever uttered, every single thing he had ever uttered in his life, seemed false to him when put up against what he had just said. There had indeed been nothing to it. He had felt nothing, thought nothing, and now could remember nothing of his ordeal except for the bare fact that people had been shooting at him and he was still alive. Other than that, *nothing*.

I know this to be true for he told me. I will tell you of the occasion later.

31. Restoration Comedy

Joy rul'd the day, and Love the night.

Dryden. 'The Secular Masque'

Bone leaned on the rail of his little balcony, sucked on the quid in his cheek, and surveyed his stage below. It was not of course *his* stage, any more than it was his theatre, he knew that, but he thought of it as his stage, and the more he thought of it so, the more solid became his ownership and the more proud. The better he became at his job too, the owner of the theatre noted silently, for he was no shirk and he liked to invent.

He loved the moment when he first arrived before a performance. The theatre would be empty. The candles had been carefully snuffed and trimmed, the corridors swept clear and doused with water the night before: he was most particular on that score, otherwise the smell of shit was impossible to get rid of. There were latrines dug out the back of the building, but no one used them. The dressing rooms had been cleared of the actors' possessions, the costumes carefully hung on racks that he had designed himself and whose making he had overseen with the carpenter. The painted scenes, an innovation that he had helped to design and make, were carefully stacked against their frames and runners in the wings.

He would enter through the stage door and check to see if the doorman had left any notes or letters or packets for him. There was usually something: a bill from the seamstress, a scrawled note on a rag from one of the stage crew that he had been called back to his ship (he made a mental note: 'Thank God for that,' the man was a born fool who had dropped a stage-weight on his foot, crushed a toe, and now walked like a gimp), a florid-handed squawk, on a margin torn from the prompt copy, from the playwright complaining that Mrs Barry had been extemporizing once again, demanding that she stick to what he wrote, and that she was getting above herself in the closet scene too, would he carefully rehearse her once more, if you please?

No, he thought, he would not. There was no telling Mrs Barry what to do. He would arrange for something to go wrong in the closet scene, perhaps a screen to fall on her, then she would behave herself or risk being laughed at. She hated that more than anything.

After he had gone through his messages, he would light all the candles in the main chandelier from a taper, and then crank it up to its full height above the auditorium. He would then enter the door in the proscenium arch and, with a slightly altered gait of which he was not aware, he would walk across with measured tread until he stood downstage centre, and he would survey the rows of empty seats. The theatre was utterly silent. He let his gaze fall along the aisles and rows of seats and benches, unconsciously checking for faults or anything askew.

What he loved was the almost palpable feel of the approaching sounds. The chatter as the audience assembled. The hush that fell as the curtain rose. The slow increase in noise, as they grew bored with the play and began to spy on the new arrivals and gossip about who was with whom. The sudden rapt silence as the lead actor went into his soliloquy. The more pregnant silence when he confesses his worthless love for the heroine. The hush when the actress first tilts her bosom at the audience. The intake of breath when she hits the rake with her fan. The faint susurrations from the aristocrats' boxes. The assignations between the middling gentlemen in the balcony and the vizards.

All of these things he could feel in the muffled silence of his theatre. The seats and boxes were pregnant with it, and here he could stand centre stage and look out in one silent moment of splendid satisfaction. Truly he felt a prince of all he surveyed. The actors thought that the stage was theirs, but as far as he was concerned, they only borrowed it for the performance.

After his silent moment of private joy, a joy that he would never let any see, he would set to work for the amusement of a hot afternoon.

And now the performance was well under way. He looked down from his position high on the wall next to the stage, leaning against one of the fly ropes, and unnoticeably checking its tension and weight. He knew rope and could detect a fault or fray just by testing one end with a callused hand. He could see the tops of the actors' heads. The women still wore wigs, though these days they were actually women, not boys. Not like when he had started. On the far side, the deputy was poring over the prompt copy, carefully inching his rule lower and lower over the lines as they were spoken. Bone knew the text backward by now, and knew there was a cue coming up.

The deputy raised his hand and looked quickly to check if Bone had seen it. Bone nodded briefly. Then he half turned and unhitched one of the ropes from its cleat. He took a length and draped it down the length of his back, up between the fork in his legs, and used the friction to take the whole weight. It was a minor chandelier, and he was slowly lowering it in order to stealthily increase the light falling on the scene below. This was hardly noticeable, but it was necessary because a night scene was coming up soon, and by quickly withdrawing the increased light, a good impression on the viewer could be effected. It was just one of the many tricks that he could do with light.

For eighteen years he had been back at sea. When the theatres had all been closed by the zealots, it was all he could do. He had been a sailor when young, but had found his true vocation when he had been laid off for a while and had discovered the skills of the back stage. That had been in the days of outdoor theatres, when his knowledge of ropes and pulleys was not needed, but now, since the new King had re-opened all the theatres, he had come into his own, for they were all indoors.

Being indoors had meant painted scenes. It had meant chandeliers and clouds hanging from the ceiling on ropes. It had even meant, in one famous masque which he had watched from the wings, a chariot descending with the King and Queen in it dressed as Greek gods, he was not sure which. He had helped crank them down, the crew sweating more from fear than effort, for God knows what would have been the punishment if they dropped the King.

He had designed ingenious pulleys and cranks and even a special windlass with variable sized rims upon it, so that many effects could be controlled by one man on the crank.

Now he awaited the deputy's signal. 'Who counts her sins may as well count the stars,' said the actress, and Bone began to let the rope slip across the length of his back. He took five good minutes letting it slide, until the light source had descended only a few feet. Then he tied it off again and went back to his rail. He looked down on the head of Betty Barry. By God, she was terrible. She staggered around with a long legged gait that looked like an ostler, and she sawed the air with her hands and declaimed at the top of her squeaky voice and generally embarrassed everyone who looked on her. Her face was not downright ugly, nor was it above handsome. She had nice white bubbies, which she levered up high, and her ankles were slim. It was said that Davenant fancied her, which could be the only explanation for the fact that she had replaced Mrs Boutel in the role of Cleopatra. Mrs Boutel could do tragedy like no other, and could also do a backward bow. Mrs Barry on the other hand was just another hopeful whore.

She couldn't act to save her life. Bone shifted the quid to the other cheek and sucked upon it silently. Something would have to be done about her. He spat and watched the dark brown blob of tobacco juice fall through the upper air, past Mistress Barry's bobbing wig, and land flop on the toe of her left slipper. She did not notice, though she did later.

It was Wilmot took her in hand, and it was obvious what he wanted from her, though why her is still a mystery. He had had all the women he could need for two life-times, and all of them beauties, but still he chose horse-faced Betty. She must have had a boudoir secret, and his taste for the theatre was well known. He certainly loved an actress.

'Now Betty you must stay with me a while if you are to learn. For you think your art is easy but it is not, and takes more time than most of your profession will put into it. I will work you hard and you will hate me for it I know, but when we are done I will promise you here and now that you will be the best tragedienne on the London stage, which is only to say the best there is in all the world. For I have been in France and seen what they do there; idle things to make a King laugh. Now to make men laugh is not so hard a thing to do. All you might do is fall over (or open that horse face of yours too wide and whinny, that would do the trick, though I would never mention it) or do an imitation or a satire. No, to make people laugh is a gift that some have, and it is nothing. I can get Mr Davenant or Mr Killigrew to write a lead for you, in the new comedies, and all you have to do is fold your fan and hit the rake on the arm with it, and twit him by saying something witty, like 'I will dwindle into a wife', you know the sort of thing, and people will gloat and clap each other on the back and then ignore you while they turn to their partner in the box and slip their hand under her skirt, just for feeling so good after a laugh.

'But to make people weep, now that would be worth a lot I think, and to make people weep, all you have to do is make them listen. Ah, you start. Well, yes of course people have been listening to you all this time my dearest, but they have not been *listening*. Not straining forward, not hanging upon your every word, nor dying to know what will come next, nor feeling your deepest emotions even as they spring from your heart. They have not been *listening*. They have simply heard you.

'Now. Read this.'

Mrs Barry took the paper from his hand, took a deep intake of breath, and struck her pose.

'Stop,' he bellowed and she jumped. 'I said read it, not proclaim it.'

She slumped a little and seemed to settle a few inches lower.

'Good,' he said, 'kick off your shoes.' With some relief, she dropped off her flax-flower-blue coloured slippers, with the green fleur-de lys and the little heels, and kicked them from under her skirt.

'Good,' he said, 'now plant your heels back and feel the ground under you.' She scowled, but swayed a little back. He walked towards her, then at the last minute dipped down, and slid a sheet of paper under the toes of her left foot.

'There,' he said, 'you are not standing firmly. Plant both feet down, so there is nothing between the earth and your legs.'

'My Lord, I simply do not under . . .'

'Do as I say,' he shouted, 'and don't be such a horse.' So she did.

'Now, begin.'

She lowered her head to the page and read the first line to herself a few times, then threw back her head and at the top of her voice began to squeak.

'Stop. I said read the speech. Don't learn it, don't pause, don't shout it, just pick it up as if it were a letter from your lover, and read it aloud as if to yourself.'

Mrs Barry paused a little longer than was necessary after this instruction. Her nostrils were wide and her breathing was audible.

Slowly she lowered her head and, again after a pause that was two heartbeats too long, she began to read.

> *'The wanton troopers riding by*
> *Have shot my fawn and it must die . . .'*

She looked up, and said, 'My Lord this is not a *play*.'

'Of course it is not a play. If I had wanted you to read a play I would have given you a play. This is a poem done by a friend of mine, 'and it is a damn sight better than anything our play writers can do at the moment. Come, start again, it was designed not quite to be read aloud, but as a singular voice.'

'The wanton troopers . . .'

'Stop. What are they?'

'Troopers.'

'And have you ever seen troopers?'

'Why yes of course. They were Parliament's cavalry and they frightened me.'

'And so they bloody should, murderous, God-bothering, Levelling, Ranting, zealot rabble the lot of them. My father killed a few. Good, think back to when you saw them, and see them again. In your mind's eye.'

'The wanton . . .'

'Stop. How do you know they are wanton?'

'Because it says so here'

'No. How do *you* know.'

'Because I have seen them. They are raucous and bloody and have no manners and are vicious, and um . . . like as not to shoot you or your beast just for fun.'

'Good, excellent, you begin to get the idea, your colour is rising in your cheeks most pretty and you are indignant. Hold on fast to that indignation that you feel. Again.'

'The wanton troopers riding by . . .' and she began to blush furiously, and then lost her thread and tears sprang to her eyes from perplexity, and then she stamped her foot, forgetting she had no shoes, and banged her heel and yelped with pain, and was embarrassed and then even more angry and gathered up her skirts and stormed off, forgetting that there were no wings and so she could only go as far as to the side of the room. And Wilmot strode fast after her.

'Good, Betty, good my dear, you see what a storm you can provoke in your breast, and see what you have done to me.'

'I am all excited, I know not what I feel.' And indeed she was trembling.

'I know exactly, I know. Here,' and he lifted her skirts, 'I will frig you a little, that will help.' He thrust up his hand and felt her bare thighs and higher, and soon her breath was coming faster and scratchier and she came quite quick, squirming her legs together, and leaned against his shoulder panting.

'There. Is that not better now?'

'Yes, my Lord, much better,' she said, sighing and breathing into his ear. 'My temper runs too high.'

'Not so, not at all, it is just what we want. The emotion was not extravagant. You did feel it from your reading of the lines and so it was not false. What I think you must do, you must frig yourself each time before you step onstage, but be careful not to come. That way you will enter the scene at just the right altitude. You will be on the crest of an emotion and the world will see your blush and imagine what a prize you may have afterwards when your speech is done, and you are alone in the tiring room. Now I find I am a little excited too, so if I may ask of you no less than I have given . . .'

And she sank to her knees, and happily did as she was told. A face like a horse and a wide mouth to match, thought Wilmot, and sighed a greedy little sigh.

'Ah,' he said finally. 'Fair quiet, I have found thee here.'

I must thank that Marvell, he thought, I would bet the man never had such a success from his own poems. And I will get on to Otway too. He must rustle up a Cleopatra or a Eurydice for this girl. She will be good, if only I can fuck some life into her.

'Now, show me your lovely face,' he said, lifting her up and kissing her deeply, the spend running between their lips.

'You taste of salt,' she said.

Strange, he thought, I can taste nothing.

32. The Lord and the Gentleman

Kindness only can persuade;
It gilds the lover's servile chain
And makes the slave grow pleased and vain.

John Wilmot, Lord Rochester. 'Give me Leave to Rail at You'

'Mr Marvell, I must thank you, sir, from the bottom of my heart.'

I stopped in the street and for once was lost for words. I had done this idle rogue no favour recently, nor did I plan to.

'Why, my Lord?' I said, in the spirit of true inquiry.

'I have found a girl who will be a great *actress*, and it was with your help I was training her, sir.'

'You mock me, my Lord,' I said, 'you know I have little taste for the theatre.'

'Mock you? Never,' he said. 'Please believe me that I will mock anything in this world, whether it deserves it or not, but never will I mock your verse. It is fine, sir, very good, I think, and it had an effect upon this actress that you would not credit.'

'From you, my Lord, I would credit anything. I would thank you if I thought you were not teasing.'

'Thank me or not, I do not care either way, sir, but believe, I beg of you, I am as nothing to you in that art.'

'I am unsure of your meaning here, my Lord, but it is kindly said, and I thank you.'

'Truly I meant it. I will say no more at present, but will show you in time the most pleasing tricks that your verses can effect. And now, sir, I am yours to my knee,' and he bowed most low.

'And I am yours, my Lord, to my shoe buckle,' and I too bowed low, though not without a little mockery.

'And I am yours to the toes,' he said bowing again and lower.

'Then I am yours to the earth,' I said bowing again.

'And I am yours to the centre,' he said pointing downwards.

'Then I am yours, my Lord, to the Antipodes.'

Finally, Wilmot drew himself up to his full height, and dropped as low as he could without falling.

'I am yours, sir, to the very ninth circle of Hell.'

'And there, my Lord,' I said, 'I will leave you.'

And I turned and walked away, feeling most pleased with myself and slightly fearful too, for he had a temper on him, that much I knew. After only two steps, I heard his roar of laughter, bellowing, rolling past me like a peal of thunder. 'By God,' he cried, 'I never thought your kind would best me.'

The Green and the Gold

I loved the man for that. He is a drunken lecher and he is all that is wrong with the court. He leads them in their activities of fighting and fucking. But he is no hypocrite and his verses do not lie. Nor does he dissemble, as I do. He has the right vein. Alone of almost all the high Ballers of the court, I cannot hate him. He is my opposite, indeed he is *my* antipodes, and so we are well balanced in our way, he at one point of the compasses, I at mine.

33. Duelling Poets

'Tis not what once it was, the world,
But a rude heap together hurled.

Marvell. 'Upon Appleton House'

I came to know him a little better at The Horn, one of the more louche drinking clubs that had sprung up about town of late. It was mainly writers and politicians that gathered there, with the occasional lawyer, though not if it could be helped. I would not normally enter one of these cradles of sedition. I don't know that many courtiers were to be found in there either, but Rochester was a writer and writers need somewhere to exchange their verses and spread their satires among their own kind. Charles had tried to close the places down, along with the coffee-houses, because too many people were circulating satires about him in them. He was dissuaded, but the King's spies still patrolled the clubs, disguised in plain clothes, listening here and there for mischief.

That is no great problem, however, for you can see them coming. It is not like it was under Oliver's regime. In his day, at least a tenth of the national exchequer went on spying activities; and the lion's share of that was spent, not on surveying foreign activities which might threaten this land with war, but on keeping a sharp eye on the inhabitants of this very land, for fear they might be getting up to such wickedness as voting Oliver out. Or, for fear that, God forbid, people might just be enjoying themselves too much for the Protector's liking. You can always recognize a despot. He fears his own people more than foreigners.

Charles is loved by his people like a father. God knows, he *is* a father to a great number of them.

I too had written a minor satire on the King, something about his revelling, drinking and whoring, which had gone down well with the courtiers, and with Charles himself too, for he sometimes is fond of a jest against himself, when in the right mood, and provided it is only rude about his love of pleasure, for he considers that no defect. He has become the most absolutely powerful monarch since the Conqueror, and so I think he could do with taking down a peg or two. He is a various man though. It is best not to tease him on an off day.

It was one of the courtiers, Lauderdale in fact, who invited me for an evening's drinking and gaming with some of his like-minded men. Lauderdale was part of the kitchen cabinet, which I named the CABAL, so derived from their initial letters. You will remember that I once used the term about my sisters. They were just as tight-knit and twice as vicious as this self-serving bunch of Lords. I can deal with little groups of schemers, thanks to my sisters. Which is about the only thing I do have to thank them for; that and a marked ability to understand women, which has left me with a perpetual mistrust of them.

I think Lauderdale wants to get me on his side for some political reason. Perhaps there will be a vote coming up in the house on some topic of his, such as how to give more tax money to the King. The King only ever wants more tax money for two reasons: either because he wants to purchase a bauble for his latest mistress at public expense, or else there is a war on. Recently in the park I think I saw that de Kerouaille woman, Charles's number one mistress at the moment, showing off an emerald green necklace nestling in her extravagant bosom. She is a mite chubby; he doesn't call her 'Fubbs' for nothing. So, it must be that he is spending more on his women. Yes, it must be that. There can't be a war on at the moment, I would have heard.

Buckingham, the unspeakable shitefire, was also there (the B of my CABAL). He is a revolting man, as I keep saying. He is a great mimic, being able to walk and talk in an exact likeness of anyone at the court; and like all mimics he is not to be trusted. It is as if his character were not fixed, for if he can be so many different people for an audience at the drop of a hat, then what is he when he is alone? I suspect that people like that do not have a very fixed nature. When alone, there is something missing in them, which they can only fill if they have an audience for their mimicry. When they speak as themselves, they often prove to be dull creatures, and if they can be anyone whom they like, for surely they could adopt the manners and sayings of a wit like Rochester quite easily, why then do they choose to be a dull man? They are inconsistent, and like a leaky vessel which you would not in all good sense take out to sea.

His enthusiasms come and go with the waxing of the moon, so that one moment he is all for chemical experiments and the next minute he is trying to learn the fiddle. All of which would be fine and harmless, if that were all, but the man is vicious. He loves making trouble for its own sake. He brought down Clarendon for no better reason than that he could, and he killed Shrewsbury in a duel, which was going too far. No one need be hurt in a duel, a simple shoulder scratch will satisfy honour.

Some say that the charge against him of buggery was trumped up. And many say not.

He is all softness when he woos, but his heart soon hardens and he throws over a woman without the least regard to her feelings. How he ever persuaded Mary Fairfax to take to his marriage bed is beyond me. She was clever as a child, and her father was so good and straight a man. I do not know how fortune could favour so good a girl so badly. He saw in her a way of special pleading to get the return of his estates which Cromwell did sequester. Quite what the internal machinations were, I have not yet inquired. Indeed I am not sure I even wish to know. It makes the blood rise in my neck and my forehead blister just to think of them being together . . . and imagining them enjoying the marriage bed . . . I will die sooner than even think of it. If I ever see them walking as a pair, I turn away and take a different route. I cannot bear it. It is the only thing that drives me close to weeping.

There were even some ladies present at this evening rout too, which did surprise me. They were playing at cards in the corner, and Rochester told me they were mainly actresses. This I can believe. I do not approve of cards.

I do not much approve of actresses either come to that. The theatres have long been places that attract debauchery and crime. I do not necessarily think that a bad thing. The populace must be amused somewhere, and it's best perhaps to contain it all in some small place, known to the authorities, but this is the first time in this country in which women have taken to the stage, and they are women of the worst kind. Moreover they seek to make a fortune for themselves, which is a troubling inversion of the natural order of things. My friend Aphra Behn was thrown into writing by circumstance, and the need to line her stomach. That is fair enough. But the huge fortunes which some ambitious whore can make by acting far outweigh her social worth.

What is worse are their natures. People of the theatre, actors, managers, play writers and so on, they are all intolerable. That is why they can only live among their own kind.

No one else could stomach them. Actresses are the worst of the lot. Have you ever met one? Then you will know what I mean. I could list their many failings, all *their little ways*, but their mere presence makes you want to run outside and shit through your teeth.

At the far end of the table several of them were clustered around a candle, playing picquet and laughing gaily. They were being advised by a small company of men, watching over their shoulders, and I could make out Rochester among them. He soon tired of their company though and joined us with a despairing shrug; a shrug which said that one had to be gallant of course and bow to their demands, but dear God it could get tedious, give me the company of a drinking man for the evening.

He slouched over to a stool, sat down, gripped the bottle by the neck and slugged himself three good cupfuls, which he threw down his throat without pausing, refilled his cup again and passed on the bottle to me. I filled and duly passed it on round. The conversation had moved on to the topic of Mr Dryden, the poet and play writer, whom I judge to be not yet in his stride, despite being very popular. Rochester loathes him for his toadying. Dryden has even tried arse-creeping up to Rochester himself, but he can spot that sort of thing a mile off, and hates it. Whatever else people say about Wilmot, he is no snob. He is not a respecter of persons either, but then he thinks himself the very worst of all, and I think that puts him in the strongest position to satirize.

Dryden tries to keep in with whomsoever is in power, even to the extent of changing his religion to suit the times, and that is not the sort of thing to impress the atheist Rochester. I have some sympathy for that kind of behaviour however, for my father was a clergyman, and I know how hard it used to be for men of the cloth to find a living. They would often have to trim their beliefs to suit a patron. Besides, I am not above a little careful tailoring myself. I had once told Rochester that I liked to sit long on a problem and think hard about it.

'And on the fence too,' he had replied. 'Trouble is, Andrew, if you sit your arse too long on a fence post, you will split up the middle.'

Still, the subject of this night was poetry, a topic which every person present had an opinion on, no matter that Rochester and I were the only poets in the room. Oh, they had all written poetry, and had scribbled love sonnets in their youth of course, the way that young Lords do, but Wilmot and I know of our worth in that respect, and knew of theirs too. He was openly scornful of their opinions; I, quietly indulgent.

Then, for some ill reason, we sank to discussing our own efforts. This was a mistake, and one from which I came off worst, and I suffered much jibing later, even though I do not hold it against the man. Writers should never talk of their own works.

Love came up.

'*Love* poetry?' said Rochester, his mouth becoming mushy about the corners. 'God almighty, I can do you love poetry all right. I can do you love poetry by the yard. It's cheap and it's easy, sir. Everyone has known the state of love, and the weak half of mankind lives for nothing else. But a man in love? He is simply labouring under the delusion that one woman differs from another.

'Which one would you like to hear? "The Constant Lover", sir, or "The Ancient Person of my Heart", or "The Nymph Complaining"? Not that I have written any of them yet, but I can rustle them up here and now, just give me half an hour, they are so easy. *Love poetry*? God almighty, it's like pissing; you live, you love, you drink, you write it, it all comes pouring out whether you want it to or not. I'll lay you ten pounds here and now, sir, I can finish a love poem quicker than you, and then write a satire on your finished poem within the same time.'

'Poets do not compete, my Lord,' I said, in that prissy tone of voice that I always regret, but can't quite throttle before it comes sliding through my clenched teeth.

'No, indeed they do not, sir, and the reason for that is nothing very high-flown. It is simply because they make no money at it. But they will. In the future they will make money. Patrons will pay for it, the same as they pay for pictures, and the moment a man can make his living with his pen then he will begin fighting to the death with his fellow scribblers exactly ten seconds later, and it will be solely to see who is the greatest writer of them all. Nothing else.'

'Horses will often race against each other without a mount just for the joy of competing,' said Mulgrave, whom I had not noticed, for he was standing back in the dark. Best place for him, the bone-head. Rochester hates him.

'True, sir, but the winning horse doesn't expect the loser to give him his oats afterwards.'

There was a telling pause, while Mulgrave desperately tried to think his way through to the meaning of this rejoinder, then gave up and settled back with a driveller's grin on his drunken face. I think he must be Scottish.

'Do you wish to make some money from your writing, sir?' I asked Rochester.

'I wouldn't be averse to it. God knows I could do with some. I've got various positions at court, but the King is not very rich and he pays late.'

'Then you should try the stage. I believe there are fortunes to made there. Look at Dryden,' I said.

He snorted at the mention of the name, and jumped in before I could tell him about the huge amount of money his play *The Indian Emperor* had made. 'Look at *Dryden*? That puling moron? I'd sooner my balls fell off from the pox,' and so saying he gripped his crotch with his left hand and hefted them a little, and continued, 'Mind you, I think they will soon, if this mercury treatment doesn't take hold.'

'It is a reasonable ambition, my Lord,' I continued,

rerouting the subject back to something more seemly. 'All you need to write a play is your reason. It is an art of logic. You do not need imagination or fancy, all you need for a good play are cause and effect. You may exercise your great capacity for reasoning, and you will emerge with a very reasonable play.'

'Do not talk to me about reason, sir, reason is a dark and useless thing, a dead end, an *ignis fatuus* of the mind. Anyway, play writers have been making fortunes out of portraying me on the stage already.'

'Indeed, I have heard it. Every heartless rake that appears in any play in town, it is always said that he is based upon you.'

'Yes, it is very tiresome. If I had done one tenth of all they suggest I would be very much more wealthy, and very much more dead. I would have worn myself out to an early grave long ago.'

'You are doing your best in that line sir,' I said, pushing the second bottle across the table towards Rochester's greedy hand. 'You are a hero in *that* line.'

'One needs more and more of this stuff to get oneself up to the right speed,' said Rochester. 'I feel nothing bites nowadays until I am two-thirds of the way down the second bottle.

'Ah, the second bottle. It is my sincerest, wisest and most impartial friend. It tells me the truth of myself and forces me to tell the truth of others. It banishes flattery from the tongue and distrust from the heart. It sets us above the policy of Court prudence, which makes us all lie to each other all day for fear of being betrayed by each other at night. Before God, the worst villain breathing is honest as long as that second bottle lives.

'But it becomes hard to keep the right buzz on all day long, and I am tiring with age too. Still, I do my best. There are standards to be kept up. I haven't fallen down drunk for some days now. To you, sir, to you.' He emptied down his glass, and not remotely exhausted by his extraordinary performance, continued:

'The stage, hmm, the stage. It is such a solemn toy, but I might well follow your advice sir. Something to do with the stage for me, I think. In the meantime, I feel the effects of the drink coming on, at last. Let me repeat the wager, sir, but let's do it quickly, before I fall face-down in my food. I know, I've got it, just recite me one of your earlier efforts, something touching on love, sir.'

'I cannot, sir. It would be boastful. You make me blush.'

'Yes, yes, of course it's boastful, and you are known for your modesty, sir, but then again, I don't actually see you blushing do I? All right, I'll do it for you. I will recite one of your verses, so we don't even have to write it down, because it's in here.'

So saying, Rochester tapped the side of his head, tapped his nose at the assembled company, and then began to recite my 'Picture of Little T.C. in a Prospect of Flowers'.

I have to say that I was so overcome with pleasure that the man had not only read my piece, but committed it to memory, that I hardly knew where to put myself with pride, and only managed to keep a straight face and unreadable demeanour by not listening to him recite my poem, but letting my thoughts wander elsewhere.

Nevertheless, he did recite it, and very exactly too, and he did not even play down the emotion, but got it just exactly so, so that the audience of men were very moved by the end. I will repeat you a part of it here, for those of you who have not yet read it:

> *See with what simplicity*
> *This nymph begins her golden days!*
> *In the green grass she loves to lie,*
> *And there with her fair aspect tames*
> *The wilder flowers, and gives them names . . .*

It goes on, in the same vein, I will not bore you with more, but it is a hymn to innocence, and what I elsewhere call 'green love, not lust'. It was of course inspired by Little Moll, when she was the twelve-year-old that I first met in the gardens of Appleton, and whom I did love with all my heart, though it took me a while to know it.

I have written it out, or at least the events surrounding our long love's day, and you will have drawn your own conclusions about the episode. I never speak of it to anyone, not even to her, though she is a woman now, and must have come to realize something of my feelings for her then. I wonder what she makes of it all now. Nothing, probably. Most children are carefree creatures, thank God, and hold things lightly. (Not me, I know. I was an exception.)

Does she ever think back on old memories like that, I wonder? Do I ever cross her mind? I hope so. For I am slowly reaching that age where I am acquiring a store of memories, and I think pretty soon, my memories will be more entertaining to me than anything more which can happen to me. Not yet though, not yet, I am not yet quite that far gone.

The company was moved to applause, which made me come around from my reveries on young Moll with a start, and I believe I did blush, and privately vowed never to let anyone read one of my poems ever again, and certainly not repeat it in my presence. I felt as though someone had just read my mind, and dug deep down into it and lugged out its gravest secret. I do not want that. I am not even sure what the secrets are exactly, nothing very terrible I am sure, but my point is that I do not want anyone looking at them. They're mine. I am sure the company thought I was blushing over my poem. Let them think so. No one will ever know that I blush over Moll.

When he had finished, he smiled and bowed most courteously, if a little too extravagantly for this occasion, and drew from his sleeve a sheet of paper on which he had already made a few marks, and even a few deletions. So it looked like it was a work in progress. He called for a pen and someone brought him one from behind the counter, and ink too. With a flourish he pulled back his cuff, and set to writing and did not stop till he was finished. It took him about five minutes, during which time his friends continued drinking and talking, but not with much animation for they were keeping a swivel-eye on him, and even leaning over his arm to catch an early glimpse as the poem took shape.

I noticed that his tongue protruded very slightly between his lips as he wrote, but otherwise his face was unmarked. Some people knit their brows and others chew the end of their pen, some rip up the paper, others screw it into a ball and aim it across the room. Some pace. But not he. It just came pouring out, and I have to say I was impressed by the man's concentration. Right here in the drinking club, surrounded by his raucous crew of merry courtiers, he could dash off a verse without pause.

I wonder if I do that thing with my tongue? It is no good checking in a glass next time I write of course, for now I will be too self-conscious about it, and if I did catch myself doing it, would never do it again.

Ye gods, but the rubbish which writers trouble their minds with! Could anything be less important?

Finally, he skewered the pen down on to the page with a full stop, splattering ink all over the bottom of the sheet, exclaimed a hissing little 'Yesss', waved the paper in the air to dry it, gave it to me, and began reciting even as I read it. He went:

> *By all love's soft, yet mighty powers,*
> *It is a thing unfit*
> *That men should fuck in time of flowers*
> *Or when the smock's beshit.*
>
> *Fair nasty nymph, be clean and kind,*
> *And all my joys restore;*
> *By using paper still behind*
> *And sponges for before.*

I nodded. It was good, I have to admit, and funny too, and a very good satire on mine. He has the right vein, I think.

'But like me sir you could not resist the pastoral touch. It is clear that you know your Virgil, sir, and your Longus. You refer to flowers,' I said. 'There I have you, sir. For all your smut, you are just as fond of nature as I.' As I spoke this, the whole company burst into horrible laughter. I smiled as best I could, but Rochester took me aside as the others fell to slapping each other on the back and choking up their food.

'Do not concern yourself with them Mr Marvell, they may be the King's men, but their humour is coarse.'

And so is yours, I thought to myself, but said nothing for he was being kind to me, and being kind in a way which I have rarely seen in his behaviour towards others.

' "*Flowers*", sir,' he said, 'it is a euphemistic way of speaking.'

'Oh and what would that be, something sexual no doubt, eh?'

'Well, yes and no.' He looked at me strangely, as if he could not quite believe that I did not understand. 'It means a woman's menses.'

I looked at him blankly.

'Her monthly flow, sir, her flux, her bloody discharge, her . . . Jesus Christ, don't tell me . . . but surely . . . I mean . . . all right, I know you are unmarried, but . . . I . . . hmm. I am so sorry, sir, I did not realize. But surely, I believe you told me you had sisters, did you not?'

'I did, but they were distant from me, sir, much older than me and, well, they taught me nothing.'

'I see, I see. Well, I will enlighten you later. Umm, well . . .'

The strange thing was that I realized that he could make great jest with this story once I had gone. Indeed he could probably dine out on it for weeks, singing for his supper with the story of how poor old Andrew Marvell knew nothing of a woman's cycle. I knew this almost instantly. I also knew within the same second that he would not, and I knew then why I liked him. Oh, I know everything that is said against him.

The court then was at its highest pitch of wanton luxury, and the behaviour of its denizens was corrupt and scandalous. I have seen the most appalling actions on his part too, even murder as I will later tell you, but he has at base a kind heart. Strangely, you can tell that from his poems, no matter that so many of them are obscene. There is a human decency shines through them, in even the most indecent parts.

I cannot say why or how I know that. It is something that strikes you immediately when you read them or you hear them, and I don't know how he achieves that effect. I could find out, if I studied them carefully I suppose, as I study my Latin poets, and my Bible, but I will leave that to bookworms, who pore over a new poem, and tease it apart line by line, until it is stone cold dead on the page, like doctors looking for signs of life by dissecting the body.

That is why I enjoy hearing my poems set to music. Nobody does that so very much any more, but it is a sure sign of whether one has caught something right, dead on, in the poem. Will Lawes did me proud with his musical version of my 'Dialogue between Thyrsis and Dorinda'. He proved to me that I had written it truly.

The only poet whom I admire who defeats any attempts to set his verses to music is Donne. Composers have tried, but his metre is so warped, and the stresses in his lines so irregular, that it cannot be done. That is partly why I like Donne. His great distortion can bring about great effects. In the main, however, I prefer the poets of a plainer sort. Regular metre, regular rime, gentle music, there is nothing sweeter.

So we had a strange duel, Rochester and I, and he won hands down, no question. I did not mind at all. Indeed I liked the man all the more for it, which is strange, for I have witnessed real duels which end in a gash to the shoulder, and leave the wounded man with an undying hatred of his opponent. I wonder whether that might be because the original offence is still festering, and has not been settled by a death.

Now that I think about it, I have seen men who were completely unknown to each other fall to fighting with their fists because of some argument, and after a few blows were struck, they then became the best of friends. I used to think that sudden violence was one way in which to get to know a man thoroughly, and perhaps come to like what you saw, but besides that, there was no original cause for the fight, and so nothing left to fester on afterwards.

I am certainly right about men doing sudden violence to each other. Watch a man when he fights and you will get the full measure of the man quickly. A cool head and a single judicious blow will always defeat a hot head who is wind-milling his arms and throwing his weight around.

Aphra Behn once said to me: 'Get a man into bed, and you will know all there is to know about him.' I asked her to elaborate, and she went on a little about how rough or gentle a man might be, or how considerate or how brutish. I muttered something about how I imagined women liked the gentler kind of man, the sort that other men might consider a fop. Her eye twinkled and she said nothing, but rocked her head side to side on her shoulders. It was one of those women's silent gestures which said: 'Maybe, maybe not. Sometimes, one likes a bit of a rough man.'

No doubt, no doubt. Another good reason not to slope into bed with just any woman who crosses your path. Women are incapable of keeping silent on any score, and before you know it, your character is talked about all over town. Actresses!

Still, Rochester likes them, as I later discovered when I passed the theatre. I had left him face down upon the table, snoring heavily. He was down to his third or fourth bottle; by God what an appetite, I don't know how he does it. The next time that I saw him, outside the theatre, he was looking distinctly the worse for wear. His eyes were heavily pouched and his hands were trembling as if he were senile. He had been so very handsome once that people often mistook him for a beautiful girl, but now his face was sagging with dissipation. And he was still far from thirty years old.

He cannot last much longer, most especially if he is still attending Fourcard's *bagnio* in Leather Lane for the pox. Ah, that disease of the Turks, rub-a-dub-dub. The mercury treatment does dreadful things to a man. He drools. The teeth blacken and fall out leaving no stumps. The hair falls out too, which is fine in this age of wigs, but does leave a man looking a mite peculiar when he lowers his trousers. There is a wig maker down my way in Clerkenwell does a roaring trade in pubic wigs for this very occasion. His merkins are kept in place by a glue of medicinal gum arabic. It must be most uncomfortable, brushing on a thick paste in the morning, sticking a dead cat's pelt to it, then waiting for it to dry. I wonder if their owners lay them on a wig-block at night to regain their shape. I wonder if they come in different shapes. I wonder if women need them.

Still, it would explain why Rochester was always scratching himself about the privities.

The next time I ran into him at The Horn, he was still up to his old tricks, whoring, and jesting about it, and getting one up on me. I am indulgent of it, and indeed I do not mind at all, he can be so pleasing a man. It is like having a puppy round the house. They are so amusing, that you forgive them when they piss on the best rug. Which they do, they do.

He came up with a lovely line from one of his poems, which went:

On this soft anvil all mankind was made.

I am sure he had been working on that for some time. 'Soft anvil', I love that phrase; it must be the best euphemism for cunt anyone ever thought up. He got drunk that night and he stayed drunk ten years.

34. Reason and Error

Reason, an ignis fatuns *of the mind,*
Which leaving the light of nature, sense behind.

John Wilmot, Lord Rochester.
'A Satire against Reason and Mankind'

A little while later we met again, in the same place, for we had decided to collaborate on a satire: he for the pleasure of it, for he had a natural talent for moral attack; me for the learning of it, for I had not strayed much into satiric territory before. Since these scurrilous sheets were all the rage about town, circulating among the wits in the coffee-houses, I thought I had better try my hand at it. The lyrical vein has deserted me since the return of the King, I am not sure why.

He spends all his days
In running to plays
When in his shop he should be poring;
And wastes all his nights
In his constant delights
Of revelling, drinking and whoring

was my contribution, on the character of the King. Rochester's was, I must admit, much better:

> *Chaste, pious prudent Charles the Second,*
> *The miracle of thy restoration*
> *May like to that of quails be reckoned*
> *Rained on the Israelite nation:*
> *The wished for blessing from heaven sent*
> *Became their curse and punishment*

– better, because more allusive, and it had some backbone in
it, thanks to the mock-learned use of the Old Testament.
Never mind that Rochester is an atheist, he knows his Bible
as well as I.

Then we put our heads together, bouncing lines off each
other and topping the other's scandalous rhymes, and we
came up with:

> *Restless he rolls about from whore to whore,*
> *A merry monarch, scandalous and poor*

– a good satire which we finished off with the strong hint
that Charles was impotent, a rumour which we got from
Ellen Gwynn. Nell had often been in his bed by this time,
and was later to have his bastard, though this was a period in
between, when Charles was enjoying the favours of another
mistress: I forget which one there are so many. They all look

the same, with their big round eyes and their milk-white bosoms.

Nell was a mite put out. Not that she had lost her sense of humour, she is irrepressible in that respect and I can see why she is as popular with the crowd at the theatre as she is with Charles. Her greatest success at that time was in Dryden's *Secret Love*, in which she took the part of Florimell, and played in a most gay fashion opposite her off-stage lover Mr Christopher Hart, in the role of Celadon. Their scenes together were so life-like, and so erotically charged, that they were imitated later by Congreve when he gave Mirabell and Millamant much the same sparky banter in *The Way of the World*.

She is a born smiler and, from the very first time that you meet her and she smiles upon you, you become very fond. She is tiny, with the most delicate hands and feet I ever saw. She has a turned up nose, a full nether lip, and her cheeks are rosy and a little blub. There are two dimples when she smiles. The French would call her *mignonne*.

Rochester loved her very much, and was often to be seen egging her on at card games and such. He always saw to it that she could pay the debt of whatever she had lost in an evening's gambling. She told him of the King's failures in bed just to get back at His Majesty for forsaking her for another. She is transparent and cannot lie at all, so we saw it for the shameless fib that it was, and Rochester knew this perfectly well, but could not resist using it anyway. We took to writing the lines turn and turn about, and he was delighted when I used 'enjoys' to rhyme with his 'thighs'. He called it a weak and feminine rhyme, to which I replied that that was most appropriate to both his line, for the thighs are feminine, and to my line, for the King is quite unmanned:

> *This you'd believe, had I but time to tell ye,*
> *The pain it costs to poor laborious Nelly,*
> *While she employs hands, fingers, lips and thighs*
> *E'er she can raise the member she enjoys.*

'You're getting the knack of this stuff a little too quick for my liking,' said Rochester. 'I'll be out of a job.'

'Or in the Tower,' I said.

'Yes, well, it is better that it is me in that place than you. I am well acquainted with one of the gaolers there. He puts me up in one of the well-appointed rooms – believe me you do not want to be thrown in with the poor – and he lets me have a key, knowing that I will be out within a day or two.'

Charles did indeed clap him in the Tower for that one, but only to see how he would charm his way out again, as he always did. It amused the King to see the variety that Rochester employed each time. Rochester stayed only an hour or two in his well-appointed room, then sent to the King the following:

The Green and the Gold

Nor are his high desires above his strength:
His sceptre and his prick are of a length.

It was a risk, but the King was in a good frame of mind that day and so was mollified and Rochester was promptly unlocked. Besides, the King does not like to cause great offence to anyone, but prefers to let sinners well alone. As he often says: 'The more you stir a turd, the more it stinks.'

Rochester went on to use the lines in a bigger poem later. 'Nothing is ever wasted,' he would tell me. 'Extemporize something at the court to amuse the Royal ear, and you will get away with murder for a day or two, but always take the trouble to note down your little squib, for you can later put it to good use in a written work, and none will be the wiser. No one remembers what was spoken very exactly, being drunk, and anyway they will all soon be dead.'

'Well, so will you and I,' I said, 'and then it won't matter.'

He affected to look shocked.

'*I* might well have said that, sir,' he replied, 'being an atheist and Hobbeist, and therefore realizing that there is nothing beyond the grave, but you, sir, *you* are a believer, though please do not at present enlighten me as to exactly what kind of believer. I could not bear it. You, sir, are a believer, and therefore must think of your afterlife. You will look down on us all from your cloud and it will please you to see that your poems are still read and prized.'

'It is not good to mock a man's religion,' I said, as gently as I could.

'I know that, I know, for look at all the trouble it has caused. They cut off the head of the King's father for religious reasons, and not what Cromwell claimed at all. And I do not, sir, believe me, I do not mock you on that score. I beg you believe me. But be frank. Are you to tell me that you have never, ever, had the slightest hope that posterity will treat your poems kindly.'

'It is true, sir, I do,' I said in a small voice, with my head bowed slightly. Never would I have confessed such a thing to anyone, but Rochester has that cursed knack of getting the truth out of me. He is so open and free with his speech, and so fair of face and demeanour. He is like a boy, and he seems completely innocent, and yet one only has to know the merest thing about him to know that he is wholly the devil. I think that John Milton must have had him in mind when he made his devil so damned attractive. Not that Milton and Rochester have ever met. At least I assume not, not yet, though I must say: *There would be a thing.* Put those two together and by God there'd be a larruping good time.

'Well, there is a thing,' said Rochester. 'So good a man as Mr Marvell, all clad in seemly grey and well behaved, and the son of a clergyman too. Yet he is vain as a peacock.'

Blood, I would have struck another man for that, if he had spoken it in company, and humiliated me, but we were alone, and Rochester said it with such a sweet air of genuine interest in me, that it purged the insult of all offence. He fascinates me.

'Is it vanity, my lord, is it truly? I think not. A man may justly hope that his virtues might be applauded; surely that is not vain.'

'Mr Marvell, I will speak frankly to you, because I know it will not make me your enemy. To others I might dissemble or give a white lie to spare their feelings. To yet others, I would curse them and damn them to hell for a time-waster. But you, you sir are worth more than most, because I can tell that you like me, which is pleasing – but what is even more pleasing is that you do not lick my arse.

'Yes, it is vanity, for everything here on earth is vanity. What you call bravery, I call fear of being branded a coward. No, do not interrupt me, I have been under fire, as you well know. I know what men call brave, and I demonstrated it myself. The King gave me a medal for it, I think. I know that all men would be cowards if only they dared. What you call public service, I call a taste for power over others, and a desire to line your own pockets. What you call love, I call a damned itch. What you call marriage, I call the end of all pleasure. What you call a man's gratitude, I call a whore's worthless promise. What you call age and wisdom, I call the final understanding of having been wrong all one's life. What you call death and heaven, I call eternal night. What you call reason, I call error. Reason makes a mite think he is the infinite.

Birds feed on beasts, beasts on each other prey
But savage man alone does man betray.

'Man undoes man, to do himself no good, and he does it with smiles, embraces, friendship, praise. And a man's love of truth is no defence for his reputation, for all the rest of the knaves will continue in their knavery and insult and oppress you. You will be wronged if you dare be less a villain than all the rest. Men are dishonest, and he who aspires to a lesser corruption will be cut down.

'Find me one honest man at the court, who raises his country up and makes it prosper as much as he enriches himself and his family, and I will recant. I will concur. But you will not find one. So allow me this at least: man differs more from man, than man from beast.'

'You take the cynic's line, sir, to put it at its best,' I said.

'Cynic? No I do not think so. I know good when I see it. It is just that I never see it in this busy life of men, and believe me, sir, I have seen it all.'

'Then why do you continue in this life, sir? Surely suicide would be the only cure for a man of such beliefs as yours.'

'Self-murder? Well, it has its attractions, but not to me. I have known poor wretches, driven to such extremity that they have done themselves in, and believe me, never would I damn a man for doing so. However, I do think it wrong – not for religious reasons, but because it loosens the bonds by which the rest of us hold on to life, and God knows many are weak enough to take a suicide as an example and follow suit. Not me. I think I do not have it in me, that streak which makes a man do himself in. I just could not do it. Besides the world amuses me still.'

'Is that all, sir, that you wish from the world? Amusement. It is not much, is it?'

'Not much, agreed, but all I have left.'

I drew a deep breath and looked around me. Men were sprawling about the place snoring, with their heads on the table or in some woman's lap. I noticed that there was a mess of empty plates before us, used but scraped clean of all food. 'Have we eaten?' I said.

'Oh yes,' said Rochester, 'the girls have brought us three different dishes, and you did not even notice what you ate.'

'I did not notice that I had eaten at all,' I said.

'Good conversation will do that,' said Rochester, and called for a third bottle. 'You have drunk nothing yet, sir, and you must be thirsty after that food. I am certainly thirsty after that speech. Here, drink with me.'

'It was a good speech, but no thank you,' I said and went to the door.

'Mr Marvell,' Rochester called after me, 'unclench a little. Smile. Unbutton. Above all, treat yourself a little more kindly.'

35. Newmarket Stakes

Royalty is a government in which the attention of the
people is concentrated on one person doing interesting actions.

Walter Bagehot. *The English Constitution*

The court used to go to Newmarket, because the King liked
to go to Newmarket and what the King likes, the court had
better like too. He had bought a stable there some years back
and restored it all at ruinous expense, which I do not think
was ever paid anyway, and there he kept horses which were
fed each day on new-laid eggs and Spanish wine. He also
kept four jockeys, though they ate less well. Why he needed
an *équipe* of jockeys I do not know, for he loved nothing
better than to take part in the racing himself. Nor did he
expect his rivals, nor even his sons, to hold back, but enjoyed
a good hard thrash around the course. He would often ride
alongside the race on his own horse, not to compete, but just
to track the race in parallel. He is a sporting King.

The evenings at Newmarket were a treat. One night, we
watched my Lord Digby walk five miles in one hour across

the heath, naked as the day he was born, and barefoot too. He did it for a bet, and damned if he didn't win it. He walked around, still in his skin, collecting his cash from the laughing Lords, then realized he had no pocket to put it in. Rochester made a lewd suggestion, which Digby promptly followed, and finally wandered off in search of his lodgings, walking somewhat bow-legged. The townsfolk tutted and rolled their eyes, as if they were used to this sort of thing by now, ever since the King started coming here. Digby's feet were badly scratched and quite bloody, though he never complained. He had bottom all right.

The next day Charles rode a race against his own son, Monmouth, and beat him. There must be a good twenty-five years difference in their ages, but the boy did not resent it, for he does love his father. As is right and proper of course, but many boys would feel put out at being bested by their father, and fathers are notoriously keen to hold on to their powers. They think that giving in to their sons would be a weakness. Not Charles though. He is canny enough to acknowledge his son is already a man, and therefore he must be treated on equal terms, and not patronized. Besides, the son won a race later, and Charles did not throw it for him.

They are on happy, easy terms, and I must say I envy them for it. I never had such a pleasant thing with my father, and I am not sure why. I think it was my sisters who came between my father and I, and stole away all his affection. But then again, it may be something in me. I do not warm to men, I know it. That pranking with Digby, well, it was great fun, and there was no harm in it, and everyone had a good laugh, and won or lost a little money, and you could say that it was altogether a harmless pleasure – and God knows that there are few enough pleasures in life which are altogether harmless – yet I could not take part. I was happy to watch, happy even to enjoy it a little, and share in the common laughter, but never could I take part in a thing like that. I am forever on the outside of a group merriment, watching, choosing which side to come down on, wondering whether I approve or not. What makes it all worse is that I know it. It would be so much easier if I was one of those purse-mouthed Puritans, who have no idea of what a pain in the fundament they are. I am cursed by knowing exactly how I am, and how unpleasant I must appear to others, especially those who are enjoying themselves and don't want unpleasant Mr Marvell watching them like an umpire. But there it is.

Rochester is all I would like to be in that respect. He follows his instinct and never thinks twice about a course of action, yet just follows it through, and I have to say he does it all with great *sprezzatura*. It goes wrong for him badly sometimes, and he even ends up in the Tower for some of his grosser jests, but he always gets out again, usually by sending the King some witty letter. Me, I'd just spend weeks there sulking about my lot.

Rochester and Nelly got together one night in a corner, and it was delightful to see them talking and laughing. I think they love each other, they are so tender, and have that good understanding that comes between people with a *tendresse* for each other. She is a wonderful woman, and full of life. I do not think even that they have shared a bed. Charles, who has not bedded her in a while now, has noticed their rapport, but he is not a jealous man. Or if he is, he is careful to hide it. As far as he and Rochester are concerned, a pang of jealousy is classed under the heading 'Conduct unbecoming a gentleman'.

Rochester waved me over with an insistent beckoning of the hand. I was reluctant to interrupt their long love's day, but he was insistent, and in fact they were not canoodling, but plotting, albeit another jape. Nelly has got a very rude laugh on her. When she laughs it is like hearing two sailors coming round the corner and finding a whorehouse which is putting it out for free. It is a welcoming laugh. It makes you smile and want to take part.

Their plot was to get one up on the King, because he had not given Nelly a good seeing to for quite a while. 'It's not fair on a girl,' said our Nell. 'Believe me, when you get a seeing to from Charles, it will last you for weeks. He is a King in all departments, and I mean size as well as power. If he lives as long as he fucks, believe me we are in for a full century monarch. He will outlast us all, and our children. Go with him, and you won't look back. He used to leave me bandy-legged from one month to the next, but now he is all over that Kerouaille woman, the Catholic whore, and here's poor Nell with the itch and no one to scratch it.'

Rochester looked at me, and I looked at Rochester, and we said to each other, as one, 'What are you looking at me for?'

And we all three burst in laughter, such as I haven't for a long time now. 'Well,' said Rochester to me, 'listen up, for here is our plan . . .'

'They are, Majesty, the finest whores in the kingdom,' said Rochester to his King. 'I do not know what they are doing wasting their time out here in the country, for they are clearly born and bred for better things. They could open a knocking shop down by your palace and earn a solid fortune to retire on after a couple of years. Instead, here they sit like silly maids milking the cows each day and watching the horses race by, all great fun no doubt, but somewhat rustic in my opinion. At any rate they need a good seeing to from some capital men, and it seems to me we are just the men to do it.'

'Mmm, ah, quite so, Rochester, mmm, very attractive, very appealing but, mmm, the royal self and all that. I mean, will I be known? Now down in town I don't think it matters too much either way. Of course I get my treats where I can, but they are mostly women of fashion who move in my own circle. Which is why I have been swerving away from pretty Nell just lately. Lovely girl, lovely girl, and I love her dearly, but you know there have been mutterings about her round the court. You know the sort of thing: no better than she ought to be, given too much money from the public purse just because she got a bastard from me, and so on. Couldn't give a fart about it all of course. Best left alone in my opinion, but after a while it starts to bite a bit, you know. Upsets the wife too, and I won't have that. She has a tender heart which is easily bruised. I have to protect her all I can . . .'

Rochester was the only man in the kingdom who could interrupt His Majesty and get away with it. He could always judge when to do it to the nearest second. Indeed I do not think it was a rational judgement at all on his part, just something that came so naturally to him that none would ever gauge it to be *lèse majesté*.

'Beards,' said Rochester, and a look of ineffable happiness spread over Charles's dark features.

We all stepped out that evening in our country clothes, wearing thick beavers, which Rochester had procured from somewhere and tied behind our ears with wool. They were horribly smelly and itched like the devil, and so I did not inquire about their provenance. Charles stalked along at his usual fast clip, striding about the place like a man who owns the kingdom, looking exactly like a King in a false beard, but very happy.

When we arrived at the house on the outskirts of town, the bawd welcomed us in as if we were simply another set of travellers or drinkers out for an evening's sport. What

Charles did not know was that Rochester had already called there and primed her, not as to who her clients were, but how to play a game upon us.

We sat in the parlour a while, enjoying a drink of hot wine, for the evening was chilly, and the company was good. The three or four girls were not quite as cracking as Rochester had played them up to be – indeed they all but had straw coming out of their ears – but they were plump and happy and willing and that is the way that Charles likes them. In fact, so long as they are willing, I do not think he minds about any other thing they possess. He might draw the line at an octogenarian hag. But then again he might not.

So we sat there, enjoying that pleasant pre-prandial sort of tension which rises in a man when he knows he is about to get some adventure. It was most pleasant, with old Mrs Wood, the bawd, telling us tales of what the folk down here get up to of an evening. My, they seem to be at it morning noon and night in the country. It seems to be all they do. No doubt it comes of having no theatre to go to of an evening for entertainment. No levees, no balls, no parties, no walking out: dear God it would bore the trousers down to half mast of any man, bar Cromwell of course, which goes without saying.

On she prattled about orgies in the hayricks and other tales of immense rudeness, and the girls carried on looking sweet and giggling much and plying us with drink, no doubt in the vain hope of increasing our desires, but reducing our performance, so that the sooner we would be finished and be on our way. By God, they didn't know Charles on that score. The man can sink ten bumpers, and still roger the arse off a score of strumpets, before cantering off to another race meet. He is six foot six of spinning energy. That is what it is to be a King.

'Oh ha,' he goes. 'God's blood, but that's a good one. Thirteen in one go eh? Did you hear that Wilmot? She took on thirteen one after t'other, in the barn out back and then called for more, so they went around one more time for seconds. Then she had the whole evening to look forward to in here as well. By God, what a game lass. Is she hereabouts by any chance? Would love to see her. Girl with a good country appetite, eh, eh? Nothing like a greedy girl. Give me a woman who likes her food every time, and you know you're on to a winner, eh?'

Mother Wood indicated with a wave of her hand one of the young lovelies sitting in the corner by the fire, who had the good sense to blush most prettily.

'You? But you are such a slight little thing, barely more than a girl, goodness what an appetite, still growing eh? How did you fit them all in?' crows Charles, and goes to sit next to her, beside the fire, and starts stroking her arms and hair in a cooing sort of way, which the girl does not object to at all. Indeed, she evidently takes a liking to him, for she reaches over and takes his beard off him, and damn me if he hardly notices that his disguise has been rumbled, and she plants a kiss straight on his mouth and I can see it's a corker, for his toes are curling up inside his boots, and he is getting quite red-faced about it all. So am I come to that, for I too have suddenly got a girl from somewhere, leaning against my upper arm and whispering wicked thoughts into my right ear, almost before I notice it happening.

Then I caught sight of Rochester who was giving me a look to remind me of our little game, and so I pushed the girl away a bit, firmly but not too unfriendly, and told her that I must talk with my friend yonder. So saying I sat before Rochester and pretended to have an earnest conversation.

'The King will go with her in a minute,' he said, 'and then our little plan will be under way. What do you want to do while it is unfurling? That girl who was licking your ear seems very accommodating. Perhaps a little of what you fancy, Mr Marvell?'

I find there is only one way that I can respond to this sort of suggestion and that is to deny it fiercely. If only he hadn't brought it up, I would happily have gone with the girl for the evening, but I just cannot bear anyone knowing my business, especially on so personal a matter.

'No, no,' I said, 'I will wait here in the parlour. I have no mood for love this evening and besides I think that someone ought to oversee our prank in some way, should it go awry. But don't let me detain you, or put you off, my Lord,' I said, out of politeness to his feeling.

'Mr Marvell, when my rod is up, nothing will detain me,

or put me off. That is my tragedy,' said Rochester, his face hanging slightly with the sadness that he spoke of. 'Well, there is nothing for it but to get it done, I suppose, but I will be quick. Remember our little plan, we must be out of here before the King, which, knowing his staying power, will not be difficult. I'll skip the foreplay then, and see you back in here within fifteen minutes.'

It was less than ten in fact when he came back down the stairs and sat by the fire again, so I can only assume she was not to his liking.

'Liquor,' he said. 'I can't get it up anymore past about eight in the evening. Will have to cut back soon; can't let this thing stay limp for too long; get a deadly back up of vital fluids in the brain, which needs draining regular. Pass me the bottle, there's a good man; can't do any more damage now.'

I passed him the wine, and said, 'What of the morning, sir, does a hangover not give you the same ill luck?'

'What? No, no, strangely enough it helps the hard-on, does a hangover. There is nothing I like more before break-fast than giving my page a good length. I don't know why, but a hangover intensifies the pleasure beyond measure.' He threw four cups of wine down in one, with hardly a pause to swallow.

'Best be on our way I suppose, Mr Marvell, Charles will be finishing off soon. It's a great pity we can't stay to see the results of our game, but that would spoil it all alas. Never mind, I have sworn the lady of the house to come and tell us the outcome, and if she sing well for her supper, I will reward her well too. I had best alert my tame gaoler at the Tower to keep my cell warm and ready for my return to London.'

'I will visit you there, my Lord, perhaps bring you some comforts.'

'Thank you, you are kind, but no need. I have all I need there, and I won't be in long, unless Charles is feeling especially peevish.' So saying, we upped and left and wandered our way home, singing a little song that was a favourite of Rochester's. It was an ancient song, and lovely, but Wilmot had written a new set of words, and had a number of fiddlers to set it to music for Charles one night and had tickled the whole court into joining in. One verse was his favourite and went:

> *The mayor of London town*
> *Is flogged by his own sheriffs;*
> *The bishops bugger up and down*
> *And all beshit their sleeves.*

Not a great lyric I would agree, and faulty on the metre and the rhyme too, but when you hear a gang of twenty drunken Lords hollering it out fit to wake the dead, accompanied by swooning violins, it has a certain charm. We were just the two of us as we staggered back to our rooms, but we were crooning right on song. We even woke a few people up, but they were happy to listen to us at the window, rather than throw things. He has a fine voice this boy, and I went to bed quite happy for once.

I got the story from Rochester the next day, who got it from both the Madame and the girl who went with Charles, and it was a great yarn which Rochester dined out on for weeks, embellishing it each time and improving it with the telling. He never even went to the Tower, so tickled was the King by it all.

When Charles had done his business and was dozing on the bed, the girl went to his suit, which was draped over a chair in the corner, with the beard neatly laid on top of it, and picked his pockets. How he did not see this I do not know, but women like her are adept at the buttock-and-twang routine, by which they can pick a man's pocket even while he is wearing his clothes, so presumably this was not a problem. Rochester had carefully told her how to do it, but carefully not told her who this man was, otherwise she would have thought twice about it all.

When Charles comes around from his post-prandial torpor, he reaches for a pipe of tobacco, and she asks for her money. 'Of course, my dear,' say Charles, ever the gent, and trots over to his clothes, only to discover the dread truth, that he has no money, although he did have his ring in his pocket, where he had hid it in case anyone might recognize it.

He and the girl go downstairs, with him looking a bit sheepish because of it all, and he throws himself on the bawd's mercy, asking, 'Could you extend me credit until the morrow, when I swear I will return with the money owed. You see, I was with my friends, and they promised to pay for it all, for I was temporarily embarrassed, but they must have had too much to drink and gone away, leaving me here in this sorry state.'

'Credit?' screamed the bawd. '*Credit?* Will I fuck. I'll be hanged for a traitor before I give credit to a saggy-arsed, black-faced, long streak of piss like you, my good fellow. Credit indeed. If you don't produce the goods soon enough, I'll call one of my gentlemen to come and take care of you.'

Charles was thus placed in a very awkward position. Either he must swallow all this insult from a common bawd, which would be tough on him – he does not mind too much his lords twitting him on occasion, though they had better not overdo it when he is feeling a touch off-key, so he has a tolerance in that direction; but to get it from a Madame, and a provincial one at that, was a mite too much – or he could draw himself up to his full six foot six, and declare himself as her King, and so teach her a nasty lesson which she won't forget in a hurry. But then of course, there is the matter of how to prove to her that he is indeed her King. People out here in the country will often live out their whole life without any clear idea of what their monarch looks like.

I well remember when the first King Charles, this one's father, was escaping for his life at the end of the wars. He disguised himself only slightly, for most people he came across in his travels would have no reason to know what he looked like. True he encountered a drover, in Devon, who had once worked in London and seen his King in a procession. The man was sure that he recognized this coachman (for such was Charles's disguise), but could not for the life of him remember where. So the King chatted to him for a while, and learned where he had been lately, and said that he had been there too, so perhaps that was where they had met, perhaps over a drink in a tavern, and the man went away satisfied, and went to his grave never knowing that he had in fact talked with his King and had been a hand's-breadth away from a large reward. I wonder how often that must have happened to all or any of us, and we have been none the wiser.

So too here.

Charles had no way of proving who he was, thus reassuring the woman that he was good for the money he owed, or of avoiding a drubbing at the hands of whatever brute the woman might summon, or of taking her down a peg or two in the process. So he takes out his regal signet ring, from where it was safe in his pocket, and puts it back on the regal finger where it always fitted snugly, and shows it to her. She, of course, does not recognize it; why should she, knowing nothing of royal signatures and seals and so on, never having had a regal missive in her life.

So Charles suggests that she wake a local jeweller to come in and have a look at it and place a value on it. Reluctantly she rouses one of her lodgers, a leery looking fellow of low brow, who went out into the dark without too much demur and got the town jeweller.

The man arrived at the brothel all of a dither. He had examined the ring carefully at his own house, and had dressed immediately and come over at a run to demand where the woman had got such a ring. He had recognized immediately what it was, but assumed that it had been stolen, and he therefore arrived at the house demanding to know straightaway who was there and how they had come by it.

'Who is here?' said the bawd. 'I'll tell you who is here. A black looking, ugly son of a whore, who has no money in his pocket and was obliged to pawn his ring.'

At this the man was about to start explaining patiently just what she had in her ownership, but Charles suddenly re-appeared at the foot of the stairs. The jeweller fell straight to his knees before the King, and begged pardon. This had some effect upon the onlookers who were loafing in the parlour. Their mouths slowly sagged, and half of them also fell to their knees, the other half pausing to see what would ensue, perhaps suspicious that this man might not actually be the King.

And that is the story. There is no more to it, except to say that the King as ever was in a good humour about it all, and twice as quick-witted as any of his subjects, or indeed the Lords who had set up the jest. With a gesture which stilled his audience and convinced everyone standing there that he could only be their King, he forgave them all in the simplest terms, said that he appreciated a joke with the best of them, and would like it very much if they would all remember this evening and tell it to their grandchildren as a good yarn.

Finally, he asked: 'Would this ring bear up another bottle?'

Indeed it would, more bottles were found in the cellar, dusted off, brought up for the crew, and they had as merry a night as they had in all their lives.

Of all the stories the King ever told, this was his favourite and he never tired of repeating it all his days, and would weep with laughter on each occasion.

Rochester never went to the Tower, and I do not think the King ever knew of my involvement in the jape. It was pleasing how well it all turned out.

36. Six Mile Bottom

Must we not pay a debt to pleasure too?

John Wilmot, Lord Rochester. 'The Imperfect Enjoyment'

Which is more than can be said about the follow-up to this story, which is also set near Newmarket. It involves Buckingham, and I have already spoken of my feelings about the despicable man, so you may well feel that my own animosity colours what I have to tell you. There is certainly much in that theory, for I would dearly like to see him done down.

The French have two phrases which mean much the same thing: either '*face à claque*' or '*tête à claque*'. Like so many of their best phrases, it is not translatable exactly without missing much of its nuance, but what it boils down to is this: there stands a person before you with a face you would dearly like to slap. In most cases it applies to a situation which is irrational. You have not a single reason to dislike that person, but just the sight of their face is enough to provoke an assault from you. Their mere existence is enough. They constitute an offence to the eye, and your desire to strike them wells up from some deep place in the mind.

It is an unpleasant thing to admit to; yet if you examine your conscience you will find that there are several instances in your life when you have taken an immediate and irrational dislike to someone.

When I ponder on it, I do not think it so irrational, for I have discovered over the years that such instincts are often proved to be correct. I have often berated myself for such a rush to judgement over a man I cannot take a liking to. I tell myself that I must give him a chance, and see how he prove himself; that no one can judge a book by its cover; that a man may smile and yet be a villain; that a hideous man may be saintly; that this or that man I dislike so much has friends with whom he is on good Christian terms and is therefore not universally despised. Why then do my hackles rise?

Well, in my experience they rise for a good reason, and that is to warn me off, and keep me away from someone who can do me danger, and even take pleasure in doing me down. For such was Buckingham. One look at the man, and I wanted to hit him. I smell danger rising from his pores like marsh gas. When he enters a room, my first instinct is to club him with my stick, and after I do not, by exercising extreme restraint, it is all I can do simply to stand up and leave the room. It is abhorrent to me, to discommode myself when in fact it is he who should leave, but I fear violence would result, and I am not a fighting man; not yet at least, though I will get better at that in time, as I will relate. For the moment I must be a good Christian and turn my cheek, and the back of my throat tastes of bitter gall just to admit this much to you.

I wonder if perhaps nature has given us this instinct for reasons of safety. In the days before we were so civilized, our life may well have depended upon such intuitions about a stranger, but I do not know for sure. Either way, I have had enough justification for my anger. The man behaves abominably enough for me to hate him anyway, no matter what my instincts tell me. He married my little Moll for one thing.

Rochester rubs along tolerably well with the man. I do not think that he admires him at all, but Buckingham is powerful, and while Rochester does not give a toss for political life, none the less, someone like Rochester will make enemies and so will need high placed friends from time to time. Except that Rochester never gives the impression of playing this game, so perhaps he genuinely likes Buckingham. I do not know. I know that Rochester can be the very devil, but I cannot help but see some angel in him. Perhaps he sees himself mirrored in Buckingham. Perhaps he sees a part of the man I cannot. It is an intriguing knot, and one I cannot unravel.

My sisters for example seemed all abhorrent to me. Yet they found men to love them and marry them, without so very much trouble, and so the good Lord did make them lovable, no matter what my feelings for them were. So with Buckingham.

No, I must stop trying to be charitable on this score. He is scum, and there's an end on it.

And so to my story. I got it from Rochester himself, but, even though he was himself involved, he did leave the ending out of it, which I had to find out from sources around the coffee-houses.

Rochester and Buckingham found themselves out of favour at the court simultaneously. One or the other was always on the black list, but to be both there together was unusual, and so they amused themselves with another jolly set-to, near Newmarket while the King was not there. They both got themselves up to look like landlords. I get this much from Rochester, who enjoys disguising himself all the time, and would have had a creditable career as an actor had he been born to a lower station in life. He was also fond of conjuring tricks, and you will hear more of that from me another time.

They then eject the landlord of the Green Mare Inn, at Six Mile Bottom, not far from Newmarket, paying him well enough for the temporary use of his tavern and the goods therein and for his trouble. Then they install themselves behind the bar, with a cheery look and an offer of free booze to all those newcomers who had not yet tried the delights of this inn. This, not surprisingly, turns out to be half the population hereabouts, who leave their nice warm home of an evening and venture out for a free drink, even taking their wives along with them, just for the free ride. Each parks his spouse in the back in a snug parlour, where she won't complain about her husband's drinking, or get in the way, or start a foolish conversation, or any of the hundred other things that a man does not want when he settles down to an evening's serious drinking among friends. He buys her the odd small beer, an innocuous drink, to be taken in to her by the landlord's wife, just to keep her happy.

While the men of the area were slowly becoming more and more drunk, so Rochester and Buckingham, still in the guise of landlords, though less so, set about making hay with the women. They would doctor their drinks with brandy, then ply the good ladies with more of it, then sneak them out the back of the parlour and, since the weather was good, have them as soon as they would permit: against the back wall, if willing; in a hay rick after a little walk and persuasion, if less willing. The pair of them got through nearly all the women in the neighbourhood, by stealth and by more honest means.

Or so they said. I get this part from Buckingham. No, I am sorry, I get it from a friend of Buckingham, since I cannot bear for the man so much as to speak to me, but he has enough cronies so in thrall that they will do his boasting for him. And boasting is certainly what it is. I tried to get that much confirmed from Rochester, but he immediately went sheepish, for he knew that they had not nearly seduced all the wives in the neighbourhood, but then again, he did not want to make Buckingham out to be a liar. I must improve my cross-examination technique.

However, I recovered myself sufficiently to ask Rochester to continue, and he did, for he does love to tell a good story and, I have to say, I do like to listen, for he has a way with him.

There was one old man who would come along with a stick to help him walk, and he supped a little, though not too much for he was quite old and losing his powers, and quite often would have to be seen home by considerate friends.

This old man had a young wife, called May, and she was fresh and lovely as that very month. She was not fond of drinking nor of the rough manners you find in an alehouse, and so the old man left her at home in the care of her older sister. Of course Rochester's interest was piqued.

He had to see her, he knew it, and he could not resist doing his favourite trick of dressing up. Buckingham stayed behind the bar to keep the old man drinking and engaging in longer conversation than usual, and Rochester sneaked off into the dark, clad in voluminous skirts and a beauty patch on his cheek, and I am sure made a very convincing wench, for he was still a pretty boy in most aspects, in spite of the addled look around the eyes from all the drink.

The sister opened the door, somewhat surprised at the intrusion of this strange woman of uncommonly broad shoulder, but Rochester lifted up his overskirt and withdrew from his drawers a large bottle of brightly coloured, sticky fluid, which he said was 'cordial'. It was no such thing of course. It was every available alcoholic drink from behind the bar all thrown together in one great mixture, thickened with sugar and coloured with dye.

A girl does have a sweet tooth, and May's was sweeter than most, and so 'Miss' Rochester and May and May's sister fell on the bottle with coos of delight and began to while away a long evening indoors. Not content with the alcohol, Rochester had also doctored the sister's cup with some opium. In no time the chaperone is lying on the settle, snoring, and Wilmot and the girl are at last alone. The lovely May turns out to be not quite as fresh and innocent as she looks. She complains the traditional complaint of the young woman married to an old dotard. The old fool can't get it up anymore, and the poor young wife is forced to take the matter in hand all the time, much to her disgust.

'Well,' says Rochester, 'I think we might just have the very thing you are looking for here.'

May looks up eagerly, imagining that old mother Rochester is about to produce some love potion from under her skirts, which will magically revive the old man's passions, and Rochester does indeed rummage around under his petticoats for a while. Imagine young May's surprise and delight when he produces, not a potion, but something that she has been equally desirous of finding.

Alas, young May has never ever had such a rogering, and, being young, she is also suggestible when in such a state.

391

Wide-eyed and still panting after catching up with half a lifetime's unrequited lust, she now succumbs quickly to Rochester's next suggestion. She runs to the hiding place where her husband keeps his savings in a box, and together they decamp into the night giggling.

On their path back to the tavern, who should they spy coming toward them, weaving a little in the moonlight, but May's old husband, mumbling to himself and banging his stick in the ground. They hide behind a hedge, and Rochester puts his hand over the girl's mouth to stifle her laughter, and also to hide her gasps as she comes for a second time thanks to his ministrations, even while her husband is scarce out of sight, still muttering as he goes home.

Back at the inn at Six Mile Bottom, the girl has acquired such a taste for it, that she goes with Buckingham too, such are the passions of young women when they are inflamed.

The pair of them have a good time, and then pack her out the back door with the advice that she leave her silly husband and head for London where a girl like her could make her fortune, they would see to it.

Well, it's a good enough story, if you like your pantomime. I am not sure I believe all of it, but some parts have the ring of truth about them. I would not put either of those rogues above trying such a jest. They got back to court and Charles all but split his sides laughing at the joke, and so the court had to split its sides too.

The Green and the Gold

But that was not the end of it, I heard the end of it later. Rochester was too cowardly to tell me. Or perhaps he holds me in too high regard. Or perhaps he wanted to spare my sensibilities. Or perhaps he was guarding his reputation, I do not know. Or perhaps, even, he had told all of the truth, and that was the end of his story as he knew it. I cannot be sure.

The old man, upon returning to his house and finding both his young wife and all his money gone, hanged himself from a beam.

37. The Poet Duels Again.

Then is the poet's time, 'tis then he draws,
And single fights forsaken virtue's cause.

Marvell. 'Tom May's Death'

There is some degree of difficulty in relating the duel between Rochester and Mulgrave – not for reasons of propriety, but the problem was that I had some trouble disentangling the truth from various observers, or people who claimed to be observers of it, for I was not present myself. It has appeared in several versions. One hears stories of true events in life all the time from people of differing narrative gift. Accordingly, not only are many events, even ones in which you have yourself participated, hard enough to assess with any degree of accuracy; many more will have to be assessed from accounts given by people whose judgement you will find it hard to confirm as just.

Even if the report is given in good faith, you will always find that one person will dwell on one aspect of the events as important, and another person will choose a different part. This truth, which I take it is obvious enough to anyone who has ever asked for witnesses to an accident or crime, is especially applicable to the following story.

I got it chiefly from the seconds, but also in a desultory account from Rochester himself, though he was loth to talk of it except obliquely. Mulgrave wrote an account of it, but that is not to be trusted, since it is self-serving. There were also a hundred different accounts, racing around the coffee-houses, all of them alas with the same conclusion concerning Rochester's reputation.

There was no large divergence between these various accounts, although when it came to sorting the truth out from picturesque detail, none of the observers could be called pedantically truthful. Rochester was in this respect the most reliable because, like most men of imagination, he had a strong appreciation of the power of graphic fact. However, he had little taste for recounting the story, not even to justify himself. Mulgrave as I have said is not to be trusted.

Colonel Aston, Mulgrave's second, was in principle a man thought of as a type more used to violent action than any of the others, being a soldier, but he was more taken by surprise by the events than any of them, and this in turn must colour his version. Like many people who have had an adventurous career, who might be said to have knocked about the world a bit, he still retained a strain of naïvety, a sort of naïvety which penetrated those very regions of the mind which in Rochester's case were not inhibited. Indeed, Rochester himself said to me once that it is often better for an artist of whatever kind to be somewhat naïve, since, when practising the arts, it is necessary to see only the one thing you are looking at, but see it with utter clarity. This put him at a disadvantage.

I understand that point of view only too well. When I am on song, I am concentrated on my vision as if the rest of the world had disappeared and died. So a man like Aston, rational, cool, tempered by the toughness of his calling, could be very misleading in his accounts. Indeed his tale when I heard it was scrappy, and served only to confirm Rochester's brief account, even at the expense of his own man, Mulgrave, to whom Aston was second. And now, to the matter:

Why Mulgrave chose this moment to challenge Rochester to a duel is still a mystery. I cannot tease it out from all the strands of the differing accounts. They loathed the sight of each other all their lives, so it might have happened at any time, and so I suppose that the occasion of it hardly matters. Some insult or slight no doubt, though Rochester spent many happy hours insulting Mulgrave without the man ever noticing, he was so thick-headed. Still, something finally got through to him and a duel was called, and that is all I know of the reason. The two of them set out to do it, but Charles got wind of it and called them to halt, for he hates this sort of behaviour. He sent out arresting officers, who banged on their doors first thing in the morning.

Alas, they missed Mulgrave, who was taking his rest with

Colonel Aston over in the Knightsbridge barracks, gaining his strength before the fight. They found Rochester all right, snoring away in his lodgings. He duly gave his word to the arresting officer that he would accompany him to the King's presence, then asked most politely if he could draw on a clean shirt and breeches in private, was granted this wish, and jumped from his window and legged it at top speed. Not that he was running away you understand, he was in fact running toward the duel. Hardly the action of a coward, and so how he acquired this slur to his name, I cannot understand even to this day. I have pondered long and hard on the matter – and will admit that Rochester was perfectly capable of cowardice as he was of bravery – but why the men of fashion should accuse him thus on this occasion is hard to fathom.

Still, he had hurt enough of them in the past with his wit. He is more clever than all of them. If he were even more clever than he is, he would cover up the fact, but he cannot, and so makes jokes at their expense, and no man likes that. Had it not been now, it would have been later that they assassinated his character, but now seemed as good a time as any, and they had the means and the occasion, no matter how slight.

In fact both Wilmot and Mulgrave were finally tracked down in a day or two, and Black Rod brought them both before the House, and they duly swore on oath they had no quarrel any more and would behave as the King required, and both would be gentle as lambs with each other. They lied.

Rochester and Mulgrave met at the appointed place, a November morning mist rising from the ground in gentle white feathers and partly masking their legs. Rochester, being the one called out, was allowed to choose how to take the fight, and he asked that it be done on horse. Mulgrave at first agreed to this, but then pointed out that Rochester's second was not the man he had originally cited, but a huge trooper of uncertain temper, though strangely he looked like one of Aston's own troop. Moreover he was seated on a massive cavalry charger, whereas Mulgrave and his second were only on pads. Mulgrave then pointed out that the sides were unevenly matched, and, should the seconds become involved, then the fight would be unfair, because unbalanced. Rochester very sweetly agreed with all this.

Alas, what he could not agree to was Mulgrave's suggestion that they fight on foot. For Rochester had chosen the option of horseback for the simple reason that he was too weak to stand. A combination of being soused with the mercury for his pox, the depredations of the pox itself, and the fact that he had been dead drunk for five years now, had all taken their toll. The man was a near ghost, a dead man standing.

All would have been well I think had Rochester either insisted upon his right to choose, which was fair after all, or else had agreed to dismount, in which case he would have collapsed before more could be done or said.

Alas, he chose to speak instead. He told Mulgrave of his condition, excused himself from the fight on account of it, and asked most gravely that Mulgrave make nothing out of it when they returned to the court. I do not know if any assurance was given, but Mulgrave and his accomplices worked it all up a treat when they got back, writing the whole abysmal affair up in the most humbug style, damning Rochester by faintly excusing his behaviour.

No matter that the man was the coolest soldier under fire that the army at sea had ever seen. No matter the King had given him medals. No matter any or all of the other things that I have related. Just one slight slip from grace and the weasels of fashion fell on him and began shredding his reputation with their little pointed teeth. Of course, he affected not to give a damn, and I must say I liked the man for that, but it hurt, I could see it. A man has little enough of any true importance in this life to call his own, except his reputation. Take that away, and he is sorely wounded down where it hurts most, in his soul.

The weak have self-esteem, for they do not know any better, but the strong man has self-respect. Rochester had enough of that to keep him afloat through all the troubles that he heaped upon himself. But a whole town turned against him, and whispering behind their hands that he is not what he thought himself to be . . . well, that can damage a man badly.

He was but twenty-two years old. Dear God, how young he was, and yet how experienced; but from that moment on he never looked for good in another man. He went black in mood, and never could see the light side of things. He was not wholly a cynic, for he still could see good when it shone before him. Yet it became harder and harder for him to find that good, and he was more loth to admit it when he saw it. Women became no more than carriers of the pox, and men simply sufferers of it.

It is a sad thing to see in a man, the loss of all optimism. God knows it happened to me, thanks to the wars and their aftermath, but the disease worked its poison through my veins more slow than it did Rochester.

Enough of this analysis, I must be more simple in my speech, and tell you how things fell out, but first I had a trip beyond sea to Muscovy, and what a trip.

38. In Muscovy

Rule 1, on page 1 of the book of war is: 'Do not march on Moscow'.

Lord Montgomery of Alamein.
Speech in the House of Lords, 1962

It was in July 1663 that I set off for an ambassadorial trip to Muscovy, a mission which was in part to restore trading privileges which we had enjoyed with Russia, until we cut the head off our King; an event which did not amuse the Tsar. He had felt a sudden spasm at the nape of his neck and had immediately forbidden all intercourse with our country. No doubt he feared that the idle peasants in his country might hear of the execution and start sharpening their scythes, their minds brooding upon former grievances

It is not a good idea to kill Kings. All the Kings of the civilized world are related, whether by marriage, family or just by the fact of Kingship, and they don't like the idea that one of their number might be knocked off the throne and disposed of by the very subjects who are supposed to love, honour, worship and obey. It makes them itchy, especially an old stinker like the Tsar Alexei.

I had written to my constituents in Hull that I would be absent beyond sea for at least a year, but that their interests would still be looked out for. I did not tell you that I was a Member of Parliament for Hull did I? Well I am, and let that be enough for you. It is certainly more than enough for me, for it is mostly dreary work and, though I do it diligently, not much to my liking. I carry out my duties, which are to represent the Mayor and the folk of Hull, as best I can. I do it just to have something to do, and I dearly wish that my fellow MPs would do the same and nothing else. However, once they enjoy a little power, then it goes to their heads and they become quite crazed with it. So they want more power, and it is a thirst which feeds upon itself, and is never diminished.

Most days in the House are tedious, which is as it should be, but every so often there is an outburst of factional intrigue, and someone loses their head: like the doing-down of Clarendon, which was quite shameful. Enough of that, politics is either boring or vicious, and so are politicians. Instead I will tell you of my Ambassadorial trip to Muscovy.

We set out from Gravesend, bound for the port of Archangel, led by the 34-year-old Earl of Carlisle. Carlisle is a Privy Counsellor. He had fought on both sides in the Civil War, being unable to make up his mind, but he had not suffered for it, for his demeanour was youthful and fair, and he was not a dissembling man. He was some eight or nine years my junior, but we saw eye to eye on most things, which is to say that we were undecided on most things, and so we rubbed along pretty well. Certainly I was pleased that he asked me along on the mission, for I was becoming mighty bored with the life of politics in London, and needed a little foreign adventure. Also the Foreign Secretary asked me to keep my eye upon all things Muscovite and write him a secret report when I got back, so there's a little spying in it all too. Not that I have any contacts in Muscovy, but I will make some none the less. There are English merchants out there, plying their trade with the Ivans, and some are in our pay.

A record of the trip was kept by a nineteen-year-old Swiss under-secretary to the mission, Guy Miège, who later published it in book form, and it proved quite popular, running to several editions.

My account does not accord with his.

The frigate docked first at Archangel, in the far North, after a month at sea. Carlisle sent me off to be the first ashore, and I must say I was greeted royally by the local Governor. This may be because Archangel was first discovered as a place for a useful port by the English, and so we enjoyed special status there, and did not have to pay a fee to anchor. Six knights were sent out to escort me to the castle, and later a full regiment of six hundred men was put at my disposal for whatever purpose I had in mind. I tried to explain that I was not about to invade Siberia and therefore had little use for them, but gave up. Besides, they looked splendid, their burnished cuirasses gleaming in the August sun, and so I murmured and nodded and said something in French to the effect that while they weren't quite up to the standard of our own Life Guards (sabretaches a little shabby and those boots could do with an extra shine), nevertheless it was a very kind gesture and we were honoured, flattered etc etc, and now could we get on with our trip to the capital please.

So, after feeding me and putting me up for the night, the Governor then sends out twenty boats with several hundred men to help see Carlisle and his crew ashore.

What a sight we made. The whole point about Ambassadorial trips is to blind the other side with splendour, and so Carlisle had spent the previous day drilling our men for a show-off. We had nearly eighty men all told, including the usual complement of Chaplain, interpreters, a few tradesmen and a couple of barber-chirurgeons, all of them necessary men. The bulk was made up with a most splendid retinue of pages, trumpeters, and footmen, all clad in regal gold, and fire-flashing in the sun.

It was a wondrous line-up and I could see that Archangel wasn't used to such pomp. The good citizens turned aside from their usual round of consuming whale blubber and breaking ice. They all lined the road, eyes bulging, and waved their hands and clapped and the local dignitaries straightened their hats and brushed their coats and threw back their shoulders a little more smartly that day. It was all very sweet of them, but then all hell broke loose.

The Green and the Gold

There were already a few Dutch ships in Archangel when we arrived, and to add to the general merriment that they could spy ashore, they started letting off gun salutes, which, as any sailor knows, are just powder shots with no cannon balls; and great fun, especially for children who like being frightened by big noises. Alas, it did not go down at all well with the locals. I do not know which law of etiquette it breached, something obscure and Russian no doubt, but it was suddenly a case of stern looks and thunderous brows all round from our hosts.

It was all that I, with little Guy Miège interpreting, could do to bring them around again. We blamed the Dutch of course; an ill bred, nouveau-riche sort of nation which scarcely had the right to call itself a country at all. We pointed out that most of it lay below the level of the sea, and was simply composed of the off-scourings of the British sand, and, since they had no history to speak of, their manners were appalling. One day they would all drown, and the world would lose a few good paintings, and a couple of dull cheeses, and that would be all.

This long and impassioned piece of lying seemed to satisfy honour all round, and so we fell to the merrymaking again, though not for too long outside. It is frightening cold up here, even though it is August, and the midges were put here by the Devil to give men a foretaste of Hades. I find cigar smoke a good way of deterring them, and have taken up smoking for that very reason.

I suspect the Dutch knew perfectly well all about local protocol and let off their cannon just to do us down with the inhabitants. I will have my revenge on them, but not now. I will brood upon it, in the Spanish fashion.

For a fortnight we enjoyed all manner of good entertainment. We kept protesting that we must move on, but your Archangelic is not one for stinting the hospitality. By mid September, however, we had been furnished with six big barges as requested and we set off for the capital on the river Duina.

Progress was slow, for we were pulled, not by horses in the English manner, but by serfs, and most of the serfs were not very willing to pull the barges of some foreigners. There was much cursing and muttering among their ranks, and they were inclined to slack, but then an overseer would appear, and they would step more lively after judicious application of the knout to their backs. I can't say that I approved. – this sort of thing disappeared from England hundreds of years ago – but there is nothing to be done about it. This is their land and they must live in it the way they wish to. I can't help but think though that Oliver would have had a field day here, liberating the poor oppressed serfs, and then making sure that they were pious and not allowed to enjoy themselves. They must wait for their own Protector I suppose.

So, we crept along at a snail's pace, but enjoying some comfort, for Carlisle had had the leading barge equipped as a kitchen, complete with a hearth and a chimney. We had cooks, but most of the rest of the entourage liked to hang around the kitchen range as well, for it was getting colder and colder outside. For the rest of the time, we slept much, swaddled in furs and rugs.

As we passed local villages, which were mean and inhospitable places, the local priest would be the one to come out and greet us, while the population stared at us from behind closed windows and the fringes of their fur hats. He would usually bring some small offering, a fresh fish, or some local fruits, and we would give him what we could, which meant a healthy amount from our barrel of brandy. We would then watch him staggering through the sleet back to his congregation, beaming incontinently and scattering blessings. It became a small sport among us to see how drunk we could make each successive priest and how quickly. By the ten-day mark it was dead drunk within the hour.

By the end of October we had only reached Vologda, by way of the Duina and Sucagna rivers via Colmogro, Arsinoa, Yagrish, Ustiga, Tetma, and Chousca, and the journey was becoming grievous and insupportable. The snow was continuous, but it would not harden and the serfs pulling us were up to their waists on the tow-paths, and unable to move, no matter how hard they were lashed. So, we stopped at Vologda, bedded down in every available garret and inn, and decided to wait, either for the snow to harden, when we could then take sledges, or, in the worst case, for the thaw.

We had little to do for three months, and so I organized

an entertainment. November the fifth was approaching by our calculations. The date meant little to the locals, but I decided that it certainly would do by the time we left.

With my interpreter, and also with much use of dog Latin and my conversational French, I spent much time explaining to the locals all about Guy Fawkes. They did not entirely understand the notion of democracy and what a Parliament was for, but they took to the idea of a man blowing up the main seat of government with undisguised glee.

My plan was that Carlisle would take the part of the Guy, since he liked a jape, and we would arraign him between two of our more burly guards and march him at the head of a torch-lit procession up to the very foot of the unlit bonfire. Then, vainly protesting his innocence and calling for justice and mercy and his mother at the top of his voice, he would be led struggling around the bonfire to the side away from the crowd. Under cover of a cloak, Carlisle would be spirited away, and his two gaolers would climb a ladder up the side of the faggots, with a dummy dressed in Carlisle's clothes and tie it to a stake at the top of the bonfire.

The assembled congregation would then throw their flaming torches on to the pyre, while emitting bloodcurdling whoops, and appropriate sentiments such as 'Death to the traitor' and 'That'll teach you to blow up your betters.' They would then feast on whatever meats they would bring to the fire and potatoes roasted in the ashes.

It all went very well at rehearsals, which for obvious

reason we did without the chanting mob. Carlisle got in just the right amount of eyeball rolling and foaming at the mouth as well as general cursing and blasphemy, and our two Sergeants made a very good show of handling him roughly. We did the business with the cloak around the back, and found that there was a little copse of silver birches on the common ground just near the bonfire into which we could easily smuggle him, just as the dummy was being lifted up the ladder.

But on the night things went horribly wrong. The dark and unwashed citizens all duly turned out for the festivities, muttering about Gee Forkshes into their beards. I find the Russian accent very melodious on the ear and a great pleasure to listen to. Even if you do not understand a word, you can gain much sense of it from the music it makes. What I had not realized was that they are permanently drunk as a boiled owl, which they do as a barrier to the cold, and so the pleasant lisping and slurring has a darker reason than mere melody. By the time all the torches were lit, the procession was swaying in time to some infernal music erupting from the depths of the crowd, and the whole column was becoming dangerously restless.

'What ho, for a good burning,' shouted Carlisle, duly stepping up to his place at the head of the column, and allowing his wrists to be gripped on either side by his executioners. 'We will skip the drawing and quartering I think Mr Marvell,' he said in an aside to me, 'but I'm all for a little warmth.' And they duly set off. The column of local peasants lurched into a shambling gait, and staggered along behind the miscreant, chanting low but strong in time to this strange music. At first they all moved at ponderous speed, but as the rear ranks began to become restless, they pressed forward and the crowd began to thicken and move too far forward.

By the time they had reached the foot of the bonfire, Carlisle and his two men were all but hemmed in. They tried to break free, and I called to several of our footmen who were nearby to try and contain the crowd while Carlisle slipped away, but they could not. The chanting was becoming louder and sparks from the torches were flying everywhere. Many had dropped their torches on the ground because of the press, and already the base of the bonfire had caught fire, and flames were licking upwards from the bottom logs. With a roar of triumphant revenge for all the past iniquities which their masters had visited on them, the mob surged forward, seized the young Earl of Carlisle, placed him in a large blanket which they produced from their ranks and were tossing him up and down higher and higher next to the bonfire.

Why they did this, and whether it was supposed to be a sport or a punishment or a ritual humiliation, I had not the faintest idea, but as their chanting grew more rhythmic and more loud, so Carlisle rose ever higher with each toss of the blanket. He rose and soared, lark-like through the darkening heavens, and warbled in delight at each lift of the blanket.

The crowd thought it a huge joke and were cackling with glee as he went ever higher.

Then, with a great shout to signal the climax of their game, they gave one final mighty heave, slanted the blanket slightly to one side, and sent our Earl flying off up a tangent, which was ended by him landing neatly on top of the bonfire. This was greeted with a mighty roar of approval, and much raising of grog to toast his final end.

Oh dear God, the locals have not got the main idea about play-acting at all. They were convinced they were attending some ancient English ritual of public execution, and had decided to show us a realistic little twist of their own for the final act. This is not how diplomacy is supposed to work.

I shouted to the Sergeants, but could not be heard above the roar, so I gripped them both by the elbow and fled around the back of the bonfire, where we had left the ladder. Fortunately the flames were lower here, but the bottom rungs were becoming charred and were smouldering. We gathered some snow and flung it as best we could around the base of the ladder, and I then jumped up over the first three or four rungs. After that it was easy and I was at the top and helping our man down again in no time. When we reached the base of the smoking ladder we jumped for it and landed in a heap next to the fire, which now was beginning to rage on this side as well.

With a shout of frustrated outrage, the mob once more

surged around him, lifted him up, and bore him struggling to the fire.

I looked about and realized that both Sergeants were armed. Pulling a pistol from the belt of the nearest, I loosed it off into the air, and a sudden quiet settled over the crowd. The second Sergeant had got the right idea by then and stood close by me, his pistol held at arm's length, aiming from person to person in the crowd. He handed me his sword and I stepped up beside him. It was a close run thing, but our interpreter then appeared, thank the Lord, and began to explain at the top of his voice just what it was that they ought not to be doing.

Slowly they melted away, with much disgruntled muttering at having had a good evening's burning spoilt. The Sergeants sheathed their swords and holstered their pistols. I brushed down Carlisle and we retired for the night. 'Close run thing, what?' he said, grinning from ear to ear. Sangfroid is this boy's middle name.

The next day, the butler's wife was brought to bed, and gave birth to a large boy. She had been big with child when we set out, and while I thought it foolish to accompany us, still she was a very strong woman. We christened the boy Guy, which I think appropriate. She lived and the child is with us yet.

It was January before the snow was sufficiently hardened, and we could finally set off on sledges, and it was February, a full seven months after leaving London, when we finally entered Moscow. We were quartered and fed and treated well before our first official audience with the Tsar.

39. In the court of the Tsar

This will last out a night in Russia,
When nights are longest there.

Shakespeare. *Measure for Measure*

At the ceremony, we were greeted by a heavenly voice, a great rounded booming bass, which could be heard echoing around the bell-shaped chamber of the highest dome of this city, and rebounding from the great south-facing doors of the greatest hall in Christian Muscovy. For we were in the Kremlin, mother-fortress of all Muscovy and of all the Muscovite Empire. That bright March morning it was as full as it had been in the centuries since its foundations had been laid, and the assembled dignitaries could not have been more exalted. The middle-aged Tsar Alexei himself and his attendant Crown Princes, Princes, Lords, chamberlains, viceroys, Patriarch, Archimandrites, Generals, Archbishops, no fewer than twelve primates, together with less eminent clergy from throughout the Orthodox world – these and hundreds more had assembled to greet our Embassy from His Devout Majesty King Charles the Second, King of England,

417

Defender of the Faith and a few other titles we forbore out of politeness to mention.

Alexei received us with stiff ceremony, which reminded me mainly of Byzantine court practice, with perhaps a hint of Mongol heritage thrown in. He was surrounded at the points of the compass by four chamberlains clad in tunics of embroidered silken brocade. Each wore a tall fur hat and carried a long-handled silver axe at the shoulder-arms position.

To the Tsar's left was Prince Vorotynski, the Keeper of the Exchequer; and to his right, Prince Dolgoruki, the Marshal of the Realm, who gently lifted the Tsar's right hand and offered it to us to be kissed. And so we all duly bowed and kissed it. Fortunately it was gloved.

We went through the hours of formalities, the Ambassador Carlisle having done it many times before, and he used me to translate into Latin, the formal wording of which was then relayed by the Tsar's translator into Russian and spoken into the Tsar's right ear. I spoke in high ecclesiastical Latin, a language unintelligible to most of the assembled court, despite the theoretical use of it in diplomatic circles and church services. This did not matter. They could recognize many of the words, and got the gist from my tone of voice.

'King Charles the Second is distinguished in matters of faith and observances (our first lie – King Charles couldn't give a damn for religion and would willingly embrace the first one which would pay him enough and leave him alone to enjoy a quiet life), enjoying respectful relations with both the Protestant and the Papal courts (bigger lies – they are both extremely suspicious that our King had gone over to the other side, but these Orthodox Ivans are close to the Pope in their worship I think, though He doesn't know it), and is held in tender esteem by his people (a monster lie – they do like him, but really they couldn't care less who was on the throne so long as taxes did not increase and they didn't allow the Puritans back to spoil their fun).'

And so we dragged on and on with the solemnities, and as I translated with half an ear and my tongue on auto-pilot, I looked about me slowly and was put in awe by the sheer size and barbarity of the setting. Apart from Brunker's great dome, the most renowned of the sights to be seen was the vast Zouravioff ceiling in commemoration of the victory over the last Mongol horde, the fruit of a decade's backbreaking work. There was nothing like it west of the Dnieper.

The East-facing coloured window by Traminsky, fired now with the morning sun, showed the birth of St Sasha, Mother of all Muscovy. Along the Western wall ran Rublev's brilliant frescoes depicting St Dismas's progress through the plague-ridden thugs of the Ukraine. Potemkin's oil painting of the Martyrdom of St Malankov hung on the facing wall, and was celebrated for the artist's journey to Siberia in the hope of getting the setting right. Alas for verisimilitude, he perished of frostbite. One of the latest additions, the Boyar

419

mosaic by Kandinsky, has attracted criticism for its retro-
grade, almost medieval style. He had been lucky to be merely
crippled by the Tsar's official hangmen.

I gaped in unreserved awe at the Tarkovsky spandrels on
the high arches of the central aisle, at the chryselephantine
gates, guarding the entrance to the inner chambers, and at
Paradjanov's Christ Pantocrator in Uzbeki marble set about
with semi-precious stones, but chiefly at the soaring columns,
broad and thick as an ancient oak, which supported the stone
roof trusses. The streaked emerald green was malachite, polished to a glowing smoothness by centuries of the passing
faithful, and all about them, a thousand smoking candles
burned gold in the morning air.

However, it was the background music, underscoring all
we said, which pressed upon us more immediately than anything: a magnificent dirge by Nacria, the crowning glory of
his old age and of all his opera. There was a story about this
work, that it had been composed out of the composer's grief
at the untimely death of a beloved young catamite from the
plague, but there was no mistaking its heavenly fire.

The attendant crowd stayed still because to move was to
risk the royal wrath. Also they were overwhelmed by the
music with a feeling that was nearly pious. Our party were
largely clad in the black vestments of diplomatic life, but with
scarlet piping to distinguish us from the Puritans.

The noonday sun increased its burning ray, illuminating
to advantage the multicoloured onion domes, and pleasantly

warming the crowds outside, who would have assembled just the same if there had been a raging blizzard, in order to gawp. Foreigners, while not forbidden in Muscovy, were not actively encouraged, and so we made a rare sight.

Soon a great bell began to toll, and the singer ceased. It seemed to be an indication, or at least a hint, that the ceremony might be coming to an end, in spite of our being only halfway through our introductions. A groan of relief ran through the crowd and subsided.

The Royal Guard, in their eau-de-nil and mauve, parted to reveal the Patriarch Nikon, in his white and carmine uniform. The ceremony reached its end. The Patriarch came forward at the stately pace of a galleon, acknowledged the Tsar's obeisance, raised him and escorted him towards us. As he approached he held out a length of paper, with writing in English upon it.

'These are the things I want from you,' the Tsar said to the Ambassador, and handed him what turned out to be a shopping list.

- The very best sort of Doctor, who can find herbal cures in Muscovy. Especially for the piles.
- An alchemist of the best kind, and an amiable fellow, who can concoct the herbs.
- A reliable herb book that deals with Russian and Polish and foreign herbs.

- A mineralogist expert in all forms of silver, copper, lead and iron ores.
- A goldsmith who can gild.
- An illustrated book in four volumes on trajectories, and someone, anyone, who can make them work.
- A pamphlet to be written on the Tsar's campaigns.
- A monthly news sheet from all the States, telling us all the news.
- Good birds – singing parrots, finches, canaries and the like.
- A master glass maker who knows how to make clear glass and all kinds of embossed and cut-glass vessels and who knows how to find the right sort of earth for making glass.
- 2 and a half cwt of Camphor.

Then he was gone, in a gilded carriage jangling through the snow, with the sun blasting off the gilt, and points of multicoloured light from the crystal with which it was decorated. It was surrounded by a troop of Palace Guard, their crimson-flagged lances at the port, trotting at a brisk pace each side of the Royal carriage. Hooves and iron-clad wheels were muffled by the snow, but the harness bells rang out clear across the cold bright air. I had seen nothing more stately since the return of my King.

'Finches I can do,' said Ambassador Carlisle to me, 'but what in the blue flying blazes is camphor for?'

'It originates in the old Sanskrit karpurum, from there into English via Latin camphora, French camphore, and

Arabic kafur,' I said. 'You can smoke it, like hemp, or like myristic acid from the nutmeg tree. It is used for medicine and for repelling moths.'

He gave me a look.

After our reception there was a nine-hour play, something called *Esther* by the Lutheran pastor Grigori. I sat through it, and it passed in what seemed like only days.

Then more addresses to the court, round and round we went, in phrases ever more meaningless. The Tsar wanted to know why we had called him 'Illustrissime', which was not only the wrong form of address, but something which he regarded as an insult just this side of being called a catamite. I patiently explained to him at considerable length that it means the most serene and exalted ruler, and one whose moral rectitude, beauty, wealth, power and general esteem were exceeded only by Jesus Christ himself. After about an hour of this abject lying, he looked a little mollified, but only to the extent that he would have looked more so had I pointed out Christ's faults as a person at the same time. When he scowled, his Chancellor scowled, and when his Chancellor scowled, then so did the four chaps with the silver axes, and pretty soon the whole palace guard was at it, knitting their woolly brows together and generally giving us the evil eye. They are an ill-tempered bunch, the result I think of being permanently hung-over from too much Vodka, which they drink instead of water.

It is filthy stuff, made from potatoes, and can also be used to strip the bark from the silver birches, which they use to make log cabins. An odd race, as I said.

Eventually Ambassador Carlisle came to me in my room one night and said: 'Much as I am loth to admit to this point, I fear that this Embassy to the Tsar is not necessarily to our advantage. I suspect . . .'

At which point I held my hand up and said, 'Please, I beg you, no more of the diplomatic language. If I hear one more euphemism, I will be tempted to extreme violence.'

He looked up at the ceiling, and down at the floor, and then at the wall, and slowly his glazed air of official inscrutability turned to one of mild resignation and then to amusement. 'We're fucked. There is nothing for us here,' he said, 'and I can't tell you what a relief it is to realize it. Let's go home.'

So that's what we did. We packed all our brass bound trunks and loaded them on a train of near thirty sledges drawn by ponies and dogs and oxen, and indeed any sort of animal to hand as the winter eventually came on and they fell by the wayside. There was an incident one morning when a surly driver refused to go another inch without extra payment for the accursed cold. He had stalactites hanging from his beard, and a couple of them broke off with a clack when I pulled out my pistol from my pocket, and clapped it to his temple. 'You will drive this sled for as long as I tell you to drive this sled,' I said, cocking the pistol with a loud click, 'or else you will lie here in the snow forever.' I pushed the gun against his head a little harder. That wiped the surly look from his face, and he was all smiles after that. Always strike the first blow.

I have become quite good at violence, I think. My father would be ashamed of me.

First we went to Riga in Latvia, and that was swampy and mosquito-ridden and not at all amenable, although it was good finally to see some greenery after all the snow of Muscovy. They were having a summer jamboree which involved all the hairy peasant folk putting oak leaves on their heads and ganging together to sing a song, the chief chorus of which went: 'Riga, Riga, Riga, tum-ti-tum-tum, Riga, Riga, Riga.' Which I can only suppose to be a quiet hymn extolling their national modesty. It was a barbarous place of no civility, though the coast line is picturesque enough, a long line of pleasant sand beaches. From there we sailed to Stockholm, where we went through the whole silly business all over again with a nine-year-old who sat on the throne, and was no use to anyone. Nothing there to our advantage either. Then it was back across to Elsinore, which is a God forsaken place and Shakespeare can never have come here. En voyage between these Hanseatic ports we were entertained by two tame bears, which the Muscovites had given us. They would lick your fingers if you put your hand near their mouth. I wouldn't.

40. Astrologer Royal

Students of the heavens are separable into astronomers and astrologers as readily as are the minor domestic ruminants into sheep and goats, but the separation of philosophers into sages and cranks seems to be more sensitive to frames of reference.

Willard Van Orman Quine. *Theories and Things*

Astrology is a disease, not a science.

Maimonides (1135–1204). *Laws of Repentance*

Rastignac arrived at the court from France, claiming to be a foreteller. He is also a monk, and has been sent by Louis as a special gift to the King, to write his charts and forecast what the future will bring. He rustles about the place in a long pistachio green cape, covered in yellow symbols of the stars and planets, which envelops him from top to toe, so he looks like a travelling tent, sliding about the place on silent wheels. He also claims to summon fairies, including Queen Titania, and when we hear their little voices, it seems to me his Adam's apple is bobbing about a surprising amount for a

man who is listening to pixies. Also, the silvery tintinnabu-
lation of fairy bells quite clearly emanates from beneath his
cloak, which he never removes in public.

He has brought with him a huge plan chest, with about
twenty drawers, all stuffed full with maps and charts of the
heavens. He pores over these with compasses and rule,
making copious notes on bits of ragged paper and muttering
all the while.

As to all that stuff, I am amazed at how strong a grip it
exercises upon the general mind. We all long to know the
future and so we all are prepared to believe whatever these
people tell us. It is rot.

The man is a spy, that much is as plain as the nose on his
face. I can't decide which I find the more unbelievable: that
Louis should think we would fall for so transparent a ploy, or
that King Charles should indeed fall for it – but, believe it
or no, both things seem to have happened. Charles spends
half the night poring over incomprehensible charts, while
the monk goes ranting on all the time about 'auspicious
conjunctions' and 'cusps' and 'prognostications' and God
knows what else besides. I really have no time to learn that
language, and anyway would never do so for fear of providing the slightest support for what is a snare and delusion.
It is an *ignis fatuus* of the mind, an escape of marsh gas which
catches fire briefly solely to delude the traveller and lead him
astray from the path. It was not so long ago they would burn
people for witchery, and I hold that it is much the same as

witchcraft. It is harmless in the sense that it has absolutely no powers to affect anything, but it is harmful in the sense that it is done with wicked intent.

The world is full enough of the credulous and the gullible. They should not be encouraged in their folly.

My Lord Rochester will have none of it, which I must say is slightly to my surprise. He is up for anything, and I would have thought it would prove to be just another good piece of sport for him to while away a few more hours in his bored life, but no, he got quite exercised about it all, which is unlike him, for he is usually an easy man. I could see him curling his lip and turning on his heel, whenever Charles engaged the attentions of this fraud. Then he set to thinking and devised a wonderful plot.

'Honourable Docteur Rastignac,' said Rochester, 'my friends and I are about to undertake a journey, and we have most urgent need of your forecasting skills.'

'Of course, of course,' says the mountebank. 'Journeys are always the most hazardous of enterprises and one should forearm oneself to the best of all possible advantage. As it happens I specialize in casting for a journey, for the patron saint of travellers was born under . . .' I will not bore you with any more of the hocus-pocus which he drivelled on for hours. It is rank and offends my ear.

Rochester let him go on; he is so cunning, stroking his chin and nodding sagely, and chinking his purse occasionally to remind the man that he will pay well for a good bit of star-reading.

'We go tomorrow to Epsom, good doctor, a place not far from town, just twenty miles or so south of here, and the route is not hazardous.' Rastignac nodded and beamed at the easy task ahead for him.

'But it is our activities when we get there that I want you to investigate. What might be the outcome.'

'What would those activities be?' says Rastignac solemnly.

'Well, I thought you might be able to divine that from the stars,' says Rochester, and gets the evil eye from Rastignac who feels he is being made a fool. Indeed he is. It is perfectly obvious what Rochester and his gang are going to be doing. One only goes down to Epsom for two things in this whole world, but then I suppose you cannot expect a Frog to know about our national habits of horse racing. Or the waters.

Why not though? He is supposed to be a spy, ain't he? Some spy! He wouldn't be so bloody ignorant of the habits of the people on whom he is watching if he had been one of my men. I train them well, and I see to all of that. Frenchmen, what can you do with them? They are so wretchedly arrogant, they send an amateur to do a professional's job.

'We plan to go to the races,' says Rochester in a placatory sort of tone, just to let the man know that he was only joshing before, and Rastignac looks relieved that he has been spared the task of guessing what the hell Wilmot and his mates were going to get up to. Then he gives a great big swallow and his eyes start to bulge slightly, because he has suddenly realized what is coming next. Races! That means jockeys and horses and betting and all the punters wanting to read in the stars what is going to win, and he feels like a rabbit caught in the flare of a lantern's beam, knowing it should flee, but unable to budge to the left or right.

He gulped again, and Rochester was trying to restrain a smile, and all but rubbing his hands in glee. There was no escape for the man, and he had to get out his charts and make as many inquiries about the field as he could. He learned that there were only three races, and that each race was only a match so he had only a choice of two horses per race. After much pulling on his beard and huffing and puffing, he came up with the three names of the winners, and took himself off back to his chamber.

As things panned out, he managed to be exactly one hundred per cent wrong. I wonder what the odds on that are eh? Three times in a row he gets a fifty-fifty bet, and three times fails completely. Anyway, Rochester is very canny with gambling, never backing more than he can comfortably let go in an evening, for while he does it to amuse himself and the company, yet he is not in thrall to it as some are, even our King.

As a matter of fact, he backed all the horses that Rasty said would come second, just to be his usual contrary self, so he did quite well that day, but a friend of his lost a packet, and vowed he would send the evil little monk back to his wretched country singing the treble roles in future.

When they got back to town, however, Rastignac had fled London with all his goods and gone home, so at least he had foresight enough for that. Perhaps he read of his castration in the stars. Or perhaps he just had a sudden attack of common sense.

In fact they didn't all get back to town in quite the easy way that I have just suggested. Something went horribly wrong.

41. A Sunny Day out at Epsom

Who can run the race with Death?

James Boswell. *Life of Samuel Johnson*

Epsom was a tiresome sort of place, mainly grass-green, stables and horsey folk. I do not know why the court has to go all the way down there just to watch a few races. Still, Charles seems to like it, so everyone else has to as well. He likes to drink the waters of the spa, which have a medicinal reputation, and he has christened them the Epsom Salts. I downed four pints and got me a week's worth of good stools in one night. The farmer who owns the well now has a Royal charter to sell the stuff. I notice that the local cattle refuse to drink it.

Rochester went with a small gang, just Mr Jefferson, Captain Bridges — an admirer of horseflesh and a man who will mount anything — Etherege the play writer, the ill-fated Mr Downs, and myself, although I do not have a taste for gambling, thanks to my upbringing. Like Wilmot, I will wager small amounts when necessary, and indeed will always gain some money in a card match, for I am shrewd, but I am suspicious of it – just as suspicious as I am of liquor, or women, or strong drugs from the apothecary, for they can take over a man's life, nay his very soul, and make it their slave. I have a fondness for drink, and I will gamble, and as to women you know my tastes, but never will I let anything govern me. I want more control over my life, not less, and the man who lets a gross object, let alone a woman, have too much governance over him is a fool.

On reflection, my Lord Rochester is no fool, and yet he is a slave to all the senses! Well, he is certainly a fool in the following respect. He will die young, and in horrid pain. That much I can see coming. The pox has had a terrible effect on him. His hair has fallen out, his teeth are black, and his bones are so brittle he needs aid to stand from his chair in the morning. They creak and crack and you can hear his hips groaning. His kidneys are ulcerated and he discharges a bloody flux when he pisses. He will die sooner than me, and he is half my age. So let him have whatever pleasures a man may have.

Which at Epsom was blue murder.

We had been to the race field and watched the horses and bet our money and duly lost all to the bookie, and done all the things one is supposed to. Then, on Saturday afternoon, after the horses had done their biz, the group started drinking and didn't stop until Sunday evening, at which point what the company realized was that they were all in dire need of some music.

I relate this at second hand, for you know my habits by now. I still will not drink in company, so I took myself off on the Saturday night, but it seems that the merry gang were lurching through the streets of Epsom late on Sunday afternoon demanding a musician who could see to their needs, though God knows what he might have played for them. In their state, it would have needed the intervention of the archangel Gabriel and the full heavenly chorus to have made an impress on their consciousness.

Anyway, they found some poor benighted fiddler, and started shouting at him for some music. Well, they had been staggering around this God-forsaken hole for two days now and had gotten themselves pretty well known as a nuisance, and the locals were beginning to look at them sideways. The fiddler refused to play for them, which, given the state they were in, was a serious mistake. All he had to do was give them a tune and they would have done a quick twirl and fallen over in a stupor and snored until the dawn. But no, he had to go and draw himself up to his full five feet, strike an air as haughty as a Hun chieftain and stand on his dignity. So they tossed him in a blanket, and I must say that he was probably the better for it.

Then a barber passed by and made some half-hearted protest and they grabbed him and fumbled with the blanket in order to give him the same treatment, but they were so sodden that he got away by promising to take them to the prettiest woman in Epsom.

The prettiest woman in Epsom! My Lord, but what an enticement! Now you or I would not exactly fall over each other to get a glimpse of the prettiest woman in Epsom. Indeed we would trample each other to death to get out of the building and off in the opposing direction. However, too much the worse for the grape, Wilmot and his lusty crew bawled for the prettiest woman in Epsom, and the barber duly obliged by leading them off to the back door of a modest little dwelling.

They hammered on the door, and what should they find but that the door belonged to the house of the local constable. Oh alas for fate's hand in human frailties.

You may picture the rest.

Etherege starts bawling the man out and demanding that he find them a woman. The constable, being a fine upstanding family man, and also having fought on Cromwell's side in the war, don't take at all kindly to a bunch of drunken nobs ordering him about, most especially when it involved procuring for them. So he goes fairly cross-eyed with indignation and legs it out the front door in search of the night watch. It is half an hour or so before this band of knock-kneed peasants get themselves together and arrive at the door with half-pikes in their hands and straw sticking out of their ears. Still, they are demanding justice and just raring to have a go at their lordships, their minds awash with ancient grievance.

During this time, Etherege had managed to sober a little

and, remembering that he is a man of the theatre, he stands on the table, strikes a pose, bows low, and addresses them in his best honeyed tones, to the effect that he is but a poor scribbler who has come hither because he has heard of the handsome nature of the local men and the beauty of their wives, and now that he has truly seen it for himself, he begs their leave, and will go back contented to London and write some small epic or other extolling the virtues of Epsom.

Well, they are not exactly weighed down with a sense of irony out here in the country. They gawped a bit, but soon blushed to the tips of their little pink ears at the flattery being heaped upon them and began to steal away one by one, to tell their wives and daughters about the great actor man they had just witnessed.

This wasn't good enough for Rochester, who was still lost on the far side of sottishness. He was drunk as a Lord, and he is the sort who can turn ugly when in his cups. Usually he is the easiest of men, and would not lift a hand to anyone, just sit there giggling like a confused boy, but occasionally, and it is impossible to tell when it is coming, just occasionally he turns as nasty as a viper.

This was one of those occasions. He drew his sword on the constable and, as if that weren't enough for a hanging offence, he threw an insult too. Called him a pig-eyed sack of ordure, or some such. His friends sobered so fast after that, it was as if someone had thrown a bucket of cold water over them. Mr Downs was behind Rochester and threw his arms about him, pinning his sword arm, but creating quite a scuffle. The constable goes all green about the gills, shrieks 'Murder!' at the top of his lungs, the night watch come hurtling back at full gallop, charge in the room, and wallop the first thing they see with a great length of pike-staff.

The first thing they saw, though, was Mr Downs's head, and they split his skull with a hideous squelch like a melon.

Even Rochester stopped short on hearing that, and he and his merry friends took to their heels in the dark and the mêlée, hoping that that would be the end of that. Downs was still staggering about, his brains completely addled now. Left all alone, he picked up a stick and started swinging it around him in the belief that he was surrounded by a thousand screaming Dutch pirates all intent on making him walk the plank, and the watch just couldn't leave him be. One of the most resentful of them stuck a pike in his side, and he died a day or so later, bereft of his friends. Though to be fair to them, they had already legged it and did not realize what had happened at all.

Now Charles as we know is an easy man. There is nothing that he cannot laugh at, including the most insulting satires directed at himself, which he even enjoys the more scurrilous they are. He forgave Rochester's kidnapping of his young bride to be, just because the man wrote him a witty letter from the Tower, and a woman only has to say a sweet word to him and he'd get her off the gallows for it, he is so soft-hearted. But fighting drunken battles and duelling for no reason at all is where he draws the line, and I have to say that I think he has his priorities right. What harm ever came from an *affaire* of the heart or from a wicked bit of satire? The worst of it would be a bruised soul or a bruised ego, but drunken swordplay is something else and was a good example of exactly the sort of thing he thought ought not to be allowed.

Actually I have never seen him in such a rage. People called him 'black' before, because of his colouring, but it took on new meaning for a couple of days. His brows knitted together and his eyes looked out from beneath them with a fury that got the whole court tiptoeing around at top speed, doing their duties as never before and keeping well out of shouting range of the man. He sent word that Rochester was to be brought before him in chains, and then he paced and fretted and fumed. I kept out of his way, and looked suitably straight-faced and penitent, while I quietly enjoyed that agreeable sensation of joy at another's discomfort and down-fall. We don't have a word for that guilty pleasure in English. The Germans call it *Schadenfreude*.

But Rochester wasn't there. He was nowhere to be found.

439

42. Dr Bendo

Huddled in dirt, the reasoning engine lies,
Who was so proud, so witty and so wise.

John Wilmot, Lord Rochester.
'A Satire against Reason and Mankind'

A handbill I found on a wall at the Tower of London:

To All Gentlemen & Ladies: Doctor Alexander Bendo wishes all health and prosperity. London has recently been infested with a company of men whose arrogant confidence has enabled them to impose on others premeditated cheating, or, at best, their deluded imaginations in physic, both chymical and Galenic, in astrology, in physiognomy, palmistry, mathematics, alchemy, and even in Government itself. Upon the last I will not pronounce, since it is not my vocation. But all of the rest I find much more safe, equally honest and therefore more profitable, thanks to my God.

Is it my fault if the cheat, by his wits, makes himself so like me that I cannot avoid resembling him? Consider, pray, the valiant man and the coward. They are the same in all but one thing, and differ in but one alone. The valiant man holds his head up, looks confidently around, wears a sword, courts a

Lord's wife, and confesses it. So does the coward. Only one point of honour, and that is courage, makes the distinction.

I will only say something more about the honour of the mountebank, in case you discover me to be one.

Reflect what kind of a creature he is: he is fain to supply some higher ability he pretends to, with craft; he draws great companies to him by undertaking things which can never be effected. The politician, finding how people are taken with miraculous impossibilities, plays the same game. He promises things, which he is sure can never be brought about. The people believe, are deluded and pleased.

The expectation of a future good, which will never befall them, draws their eyes off a present evil. Thus are they kept in subjection, he in greatness, wealth and power. So you see, the politician is a mountebank in State affairs, and the mountebank is an arrant politician in physic.

There it was on the wall for all to see, and anyone who read it and knew the man, could not mistake who had put it there. For this really was Wilmot's true opinion of all politicians, and not just taken from his beloved Hobbes either, but what he had formed from close observation. Still, you had to know the man first to read between the lines of his notice. I doubt if the King's constabulary bothered to read handbills much, and if they did, they would not have spotted Wilmot's true hand behind it.

And there he was, on a small cart which he used as a platform, in front of his tent, swanning around in a great overgrown green gown, which he swore he wore in memory of his master Rabelais, and which he got at the reception of his Doctor's degree at Montpellier university, or so he said. It was lined with exotic fur of various colours. He was also sporting a huge beard, held on behind his ears with string, and a magnificent medal, set about with glittering pearls, rubies, and diamonds, which he hung from his neck on a massive gold chain. It was actually made of a cheap alloy of copper and zinc, which looks like gold. He claimed in his patter that it had been given him by the King of Cyprus, after he had cured his darling daughter, the Princess Aloephangina, of a fearful, but unspecified, disease.

He used scales and weights to make up his quack remedies, sealing the wax tops of the bottles with his signet ring and giving orders to his band of assistants in a language which was wholly invented, of which neither he nor they understood one word. The people bought the potions by the thousand and he made a tidy sum in ready cash from selling them what was a boiled up mixture of soot, urine, asafoetida, and any other vile smelling substance he could lay his hands on. His gang of servants, suitably got up like Macbeth's witches, would toil away in the heat of the kitchen, scraping scum off the walls, pounding bricks to dust on a marble slab, pissing away fit to bust, and boiling it all up in a huge dirty kettle. What a laugh they had.

Bendo also did chart readings and predicted the future, no doubt mindful of what old Rastignac had tried on before he scuttled off home *tout de suite*. He also made medical pronouncement on the state of moles, wens, warts and birthmarks, no doubt thinking of the late Lord Protector's face as he did so. There were plenty of ladies stepped up to confide about some blemish in an unmentionable place, whereupon Bendo would tell them that his female assistant, a venerable old matron, would inspect them if they would just wait for a few minutes behind the privacy curtain.

I think that many of them saw through Rochester's disguise, for, handsome as he was, he did not make a very convincing old woman, but none of them complained. I have noted that about women. They will make themselves open to their doctor sooner and more brazenly than to their husband. It is the licence to do it I think. They have been granted a special dispensation to do what they would really like to, but would be embarrassed about at home.

I noted that Bendo took no payment for any of these inspections, only for his medicines, which makes him I suppose slightly less of a rogue.

It was no small matter. His fame spread throughout the city and even beyond. He had only been practising for about a month, but the queues were huge and coiled halfway round the Tower. I saw several from the court standing there in the line, looking about them quickly in the hope that no one would see them, but still paying good money for a glass jar of servant's urine and soot. If only they had realized that they could have won the brief affections of the King by spotting who it was behind the false whiskers. Actually, they would not. No doubt the King would have done the proper thing and imprisoned the rogue until he duly apologized with one of his witty letters, but the King never could stand a tattle-tale and would have disliked the man who betrayed Rochester as much as the miscreant himself.

Among them, the great and the good lining up for the quack's cures, I saw many of Rochester's enemies, who had been combing every dark alley in London for him, one hand upon their hilt.

How that must have pleased my man! He must have felt like one of those waiters who gets revenge upon a rude customer by going out back and spitting in the man's soup.

The ostracism was lifted, for the King was quick to forgive, even so heinous a crime as an affray leading to murder. He just did not have it in him to hate for very long. I must say that I think that is a good thing in a man. He is lazy, and hopeless with his ministers, but I cannot find it in my heart to dislike him at all. Perhaps I am just getting old, but he strikes me as ten times the man his poor father was, and twenty of that wretch Oliver. When a man has a large and soft heart, he will be forgiven much.

Doctor Bendo made his first and only appearance at court, for such was the man's fame that the Master of the Revels had summoned him to appear before His Majesty. He made a good evening's entertainment, sawing the air with his hands and muttering mumbo-jumbo from inside his beard and producing white mice from up his sleeve and so on. Eventually, he claimed that he was affianced to the niece of the Great Cham of Tartary and that rather gave the game away. Not that Charles hadn't spotted Rochester from the word go, it was just that he was happy to play along, being so polite a king, but he had heard Rochester often talk of the Cham of Tartary as a sort of joke figure, someone out there who doesn't exist, like Oberon, and so when he let it slip, the game was over for both of them, though Charles rallied nicely. 'Has anyone here seen Rochester?' says the King. 'I have not seen him for a month or two, and, d'you know, I do miss the naughty rogue.'

'I have a spell, Majesty,' says Dr Bendo with a flourish, 'that will make the man himself appear before you within a trice.'

'That I would dearly like to see,' says Charles, hiding a smile.

'But it must be affected in utter darkness, Majesty,' says Bendo, stroking his beard, 'and when Rochester has appeared, he must be refreshed with champagne.'

'He may have it,' says the King. 'So will we all, as many bottles as we can lift.' And so it all came about, and Rochester was back in fortune and men's eyes, as he knew he would be in time. His confidence in himself is extraordinary.

Where do they get that from, the aristocrats I mean? There is never a day goes by when I do not doubt myself about even the easiest course of action, let alone the way my life is going, but Rochester is completely untroubled by any thought that he might be doing the wrong thing. Of course, when he does do the wrong thing, he carries on blithely as before, confident of eventual success. I suppose it is the difference between an aristocrat and a gentleman. Not that it makes me like aristocrats any the more, but I would certainly have liked to have had their confidence, when young.

No I wouldn't, it would have made me intolerably arrogant. Yes I would, I am beginning not to care what others think of me. I don't know. And if I don't know . . . ?

It was the last time I saw Rochester, though not I believe the last time that he saw me.

43. Violence and its Uses

Whereas truth for the most part lies in the middle,
but men ordinarily look for it in the extremities.

Marvell. 'A Short Essay touching General Councils,
Creeds and Impositions in Religion'

It was shortly after Rochester's capers that I encountered
Sam Parker yet again. He is the nastiest of clergymen, and I
have often had occasion to argue with him in print. In his
youth he was the archest of Presbyterian bores, eating
nothing but thin gruel and proclaiming that anybody other
than a Non-conformist would never see the kingdom of
heaven. Then, when the King is restored, he throws off his
disguise and announces himself a true Anglican and all other
religions should be consigned to the flames.

He was mumbling along the road looking pious and arrogant, the way he does, even though he is still only a curate to
the Bishop of Rochester, a paltry place with no cathedral
worth seeing.

As we are about to pass, he sees me, his foxy little eyes
light up, and he rudely takes the wall side of the pavement
and tries to shove me aside to the gutter. Ha, but I have him

now. I have been working on my tricks, and can use them when it is needed, which is right now, on him. So I stopped dead where I was and even back-stepped one pace so that I was moving in the same direction and speed as Mr Parker. I seized his lapels and pushed my leg between his, and wrenched over sideways. He sprawled in the gutter and got covered with shit, which was the best sight I have seen for many a long year. Christ I liked that. Always strike the first blow, and thank you Mr Higgins.

My saintly father taught me once that violence solves nothing. He was wrong. It can solve a lot in very short order, and also can be very satisfying. I laughed out loud at his predicament and told him to 'Lie there for a son of a whore.' What the French call '*Une réponse verte*' or a sharp reply.

He was spluttering too much filth out of his mouth to have a comeback, but he later complained to his Bishop that he had not been shown the respect due to him. The Bishop called me in, the prig.

'I only called him exactly what he has previously called himself, my Lord Bishop,' I said.

'Eh?'

At this I took out a book which Parker had recently written, that I just happened to have in my pocket, and pointed to something I had underlined in the preface.

'He says here my Lord that he is a "true son of his mother Church of England".'

450

'What of it?' said the Bishop, his jowls rattling with indignation.

'He then goes on, my Lord, "The Church of England has spawned two bastards, the Presbyterians and the Congregationals." There you have it my Lord, he clearly states that he is a son of a whore.'

Even the Bishop laughed at that. Finally he managed to purse his lips slightly and begged me to show more respect to the cloth in future. I said that I would not, for he showed no respect to a man who is an MP. What I thought, but did not say, was that I will continue to attack the smutty lubber in print; and if that does not mend his nasty ways, I will get Rochester to cudgel his brains out in an alley. Rochester is good at that.

That time when Coventry was pulled from his carriage and had his nose slit open for insulting the King in Parliament; it was said that Rochester was behind it.

I have changed. In my youth I was never so vehement. I do not know what has happened to me, and I do not care any more.

44. Geraniums

A Frenchman has been indicted for the rape of a ten-year-old girl. And another man for the buggery of a mare. Also a woman, for 'beastliness with a dog, for which she is condemned and will be executed'.

Extract from A Letter to the Mayor of Hull
from Andrew Marvell, MP for Hull

The French, I ask you, typical. Though, I must say that I do understand, for I too came perilously close, once. Not to a mare, you understand, but there was a girl of some twelve or thirteen years, too green for lust. Love was something I knew about when young. It has gone from me now, and all that I can recall of it is in my 'Mower' poems. Besides what I am naturally, I am more inclined by my age to keep my thoughts private, but when I look over some of my work of an evening when I drink alone, it strikes me I had a lyric vein once. Nowadays I am all satire, partly because of what I am, partly because of what the King has become, but then, I was young, and I can bring it all back to mind if I want to.

I take a small red geranium that I keep in a pot on my windowsill and water daily. I bruise the leaves slightly between my thumb and first finger, and if the flower be dead then I pull off the dead petals and crush them in my palm. Then I lie back with my hand over my nose and mouth and gently inhale. I have no words for the smell. It makes me think of graveyards and women, but not because they smell like geraniums; all I can say is that that is what it makes me think of, and I am young again. I do not say it reminds me of my youth, or it makes me recover things past; no, when I smell it, I am young again, and, without pause for thought, I can recite my 'Mower' poems to myself. Normally I cannot, and need to look at the page to refresh my memory, but when wrapped in geranium, then I am word perfect.

> *While thus he threw his elbow round*
> *Depopulating all the ground.*

I once thought that the best of couplets, purely for its pictorial power. I believe I told you: when a child, I used to watch the gardener, van Dieman, as he showed me how to scythe, and it was his elbow that caught my young attention, the way he threw it round.

I still think it one of my best pairs of lines, but now for different reasons. All the dead I have seen, it has been too much, too many, too cruel. When I was young I had a cool heart and a strong mind, and I still do, but the sheer weight of numbers has a bad effect. It brings a man down.

That 'depopulating' is a master stroke isn't it? When I was

young, it applied to the grass. Of course it was a conceit too – one I took from my Pliny and I think it is also in beloved Horace, the suggestion that grass was like people and all flesh would perish as the grass – but it was a youthful conceit and so one I had got from my books. I only learned its truth with age. Once that truth bore down upon me, then I could never write so blithe again. There is a greater truth in those lines that I did not see till long after I had written them, and I was old. Once they brought tears of love to my eyes, now they make me weep for pity.

I cannot overdo the geranium odour any more, for too much of it will make me vomit.

46. The Attempt on the Crown Jewels by one Captain Blood, May 1671

*When daring Blood to have his rents regain'd
Upon the English diadem distrain'd,
He chose the Cassock, Circingle and Gown
The fittest mask for one that robs a crown.*

Marvell, 'Blood and the Crown'

I sent out a boy to warn Chiffinch that I was coming, and sure enough he was ready for me when I arrived. Chiffinch's official title, Keeper of the Royal Closet... He is in fact the King's pimp, and procures fresh meat for his Majesty when and where he wishes. As such, he lodges close to the Royal bedchamber, and has complete control of the secret back stairs up to the King's suite. This makes him closer to his Majesty than any of his favourites, courtiers, ministers or even mistresses. And this is not surprising, he is a spy for Charles and altogether he is the one man that you want to be on the right side of. Keep well in with little Mr Chiffinch and you would be

45. The Attempt on the Crown Jewels by one Captain Blood. May 1671

When daring Blood to have his rents regained
Upon the English diadem distrained,
He chose the Cassock Circingle and Gown,
The fittest mask for one that robs a crown.

Marvell. 'Blood and the Crown'

I sent out a boy to warn Chiffinch that I was coming, and sure enough he was ready for me when I arrived. I forget Chiffinch's official title: Keeper of the Royal Closet perhaps. He is in fact the King's pimp, and it is his duty to provide fresh meat for his Majesty when and where he wants it. As such, he lodges close to the Royal bedchamber, and has complete control of the secret back staircase up to the King's suite. This makes him closer to his Majesty than any of his favourites, courtiers, ministers or even mistresses. Also, and this is not surprising, he is a spy for Charles, and altogether he is the one man that you want to be on the right side of. Keep well in with little Mr Chiffinch and you would be surprised how easy it is to get a royal audience; but keeping in with Chiffinch is very difficult for most people, because he is a pointy-nosed little rat, who makes you want to heave just by looking at him. He leaves a trail of slime wherever he slithers, and is living proof that God put infanticide on this earth for a good reason. The problem was that his mother did not practise it.

Most people try an unctuous mixture of flattery and bribery, which only goes to show how stupid most people are.

It only took me about a week of stalking little Finchy to discover what his tastes were, and while it is not strictly illegal, I do not think His Majesty would take kindly to a man in his close contact who liked his mouth being used as a chamberpot by dirty women.

Dirty women are notoriously diseased, and that disease might be catching, just from using the same cutlery. HM does not like the idea of disease. Indeed he spends most of his time curing it in others, the scrofula I mean, just by touching them. I don't know whether it works, but those with the King's Evil queue up by the hundreds.

Anyway, Chiffinch and I get along just fine now. He flinches when he first sees me, and then affects a haughty air, which I let him get away with, but still has never barred me from seeing HM at short notice. It is a privilege I do not over-use, but it is nice to have the little man jump when I say so.

This night he ushered me up the tiny, narrow staircase, which is panelled on both sides, and goes straight from the ground to the third floor, without stopping at the second. I have a theory that if Charles hears his wife or some unwanted harridan climbing the main stairs, he can leg it out the back and be clear out the front door, while she is still passing the second floor. It is only a theory.

Chiffinch knocked and after a while there was a short bark of 'Come'. I walked in and bowed at the door. Chiffinch ushered me forward, and then, as usual, disappeared, without me being able to tell whether he had exited the door, or hidden himself among the copious hanging tapestries. The latter, I am sure, for how else would he have his finger on the pulse of all that happens in court? Charles was sitting in a chair by the window, gazing out, even though it was dark. His spaniel dogs were sleeping at his feet, except for one puppy that sat on his head. He affected an ignorance of my presence for some minutes before removing the dog, replacing his wig, and turning his chair toward me.

'Must be something urgent Mr Marvell,' he said, 'at such short notice. Spying again I suppose?' He sighed a massive sigh, which rippled the extent of his lanky body. He stretched out a little and crossed his long legs at the ankle.

Before I could continue, Charles suddenly looked a good deal sharper about the features, than previously. 'Oh, God, it's that Captain Blood business, isn't it?' he said.

'Yes, Your Majesty,' I said, 'I think it is pressing. He is

safely in the lock up, and I have conducted a brief initial interrogation, but he says that he will confess to the whole thing only to you in person.'

'So he has confessed?' said Charles.

'Not exactly, Majesty. He says he will, but, as I say, only to the royal ear.'

'Damned odd,' said Charles, rootling away in the spaniel's ear with a middle finger, and inspecting the result on the end of his fingernail. 'Anyway, why on earth should I bother with the damned rogue? He was caught red handed wasn't he? Don't need a blasted confession. Take him away and string him up.'

'Of course, Your Majesty, that is exactly what the man deserves,' I said. Except of course that Charles didn't really mean it. He would never hurt a fly. So I paused, while still leaning forward slightly, and let the silence hang in the air for a minute. It is a way I have.

'But?' said the King. 'But, eh Mr Marvell? Do I hear a "but" in your voice?'

'Your Majesty reads me too easily,' I said, noting that he raised his broad black eyebrows heavenwards, thus letting me know that he didn't and furthermore didn't know any man who could.

'There are complications, Majesty, in the case, and, moreover, we could possibly turn the whole strange business to our advantage.'

Charles looked ill-tempered again. 'Not sure I want to

really,' he said. 'After all, the poxy bog-trotter did try to make off my with crown jewels.' He thought on this a while, stroking his moustache gently between thumb and fore-finger, teasing it out to a spike. When he let go, it drooped down his long upper lip as usual, so he tried again. Finally he let out a little wail of frustration.

'And I like my jewels, I do, I do. They are so pretty. They sit there on their velvet pillows in the strong room, and they cheer me when I go to see them. It's not as if they are exactly mine, I know, but that's not the point is it? We can't have any old hairy Irish jackanapes coming in and trying 'em on for size, and legging it out the back stairs with them under his shirt just 'cos he likes the fit of 'em. Eh? Can we? No, no, no, string him up, it won't do at all. Is he from a good family? If he is, we might have to cut his head off instead.'

'Indeed Majesty, those are his just deserts. He is Irish, and therefore not to be trusted an inch. He is no peer, but is a landowner in a medium sort of way, and claims that he was just trying to gain your attention in order that some of his lands, which Cromwell sequestered, might be returned to him.'

Charles thought some more on that, and I could see him softening. 'Suffered under Cromwell, did he? Hmmm, well I have some sympathy with the fellow then. Though we haven't been able to make much restitution to any of the others have we, eh? Much too complicated. Mmm, mmm, perhaps I had better see him then.'

'A good idea, Majesty, but there is more.'

He began to smile wearily. 'There always is from you Mr Marvell. Do I need to hear it?' He is a very clever man, but bone idle, and would rather be distracted by something more pleasurable, such as a trio of waiting maid servants with their stays neatly loosened before they enter. I did not answer his question, but pressed on quickly while I had his sole attention.

'Captain Blood is, or was, in fact the head of a notorious gang, Your Majesty. They have no name, but are quite fearless, and have undertaken the most outrageous exploits in open defiance of the law. You remember the kidnapping of Ormonde?'

Indeed he did. It was the talk of the town for months. The poor old Duke of Ormonde, a man getting on in years, but still quite spry, and damnably rich to boot, was pulled out of his carriage in broad daylight, by six bent-nosed villains on horseback, and right in the middle of town too, St James I think it was. He was hoiked up by his armpits and dumped like a sack of flour behind one of the riders. Now, Ormonde might be a bit wrinkly as I said, but he was a game old bird, and nobody's fool either. Instead of having a fit of the vapours at his treatment, he looked about himself carefully, and noted that the rider, on whose horse he had been dumped, had his hands full of pistols and swords, which he was trying to sort out by passing them from hand to hand

and gripping the reins in his teeth while he juggled all the different bits.

'He must be Irish,' thought Ormonde, who had spent much time in that misbegotten land, and boxed the man's ears with a ferocious double-hander blow. Then, with the Paddy's ears ringing like a church steeple at Whitsun, Ormonde jumps clear from the back of the cantering horse, and legs it off down the street as fast as his aged pins will carry him, with the gang loosing off all their pistols at him, which I must say I thought a bit unnecessary. Just because they couldn't kidnap him, it seemed a mite unfair to spoil anyone else's chances too. At least a dozen bullet scars were counted in the brickwork down the street, so old Ormonde must have been prancing along at a fair old pace, his little chicken-legs going like the very devil. Not once did he later boast of it all, nor gain so much as an extra grey hair on his head. He is a seasoned old campaigner.

My intelligencers told me that the gang was led by Captain Blood, though we never found them. They specialize in long riding, which means that they prepare for each piece of mayhem by placing horses at strategic points around the country, and once they have done their wicked business, they ride like hell all through the night and the next day, changing horses as they go. No one can track them down, and they are probably back in Ireland before the watch has even got out of bed.

Then the son of a whore came back and tried to steal the

crown jewels from the Tower. Well, you have to admire the brass neck of the man. He don't do things by halves. Unless of course he is brain-addled, which is always a possibility with the bog-dwellers.

I took evidence from the guards and spoke to the man too, as I said, and he is no fool. Indeed he is very charming, and, like so many Irish mischief-men, has a plausible air about him.

He is also a master of disguise, and for this occasion had donned a priest's robes and befriended a young chap, called Edwards, who is the son of the keeper. Edwards actually left him alone in the inner sanctum, but then couldn't find his handkerchief, so returned in search of it after a few minutes, only to find Blood stuffing the crown up his surplice. The boy was so perplexed he didn't know what to say, but Blood simply beamed a smile, and said, 'It was a bold attempt, but it was for a crown.'

And now he awaits the King's pleasure.

'Very well,' said Charles. 'I may enjoy seeing so bold a ruffian. Send him to me.'

So we did, and the man confessed his crimes to Charles and was perfectly charming about it all, saying he was terribly sorry, but he just couldn't resist such pretty jewels, and he would abide by the King's sentence. He was altogether wooing the boots off the man's feet. Had he been a woman, he would have been in Charles's bed within minutes. I had briefed Blood carefully beforehand as to my plans for him, and when he had been escorted back to the chokey, I again saw the King.

'He was also a Fifth Monarchist man, Majesty,' I said, and saw Charles start, and grow an inch or two. I forget exactly what it was they stood for, but it had something to do with the overthrow of the King. They were an egregious nuisance a few years ago, and prompted Charles to one of his few draconian measures. He had as many put to death as could be found. Serve them right too, stupid regicidal lot. 'And he mixes with Republican men. And dissenting clods to boot.'

'Well, so do many good men,' said the King, 'and I seem to remember you weren't above doing Oliver the odd favour by way of a flattering poem or two.'

'Yes, Majesty,' I said, putting on my smoothest air, and changing that subject very rapidly. 'The point is that he is a landowner, but he mingles with the cut-throat scum of two continents. He will dine with the Irish quality and then bed down with highwaymen and pirates.'

'So,' said the King, 'let him swing for it.'

Really I sometimes think that the only way to force a change of mind through the King's brain would be by major surgery. 'He could be very useful to us, Majesty,' I said. 'He has all the names, and he knows where they live.'

A look of elephantine cunning spread over Charles's handsome face. 'Aha,' he said with a sharp whoop. 'A double agent, eh?'

'*Exactly*, Majesty,' I said with an exhausted bow, and a smile.

'Well, why didn't you say so. By God, it takes an age to get you to the point Mr Marvell. Still, that's why we use you I suppose, you think your way through it and all around it, and come out the other side with some brainy scheme.' He paused and gave his moustache a vicious tweak. 'How will you do it?' he said.

'Majesty, it is simplicity itself. We have him in an unbreakable headlock. Unless he help us by providing top quality information, he will swing for his crime. It's perfect.'

'Can we trust what he tells us?'

'Of course not, he is Irish, but it can be checked upon, and we would be fools not to do so,' I said.

'Very well, get it done, busy Mr Marvell. Where would I be without you, eh?' And he went back to kissing his spaniel on the nose.

So I turned the man around and used him for all sorts of wicked things, and I even went on a foreign trip with him to the continent and France in the company of my Lord Buckingham, which was full of mischief. We were there to reassure all the expatriates that the whispering of Charles's *rapprochement* with King Louis of France was only an ugly rumour put about by Papists. Actually, it wasn't. Charles truly was thinking of going over to Rome, just so that he could get his hands on some of Louis's fabled wealth. But that is another story, and I am wearying of all this.

I could tell you a lot about Buckingham, for he is the worst rogue in the whole gallery of court ballers. His behaviour is abominable. It was he who seduced Mary Fairfax, my Little Moll, into marrying him, in order to regain his confiscated land, and afterwards sported with other women continually. But I have told you all this. I tolerated him for professional reasons. He tolerated me because he needed me. Not once, never, ever, did I ask him about his wife, or how she was.

When I was young I would have said that the trip was a good story. I would have given you all the details, but now . . . I just do not have the energy. Nor the desire. I am sorry. The spring has gone from my step, and I have no stuffing left in me. I have petered out.

In fact it's worse than that. The point of my story of Captain Blood was not that it was a yarn of passing interest. I see now that my point was how low I have sunk. Blackmail, spying, murder and worse; I don't know how I got here, but nothing is beneath me now. I was green in my youth, but now I have gone quite black.

467

Nunc Dimittis

There was a war within this one country, which set man against son, brother against brother, friend against neighbour, and many were mown down, but the true damage was the corrosion of the soul.

That is enough of me. You will know me well enough by now. I will walk forward, for I always walk forward, but I am no longer driven. Now I am pulled by the abyss, and I march toward it in step to the soft drum of my pulse. I would welcome extinction, and hug it to me as a bride. I still have some poison left, and also my pistol, but I dread to do the deed. I will do things of great risk in the future, even though age is committing its stealthy robbery on me. I will take risks, not to rekindle life in me, but in the hope it will do to me what I dare not.

She was my one, my only love, and I did not know it at the time. Now she is gone. I had lost the lyric vein, since the civil wars killed it in me, but still I could write. Then she left and she took the best of me with her. Now I am only a savage. I am hollow, as if I had been scooped out with a spoon. There is no God, for He would not have taken her from me. There is no wisdom, only knowledge; no light, only false orange glimmers on the edge of night. There is no hope, nor even fear. There are no rhymes, for the words do not chime any more. I feel no pang of all she felt for me. I am nothing, not even sorrow lodges in my soul.

I am not even nothing, for nothing is a thing that might exist. I am the dark that lives in darkness at the heart of eternal night, that place where the eyes of the damned do not become accustomed to the dark and never make out shapes or shadows. In my place, men have eyes, but they see nothing, for there is nothing to see. I am that void that did not exist before the world was created. She is dead to me, for when I call she does not answer, and I will not be consoled.

Finis

Afternote

Andrew Marvell died on 16 August 1678, killed by his doctor, who had bled him for malaria, instead of giving him quinine. He was fifty-seven.

Mary 'Moll' Fairfax contracted a bad marriage to the dissolute Duke of Buckingham (Dryden's 'Zimri'). She died childless.

Rochester died in 1680, aged thirty-three, poisoned by the mercury treatment for the pox, and adrift in a sea of alcohol. They say he converted from Hobbes to Rome on his deathbed.